PEN

A PASSION

WITH A T

A Passionate Love Affair with a Total Stranger is Lucy Robinson's second novel and follows on from her successful debut, *The Greatest Love Story of All Time*. Prior to writing, Lucy earned her crust in theatre production and then factual television, working on documentaries for all of the UK's major broadcasters. Her writing career began when she started a dating blog for *Marie Claire*, where she entertained readers with frank tales from her laughably unsuccessful foray into the world of Internet dating.

Lucy was brought up in Gloucestershire, surrounded by various stupid animals. She studied at Birmingham University and lived in London for many years before disappearing off to South America for eighteen months with hopes of becoming a bohemian novelist. This novel was written entirely on the road as she travelled through Argentina, Chile, Mexico, Ecuador and Colombia – although, fortunately, it does not feature so much as one crusty backpacker.

Lucy lives in South London with her partner, The Man.

www.lucy-robinson.co.uk

A Passionate Love Affair
with a Total Stranger

LUCY ROBINSON

PENGUIN BOOKS

PENGUIN BOOKS

Published by the Penguin Group
Penguin Books Ltd, 80 Strand, London WC2R ORL, England
Penguin Group (USA) Inc., 375 Hudson Street, New York, New York 10014, USA
Penguin Group (Canada), 90 Eglinton Avenue East, Suite 700, Toronto, Ontario, Canada M4P 2Y3
(a division of Pearson Penguin Canada Inc.)
Penguin Ireland, 25 St Stephen's Green, Dublin 2, Ireland (a division of Penguin Books Ltd)
Penguin Group (Australia), 707 Collins Street, Melbourne, Victoria 3008, Australia
(a division of Pearson Australia Group Pty Ltd)
Penguin Books India Pvt Ltd, 11 Community Centre, Panchsheel Park, New Delhi – 110 017, India
Penguin Group (NZ), 67 Apollo Drive, Rosedale, Auckland 0632, New Zealand
(a division of Pearson New Zealand Ltd)
Penguin Books (South Africa) (Pty) Ltd, Block D, Rosebank Office Park,
181 Jan Smuts Avenue, Parktown North, Gauteng 2193, South Africa

Penguin Books Ltd, Registered Offices: 80 Strand, London WC2R ORL, England

www.penguin.com

First published 2013
003

Set in 12.5/14.75pt Garamond MT Std
Typeset by Jouve (UK), Milton Keynes
Printed in England by Clays Ltd, St Ives plc

ISBN: 978-0-718-15766-1

www.greenpenguin.co.uk

Penguin Books is committed to a sustainable
future for our business, our readers and our planet.
This book is made from Forest Stewardship
Council™ certified paper.

ALWAYS LEARNING　　　　　**PEARSON**

For George
Thank you for waiting

Chapter One

Is this it? I wondered, gazing down at the scene spread out below me. *Is my life perfect?*

Suddenly embarrassed I hugged my knees. Only the most foolish of knobs sat around trying to decide whether or not their lives were perfect.

But, as I gazed down at my hand-crafted picnic – with all the bashful pride of Leonardo stepping back to admire his *Last Supper* – I couldn't deny that it did *look* rather good. Not unlike the front cover of a *Visit Edinburgh* brochure, in fact. It was one of the city's rare sunny days and the people drinking champagne below me seemed extremely aspirational and good-looking. When I was an awkward teenager dreaming about Making It, I had fantasized about having friends who looked like this. And now here they were, arranged at tasteful intervals around a large tartan picnic blanket on Salisbury Crags, holding plates of fashionable food from the farmers' market.

I beamed. *I* had done this! *I*'d put together this picnic! I allowed myself a discreet self-hug and wondered how that awkward teenager – Too Tall Charley from East Linton – had become Charlotte Lambert, director of communications at one of the world's largest pharmaceutical companies, owner of a flat off Broughton Street and a woman in possession of sufficient cool friends to be able to organize brochure-worthy picnics at only a few hours' notice. What more was there, save perhaps a relationship with a handsome man who knew about fine wines and vintage cheeses?

'Look at this!' I whispered to Malcolm the Labrador. I was dog-sitting for my parents while they Found Themselves in a four-star hotel in India again. Malcolm bestowed upon me a look of great love, inviting me to donate to him my sandwich.

'Of course, of course,' I muttered, handing it over. 'Sorry, Malcolm, you must be starving.'

Hailey, my small and bawdy best friend, detached herself from her boyfriend, Matty, and walked up the hill towards me, grinning at the sandwich-gobbling Labrador at my side. 'Hello, Malcolm!' she shouted. Hailey adored Malcolm.

Malcolm adored Hailey right back but he was too busy to hear her.

'I said, hello, Malcolm.' She drew level, laughing.

Malcolm finished the sandwich, then gave her his full attention, wagging his tail as if his life depended on it. Hailey hugged him hard, smothering his delighted face with her ample bosom. 'Well done, Chas,' she said, freeing Malcolm from her chest. 'This is bloody brilliant!'

I grinned modestly. 'It's not bad, Hails, I'll warrant you that. Not bad at all.'

She sat down next to me on the grass. 'You OK?' she asked casually.

'Of course!'

She raised an eyebrow.

'What's that face for?' I demanded.

She responded with a knowing look that clarified nothing.

'I just want to know if you're OK,' she said, in the sort of gentle voice one would normally reserve for a challenging toddler.

'I'm really happy, Hails! Sam got engaged last night . . . And here we all are having a great time!'

Hailey shook her head. 'What I meant, Chas, was did you make it to bed last night?'

Ah.

'Of course I did,' I answered spiritedly.

I was lying, of course. Sam and Yvonne, newly betrothed and very drunk, had left my flat in search of cocktails at four thirty a.m., dragging Hailey and my twin sister, Ness, with them. Once they'd gone I had compiled a shopping list, a to-do list and my wardrobe for the day, and when I'd finished it was six a.m. and time to drive to the farmers' market. I'd then spent the morning hiring glasses and plates, buying champagne and rugs, and tracking down unnecessary things, such as little potted orchids and plastic ponchos in case it rained. I had felt madly invigorated by the task and had driven around in a craze of adrenalin and coffee, fantasizing wildly about how it would feel to achieve the most perfect engagement picnic in history. It couldn't just be good, it had to be hair-raisingly *amazing*.

As with any Challenge Charley, tiredness hadn't so much as crossed my mind.

But now that I came to think of it, I was tired. Devastatingly so, in fact. Looking at the people below me, I felt suddenly alarmed about today. As the housemate of Dirty Samuel Bowes (who had stunned the world by sustaining a three-month relationship with Yvonne and then *proposing* to her last night), I had an unquestionable duty to be a sparkly and capable hostess until the celebrations ended, probably no earlier than three a.m. And tomorrow – Sunday – I had an early-morning Mandarin class, then personal training, and I needed to compose a work letter, which would be picked up by a courier at one p.m. I would spend the afternoon volunteering at the dog sanctuary, then have tea with my cousin and do at least four hours' prepping for an eight a.m. presentation at work on Monday morning. Ideally I needed to give the flat a good clean, too, and try to get to John Lewis for a baking tray. And shave my legs. Do my monthly accounting. Do my . . . I stopped, deflated. How the feck was I ever going to sleep with a to-do list this long?

A vision of my bed sprang into my head – all clean and square and fragrant – and I felt weak with desire. But I batted it away. Even people with perfect lives suffered sleep deprivation at times.

'How did this happen?' Hailey asked, breaking into my thoughts. She was looking at Sam, who, in spite of my efforts to provide a tasteful feast, was wandering around with a loaf of value bread and a jar of Nutella tucked under one arm. Periodically he would absent himself from conversation to remove a slice of bread and dunk it in the jar, all the while looking madly, uncontrollably happy. I shook my head, as bemused as Hailey by last night's turn of events.

'I don't get it, Chas,' she continued. 'I mean, *Sam*? How on earth did he get engaged before us? It's . . . it's . . .' She trailed off, utterly confused.

'Mental,' I said. She nodded.

It *was* mental. Sam was a dog! Every Saturday morning

4

since the dawn of time a different young woman with a Friday-night outfit and sex hair had snuck out of Sam's bedroom and disappeared silently out of the flat. An hour or two later, Sam would shuffle into the sitting room in his dressing-gown, ready to spend the day eating bread and Nutella. He would sometimes call for a pizza; occasionally he'd disappear for a long bath, but he would never reply to the 'I had a GREAT time last night' messages that invariably arrived on his phone a few hours later. Girls went wild for Sam: he was a knockout and a charmer. And also a dirty shagging shagger.

Sam's loose women had been as integral a part of Saturday morning as my ten-K run round Holyrood Park and the wholegrain teacake I had afterwards. But then Yvonne had arrived and everything had changed.

I didn't much like change or uncertainty. Yvonne, with her little floral skirts that would have made me look like a hulking transvestite, brought with her a distinct whiff of both change and uncertainty. She also brought with her a distinct whiff of Miss Dior and something Sam-related that I didn't want to think about, but that was beside the point. The point was that I appeared to have lost my reliably lazy, womanizing housemate and had instead been given a thoroughly unpredictable puppy, who did things like proposing while we were in the middle of my finest fusion risotto.

Below us, Sam's friend Nelson grabbed a baguette from the rug and tried to roger Sam with it. Sam ignored him, his eyes instead seeking out Yvonne, who gave him a little wave from across the rug. He broke into a mushy smile, and Hailey and I burst out laughing simultaneously.

'Look at him!' she cried.

'I know. How will we ever get over this, Hailey?'

'We probably won't. So when's he going to move out?'

I shrugged. 'No idea. I haven't actually talked to him since they went scampering off into the night.'

But it was inevitable that he'd go, I thought, not without a twinge of sadness. When I'd first rented the room to him we'd agreed that if either of us Met Someone then Sam would move out. But it had never happened. In the last eight years I had had only one doomed relationship, and Sam had got through most of the women in Edinburgh without returning a single phone call. We'd become a sort of dysfunctional couple, me with my high-powered job and obsession with healthy eating and exercise, Sam a perpetually resting actor with filthy standards of nutrition and a great love of inactivity.

But in spite of his slovenly ways I knew I'd really miss him.

'What will you do?' Hailey asked me.

'Eh?' My BlackBerry started to vibrate in my pocket.

'Will you get another lodger?' Hailey watched my hand irritably as it reached into my pocket and, for a split second, I considered not answering the phone.

But the thought lasted only a second. Things at work were absolutely critical at the moment; for me to become unavailable suddenly would be unacceptable. Sackable, probably. A flash of exasperation crossed Hailey's face as I answered: 'Charlotte Lambert.'

'Charlotte, hi, it is Birgitte from the German office.'

'Hi, Birgitte,' I muttered, hunching away from Hailey in a futile attempt to disguise what I was doing.

Hailey, clearly, was not fooled – it was the sixth work call I'd taken since the picnic began – but, to my relief, she let it go. If nothing else, she was used to the insane demands of my job.

When I finished the call, a few minutes later, she merely carried on where she'd left off, a resigned expression on her face. 'Will you get another lodger?'

'Jesus, no! I've not needed a lodger for years. I just love Sam, that's all.' I yawned, leaden with tiredness.

Hailey smiled. 'He's a stinker. But it's very hard not to love him.'

Sam, below us, loped over to Yvonne, putting his arms round her tiny waist and kissing her all over her face. Yvonne responded by jumping up and down and making little screaming noises.

'Fucking hell,' Hailey said, shaking her head.

'You next, Hailey,' I said. As if he could hear us, Matty blew her a kiss and I giggled. Matty was more enslaved to Hailey even than Sam was to Yvonne. He was a chirpy, Gore-texed, ruddy-cheeked man who was not much taller than her, and they were mad about each other. He worshipped every inch of her, right down to her strange little hammer toes.

'Stop it!' She blushed, suddenly girly. 'But fuck me, Chas, I'd love that,' she added, lowering her voice. 'Can you imagine? Me as a bride? You as my bridesmaid?'

I could imagine it. Hailey would march down the aisle like a little powerhouse, knocking out anyone who got in her way with her gigantic stiff white bosom. Even on a normal day it was big enough to set up a chessboard on; I could only imagine what a bit of corsetry would do to it.

'God, Charley, I'm so grateful,' she said suddenly. 'Without you I'd never have got so much as a date out of Matty.'

'Don't be silly. It was you he liked. I just did the admin.'

'Not true,' Hailey replied, as Matty beckoned her down the hill. 'You worked absolute wonders, Chasman. I'm in your debt.'

I enjoyed doing things for my friends, and reeling Matty in for Hailey had not been hard. He'd been keen as mustard.

'Ah, now, Chas,' she said, getting up to return to her boyfriend. 'I nearly forgot. There was a cracking article in the paper yesterday about an American dude who set up a business doing what you did for me and Matty.' She scrabbled around in her handbag, which was so large that she could probably have zipped herself into it. 'Here you go.' She handed me a folded-up newspaper page. 'I think you should set up the UK arm of this guy's company.'

She brushed herself off, then leaned down and kissed me on the cheek. 'Well done, Charleypops,' she said. 'Today is another triumph. You are super-amazing and capable . . . so now please give yourself a break. The party can run itself from here.'

I nodded obediently, knowing that it could do no such thing. It was all very well enjoying a party but *someone* had to work behind the scenes or it would turn into a big wet fart. It was my job, plain and simple. I bit my thumb, wondering if I should top up everyone's glass. But, after a warning glance from Hailey as she made her way back down the hill, I decided a few minutes' relaxing was reasonable.

Yawning again, I unfolded the newspaper.

The Blindest Date

Romance Blossoms as the Busy and Inept Subcontract Their Love Lives to Witty Strangers

Gilly, 29, is an A&R assistant for EMI Records in New York. Having recently got engaged to Aldo, 37, a men's fashion buyer – whom she met online in 2009 – Gilly is saving for her dream wedding in the Hamptons. She's cut back her monthly expenditure by 20 per cent, opened a CD account and taken on extra work.

Her additional income is, in many respects, a classic twenty-first-century income booster – she works remotely from her home in Brooklyn and dictates her own hours.

But Gilly isn't in data entry or cosmetics sales.

Gilly is flirting with other men.

While fiancé Aldo cooks their dinner in the evening, Gilly drives strange men wild with flirty emails and then closes the deal with the promise of a date.

Welcome to the fascinating world of the Cyber Love Assistant, a new breed of digital writer who is bringing hope – and often love – to America's most incapable daters.

Cyber Love Assistants – the brainchild of Steve Sampson, originally from Boston, MA – hires Internet dating ghost-writers to secure dates for those with insufficient time or talent for online dating. The writers, paid at roughly $15 per message, write on behalf of men and women of all ages who are united in one thing: a chronic inability to write the language of love.

Peter, 46, from Hoboken, is the director of a multimillion-dollar software development consultancy. Widowed ten years ago by his childhood sweetheart, Peter has finally begun to seek a new partner. But, he says, 'I just don't have it in me. I look at profiles of all of these ballsy women and have no idea what to say to them.'

Peter has a date on Friday with Lindsey, a marketing director from the West Village. Lindsey has no idea that the warm and witty emails that have persuaded her to spend Friday night with Peter have in fact been written by a faceless stranger hired by Cyber Love Assistants.

'Of course I wish I'd written the emails myself. But I can't just sit there and let life and opportunity pass me by,' he says. 'If I didn't farm this stage of the court-ship out to someone else I'd be on my own for ever.'

Will he 'fess up to Lindsey if romance should strike up between them?

'I don't know. It's pretty shameful to contract out your love life.'

Gilly disagrees. 'It's a wonderful idea! The girls who I write for are really grateful!' she enthuses. 'Why should people lose out on the chance of love just because they're not cut out for written banter?'

I glanced fondly down the hill at Hailey, who was throwing strawberries into Matty's open mouth. Hailey was a hot little property and a brilliant human being. But could she banter? Not to save her life! I remembered the first message she'd written when she started Internet dating. It had been piteous: *'Hey!! Loved your profile!! Altho less keen on the bird you've got your arm round, ex-wife maybe?!? I've got the whole weekend free if you fancy . . .;)'*

When I'd told her that was the worst first approach I'd ever seen she had been genuinely baffled.

'What do you *mean* I have to be all mysterious and reserved? Who says?' she'd grumbled, red-faced.

I'd been lost for words. And then I'd realized that there was no point in explaining: you either had it or you hadn't. Without further delay, I'd forbidden her to write a single word to anyone and had appointed myself her official ghost-writer. Matty, who had popped her into his Favourites that night, had been a breeze.

It sounded like Gilly, 29, from Brooklyn, had a similar talent for philanthropic meddling. I liked the sound of Gilly.

I resumed reading and started to chuckle. Yep. She knew the formula. Funny, a tiny bit cheeky and playfully ironic.

Saturday would be great, Gilly had written, on behalf of Sarah from North Arlington. *But I don't do midday dates. If you saw me in daylight my ethereal beauty would blind you and you'd fall into the Hudson. How about we meet early evening instead?*

I nodded approvingly. Could do with a bit more warmth but it was definitely better than anything that poor Sarah from North Arlington would have written. Poor Sarah from North Arlington agreed: *Having a ghost-writer is amazing*, she enthused. *I don't know what to say to ANYONE online. I used to rant about my ex-husband when men emailed me . . . This mystery girl saved my life!*

Cyber Love Assistants CEO Steve Sampson is keen to point out that while the nature of his business might be light-hearted, its success is not to be laughed at. 'We currently have over one hundred ghost-writers on our books,' he said, 'providing service for more than four thousand would-be daters. At present we're only operating in the US but you don't have to be American to need help. I'm hoping to take the business into the UK in the next couple of years.'

I sat back. 'No, you're not,' I said out loud. 'I am.'

Oh, are you now? I asked myself, laughing. It had been a reflexive response but, in truth, I rather liked the sound of it.

I would never dream of charging my hapless friends for ghost-writing services. After all, written banter came more easily to me than the thunderous passing of wind came to Sam. But throw in a business plan and some nifty little ideas . . . a bit of clever creativity, then a deadly publicity campaign . . . *There* was a challenge I'd relish. Business Charley sat up hungrily. There was something a little bit annoying about Steve Sampson from Boston: I quite liked the idea of taking him on.

My phone beeped in my handbag and I dug it out, sighing. Appealing as the idea was, it was no more than a pipe dream. Work was busier than ever and my deputy, Margot, had recently abandoned any pretence that she wasn't after my job. I had to guard my position as if my life depended on it: extra-curriculars, however appealing, were completely out of the question until further notice.

Then I looked at my phone and forgot instantly about Margot.

Because the person who had texted me was John. I felt an explosion of excitement go off somewhere in my reproductive system. John MacAllister? On a Saturday? *Lambert. Are you in town this weekend? I want to take you to dinner tomorrow please. 8 pm, The Tower. Jx.*

J with a kiss? J WITH A KISS? *Steady on, Charley*, I told myself. *Keep it real.* 'HAILEY!' I yelled, keeping it anything but real. Hailey was in a cheesy embrace with Matty, looking out towards the Castle. *I said, keep it real, Charley.* 'HAILEEEEEEEEEEEE!' I screamed, at the top of my lungs, getting up and running down the slope towards the picnickers. Finally! Finally! John and I were going on a date! A WEEKEND DATE! The significance of this invitation could not be overstated.

Matty continued to whisper cheesy Wotsits into Hailey's ear and I picked up speed.

My downward velocity might have been safe had I been wearing my running shoes; in my strappy sandals it was nothing of the sort. As I opened my mouth to yell, 'HAILEY!' again, my woefully inadequate leather sole hit a flat stone and my leg shot forward, wrenching me into an agonizing splits position. In slow motion I felt myself veer off sideways in mid-air, my skirt flying up round my head. As I came in to land on some far more serious-looking rocks I started planning emergency cover for the picnic so that Sam wasn't left without a hostess.

And then my head hit the ground, forcing my brain to stop whirring for probably the first time in thirty-two years.

Chapter Two

Confused and more than a little surprised, I closed my eyes, then reopened one in a subtle squint. Good God. It was as I'd thought. John MacAllister was sitting on my bed.

I was too shocked to be happy, let alone aroused. This situation – which I'd fantasized over for seven years – was far too implausible to be real.

Was I daydreaming?

After a brief mental consideration I stopped squinting and opened both eyes fully. If John really *was* sitting on my bed I'd be quite mad to waste the opportunity.

John MacAllister really *was* sitting on my bed. He was tapping abstractedly at his BlackBerry and not looking in my direction. *But he was sitting on my bed*. What the hell was going on?

I backtracked furiously.

Somewhere at the edge of my mind I had a sense that John and I were going on a date. Had it already happened, perhaps? Was I waking up, hung-over, after a night of wild and glorious sex? I bloody well hoped not. It would be devastating beyond measure to have slept with John MacAllister after all these years and be unable to remember it.

A cursory look down at myself revealed that we had not had sex. For there, where I'd hoped to see a pair of perky nipples and some crotchless pants (although I'd never owned any), was a long blue nightie and one of those holey yellow blankets with the wide polyester hems. My heart sank. This was not a post-coital set-up.

I concentrated hard, trying to work out what was going on. It was a confusing state of affairs, that was for sure. I no more owned long blue nighties and yellow blankets than I did crotchless knickers. And to add to the confusion, John seemed to be holding my foot, not in a blissful, post-coital sort of way, but rather in a . . . Oh, no. Oh, please, *NO*. In a giant, broken-leg-in-plaster-with-a-cute-foot-poking-out-of-it sort of a way.

There was a plastic identity tag on my wrist. A line of something going into my forearm under a neat white plaster. The sound of hushed conversations, flabby snoring, quiet beeping. Searing pain in my throat, terrible pain everywhere south of my belly-button, and the deadening, horrible certainty that I was in hospital.

A grey curtain enclosed John and me in a cubicle of doom; he continued to tap away on his BlackBerry.

I closed my eyes, devastated. What on earth had happened? Had I been hit by a bus during our date? Gone down drunk?

No, my head told me resignedly, as the events of the last twenty-four hours came limping back in. *No, it did not happen during your date with John. Because there was no date with John. You ruined any chance of that happening by hurling yourself down the hill like a great big six-foot ELEPHANT.*

Great work, moron.

I despaired silently under my yellow polyester blanket. Why had John chosen this – this *dog turd* of all the moments in my life – to sit on my bed?

15

When I opened my eyes again, he was looking at me with a smile that rendered me closer to crying than I had been in years. I swallowed hard. Charley Lambert was not a crier.

'Well well well,' he said. 'Hello, sleepy.'

'Fuck,' I replied sadly.

John snorted, pushing his BlackBerry into a leather pouch. His bright, X-ray eyes bored merrily into mine. 'Charlotte Lambert. That is not the kind of talk I was looking for!'

'Sorry. But I . . . I . . .' I bit my lip. *Get a grip, lame-arse*, I ordered myself. *If you cry in front of him it'll all be over.*

From the first day I'd met John it had been clear that the armour of outlandish toughness that I donned at work was a major factor in his feelings for me. Now I unleashed the full force of my iron will on my tears. *Stand down*, I told them sternly.

Watching this furious battle take place in my face, John smiled. And then did something extraordinary. He took my hand. *John MacAllister took my hand.* I felt suddenly dizzy. My gloriously attractive, powerful and downright sexual boss – one of the only three men in Edinburgh tall enough to court me – was sitting on my bed holding my hand. I fizzed all over, suddenly helpless, broken leg an irrelevance.

John had been driving me insane from the moment he walked into the communications office at Salutech Pharmaceutical Holdings seven years ago – 26 June 2005, to be precise – the day I'd set up shop at the tiny temp's desk in the corner.

I had been embarrassingly full of it. Twenty-five years old, the recently departed star of Hibernian FC's press and marketing office, and dating a handsome man named Dr Nathan Gillies. I was bristling with enthusiasm for my (extremely) important new role as deputy communications officer at Salutech: one of the biggest pharmaceutical multinationals in the world, never mind Scotland. I radiated misplaced professional confidence like Malcolm the Labrador radiated bad smells when he needed to go for a walk. I was ready to be a Big Shot.

On my arrival at Salutech's vast, space-hangar-like premises on the A1 near Newcraighall, it had become immediately clear that I was not there to be a Big Shot. Or even a small shot. I was there solely to help the Big Shots *above* me, or to suck a lot of cocks, as Hailey helpfully put it. Within three hours I knew that leaving my last job at Hibernian FC had been a mistake. My new boss, Angélique, was small, evil and Canadian, and her boss, the director of communications, was a man whose refusal to engage with me was so absolute that I was forced to go to the toilet to check that I did actually exist.

Looking in the mirror, I was able to confirm that I did. But only just. Suddenly Big Guns Lambert resembled a frightened child. In fact, the image in the mirror reminded me strongly of a photo of eleven-year-old me, minutes before curtain up on the East Linton Primary School's production of *The Wizard of Oz*. I was playing the Tin Man, feigning confidence, oozing terror. Now, fourteen years later, a similarly terrified girl stared back at me from the mirror. A whitehead was emerging next to her right eyebrow (a *whitehead*? Who, aged twenty-five had *whiteheads*?) and her 'natty' cerise fitted blouse clashed horribly with her not-so-natty but equally cerise face.

Why on earth had I left Hibs? Where I laughed every day, where I knew everyone, where my best bloody friend worked?

Hailey. I needed Hailey. I hit speed dial two and tried not to faint with fear.

'All right, Chas. What gives?' Hailey, wheezy and businesslike, accompanied by the clatter of plates and the yell of sweaty chefs. I felt my heart wrench.

'Well, in short, I hate my new job, my boss is evil, and the comms director won't even look at me,' I said. I contemplated squeezing the whitehead but decided against it.

'Have you actually tried saying hello to him?' Hailey asked. 'Oi! Paul! Put her down! You've got five minutes to finish plating up two hundred covers,' she yelled. A distant shriek and the sound of a swearing chef came down the line. Hailey was the operations manager at the Hibs Banqueting Centre and spent a lot of time shouting at people. When I had worked there in the public relations office, a good hundred metres down the second-floor corridor, I could hear her as clearly as if she was yelling into my ear.

I grinned briefly. 'Oh, Hailey, I miss that place. I miss those dirty chefs. I miss you. Do you think if I just stormed Salutech security they'd be able to sue me for defection?'

'Get a fucking grip.' She chuckled. I liked calling Hailey for operational advice. She didn't fuck around. 'Charley, I'm not listening to this. You left us here to go and do your big posh pharmaceuticals job because you're destined for big things. *Huge* things. It's your first day. What were you expecting?'

I'd thought about this briefly. It was true. This new job *was* a big deal; a huge coup for someone my age in a company the size of Salutech. 'It's not easy to do big things when no one will talk to you,' I said stubbornly.

I heard Hailey light a completely illegal cigarette, pulling the phone over to the window that overlooked the cemetery. 'Ahmad! What the fuck? MOVE!' she yelled. 'Right, Chas. As I said, it's your first day. Not even you can win everyone over in three hours, you dick. Second, you're well fit. Useful in this sort of situation. Is there anyone you can flirt with?'

I stood up straight and in so doing set off a hand-drier. 'Hailey Bresner,' I shouted. 'I got this job because of my abilities, not my sex appeal. I'm not here to make eyes at my boss! I'm here to bring in new ideas, implement new strategy and help strengthen Salutech's external relations.' The hand-drier stopped and I found myself shouting into an echoey toilet.

There was a brief pause and then Hailey giggled. 'Exactly,' she said quietly.

'Oh,' I said, starting to smile. 'Oh, right. Yes. Thank you, Hails.'

'No worries. RORY! WASH YOUR FUCKING HANDS AFTER HANDLING YOUR DICK, FOR FUCK'S SAKE! Charley, my love, you have a mountain-scaling sense of can-do. This is a walk in the park for you!'

I liked that. Mountain-scaling sense of can-do. 'Thanks, Big Tits.'

'OK, Chas, much as I'd like to stay blowing smoke up your arse, I've got two hundred covers coming in shortly for the Lord Provost's birthday lunch. You can do it!'

'Thanks, Hails. I miss you.' I sighed.

She took a puff of her cigarette and I could hear her smiling. 'Piss off,' she replied, not unkindly. Then: 'AHMAAAAAD! FOR FUCK'S FUCKING SAKE!'

The line went dead.

Right, I thought, squaring up to the mirror. *Time for action. I am Charley Lambert. A Scottish Amazon. The most fearless woman in the town of East Linton, in the country of Scotland, in the whole of the WORLD. I can do this!* When all else failed, I repeated this mantra and it generally did the trick.

I tucked my phone into my pocket and decided to squeeze the whitehead anyway. Leaning forward, I pressed in with two newly manicured nails and was instantly repaid with a tidy expulsion.

'That is disgusting,' said Angélique, walking in.

I died.

But then, ten minutes later, just as the nail marks faded away, I found myself alive. Very much alive. For into my office walked a very tall man, who looked at me once and instantly enslaved me. He had piercing dark eyes that were edged with amusement and dirtiness. He'd removed his tie – it was a warm June day – and the small triangle of visible chest, brown, sprinkled with hair and perspiring ever so slightly, finished me off. Before he even opened his mouth, I wanted to sink my face into that triangle and undo his shirt buttons with my teeth.

'Hello, who are you?' he said. His voice was deep and silky and slightly accented. His smile was more than I could handle. It was an X-ray smile. He could see everything.

'Is that rude shorthand for "Hello, welcome, what's your name?" ' I shot back. Angélique gasped.

The man grinned and bits of my body began to disintegrate. Brain cells began to fry, rude parts began to explode, my skin started to singe off. He chuckled languidly. The Bermuda Triangle at the top of his chest vibrated slightly and I had to look away before I got lost in it, never to be found again. 'Hmm. You're right, it was a bit rude. But then again, so am I . . .' he added, with just enough of a pause for me to know that I had to have this man or die trying. 'So I'll start again. Hello, welcome. I'm John MacAllister, CEO. What's your name?'

Gripped, I didn't turn a hair. 'Hello, John MacAllister, CEO. I'm Charlotte Lambert, deputy communications officer as of this morning. I'm here to help implement the new brand PR strategy.'

'She's actually just helping me organize last year's press cleepings,' Angélique butted in.

John MacAllister held up his hand and I noted the absence of a wedding ring. *YES*. 'I'm sure she's up to something more challenging than press clippings,' he said, eyes flicking down briefly at my legs.

Thank God for all those six a.m. runs, I thought. Thank God. 'I hope so,' I responded crisply. 'I like a challenging project.' John smiled straight at me with an unbearably knowing twinkle in his eye. All I could hear was the screech of gears changing as everything I'd thought I knew about men fell out of my bottom and I shifted into a whole new understanding of the word 'desire'. Me and Dr Nathan Gillies were over. He might be handsome – and a doctor at that – but in the warm glow of John's gaze I found myself suddenly able to face the truth: Dr Nathan Gillies was basically a wanker. He made constant jokes about my height and only wanted to have sex on Wednesdays when he came off shift early. He frequently made bitchy comments about lesbians when he was around my lesbian twin sister and, worst of all, Granny Helen intensely disliked him. Which was never a good sign. 'A self-important turnip of a man,' she'd sniffed, after their first meeting.

She'd approve of the man standing in front of me, though. Oh, Granny Helen would approve of this one, all right. I would finish with Dr Nathan Gillies without delay. *This*, this cheeky and more-than-tall-enough god standing in front of me, was what I wanted.

'I'm not here to make eyes at some man,' I'd roared, only fifteen minutes ago.

'Poor little Lambert,' John said quietly, moving a few inches further up my yellow polyester blanket.

I stiffened suspiciously. Dirty flirting I was used to from John MacAllister; compassion and kindness I was not. Was he here to sack me? He looked down at me with a complicated expression on his face.

'Why are you here?' I asked timidly. *Because you are all small and poorly with a broken leg and I want to sweep you up in my arms, drive you off in my Jaguar and take you to my architecturally significant house by a loch*, I willed him to say. *We will sit drinking single malt as the sun goes down and I will gently cut out a section of your plaster so we can make love.*

John smiled again, only this time with a plastic veneer

that did not make my plaster-bound crotch tingle. It made my plaster-bound crotch contract with fear.

'John? Is my leg really bad?' I asked, trying to sound calm. 'Are you going to make me resign?'

Something odd flashed across his face. Then he shook his head. 'Lambert,' he said quietly, looking me straight in the eye. 'Trust me when I tell you that absolutely *nothing* would persuade me to lose you from my team.' He stroked my palm gently with his thumb.

Damn him. Damn his deep, soft, silky voice. Damn those *eyes*. And that lovely warm caressing thumb.

For the millionth, billionth time in the last seven years, a little lamp of hope ignited in my chest. Men in happy relationships didn't speak to women like this unless they . . . They didn't come and visit their director of comms in hospital unless they . . . And holding hands! That was flirting! His affair with Married Woman must be over. *He wanted me.*

'Well, John MacAllister,' I demurred. Providing John flirted with me I was at ease: I knew exactly how to handle him. 'I'd say I'm in pretty good shape, give or take the odd broken limb. I'm sure it won't be long before I'm hobbling around the office.' John grinned. 'Or at least hobbling over to Old Town for dinner. Providing the offer still stands.'

'Excellent news, Lambert. Your doctor believes you'll be hobbling soon, then?'

I tried to shrug but was too weak, so instead ended up making a retarded sort of a face. 'Don't know. You're the first person I've seen since I woke up.'

John's eyes twinkled. 'That's not true. You had surgery and then came round eight hours ago,' he said. 'Your twin sister was here. Vanessa, is it? She told me your parents are on their way from India and your younger sister's coming up from London.'

'Yes, Katy lives in London . . .' Then I stared at him. 'Hang on. I came round from an anaesthetic and then slept for *eight hours*? Seriously?'

'Yes, seriously. Apparently you stared at Vanessa, then fell asleep hugging her elbow. Very sweet, Lambert. The nurses said they'd never seen anyone so desperate for a good kip.'

He stroked my palm with his thumb again. I felt suddenly grateful for my broken leg. It had brought John MacAllister to me, finally.

'How did you know I was here?' I asked.

'Fraser Cassidy called me. He said you were recovering from major surgery. I was close to the hospital so thought I should swing by. Employee relations and all that.'

'If Fraser Cassidy told you I was here, he's a very bad doctor,' I said. 'Since when did he have the right to share confidential patient information with the head of the local pharmaceutical company?'

John's X-ray eyes stared straight through me to the Lamp of Hope in my chest. 'Given that he's one of our most valued medical consultants, and you're one of our most valued staffers, I think it's quite reasonable. And he knows we have a special relationship.'

Damn him. The Lamp of Hope had now taken on the form of a furnace. 'We do not have a special relationship,' I told him. 'Unless you took advantage of me while I was under anaesthetic.'

John chortled. 'Oh, Lambert,' he murmured, staring at

me. 'What are we to do with you? Eight hours out of theatre and you're already fantasizing about molestation.'

I fiddled with my horrible yellow blanket and said nothing. I was far too confused to speak. I had not received this level of attention from John since our ill-fated snog that I'd spent three years trying unsuccessfully to forget. It had taken place on 26 June 2009, almost exactly four years since I'd met John. Things were going well for me at Salutech: I'd made it to brand communications manager and now had my sights on director of comms. It was five thirty-seven a.m. on the night of our end-of-financial-year jolly and John and I were in a cleaning cupboard at one of the most expensive country clubs in Scotland.

I had spent those four years longing for him to hold my hand and now, finally, he was holding my hand. Furthermore, he had been holding my hand for three whole minutes, having led me from the lounge down to the empty basement where he had found a cupboard full of mops. He had seated me on a bench among them and was now looking me full in the face – at point-blank range – in a way that left me speechless and rubbery.

'I've been trying every day for four years not to do this,' he was saying. 'Charley bloody Lambert, you *witch*, with that waist and those legs and that *confidence* and that . . . Oh, God, Lambert, I can't take any more.'

His eyes – hungry and slightly mad – told me everything I needed to know. Sex with him was going to be the most outrageous and dirty act I would ever commit.

And with that I lunged. There was no other option. It was that or die of an exploding vagina.

He was hot, dry and delicious. I was mad, crazed and damp. He immediately flipped me round and pushed me back against the wall by my throat. 'Fuck,' he muttered. 'Fuck.'

'Yes,' I replied breathlessly. 'Now. Your room?' He moved his head down and started kissing my neck, hard and urgently. Explosions and alarms fired off all the way through my body. A strange moan filled the cleaning cupboard and I realized it was me. I sounded like an animal.

John pulled back for a second and looked at me. 'Yes. My room. Oh, Christ, Lambert, I won't last. I won't.' He, too, made a sort of animalistic groan.

I did the only sensible thing; I started to unbuckle his jeans.

But then it came. The Greatest Rejection of My Life. The End of the Universe. 'Lambert, no, I can't do this,' he gasped suddenly. 'I can't. I promised myself . . . I . . .' A gurgling noise came out of his throat as if he were in the process of hanging himself, rather than in the process of having his manhood liberated from his jeans.

'Don't be fucking ridiculous,' I hissed. 'We'll both die if we don't. I order you, John MacAllister, to TAKE ME *NOW*.'

John stared at me with a sort of crazed desperation. 'I can't, Charley. If it went wrong and I lost you from Salutech I'd be totally buggered. I can't take that risk.'

'I'll RESIGN,' I yelled. 'IT DOESN'T MATTER. DON'T DO THIS. I BEG YOU, DON'T DO THIS!'

John was panting. 'The thing is . . .' he said vaguely, eyes crossing, 'The thing is, we're making you director of comms. Across everything. Brands, corporate, internal.

You got the job, Lambert – *Oh, Christ, I want to be inside you*. You've got a while to get it all running smoothly and then you'll be starting the biggest drug launch we've ever staged. I cannot start sleeping with you now, of all times.' In desperation he took a handful of my hair and scrunched it. 'Aaargh,' he added.

'What do you MEAN I got the job?' I croaked. 'You can't just announce that! You need to offer me a financial package and then I'll get back to you and then – Oh, God, what am I saying, who *cares*? That's tomorrow. This is now. Please. I beg you. Stop doing this to me. To both of us.'

John looked at me for a few more anguished seconds, then pulled me back, ramming me down on his lap and kissing me hard, stopping only to pull my dress off over my head. I wriggled, gasping, feeling an outlandishly strong, hard MacAllister between my legs, and moved in so he could take off my bra. He reached round to undo it, burying his head between my breasts. He definitely bit one of my nipples but it didn't hurt. At all. I began to lose myself. It was finally happening. My privates had gone completely barmy and volcanic, full of pulsating molten lava. Soon they would not be private. Soon they would be filled with John. Jesus, Mary and Joseph! At last!

'Jesus, Mary and Joseph!' It was a scream. A high-pitched scream. 'And all the saints!'

Was it me? No. I had not just said that. Was it John? No. John was frozen, his head still between my breasts, hand on the back of my bra strap.

Slowly, I looked round. The door was open. A woman of around Granny Helen's age was standing at the door wearing a black dress with a white apron. She had a little white hat thing on her head and was carrying a bucket. She looked like she might drop dead of a heart-attack.

I looked back down at John, who had become the CEO of Salutech Pharmaceutical once more. He couldn't meet my eye.

It was over.

As, I realized, with great irritation, it was now. John had his hand in mine and was looking at me in the exact same way he'd looked at me that night. But I was swaddled in nylon, my Temple of Lady buried behind a wall of plaster and bandage, a coterie of fierce nurses, the sick and injured metres away. There would be no sex. No passion. Just the agony of John's hand in mine and the possibility of absolutely nothing further until a later date.

As I tried to douse the Furnace of Hope in my chest – not to mention the one in my gynaecological parts – it began to dawn on me that physically I was feeling terrible. I had no sensation in my left leg, my throat was still on fire and I was freezing cold. John swam before me for a few seconds.

'Charley? Are you OK?'

His face was a lot closer to mine. I could smell toothpaste and a very light, delicate man perfume. (Toothpaste? Scent? Surely significant?) 'Yes,' I said weakly. 'I just suddenly felt tired. I . . . I think I need to sleep.' *Offer to hop in and spoon me*, my eyes implored.

John put his hand on the side of my face. 'I'm going to bugger off,' he said. 'Promise you'll get some rest. Work can wait, OK?'

'I can work from here till I'm on crutches –' I began,

but he put a finger over my mouth. Had I not been feeling so nauseous I might have bitten it. 'OK,' I said meekly. 'I'll rest.'

We both knew that I would do no such thing.

Then something even more incredible happened. John leaned down and kissed me gently on the mouth, lingering for just a second before straightening up, smiling at me. My brain went funny and fizzy. I had just received a Tender Kiss. From John MacAllister! The man who, I was quite happy to admit, was the only reason I'd been single since I'd split up with Dr Nathan Gillies six years ago. Too busy for love, my arse. I just wanted John.

John MacAllister, John MacAllister! my head sang, to the tune of 'Bread of Heaven'. Kiss me till I want no more! (Want no more . . .)

'John MacAllister!' said a voice that was not in my head. My jubilation dispersed rapidly into the stale hospital air. It was a voice that was rather pleased with itself; a voice that I did not under any circumstances want to hear. *Please, let it not be Dr Nathan Gillies*, I prayed, as the curtain was swished grandly to one side and in strode Dr Nathan Gillies.

Of all the wards in Edinburgh, I'd had to end up on his? Seriously? He smiled briefly and picked up the chart at the end of my bed. 'Hi, Charley,' he said briskly. 'John.' They shook hands.

I closed my eyes. The last time I had seen Dr Nathan Gillies, in 2006, he had told me that I was 'dysfunctional and remote' and a 'messed-up workaholic', who was entertaining 'a pathetic obsession with a boss who will *never* get together with you'. Too stunned to say a word, I had sat on my bed and watched him round up the belongings he had kept at my flat during our time together – a solo toothbrush – and march out of my life.

After twenty-four hours spent sobbing on the sofa with Ness patting my hand, Hailey telling me to get a grip and Sam, my flatmate, staring awkwardly at me from the furthest corner of the room, I had come to the conclusion that Dr Nathan Gillies was a cunt. Once this had been established, I had got over him almost immediately but, deep down, my pride had remained bruised. I had formulated several revenge plans, the best of which ran along the lines of

1. John and I got married (reported in the nationals).
2. We ran Salutech together (ditto).
3. We oversaw the discovery of a complete cure for cancer (reported in the internationals).
4. We therefore saved the world (same).
5. Dr Nathan Gillies read about us and choked slowly and painfully on his own bile. (Reported nowhere because no one really cared.)

So the fact that he was currently standing in my cubicle, my fate in his hands, chatting pompously away to John (who had indeed declined to get together with me – thus far) was pretty devastating.

'Congratulations!' Dr Nathan Gillies said to John, doing that pointless elbow-clasping thing that men do. He must have read the medical-profession-only introduction to our new breakthrough drug, Simitol, which I had recently started circulating. It was easily the biggest story the pharmaceutical industry had seen in the last twenty years.

'Thanks, Nathan,' John said, looking uncomfortable.

'We've been awaiting this news a long time,' Dr Nathan Gillies barked. There was something ratty in his eyes that I didn't like. Clearly, John felt the same for, without further ado, he nodded curtly to us both, swished back the curtain and strode off. I closed my eyes and listened to the clip of his leather loafers striding off down the corridor. *Things were happening in this cubicle*, I screamed silently at Dr Nathan Gillies. *He just kissed me! And didn't you see the way he was looking at me? He was about to Say Something! You rotten bastard, just marching in here!*

When I opened my eyes again, Dr Nathan Gillies was looking at me over the clipboard with an ever-so-slightly malevolent expression. 'So, Charlotte,' he said. The only people who called me Charlotte were Granny Helen, when she was being terrifying, and myself, when I needed a pep talk. Dr Nathan Gillies was enjoying this situation immensely.

'So, Nathan. This is a nice surprise,' I said awkwardly. It was nothing of the sort and he ignored me.

'You've fractured your tibia in two places. It's going to take a long time to heal. But the good news is that the operation was a success and you should be out of here in about a week.'

I stared at him, stunned. 'I've broken my leg in two places?'

'Yes. You also had a potential fractured skull, which

turned out to be OK. You've suffered quite a lot of soft-tissue damage, with various superficial wounds on your arms and legs from the rocks you fell on. Oh, and I suspected you may have fractured your pelvis, too, so I'm sending you for a CT scan shortly.'

'So – and *you* operated on me?' I asked. He nodded curtly.

Even worse.

My mind was racing, trying to figure out the implications of a properly broken leg and maybe even a broken pelvis. Dr Nathan Gillies watched me with malignant amusement, knowing full well what was happening in my head. 'No, Charlotte, you will not be able to run again this year. Possibly never. No, you cannot go back to work soon. And, no, I do not recommend that you transfer to a private hospital.'

I had yet to come up with a satisfactory explanation for why I had gone out with Dr Nathan Gillies for so long. Hailey had insisted that it was because of my obsession with men of medicine but I wasn't convinced. Deep down, I suspected it had more to do with the fact that he was so chronically unavailable, both mentally and physically, he was actually my perfect man. During our relationship I'd got all the nourishment I needed from work, and for four years we had seen each other three times a week (sex on Wednesdays), with my emotional state remaining entirely unaltered.

But today my emotional state was in grave danger. *Don't give in to the fucker*, I imagined Hailey hissing in my ear. 'So . . . just to clarify, how long until I can get back to work, more or less?' I asked him.

He seemed bored. 'I don't know. A few weeks. Longer if your pelvis is fractured.'

I stared dumbly. '*Weeks?* But . . . we're just launching Simitol! It's going to change the face of medicine!'

He interrupted me with an upturned hand. 'Charley, this is non-negotiable. I'm sure John will be able to find someone else to do your job while you're recuperating.' Aware that this was just about the worst thing anyone could say to me, he positively beamed.

I felt my face crumple. 'This is the most crucial time in Salutech's history,' I whispered. 'I can't not be there. I just can't.'

Dr Nathan Gillies shook his head. 'It's as I said, Charley. And I will be making sure John MacAllister is fully briefed, should you be tempted to return to work earlier than advised.'

I swallowed hard, my eyes stinging. This was too much. 'How many weeks. Three? Four?' I whispered.

He put my chart back at the end of my bed and shrugged noncommittally. 'We'll see.' He shot a shrewish look in my direction. 'Speaking of John, what do you think? Interesting news, eh?'

I felt exhausted. 'What? Us getting the health secretary behind Simitol?'

'No. John and Susan Faulkner getting engaged,' he said, watching me intently.

I stared at him. 'Susan Faulkner is married,' I said uncertainly. 'It's just a silly little affair.' I didn't acknowledge the fact that John had been having this silly little affair for three years.

Dr Nathan Gillies smiled. 'Not any more! John called

Fraser Cassidy earlier to tell him the good news. Apparently Susan's divorce came through yesterday and John proposed to her on the spot. I'm surprised he didn't mention it.'

I swallowed, bolts of pain shooting down the back of my throat. Dr Nathan Gillies pressed on, smelling blood. 'At long last, eh? John's been begging Susan to leave her husband for, what, three years now?'

'But . . .' My voice caught in my throat. I no longer cared what Dr Nathan Gillies thought. 'But . . . he invited me out on a date . . . A date tomorrow night . . . It was going to be our first date together . . .'

Dr Nathan Gillies clipped my chart to the end of the bed with a triumphant grin on his face. Revenge, finally, was his. 'I rather doubt that, Charlotte.'

Chapter Three

Someone was playing 'You Are My Sunshine' on a banjo in my cubicle. It was a very poor rendition, made still poorer when a thin, reedy voice started singing along about a semitone sharp.

'For God's sake, Christian,' Mum's voice said. 'The poor girl's in trauma.'

'It'll help her,' Dad replied with certainty. 'Tomatoes grow if you sing to them. Look, Jane! She's waking up! It worked!'

Mum, tall and tanned, broke into a smile. Looking at her standing above me, all strong and capable, I felt safe. Mum would sort this mess out.

'Hello, my poor love,' she said gently.

'Charlotte! My dear girl!' Dad bounded up, thumping his banjo down on the bed next to my healthy leg. Mum sighed despairingly as he swooped in and kissed me on the forehead. 'Christian . . . will you please be careful with her?'

I laughed, then winced as a monstrous wave of pain shot up from somewhere below my hips. 'Hi, Dad. Hi, Mum. Um, sorry.'

Mum smoothed my hair out of my face. 'Charley, darling, there's nothing to apologize for. *We*'re sorry. We got back as quickly as we could but you know what it's like, trying to make something happen quickly in India –' She broke off, alarmed, as a series of beeps started going off somewhere above my head. 'What does that mean, Christian?' she asked.

Dad peered at the machines. 'No idea!' he said cheerfully. 'But she's alive! Look at her, eh? Our fine little girl! Battling on!'

Mum shot a stern look at him and opened the curtain of my cubicle. 'Nurse, could you please come in and help my daughter?' she said firmly. So direct and confident, Mum. Calm in a crisis. My best qualities had come from my mother.

Well, most of them, I thought, looking fondly at Dad, who had pulled the blanket off my leg and was examining the plastering with a face of great wonder. 'Do you know what, Charlotte? This technique hasn't changed since I was a senior house officer! Not a jot! Oh, hello, Nurse. A few bells and whistles going off in here. Any thoughts?'

I giggled, in spite of the alarms. Dad was still wearing the swimming trunks he must have had on when they got the call.

The nurse strode over. It was the same moody one who had refused to euthanase me when Dr Nathan Gillies had left earlier. In the face of Dad's most childlike smile, though, she melted a little. 'Nothing to worry about,' she said gruffly. 'Just time for her next dose of Diclofenac.'

'We used to eat Diclofenac on Friday nights when I was a registrar,' he said. The nurse blanched. 'Oh, we had some merry old times!' he added, gazing happily into the distance.

The nurse retreated from the cubicle, clearly disgusted.

'What time is it, Mum?' I asked.

'Just gone half twelve.'

'Oh, Mum, it's way too late . . . You guys should go and get some sleep. Come back in the morning,' I said weakly.

Mum took my hand. 'Charley, dear, it's half twelve in the afternoon.'

'What? How?'

Dad chuckled. 'You've been in a coma, Charleychops!'

'*What?*' I clutched the side of the bed.

'CHRISTIAN!' Mum roared. She shouted rarely, but when she did, it brought traffic to a standstill. The ward beyond the curtain froze in abject terror. Only the timid beep, beep, beep of a machine convinced me that her blast hadn't turned them all to stone.

'*Christian*, your daughter has gone through the most frightening experience of her life. Pull yourself together, man, and don't you *DARE* make jokes about comas.'

'It was a figure of speech, Jane,' Dad said reproachfully, slinking back to the corner with his banjo. I caught his eye and smiled quickly while Mum rearranged my blanket. Dad spent his life being sent off to the naughty corner. I had hundreds of photos from family get-togethers of me, Mum, Ness and Katy sitting around the dining table with Dad relegated to the corner, hugging Malcolm or pulling a face of comic remorse behind Mum's back.

'Yes, Charley,' Mum continued quietly. 'It's Sunday afternoon. Apparently you saw your boss yesterday afternoon, then slept for fifteen hours!'

Dad stretched out his arms and fingers and pretended to be a sloth from behind Mum's back in the corner of the room.

37

I found myself suddenly mirthless.

John. Of course. John was engaged. I was assailed by a terrible emptiness and had to focus hard on the dog-tag on my wrist for a moment. (1) *Don't cry.* (2) *DON'T CRY*, my head commanded sternly. I did what I was told but I wasn't sure I'd be able to keep it up much longer. My aversion to crying seemed less explicable by the minute.

Mum pulled up the other chair and sat down. 'Now, dear,' she said briskly, getting out a pad and pencil. That businesslike voice meant she would Take Care of Things. Dad began to tinkle away at his banjo.

Mum shot a frustrated glance in his direction. 'Now, Ness said you wanted to move hospitals. I think not, dear. It sounds like you shouldn't be moved for at least another week. OK?'

'I told Ness that?'

'Yes, she was here when you came round from your op. You told her that you wanted to move to a private hospital where you could get on with work.'

I smiled. 'That sounds about right.'

'Well, it's out of the question. These people operated on you so you will remain here,' Mum continued. 'And when you're well enough to be discharged, you'll be coming back to East Linton with us. You will not be working during that time.'

I nodded, crossing my fingers under the blanket. If anything was going to help me deal with the wreck my life had suddenly become, it would be work. The great panacea. My own personal cure-all.

'Also, I've spoken to Sam and transferred him some money to hire a cleaner while you're in hospital. I shudder to imagine what will happen to your flat otherwise,' she continued.

'Thanks, Mum. Good idea.'

'Now, I know you've seen your boss but I did put in a formal call to the duty HR mobile at Salutech,' Mum said. 'Everything's fine, there'll probably be forms to fill in but you're not to worry about that now.'

I felt a twinge of fear. 'Did everything sound OK?'

'In what sense, dear?'

'In the sense that my job's never been busier or more important than it is right now. I'm really worried that they'll have to get rid of me, Mum.'

Mum shook her head. 'Don't be silly. That would be against every employment law in Scotland.'

I rather wished I had inherited Mum's unshakeable conviction in absolutely everything she said.

Mum was the practice manager, receptionist and head nurse at Dad's general practice in East Linton, the pretty but functional little town where I had grown up. Even though Dad was the doctor I was fairly sure that it was Mum's no-nonsense bedside manner that convinced locals to reject the new medical centre in Dunbar and keep on coming to Dad.

'As long as you're sure,' I said gingerly. 'I'm just worried. I've worked hard, Mum.'

'Yes, dear, I know. Hard work gets rewarded. Everything will be fine.'

'And, if not, I'll bomb them,' Dad offered. Mum ignored him.

Please, please, let her be right, I thought. The scientists at Salutech had spent more than a decade developing

Simitol, the first ever HIV vaccine. It was a breakthrough that no other pharmaceutical company had come close to, and after years of clinical trials, it was ready to go. Now, in the final few months before it was launched, it was my turn to take the reins. My job to make sure the government and medical industry were clear that Simitol was *the* most innovative product in the last twenty years. That it could actually prevent HIV, which, even in recent memory, had been a death sentence – and deserved long-term funding. I had to bottle up the support we had from patient groups and transmit it to our drug reps so that they could sell Simitol with total confidence.

Being responsible for the public face of a company while it changed the course of medical history was a gigantic feat for anyone, let alone a girl of thirty-two. Being bed-bound was simply not acceptable. *I'*d sack me.

'Now, my love, can you please tell us what happened?' Mum said, taking my hand. 'Why were you running down Salisbury Crags in sandals?'

A large pair of breasts arrived in the cubicle, followed by Hailey and then Matty. 'Because she never stops bloody well running!' she said. 'Hello, Chas! You poor thing, how're you feeling?' She kissed my parents.

Dad loved Hailey. 'Ah, wonderful!' he exclaimed delightedly. 'And you must be the famous Matthew! Welcome to the family, young man!'

Matty beamed all over his round little face. 'How lovely to meet you, Dr Lambert,' he said excitedly, as if he were meeting Hailey's father, not mine. 'Hello, Charley,' he said brightly. 'Are you OK?'

'Not amazing,' I mumbled. I'd put on a brave face for

John but it looked like that was my limit. 'It's hard to say what part of me hurts the most.' *Probably my broken heart*, I thought sadly. Matty nodded sympathetically but was quickly distracted by the amount of electronic equipment behind me. Hailey, meanwhile, got stuck into the opened box of Milk Tray by my bed. What a fantastically odd couple they were. Hailey, small and curvy, looking like a slutty country-and-western singer with her long golden curls and a cowboy shirt; Matty, in hiking pants and a multi-function fleece, mirrored sunglasses on his head and probably a compass in his pocket.

I glazed over a little while my parents chatted to them, Hailey popping chocolates into her mouth as if they were grapes. I wished I cared as little about my figure as she did about hers.

Then it struck me: in the wake of John's engagement, my figure had ceased to matter. *Fuck my waist*, I thought grimly. *In fact, fuck everything.* 'You know what?' I interrupted. Everyone looked at me. 'I'm *STARVING*,' I said. 'Gizza chocolate, Hailey!'

Hailey was surprised. 'I didn't think you ate chocolate,' she said.

'I do now. Who brought them?'

'Me,' Hailey said.

I giggled, stopping abruptly when bolts of pain attacked my throat. 'Thanks, Hails. Kind of you to purchase a present that you could eat yourself.'

Dad roared with laughter. 'She's always had an appetite, this one! I don't blame you, Hailey, someone's got to eat some chocolate round here! That crackpot organic diet Charley follows!' He rolled his eyes and winked at her.

At that point Sam ambled in, raffish and beautiful, poncy sunglasses on his head, a present under his arm. In spite of it being June, the present was wrapped in Christmas paper. 'Hiya, Chas,' he said, as if he'd just walked into our sitting room. 'What's up?'

Hailey gave him a despairing look. 'What's up? She got carted off from your engagement party unconscious, Sam. That's what.'

Sam picked up the box of chocolates. 'True.' As he pored over them, large green eyes alight with childish pleasure, I found myself smiling like an indulgent mother. Although he was the best-looking man in Edinburgh, I had never wanted to do any more than parent him: give his neck a good scrub; get some healthy food down him, that sort of thing. Sexually I wouldn't have touched him with a barge pole. Partly because he was a grubby pig with women but mostly because, having lived with him so long, I knew he was basically a big child in a beautiful man's body and that it would be tantamount to paedophilia.

The day I'd met Sam he was wearing his T-shirt inside out and – apart from his incredibly good looks – he was indistinguishable from the sea of nice boys who were shuffling around my halls of residence. They all had an air of having been cast adrift; lost without their comfortable homes and clothes-laundering mothers (but greatly comforted by the opportunities for unlimited drinking and sexual intercourse that university life was offering). Sam had been suffering a terrible hangover and had exited the lift too early by mistake; when he walked into Hailey's and my room on floor nine, he'd believed he was walking into his own on floor ten. 'Oh, hi there,' he'd said, surprised but unperturbed to find two girls on the floor, poring over an Edgar Allan Poe poem that they claimed to love but couldn't really understand.

'Hello,' we'd bleated, slightly awed by the beautiful man who'd just walked – *voluntarily* – into our room. Sam eventually realized he'd made a mistake but showed no signs of departing. Instead he wandered over and opened the bottle of Glenfiddich that Dad had given me as a going-away present. He drank it on our sofa while trying to figure out – with an expression of genuine puzzlement – how he had slept with so many girls since arriving in Glasgow. 'I really haven't been trying,' he mused, sleepy green eyes clouded with confusion. 'I even went to the theatre the other night and some girl bought me a drink and pretty much stuck her wangers in my face. It was the weirdest thing . . .'

Hailey and I had shaken our heads in surprise, even though we knew full well why the girl had stuck her wangers in his face.

And yet, awed though we might be by his looks, we both knew instantly that we would never want to Go There. It would just be wrong. Instead we became an unlikely triumvirate: me, a lanky nerd who got twitchy when out of the library; Hailey, leading a more classic life of drinking, occasional lectures and failed romances; and Sam, drifting around studying something called 'Drama', growing mad hair for his theatrical productions and leaving a trail of crazed girls in his wake. He picked them up everywhere. I even saw him pick one up in the university Spar shop while wearing an inexcusable pair of ethnic 'rehearsal pants'. I concealed myself behind a huge display tower of Haribo and watched enviously, wondering why, when I always made an effort to dress well, I couldn't so much as muster a smile out of other men. They just ran from me, seemingly terrified.

Sam popped a chocolate into his mouth while Dad struck an excitable and tuneless chord on his banjo. 'Well, the gang are all here now. All we need is Nessie and little Katy and then we can have a party! Shall I go out and get some pizzas in?'

'Christian.' Mum sighed. 'I . . . Oh, it doesn't matter. Come on, let's give Charley and her friends some space. We can come back later.'

Dad looked disappointed but gathered up his banjo. 'OK. Bye, darling!' he said, planting a smacker on my forehead. 'I'll sneak Malcolm in later. Never understood why you can't bring animals into a hospital.' He wandered out of the cubicle, whistling 'You Are My Sunshine' even more tunelessly than he had sung it. Sam, grinning, took his seat in the corner.

'Dear God,' Mum said, following Dad out. 'I really could punch him at times, Charley.'

I tried to laugh but it hurt. 'You're made for each other,' I croaked. Mum shrugged, blowing me a kiss as she left. However improbable their marriage might seem to an outsider – in fact, even to them – it worked.

I'd often imagined John and me as a married couple. We'd be busy, of course, with Salutech, but we'd make sure we created time to eat around our large scrubbed-pine table in John's loch-side house. Our children would be naughty, clever and beautiful and would speak at least five languages by the age of ten. They'd be skilled at sports and music, and the most popular kids in school by some margin.

Stop it, I told myself. *Don't do this.*

For once, I obeyed. I didn't remotely wish to believe that a long-term future with John was now impossible. *It was impossible in the first place, you moron*, my head snapped. *Why would he want a gigantic weird-looking fool like you?*

Hailey removed the chocolates from Sam and handed one to me but I felt so engulfed by sadness that I was unable to do much more than roll it around in the palm of my hand. 'Where's Ness?' I asked eventually. When I was feeling vulnerable I felt a visceral longing for Ness who, born a mere twenty-six minutes before me, was pretty much part of me. Our younger sister Katy, who had followed nearly ten years later (the result of one of Mum and Dad's pseudo-spiritual holidays to Asia), often grumbled about being the Lambert family wallflower, what with Ness and I 'living up each other's arses'. We were the exact opposite; in my eyes I was a big, tall, corporate beast while Ness was a little, soft, chilled-out flower fairy. I imagined her kind blue eyes set in her delicate face, framed by her dark pixie-cut hair, and struggled not to weep.

'She'll be here any minute,' Hailey replied. 'She sat up with you all night; your parents sent her home to sleep.'

'Wow,' I mumbled, moved and grateful. I had a feeling I'd really need Ness in the coming weeks.

There was a pause.

'Sorry I ruined your party, Sam,' I said eventually.

He chuckled, shaking his head. 'Chas, you fucking

45

rocked that party, brother,' he said. 'How often does an out-of-work actor get to fly across Edinburgh in an air ambulance? It was AWESOME!'

'Oh, Samuel Bowes. You really are an insufferable penis.' Hailey sighed.

'Takes one to know one, Hai—'

I interrupted. 'Er, *what*? I came here in a helicopter?'

Sam got a can of beer out of his satchel. 'Course you did. What sort of an ambulance gets up the Salisbury Crags?'

I stared at him, shocked. 'And you came with me?'

Sam nodded enthusiastically. 'Fuck, yeah! I got shotgun what with it being my party and all. I wasn't going to miss out on that!'

Hailey tried to look disapproving but couldn't help laughing. 'I did try to come with you, Chas,' she said. 'And Ness really wanted to but, of course, she's terrified of flying. Sam just basically shoved his way in shouting, "SHOTGUN."' Matty nodded confirmation, looking green with envy. An emergency helicopter ride would be just up his street.

I smiled. 'And how was the flight, Bowes?'

'Wicked! A bit too short, plus there was this bird making horrible noises, but the paramedics pumped her full of tranquillizers and she shut up.' He looked up at me sharply to check I was still amused. I was, just. His face softened. 'Chas, it was pretty horrible. We're all really glad you're OK.'

I realized I still had the chocolate in my hand and popped it into my mouth. My wholesome home-cooked diet could go and fuck itself. What good had it done me?

I had never been attractive enough for John. Six a.m. runs, endless trips to Beetroot Deli, the farmers' market, Crombies. Everything organic, fair-trade, high-quality, sodding expensive. *What a pitiful waste of time*, my head mocked. It would be all about chocolate from now on.

A second later I spat out a mouthful of Turkish Delight. 'Hailey!' I cried, appalled yet unsurprised. Hailey did not take chocolate-sharing lightly. 'I've broken my leg! Give me a good one, you horrible girl!' She handed me a caramel.

'And you're calling me an insufferable penis?' Sam asked her mildly. He scratched his testicles and, watching him with the usual horrified fascination, I felt a renewed sense of shock at his engagement.

Then the curtain was thrown aside and Katy came sauntering in, like a scene from an east London art gallery. She wore vintage sporting breeches, a sparkly cropped bustier and some sort of feather construction clipped into her cropped hair. A pair of vintage pearls hung from her earlobes and she had smudges from last night's make-up under her eyes, making her look simultaneously dirty and vulnerable. I began to smile. I didn't see anywhere near enough of Katy: she was too busy being a fashionable electropop singer in London to hang out with her two old-granny sisters in Edinburgh.

'Charley!' she cried, bounding over and kissing me. 'Oh, my God!'

'I know,' I said ruefully, as she squeezed my hand. 'This is what happens when someone my height suffers the misapprehension that they're athletic.'

'No!' she protested. 'You're super-athletic! You put me and Nessie to shame with all that running.' She peered into the box of chocolates and I took a quick look at Sam who was, as usual, eyeing her up fairly unsubtly. He caught my frown and held up his hands. Quite apart from the fact that Sam no longer had any business perving at girls, I had told him a few years back (when I'd caught him using his infamous Shakespearean chat-up line on Katy at my birthday party) that I would personally cut off his scrotum if he so much as touched her arm.

Katy, unaware of my fatwah, flopped down on Sam's knee. 'Hi, babe,' she said, patting his leg. Katy was enviably aware of her own sexuality and Sam peeped out at me from underneath her arm, powerless and afraid. I raised a warning eyebrow.

But I knew it was OK. Sam was in love. He was getting married. The impossible had happened.

'Sorry, Charley, I look like a Blitz prostitute,' Katy said, pulling off her painful-looking vintage heels. 'I haven't been to bed. Gig till three a.m. and then I got Nessie's messages about you being here. There wasn't anyone sober enough to drive me up to Edinburgh so Ruben and I waited at King's Cross for the first train.'

'You didn't need to do that!' I said, coughing. Christ, the pain in my throat. 'And who's Ruben?'

'Oh, he's our temporary bassist. We're having a bit of a fling – it's nothing.' She turned round and squeezed Sam's nose. 'I heard your news!' she said. 'Fucking mental, Sam!'

Sam looked pleased and embarrassed. I tried to shift slightly up the bed, to check that he wasn't enjoying having Katy on his knee too much, but was met with a stab of pain from my pelvis so acute that I whited out for a second.

When I came to, Hailey was standing over me, frightened, and Matty was dragging Moody Nurse in. 'She just sort of sank,' he was saying anxiously.

'What happen?' the nurse asked, looking irritably round the cubicle.

'I tried to move and it really hurt,' I said faintly.

Moody Nurse tutted. 'Girl, don't move. We told you that. Don't you move an *inch*, hear me?'

I closed my eyes, exhausted. 'I increase your painkillers,' she said. 'The CT-scan results arrive. The doctor come and talk to you soon.'

She shuffled out. Katy was appalled. 'Blimey, Charley, are you OK?' she said, visibly shaken.

'Yes, great!' I said weakly. I didn't fool anyone, least of all myself. I felt terrible, mentally and physically. I was frightened by the amount of pain I was in and terrified of being there for ever, rotting away in the evil clutches of Dr Nathan Gillies, while back at Salutech Margot stormed my office and took over my job. And far worse than *any* of this was the pain of John having got engaged. That was the end. I had no fight left; I was spent.

'John got engaged,' I blurted out. 'To Married Woman. Who isn't married any more, apparently.'

There was a silence.

Then: 'Fuuuuuuuck,' Hailey said quietly. I felt my face disintegrate and tried once again to keep it together.

Sam, who felt comfortable with emotion only when it was his own and he was on stage, scratched his head. 'I brought you a present, Chas,' he announced. The others looked at him, awed as ever by his timing.

'Um, thanks,' I mumbled, grateful for the distraction.

I smiled bravely at the Christmas wrapping paper. Sam had cocooned it in Sellotape, so tightly that Matty had to step in with his sixteen-tool Swiss Army knife. My hands were pretty much lifeless.

'Wow,' I said, surprised, as something smooth and shiny fell out of the wrapping paper. It was a brand new generation-something iPhone. 'Sam . . . You haven't got the money to be buying things like this. What . . . ?'

Sam smiled in a saintly way. 'You were carrying your phone when you came running down the hill,' he explained. 'It smashed to pieces. I bought you a new one with some of my money from that clinical trial work you got me. Look – it's all ready to go, your numbers are there and everything. Your network even threw in a load of pay-for apps free of charge as a get-well-soon present!' He beamed, delighted with himself. In spite of my suffering I smiled, enjoying his pleasure at having achieved something reasonably adult. The atmosphere in the cubicle lightened a little and Hailey inched back to my chocolates.

'Come here,' I told Sam, giving him a big kiss on the cheek. 'You are truly precious. Thank you.'

'Er, there's a maximum of three visitors per cubicle on this ward,' said a nasal voice.

Hailey froze, strawberry cream hovering centimetres from her mouth. 'It's Dr Nathan Gillies,' she said slowly, eyes widening.

Dr Nathan Gillies looked irritated. 'I'm a surgeon, Hailey, as I've pointed out before,' he said. 'Quite a senior one, in fact. So it's Mr, not Dr.'

'Still a cock, though,' Hailey muttered loudly. Katy

laughed and I blushed. Dr Nathan Gillies had my fate in his hands: I did not want to piss him off.

He looked round the rather busy cubicle. 'Could we have a bit of privacy, please?' he said peevishly. Hailey, an ominous expression on her face, jerked her thumb at the others. They left and the curtain closed behind them.

I smiled: four eavesdropping pairs of shoes stood stationary on the other side of the curtain.

Dr Nathan Gillies cleared his throat. 'Charlotte, I have some rather bad news. The CT scan is back and it appears that the fracture to your pelvic bone is as we suspected. Which does mean your recovery time will be longer.'

A large swell of panic rose up inside me but I feigned calm. 'How much longer?'

'It's impossible to say at this stage,' he said, sounding bored.

I breathed slowly. 'You must have some idea?' I asked, with as much patience as I could muster.

A phone was ringing; I realized it was the new iPhone sitting on my stomach.

'I doubt you'll be back at work until probably October,' Dr Nathan Gillies said smoothly.

I did a brief mental calculation. He must have made a mistake. It was the end of June. 'No. That's three months,' I said, in as level a tone as I could muster. 'You've got it wrong.'

The phone stopped ringing and Dr Nathan Gillies shook his head. 'I'm sorry, Charlotte, it's going to take a lot of time to mend all the damage. I'll come and visit you tomorrow.'

As he swished the curtain open, I saw four horrified

faces. When the curtain closed behind him, no one moved. Four pairs of feet remained rooted to the spot.

My phone started ringing again and I looked at it numbly. Then I jumped out of my coma. *It was John.* 'Sam,' I called urgently. 'How do I answer this thing? SAM.'

Sam bounded in. 'You slide your finger along this bi– Maybe you should just get some rest, Chas,' he said, seeing it was John.

I ignored him. 'John?'

'Charley. How are you feeling?'

My heart broke just a little bit more. John really was engaged if he wasn't calling me Lambert. 'Bleugh.'

He paused. 'I know this isn't great medical protocol but I heard about your pelvis. Er . . . bad luck, eh? Look, Charley, I'm at the airport so I can't stay for long but I wanted to reassure you about your job. I've decided to move Margot Pearson up to your position until you come back, so as to keep outsiders out and maintain continuity. And I'm not letting you anywhere near the building for at least three months. You need proper rest, OK?'

I reached for the chocolate box and stuck something large and square into my mouth, ignoring Dr Nathan Gillies's pre-surgery orders. Of all people, please, not Margot. *Seriously, God*, I repeated, *please not Margot.* I would never see my job again if she took it over.

'I think I should be fine to work from here, John,' I said, without conviction.

'No,' John said briskly, raising his voice to combat a departure announcement in the background. 'No, you're far too weak to be working. Margot may not be a patch on you but she's familiar with the brand, the corporate protocol and all of your contacts. I have no choice.'

I said nothing. I felt like someone had turned a light out.

'Well, Charley, I just wanted to let you know. I thought you'd be pleased we're keeping it internal –'

'Anything else you wanted to tell me?' I interrupted.

There was a brief silence. 'This is the final boarding call for flight V6000 to Los Angeles LAX,' said an impersonal voice in the background.

'Yes, Charley, I . . .' John was speechless for once. Then: 'I thought you'd be pleased to hear that I got engaged,' he said lamely.

My first tear in six years began to slide down my nose. 'Wow,' I whispered. 'I'm delighted. Absolutely delighted.'

'I, um, wanted to let you know in person,' John muttered. He didn't sound far off tears himself. 'But you had your accident and . . . Look, I have to go. Susan and I are going to go and get married on a wine estate in California. Just a quick, quiet affair. Not a big deal. Another reason why I want Margot to take the reins. I need to be able to go away knowing the company's in the hands of someone who understands and cares about our corporate profile.'

I nodded, tears falling silently down my face. 'Bye, John.' I ended the call.

Matty and Sam left first. They exchanged a look that said, *This is not a place for a man.* Matty kissed Hailey quickly and slid out; Sam gave me a lopsided smile and waved formally at Katy, just to be on the safe side.

Hailey was clearly stumped by the wreck that quivered

before her. For what seemed like eternity, she stood by my bed, blotting tears as they fell, holding my hand and saying nothing. I howled all the louder. If Hailey couldn't solve this, no one could. But, after a long and painful interval, during which I thought I would never recover, I made a decision and signalled to Hailey to hold a tissue over my nose.

I had decided to get a to-do list going. Organization was the only way I knew how to claw back control when the world around me went mad: it gave me certainty, calm and purpose. 'Right,' I said, sliding wearily into Business Charley mode. 'Katy, go to my house and sleep. Actually, no, go to Ness's. I don't want Sam molesting you. And, Hailey, I need you to help me clear my diary.'

Hailey nodded, relieved. 'Excellent plan,' she muttered, getting my Moleskine off the bedside table. 'Although, God knows, Chas, it's going to be quite a job.' We both smiled bravely.

Katy gathered up her stuff. 'I'll come back later, sis,' she said tiredly. 'You'll be OK. I only met John once but I thought he wore terrible middle-aged clothes. Chinos. I mean, *Christ*.' She kissed me and wandered out.

Hailey, viewing my diary with alarm, pulled up a chair next to my bed. 'Bloody hell, Chas,' she said, gazing at the boxes filled with neatly written appointments. 'I feel dizzy just looking at this.'

For a few minutes, it went well. Hailey copied down several phone numbers and agreed to call several people: the dog kennels where I volunteered; the chef at the French bistro on Broughton Street, who was going to teach me perfect pastry; the little woman who taught me

Mandarin; and the noisy multi-bangled girl who waxed my muff. The decorators, who were booked in throughout July; my personal trainer; the man I'd approached about starting piano lessons. And many more. When we got to my gym membership, though, things got harder. 'Well, presumably I should cancel it ASAP,' Hailey said, scribbling something.

'No! Absolutely not!'

Hailey looked pointedly at my broken leg and I implored her silently not to say anything. I couldn't give up the gym. It would mean defeat. I simply had to know I could go back there one day and, if I wasted four months' subscription in the meantime, then fine. Hailey, watching my face, said nothing but crossed out 'cancel gym membership' from her to-do list. I felt a fleeting moment of gratitude for my bosomy friend.

'Tuesday, video conference with the German office at seven thirty a.m., catch up with John at ten, meeting with Edward from the *BMJ* at one o'clock, French reps at three, board of directors at six. What the fuck? Who has meetings after the working day has finished?'

'The working day has not finished at six,' I muttered. 'Don't worry about the work meetings. Margot will no doubt be hacking into my Outlook diary already. Just concentrate on the extra-curriculars.'

'With a schedule like this you should not have fucking extra-curriculars, Charley Lambert,' Hailey said.

There was an uncomfortable pause while I tried and failed to come up with a defence. *She doesn't understand*, I told myself. *She may want to spend her Tuesday night sitting on the sofa with Matty, but I want more than that!*

And then I felt a sudden stab of panic. I had no option *but* to spend the next few months sitting on the sofa on a Tuesday night. *How* the fuck would I do this? WE WERE LAUNCHING SIMITOL! I HAD TO BE THERE! I eyed up the controls on my drip and wondered if I could make myself unconscious.

'OK, Chas, what's left?' Hailey asked, a few minutes later.

I thought about the lonely desert of silence and inactivity that stretched ahead of me, hours, days, weeks and months. No projects, no appointments, no warm glow of satisfaction as I crossed something off my to-do list, no building adrenalin as the Simitol launch got closer.

'Nothing,' I said softly. 'Nothing's left.'

'Oh, Charleypops,' Hailey said, reaching out to touch my hand. 'Don't say that! You needed a break! We could hang out for once. I miss you,' she added pointedly.

I tried but failed to resist asking her what she meant by that.

'I mean that every time we arrange something you either arrive at, like, midnight or something . . . or you cancel,' she replied. 'Which means I'm in a good position to tell you to rest.'

'I don't want to,' I muttered as Ness slid quietly into the cubicle. The very sight of her made tears spring from my eyes again. 'I've just got too much to do. You don't understand. I'll take a rest next year . . .'

Ness jumped over and kissed my forehead. 'Rest sounds like a lovely idea,' she said gently. 'But, oh, poor old Charley, I'm so sorry you're having to rest in, um, these sorts of circumstances.' She grimaced, guessing correctly how much pain I was in.

'I don't want to rest,' I told her. My breath caught in my throat and it came out in a sob that sailed out way beyond the confines of my cubicle.

'Here we fuckin' go,' muttered a man in the one next to mine. He sounded like an early species of caveman.

'Fucking shut up,' Hailey replied to the curtain between us.

Ness took the tissues from Hailey and dabbed at my cheeks. She looked beautifully healthy in her high-waisted shorts and stripy vest. I felt vast and lumpen. 'Charley, you need to take a rest!' she protested. 'You've got a broken leg! My love, you –'

But I wasn't having it. 'You just don't understand,' I cried, knowing how juvenile and horrid I sounded, but finding myself strangely unable to stop. There was a terrible panic welling in me and it was gaining momentum every second. 'You don't know what it's like to be as busy as me. Fine, maybe I *do* do too much and, fine, I'll maybe look at that in the future, but for now, Nessie, I have to *work*. I – Ah, God, it's pointless –' I broke off, agonized. What was the use in trying to explain or justify my schedule to someone who had the luxury of working an eight-hour day? Who was able to sit in the bath and cook dinner and play board games? Jesus! If only!

'Being busy is a choice,' Hailey said mildly, as if reading my mind.

I ignored her, crying with renewed despair as I caught sight of my diary, every appointment now scored through with Hailey's pink pen. 'I literally cannot do this,' I sobbed. 'I can't. If you don't understand, fine, but you'll have to believe me when I tell you this is an *absolute disaster*.'

Hailey's face suggested she wasn't very interested in believing me. Ness tried a bit harder than Hailey, but I could tell she, too, was struggling. And so, feeling completely alone, I gave up. I covered my face with my hands and wept. And wept and wept, not pausing even when the drunk next door started yelling about me being a 'fuckin' loser' and Hailey stepped out to deck him and Ness had to drag her back into my cubicle.

At first I cried out of sheer frustration at being trapped in plaster for an interminable length of time, but then further causes for despair erupted brilliantly into my head like a toxic cabaret show. I cried over the agony of handing my precious job to Margot Pearson, at the loss of my independence, at the possibility of permanent damage to my leg. And then I found myself crying for the years I'd wasted trying, with futile desperation, to reel in John. All that brown rice, all those expensive haircuts, all of those painstakingly composed witty emails. All for nothing! John had opted to propose to a married woman he'd started an affair with soon after kissing my bosoms in the cleaning cupboard three years ago. *You idiot!* my head crowed, delighted. *You could have got married in the time you've wasted following him around! Had a child. Learned to play another instrument. Been happy!* I wept for all this and more.

I wept until, after half an hour, my best friend and my sister gave up. They called the nurse in. 'Any chance you could knock her out?' Hailey asked politely.

The nurse was only too happy to oblige.

At some point in the night, I woke up, my strange dreams interrupted by the persistent ring tone of the hospital phone beside my bed. It swam into focus as I opened my eyes; a red light flashing benignly above the receiver.

For a second or two I considered ignoring it. Nobody called in the middle of the night. But what if it was John, calling from California to tell me he'd made a mistake? That was a call I'd be glad to take, I reflected, reaching out and picking it up.

'Hello?' I whispered furtively. I did not under any circumstances want to wake up the caveman in the cubicle next door.

There was a short pause. Then: 'Hello,' Granny Helen replied regally.

I checked the clock. It was four thirty-six a.m. And, for the first time in more than twenty-four hours, I smiled. Of course Granny Helen would call at four thirty-six a.m. Of course. 'Hello, Granny Helen.' I settled back on the pillows. 'Bit late, isn't it?'

Granny Helen ignored me. 'I hear from Vanessa that you're feeling sorry for yourself,' she said. It sounded like she was eating. I knew what she'd be eating too: it would be Jamaican ginger cake. Granny Helen lived in the cottage attached to our house and she often sat up in there until the wee hours, eating ginger cake and reading fearsome-sounding books with her glasses perched on the end of her nose. There would be a tumbler of Scotch nearby and probably a dramatic Dvořák symphony playing quietly from her gramophone. Imagining her in that very familiar setting I felt suddenly comforted. 'Well?' she prompted, when I failed to respond. 'Are you splashing around in the pond of self-pity?'

I considered lying but thirty-two years of experience

with Granny Helen convinced me otherwise. 'Yes,' I admitted. 'But, Granny Helen, you can hardly blame me . . .'

'Nonsense!' she snapped. 'When those boys started coming back from the war they had broken bones in places where there weren't any bones, Charlotte. They didn't just break their legs in three places like you, they broke them in twenty! But they were still limping around on sticks, getting on with it. Where's your wartime spirit?'

'It's 2012,' I replied. 'I went for a picnic, not to fight the Germans. Allow me a little bit of frustration.' I knew, of course, that she wouldn't.

'No,' she replied crisply. 'No, Charlotte, I shall not. I'm going to ask Christian to bring me to the hospital tomorrow and by then I want you to have brushed yourself down and stopped sulking. Good heavens above, girl! You'll be right as rain in a few weeks! Think how much worse it could be!'

There was a silence: sullen from my end; ferocious from hers.

'Now listen, Charlotte,' she continued after a few seconds. Her voice was fractionally less scary. 'Have a think about what will keep you occupied while you recuperate and tell me what that thing is tomorrow. There's got to be something you can do. I personally recommend model-making. Your grandfather loved it. Kept that busy mind of his ticking over.'

'OK,' I replied automatically, knowing that there was no such thing. Nothing would make me happy until I could get up and get back to work.

'Excellent. Now sleep,' she ordered, as if I hadn't been trying to do that before.

'Bye, Granny Helen.' I replaced the receiver. I switched on my little reading lamp and stared glumly at the pile of magazines and books by my bed, wondering if Granny Helen had any understanding of what my life was like. What single activity did she think was going to replace all the things I did every day?

Trying not to pout or scowl – I often felt Granny Helen watching me long after we'd had a conversation – I pulled out a newspaper from halfway up the pile and scanned the open page blankly, as if this might help.

And, to my surprise, it did.

'Oh, my God!' I whispered. I'd had a brainwave. 'That's the solution!'

'Shove yer solution up yer arse,' muttered the caveman from next door.

I froze until his oaf-like snores recommenced, then opened a notebook. Hope was coursing through my veins once more. Granny Helen had been right, as usual. All I needed was a hobby to keep me sane. And I had just the thing.

Chapter Four

12 September 2012, ten weeks later

> I had to leave my desk I was laughing so much, Iain wrote.
>
> Why the hell have I been searching slutty bars for a girl like you?
>
> Any chance we can meet tonight?

'Ha ha!' I giggled. 'Twonk!'

Sam looked round from the cooker. 'Eh?'

'Oh, nothing. Just a guy who's fallen for one of my clients. He's jizzing his pants trying to meet up with her. I LOVE it, Sam!'

Sam came over, stirring the wreckage of the world's worst omelette around a pan.

'Oh, my love,' I said, looking at the mess inside. 'Yvonne is a lucky girl marrying a talented chef like you.'

He grinned. 'Fair fucks, Chas. But it's got protein and vegetables, just like you said. And, look, I've made some mashed potato for your healthy carbs or whatever it was,' he added, pointing towards a bowl of white purée flecked with shreds of potato skin.

I suddenly felt a great big surge of love for Sam, followed quickly by a surge of irritation that I couldn't just jump up and hug him. He had been an angel over the last couple of weeks since Mum had released me from home. He'd cooked endless meals, which, though consistently terrible, had not once featured value bread or Nutella. He'd hauled me in and out of my wheelchair ('The Tank', he'd named it), helped me swing around on my crutches once I was upright, and had thrown himself into helping with my fledgling company, First Date Aid, with heart-warming enthusiasm.

His contribution to the business had been unexpected. He'd spent August flyering the entire city and recently, completely unprompted, he'd spent a week on the phone negotiating with self-important sales executives for cheap ad space. I'd watched him, sprawled across my sofa in a pair of jogging bottoms, haggling away, and marvelled. Who would have known there was a businessman in Samuel Bowes? The jobs that Sam normally took to tide him over as a resting actor were as unchallenging as possible. Mostly he worked for promo companies as a host for posh events because he was gorgeous and made older ladies feel young and special. He regularly badgered me to get him on clinical trials at Salutech, which he viewed (alarmingly) as money for nothing. 'I mean, basically I just take some drugs, answer some questions and then live or die,' he told me. 'What's not to love?' Recently I'd managed to get him on a trial for a concentration-enhancing product and he'd been thrilled. 'I'm being paid to take speed!' I'd heard him chuckle to Yvonne.

It was with good reason that I'd written off Sam as a potential businessman.

And yet, thanks to him, First Date Aid was now everywhere, even the *Scotsman*. He'd somehow got me a brilliant feature and the emails had flooded in ever since. I was now the proud manager of no less than sixty-eight hopeless daters. Sixty-eight clients! Only three weeks after the business had been launched!

For what he'd done I was prepared to eat as many of Sam's mangled omelettes and potato slops as was necessary. The business was all that was keeping me from complete insanity. 'Those look like perfect healthy carbs to me,' I told him. 'Bowes, I don't think you'll ever know how grateful I am. For the food, the help with First Date Aid, everything.' I opened up a dialogue box to start my client Joanna's reply to poor old pant-jizzing Iain.

'Feels like the least I can do,' Sam said, after a second. 'I know I'm a bit of a thorn in your side, Chas. Messy, you know. All those girls. Crap with rent.'

I looked up at him, surprised. I'd had no idea that Sam possessed self-awareness.

'And besides,' he added, 'I'm enjoying it. It's been good to have something to do.'

He turned abruptly and I felt a little moment of melancholy on his behalf. Of *course* it was nice for him to have something to get his teeth into. The Fringe Festival had passed us by for yet another summer, with its shouty actors getting drunk all over the Royal Mile, and he hadn't had so much as an audition in two years. Had I not started up First Date Aid I would have gone completely, totally, utterly mad, so I could only imagine what it was like for him to have years pass without a whiff of acting work. As he scraped the omelette off the bottom of the pan, I willed some director out there to give him a break.

I turned back to my screen and, without thought or preparation, started writing Joanna's reply to Iain. It never ceased to amaze me how easy the banter was: I just put hand to keyboard and out it came. Of course, it was years of email and messenger flirtation with John that had landed me with this talent, but I was trying my best to forget that John existed.

> Oh, Iain. I do understand how urgently you want me. You're only
> human . . . Careful, though. I could have the physique of a Cornish
> pasty. How would you feel about that? If you're willing to
> take the chance, I can meet you next week on Wednesday.
> We can meet in a slutty bar if you like, so you feel at home.
> I'm looking forward to it. Jo X

'Bang on,' Sam said, reading over my shoulder. 'Cheeky. Doesn't take herself too seriously . . . Registers her interest but makes him wait for a date. Chas, my friend, you're the bomb.'

He went off to plate up tonight's atrocity and I looked in the mirror to see what a bomb was meant to look like. A smart and reasonably well-groomed girl looked back at me, her face framed by a neat brown bob, with ultra-straight fringe. She was tall, athletic and she could see (today, but by no means always) that she was reasonably attractive.

'You're doing your weird mirror face!' Sam sniggered from the cooker.

I winced, knowing he was right. My mirror face was designed to make me look clever and interesting but it actually made me look frightening and constipated. I knew this because I'd tried it out in photos, repeatedly, without success. 'Um, how's Yvonne?' I asked, keen to deflect attention from myself. 'I've not seen her in, what, three days?'

'Here you go.' Sam slopped down a plate of multi-coloured lumps in front of me. I got stuck straight in to avoid causing offence. 'Yvonne is great,' he said, breaking into a cheesy grin. 'And the reason you've not seen her is that she's just started a part-time degree.'

'Oh, really? Good on her! What in?'

'Communications, actually. Your gig is Yvonne's dream job.'

'*Really?*'

'Yes, Chas, really,' Sam said, clearly offended. 'She might be a bit silly but she's fucking clever.'

There was an awkward silence.

'Sam, I'm sorry. That sounded awful.' I put my fork down. 'I didn't mean it like that. I'm quite sure Yvonne'll make a great comms person. I suppose I'm just a bit protective of my job just now. The situation with Margot . . . Eurgh.'

'Margot's the slapper who's doing it at the moment?' Sam asked, squirting ketchup all over his meal.

'I don't think she's an actual slapper – she just wears very short skirts and high heels.'

'Slapper,' Sam confirmed. 'Trust me, Chas, I've met a few in my time.'

But I was out of smiles already, back in the Margot-related anxiety that I'd been battling for weeks. The experience of having to hand over every single detail of my precious job to her had been even more humiliating than I'd imagined and – worse still – she seemed to be getting on absolutely fine without me. 'Please just call me any time of day,' I'd said to her, back in June, when she'd breezed into the hospital for a gloaty briefing. 'There's no need to suffer in silence.' After all, I'd basically handed her the responsibility of getting the government and entire medical industry onside with our new drug. A huge job. A monumental job. *My* job. My chance to show the company what I could do.

'Sure,' she'd said briskly. 'Remember, though, I'm used to this. I ran the comms for a £3.5 billion brand launch in my last company.' And she'd walked out of the cubicle with the job I'd spent my entire career working for, positively radiating joy at my multiple fractures.

'So, Chas. What're the latest stats?' Sam broke off from mashing ketchup into his potato to nod at my computer.

I was relieved that he hadn't taken offence about Yvonne. 'The stats, Samuel Bowes, are good! I've got sixty-eight people signed up and sixteen active cases. Sixteen! Sixteen people glued to their screens waiting for messages from me *right now*! Can you imagine how exciting that feels?'

Sam grinned. 'Ace . . . Any fitties in there?'

'Bowes! Butt out!'

He shrugged. A leopard never lost its spots. I had another mouthful of eggy massacre (which was surprisingly good), then put my fork down again. 'Look, Sam,' I said. 'Without this project I would have gone mad. Proper raving loony. Thank you so much for all of your help and encouragement.'

'It's in my interests to keep you busy, Chas. You being cooped up here with nothing to do . . . God.' He shuddered.

In spite of myself, I laughed. 'I'm just a born doer. It's how I roll, man. I ain't no freak.'

'I know. But when you're not doing you *are* a freak. A monster. One of the worst I've ever encountered.'

This was fair.

There was a companionable silence.

'Um, Chas.'

'Yes?' An awkward flush was spreading across his face.

'I . . . we . . . have been wondering how you're feeling about, erm, stuff. Ness told me you were spouting shit in hospital about having wasted your life . . .' He was picking at a burnt onion. 'I know you don't want to talk about it but . . . mffppfff . . .' He trailed off and it occurred to me that I'd probably never seen him look so uncomfortable.

And I felt suddenly ashamed. What kind of a monster was I? Poor, lovely, silly Sam had gone to war with a sack of potatoes and a box of eggs – all for me – but was afraid to ask how I *was*?

'Sam, you can ask me how I am! The only reason I said, "I don't want to talk about it," is that there *is* nothing to talk about. That stuff I said to Ness was just a load of self-pitying bollocks! I was still off my face.'

He raised an eyebrow, but failed to make eye contact with me. Instead he scooped up a very large piece of egg with his fingers, dipped it into a pool of sauce and shovelled it into his mouth.

'Sam,' I tried again, determined that he should believe me, 'things are great for me. I've started my own business, I'm managing to have Mandarin lessons and my physio

68

says I'm way ahead of schedule with the crutches. I should be going back to work soon! I'll definitely be there in time for the Simitol launch! My life is fine!'

Sam looked very relieved. 'Excellent, Chas.'

I found myself hoping fiercely that he believed me. My life *was* fine. Not only was I continuing language classes and running a business, I was writing a blog and consistently meeting my reading target of one historical novel a week (anything low-brow had to be extra) *and* I'd started up an anonymous Twitter account, which had gained more than two hundred followers in five weeks. I might not be able to do as much as usual, but I'd not been anywhere near as bored as I'd predicted.

I rather prided myself on being so busy and creative even when bed-bound.

Later, after poor Sam had shovelled me sideways into bed from The Tank, I fired up my laptop. Pants-jizzing Iain had replied to Joanna already (of course) and was waiting, breathlessly, for 'her' response. 'Member online right now!!' screamed his profile. I felt a little bit sorry for poor old Iain, pacing around his bedroom in Tooting, refreshing his browser every few minutes 'just to be sure'. He was definitely in Internet love, that one.

My younger sister, Katy, had tried Internet dating last year, not because she needed to, but simply because, in her words, it looked 'fucking hilarious!'. But she had scrapped her profile two weeks later because she'd 'fallen in Internet love three times in a fucking fortnight! Mental!' She had reported all-night email conversations and social situations where she'd been unable to listen to a word that anyone was saying, so busy was she checking her phone. Apparently she had even spent an afternoon casually strolling up and down Columbia Road because some boy she had 'fallen for' worked there and she couldn't wait three more days until their date.

Katy wasn't mad. Young, yes, irresponsible, definitely . . . but mad, no. Internet love must, therefore, be a phenomenon.

When I'd hauled Matty in for Hailey, I'd seen just how real this phenomenon was. In spite of the fact that he was a landscape gardener who was out in the wilds of Fife all day, he appeared to be online all the time and always responded in seconds. (Knowing Matty, he'd probably rustled up a Wi-Fi hotspot in the grounds of Falkland Palace using a coat-hanger and an egg box.)

And then I'd done the same for my cousin Anna with Peter from Glasgow, for my school friend Michelle with Sean from Berwick and for pretty much anyone else who asked. They picked the men; I wrote the emails.

All the men had been hooked, yet I'd felt nothing during the courtships. Maybe it was because I was pretending to be someone else, which did rather take the edge off things; maybe I was just frozen. But I could see that it was no joke, this Internet love thing. Fully grown men abandoning their pride and begging, throwing themselves at the perfect cyber feet of all of these perfect cyber girls?

'I know what you're going through, Iain old chap,' I said to the computer. 'Hang on in there.'

'SHIIIIIT!!!!!!' Joanna wrote on MSN as soon as I logged on (under the catchy moniker of First Date Aid

Charlotte). Obviously she was in as much of a state as Iain. I grinned.

> First Date Aid Charlotte: Hi Jo
> FluffyJo 79: Hi!!!!!!!!!!!!!!!!!!!
> First Date Aid Charlotte: I think it's best to wait until tomorrow to reply to Iain, OK? All best, Charlotte.
> FluffyJo 79: GREAT!!! I know you're right but I just want to reply RIGHT NOW!!!!!
> First Date Aid Charlotte: That's why you need me! ☺

The smiley was added for good measure, even though it went against everything I believed in.

> FluffyJo 79: Thanks Charlotte!! This date would NOT be happening without you!! Now I've got time to go and buy some clothes and get my hair done this weekend! Wicked!!
> First Date Aid Charlotte: No! Don't go and buy clo

I started, then deleted. At times I struggled to remember that I was simply a ghost-writer, not a dating coach.

The *modus operandi* I'd established for First Date Aid was straightforward. If a client contacted me I familiarized myself with them as best I possibly could and, thus armed, set up an Internet dating account on their behalf. They had full access to their profile, so they could see the emails that were passing back and forth on their behalf. So far this was working well, but Jo had got so excited about Iain that she was messaging me several thousand times per day to comment on the action.

I looked at poor Iain's 'Online Now!' profile.

I closed the messenger window and went back to my inbox. A new client, Shelley Cartwright, had contacted me since dinner and I hovered the mouse over her name, toying with the idea of reading the message tomorrow. It was late and I was tired. But, of course, I clicked. Running First Date Aid might not be high-profile communications work for one of the world's leading pharmaceutical companies but it was staving off the madness.

I opened her email and groaned. It was like standing in front of an angry bear armed with a machine gun and a mallet and a knife.

Hi.

I saw the ad in the *Evening Standard*. (*The* Evening Standard *had been Sam's latest triumph; thanks to him I'd paid about a sixth of the going rate*.) I'm far too busy to be fiddling around on the Internet so would like to contract you for two weeks. I've looked on love.com and have selected two suitable men, Stuart and William; links to their profiles are below. Please could you schedule dates with both if they are available. I have openings on 26 and 29 September and would prefer a meeting in either Canary Wharf, where I work, or London Bridge, where I live. I request that you do not use abbreviated text or swear words

in any messages you send on my behalf. Please email an
invoice and note that I accept your rates and terms. You can
use the attached photo to create my online dating account
and I have written a short summary of myself in addition,
also attached.

Regards,
Shelley

I chuckled. 'I'm far too busy to be fiddling around on
the Internet'? Why did so many clients need to let me
know that they were above Internet dating? Who were
they trying to fool? I had lost count of the number of
emails I'd seen like this. *Hey, you, Internet woman, I've failed
completely to find someone, I can't even get myself an Internet date
and guess what? It's YOUR fault. Write me some emails, you
slave, and I shall throw you some pennies. P. S. I AM BETTER
THAN YOU.*

But business was business. And Business Charley liked
a challenge.

Dear Shelley,

Thanks for contacting us. We'd be delighted to work with you
but I'm afraid we need a few more details first. If you could take
a quick look at the 'How it works' page you'll get an idea of the
level of knowledge we require before we can send emails on a
client's behalf.

Normally this knowledge can be gathered in a quick painless
phone call. Although we are not a dating service we do aim for
maximum success and therefore it's important that we know our

73

clients well enough to send messages which represent them faithfully.

Please either indicate a time when we can speak or send us 600 words about yourself (there's an online breakdown of the kind of info we need) and in the meantime we'll start your profile and acquaint ourselves with the two men you like.

All best,
Charlotte Lambert
Director
First Date Aid

I logged into love.com and opened up Shelley's photo. Sighing, I got my notebook out and started scribbling. She was wearing a suit. 'Educated; professional; salary above £100 K,' she had written in the 'searching for' box. Again, never a good sign. As I had had to explain to an angry woman called Jenny, from Manchester, yesterday, the reason that Giles (also from Manchester) had not replied to the email I had written for her was not that I'd failed but rather that she had terrified the living shit out of him with the financial 'requirements' listed on her profile. Poor Giles was a shy millionaire and I was quite sure that write-ups like Jenny's ('I like to be taken out for expensive cocktails and can't pretend that I don't appreciate the odd Swarovski necklace!') had filled him with fear.

Shelley's summary of herself was a disaster: *I'm ambitious, successful and extremely hard-working: time-wasters need not apply.*

Great opening gambit, I thought grimly, scribbling some notes.

I am not here to make friends and am looking for a man whose aim is to meet a like-minded professional female with the view to settling down. [*I winced.*]

I'm single because I'm very busy with my job as an executive management consultant. However, I believe I have a lot to give and therefore am seizing the day with online dating! If you are based in London and like what you see on my profile please contact me to arrange a meet.

Best, Shelley

I sighed. If Shelley's best shot at 'warmth' was an exclamation-marked line about seizing the day, then God save the educated professionals she was expecting to snare. I stared at her uncompromising face. She was very attractive and well presented – she had a well-kept, fringed bob and very expensive-looking glasses . . . And her suit was clearly a knock-out. But where was the warmth? What would a potential partner see in this face other than a cold career fiend who would never be available to have a glass of wine with him of an evening? Before Yvonne had arrived tonight, screaming about her communications course, Sam and I had sat by the window and shared a bottle of wine. Granted, we were not a couple, but the point was that this was what people *did* when they were together. Chilled. Chatted. Relaxed. I was going to have to completely rewrite her profile before I did anything else.

Needs to calm the hell down, I wrote in my book as I logged on to love.com to view the first of her selected men.

Then I stopped.

Needs to calm the hell down? This was a phrase I had heard recently. I opened Shelley's profile write-up again. *I'm single because I'm too busy.* I swallowed and clicked on her picture once more. *I'm ambitious, successful and extremely hard-working,* said Shelley, with her ultra-straight fringe and her glasses and her smart, well-made clothes. Shelley, whose profile men would delete from their search, knowing that she would never be home from work before ten p.m. Shelley, whose profile screamed **NIGHTMARE**.

You're a man who's never seen me before. At first glance do you think I'm a nightmare? I texted Hailey and Ness.

Yes, my love, Hailey responded.

Of course not! Ness replied, which meant yes.

Fuck it. Fuck *me*! I was a nightmare!

'Was, Charley, was,' I muttered, turning my phone off. *You've changed since you broke your leg! You sit and have wine with your housemate. You chat to your friends on the phone. You hang out with your parents in the countryside. And you haven't done any* real *work for weeks!*

Yes, only because you're bloody immobile and have absolutely no other option, I admitted. In a part of my brain that I was trying hard to bury, a voice was suggesting that perhaps I hadn't changed all that much. And that perhaps I was actually quite similar to this sharply fringed woman on the screen.

I looked in the mirror. I saw a girl who also had short dark hair and a very straight fringe. Very similar glasses and, if not smart *clothes*, at least smart pyjamas.

This was not a comfortable state of affairs. Shelley, whom I'd never even met, felt more like my twin sister than lovely laid-back arty Ness ever had.

I popped Shelley's two desired dates into her Favourites folder and opened one of their profiles to take my mind off the situation. Stuart was what I liked to describe as 'meh'. There was nothing wrong with him at all – nice-looking, clearly wealthy, probably quite intelligent . . . but . . . meh. Just nothing there. Nothing silly or odd or out-of-the-ordinary. Nothing that distinguished him from the rest of humanity. He worked in finance and probably already lived in the redbrick detached house in Surrey that his woman of choice from love.com would one day move into.

I didn't understand why clients wanted me to compose emails to men like Stuart. What was the point? Men like him didn't *want* imagination or humour; they didn't want clever flirting and subtle affection. In fact, they probably responded a lot better to a message from some woman's PA asking if they were available for a forty-five-minute lunch at Club Gascon.

I yawned, suddenly exhausted. It was time for bed. I'd look at the other man (William?) tomorrow. Until Shelley allowed me further access to her inner workings, this was a waste of my time.

I turned the light off and rolled over into the Beatles-crossing-Abbey-Road posture that seemed to be the only way of getting to sleep at the moment. It hadn't been too bad a day, really: I had thought about John's marriage only twice, the physio had said that I'd be off crutches soon and, best of all, my PA Cassie had sent me a text saying that everyone in the office was being driven mad by Margot.

Forty minutes later, I still hadn't slept. I was being tortured by Shelley too-busy-for-love Cartwright. I was *not* as bad as her. Surely! I'd had Dr Nathan Gillies after all! We'd gone out for four years!

No, that didn't help. Not once in those four years had we woken up on a Sunday morning, stretched, shagged, rolled back over and gone to sleep, only to surface hours later for some bacon and the newspaper. The truth was that Dr Nathan Gillies normally saw private patients on Sundays and I generally went running, had a power brunch with Hailey, did some work, then spent the rest of the day helping at the Edinburgh Dog and Cat Home. And sometimes took charcoal sketching classes with a softly spoken transvestite in Bruntsfield when I felt my cultural life needed boosting.

Dammit. No chilling at all, then. Just a load of engagements.

But my face was warmer than Shelley's! And I had a sense of humour! A warm, silly, self-deprecating sense of humour, according to my friends. Poor old Iain was in Internet love with Joanna because of *my* emails! Me! Nice! Warm!

My leg began to itch unbearably and I turned the light on, reaching over for the straightened-out wire coat-hanger that Dad had given me so I could scratch underneath the plaster. ('Ignore those silly doctors,' he'd whispered. 'No one's leg ever fell off after they scratched it with a coat-hanger, my girl!')

As I retrieved it, I caught sight of my Salutech security pass, which was still on the peg next to my door. I took it down and studied it. Bugger, bugger and bugger. My face was *not* warmer than Shelley's. I might have the sense of humour that she lacked, but you'd struggle to see it in my stern, self-important pose.

'Damn you, Shelley Cartwright,' I said, shoving the coat-hanger down my plaster. It felt horrible down there, like my skin was covered with melted toffee. I winced.

I turned the light off and wriggled down again, then turned it back on and wriggled up. 'Cocking Cartwright,' I muttered, firing up my laptop. I was wide awake and very pissed off, and I knew there was only one thing that would help. When in doubt: work. I logged back on to love. com and knocked out a profile for Shelley in ten minutes. As I sat back to admire my handiwork I saw, to my amusement, that Mervyn from West Glamorgan, aged twenty-two, had already added her to his Favourites. 'Good luck, young man.'

Good grief! Mervyn had sent her a message too! Knowing it was probably a bit naughty to go into Shelley's mailbox before she and I had spoken on the phone, I clicked. After all, I was stuck in bed with a toffee leg while my deputy stole my job and my housemate created strange concoctions in pans. Surely I was allowed some merriment.

Hi Shelli [*I smirked*]

I'm Mervyn, your Welsh lover, a woman like you needs a man in every port, right, so I reckon you should pick me for your Welsh port love, ive just finished reading psychology at Bangor and I got a first [*You stinking liar! I sniggered*] and just in case your wondering i got a massive cock and baby i just want to put it up your tight frustrated little –

'MERVYN!' I yelled. 'GOOD GOD!'

I heard Sam get out of bed and held my breath, hoping he would just ignore me.

He didn't. 'Chas? What the hell's going on? Are you OK?' he asked, walking into my room without knocking. Apart from his reading glasses he was naked, his manhood cradled in his hands.

'Oh, my God! Get out! You horrible boy!'

Sam didn't move. My eyes were carefully averted but I could see that he was doing a little rearranging while he waited for an answer. Yuk.

I sighed. 'Sorry for the yelling, Bowes. I couldn't sleep so I logged on to love.com and this kid just sent my new client a message about taking her up the . . . and then . . . urgh, I don't think I can even bring myself to repeat it.'

Sam was chuckling. 'I like his style.'

'You're disgusting. I'm sorry I woke you up, Sam, but please feel free to go back to bed. And take your privates with you.'

Sam shuffled off and I covered my face with a pillow to avoid having to look at his naked backside as he left. He had been wonderfully kind looking after me, but there were limits. Perhaps he'd move in with Yvonne soon. After all, they were engaged . . .

Aha! See? You are nice. You're not like Shelley! You're niiiice. You can't throw Sam out even though he's disgusting and wrong and rearranges his balls in front of you! Nice Charley! Soft! Kind!

Pathetic, said another voice. I chose to ignore it.

'Well, I think I won't reply to Mervyn,' I muttered briskly. Was this what it was like on the Internet dating scene if you were twenty-two? Cocks and bums at first approach?

I clicked on to Shelley's next victim, William, thirty-six, London. On the photo alone, I was far more impressed by this choice. William was really very handsome. He was wearing a sort of rolled-over thick-ribbed jumper, which, on a fashion victim like Sam, would have seemed unbearably pretentious but on classically handsome William, who wore it with a strong chin of dark, noble stubble, was rather dashing. It made him look like a Farringdon architect with large hands and not a . . . Oh dear, a doctor.

William was a doctor. An ENT surgeon at that. I had an unhealthy love for doctors. Now interested, I began to scroll through his profile.

Shelley Cartwright certainly wasn't wrong with this one. He had written:

Oh blooming heck, an entire box looms ahead of me. Did anyone else find this horribly difficult? I feel like I should write something extremely clever and pepper in references to the Balzac novel I'm reading and the eclectic collection of music I own but really I haven't got the energy. Is it OK to be honest? Because, really, I'm not here to spend months being all clever and dating a million women, I'm just looking for the rhubarb to my crumble. The jelly to my ice-cream. The spotted to my dick.

Sorry. Knob gags probably aren't going to impress anyone, if they even get through the love.com filter. But you get the general idea.

As for what I'm looking for . . . just a nice girl. That's the long and short of it.

After a few seconds I realized I was smiling at William's profile. Actually grinning, childishly, into his eyes. I often wrote to attractive men on behalf of clients but there was something about William that was just . . . lovely.

Briefly I entertained the idea of joining love.com myself in the hope of maybe scoring a date with him. I liked this stubbly doctor. His eyes (calm, brown), his smile (lips slightly upturned as if someone had just made a knob gag in a silent library) and his hair (classic man style but with just the tiniest hint of disorder) – mmm. He was rather divine, I thought, in a Sean Connery accent. He even looked like a grown-up. But a fun one.

I imagined what it would be like to wake up on a Sunday morning with William. The stubble would be there; the jumper would not. He'd be tall and warm and calm, and would wake up, then drift out for a while, to return with organic wholegrain bread and poached eggs. He would have a bottom like two perfectly baked muffins. He would not go off to work and I would not run off to the dog shelter. We'd probably roast a guinea fowl later on.

I frowned and pinched myself hard on the boob. *This, Charlotte Lambert, is not how one gets started with a new client.* But within seconds I was back with William, grinning helplessly at his face.

Fancy a client's love interest, I texted Hailey. It was Wednesday night, one thirty a.m. They'd had a big dinner at Hibs tonight and I knew she'd be striding around a sea of stripped-down chipboard tables, throwing wine-splattered tablecloths into a huge pile and having the *craic* with the bar staff. Knowing Hailey she would probably have deactivated the smoke detectors so they could puff their way through clear-up.

No, she replied immediately. *Leave him alone.*

Good advice.

I looked back at the screen. A glowing blue bubble had popped up in the bottom left-hand corner of the screen. 'Someone has added you to their Favourites!' it said. I clicked through.

It was William, Favouriting me back. William thought I was hot! He was interested!

Just as quickly, I remembered. William did not think *I* was hot. He thought Shelley was hot. I bristled. *Why?* Shelley was hard and cold! I was warm and funny! Or at least it was my ambition to become warm and funny! Was it her ambition? No! Damn Shelley cocking Cartwright! Damn her!

Another bubble popped up. 'Someone has sent you a message!'

To my astonishment, I registered my pulse speeding up. I looked across the room at the mirror. 'Are you actually hoping this is William?' I asked myself.

'Yes. What of it?' I snapped.

I clicked through. It was William.

Hello! Thanks for favouriting me. Are you sure? I just spent the day with my hand up an elderly man's nose. Understand if you wish to withdraw the interest now. I liked your capable businessy photo, though, so thought I'd hit you up.
(Hit you up? Apparently I am eighteen years old. Are we in fact on Facebook?)

I tried not to smile but it was hopeless. William wasn't just handsome, he was funny. And maybe even quite sweet. I couldn't let him go on a date with brisk Shelley! He was right up my street! Good looks, sense of humour, *doctor* . . . Boom! My holy trinity! He didn't have that utterly devilish sexuality that John had, but, realistically, that had got me all of nowhere. And in fairness I didn't actually know him: there was nothing to say that beneath the sheets he wasn't hotter than . . . My mind drew a blank. Than a hot dog, or something.

I read his email again. What seemed clear was that William wasn't the kind of guy to drag you off for a randy fuck in a cupboard full of mops, then change his mind and hook up with a married multi-trillionairess soon after. He was similarly unlikely to sit flirting on your hospital bed, kissing you ON THE MOUTH, then driving to the airport to meet his new fiancée. No. William would sit on your bed, hold your hand and kiss you until you passed out before he resumed his ward rounds. The nurses would be in love with him, the patients even more so, but he'd have eyes only for one woman . . .

SHELLEY. Damn her. I looked at her profile again. She was frostier than the rock-hard beefburger in the back of my freezer. Pretty, definitely. But frozen. I was strongly tempted to send an early reply on her behalf, simply copy-ing and pasting her dismissive statement about being 'far too busy to mess around looking for love on the Internet'. But it was probably a bit early in the development of First Date Aid to start defecating on my own doorstep.

I sighed, knowing what I had to do. I had to help Shel-ley find love. And if it was love with William, the perfect, handsome, definitely-my-cup-of-tea doctor, then that was absolutely that and there would be no argument.

I was, after all, Charley Lambert, the Scottish Amazon. I might be too incapacitated to change the face of the pharmaceutical industry at the moment, but that didn't stop me taking over the world by other means. First Date Aid was going places and no one, not even lovely William, could threaten that.

I sneaked a quick look at him before going to sleep. And watched in the third person as my hand went to the mouse, hit reply and started typing him a message.

Chapter Five

'So, yes, I thought that William was such a good opportunity for you that I replied to him straight away,' I said breezily. 'We had a few emails and I think he'll be an excellent choice for your date slot on the 26th of September.'

'I see,' Shelley barked. 'Can we get on with this, please? I've got four minutes.'

It was safe to say that I didn't much like Shelley Cartwright. According to her, she was currently in Executive Boardroom 2305 in the Smithson International headquarters. I imagined the scene: a frustrated, smart woman who looked rather like me, scowling out at the sci-fi sprawl of London's Canary Wharf. Stressed, busy and embarrassed.

I imagined having to do the same. I would be standing in the executive boardroom at Salutech, gazing across the relentless flow of the A1 to Fort Kinnard's unappealing sprawl. Also stressed, also busy and also embarrassed. I didn't blame Shelley for feeling so uncomfortable, but I wouldn't be so damned rude.

'Of course we can be brief,' I said brightly. 'Perhaps we could start with your dating history. Have you been on your own for ages?' *You twat, Charley*, I thought, feeling Shelley's hackles rise.

'I've been single for five years,' she said curtly. I imagined an angry red blush spreading across her businesslike face. 'This is because of my job. I don't think it's a relevant point.'

'It's just so I can answer questions correctly on your behalf,' I replied. 'Some men ask that sort of stuff early on.'

'Well, they're not for me,' Shelley snapped. 'Bad manners.'

In spite of my mounting irritation, I smiled. That was exactly the sort of thing I'd say. 'There are lots of men with bad manners out there,' I agreed. 'I'll do my best to filter them out.' I cleared my throat. 'Well, the first man on your list, Stuart, sounds like he's in the same sort of place as you. Busy, but genuinely looking for someone.'

'So does the second, William,' Shelley said. 'I think he's my preferred choice.'

I tried to stop my heart sinking. 'Well, as I said I've already begun emailing him. I think we can confirm a date soon.'

'I thought you were unable to enter into correspondence unless you'd been fully briefed as to your client's character.'

'Absolutely, which was why I kept it light. We didn't get into specifics.'

Light? A mild panic washed around my stomach. I was playing a dangerous game.

'Very well, Charlotte. The testimonials on your site were excellent. I trust you.'

She'll slice your hands off if she ever finds out what you've done, I thought.

'So, just how busy is your life at the moment?' I asked Shelley, trying to hide my fear under a businesslike tone.

'Very. I leave home at six twenty a.m. and return no earlier than eight thirty p.m.,' she said. 'I'm currently taking business Spanish two evenings a week because I'm involved with facilitating an expansion into Central America, and I chair a weekly book club to make sure my brain isn't dominated by business. I run daily and go to the gym when I can. I work most weekends too, unfortunately.'

I grimaced. 'Wow.'

'Yes. I have a full life. I find it very satisfying. But I don't think it should inhibit my ability to conduct a relationship,' Shelley continued spiritedly.

I felt like we were discussing her ability to manage a hedge fund. 'So what sort of thing do you like to do in your free time?'

There was a pause.

'When I'm not busy it's normally the middle of the night and I'm asleep.' She gave an awkward, empty guffaw.

I sighed. Shelley was a lost cause. And, clearly, so was I. Our schedules were almost identical. Although I was now feeling sad and flat, I turned my brightest client voice back on. 'Right. Well, let's talk about what you're looking for in a man.'

Twelve hours earlier

01.46 a.m.
Hi William.

Can I ask why you had your hand up someone's nose? I thought ENT surgery was a little more subtle these days.
I don't *think* you've put me off . . . but it does rather depend on your answer to the above.

Shelley

88

02.14 a.m.

Sorry, I was being crude. I didn't literally have my hand up someone's nose. I was in fact guiding a fibre-optic cable up someone's
nose. There are strange things happening up this nose and it was
my job to investigate. Can we stop talking about it now, though?
I should never have brought it up. It must sound disgusting.
Tell me about your high-powered city job! People like you
fascinate me. Do you break balls? (Literally, metaphorically,
whatever.) Do you wear suits like that every day? I think you look
very nice in it. I used to be frightened of women in suits until I
saw your photo.

William

02.45 a.m.
Hello William

My job isn't all that bad. Quite high-powered I suppose, as you
say, but I actually love it. As for what I do, it involves a lot of
strategic thinking and single-mindedness. A sprinkling of bravery.
Not unlike dating, really.
But I'm not fierce! There is nothing to be afraid of. My suit is a
coat of armour designed to scare competitors. Not nice men.

S

As soon as I'd despatched this message I felt stupid. Was
it too keen to call William a 'nice man'? I buzzed with
nerves as I looked in my outbox and saw that William had
already opened the message. Somewhere, down in London, he was reading my words right now. I felt slightly
sick. Were my words OK? Was I selling myself well?

'Argh!' I told my bedroom. 'This is not your correspondence to worry about! STOP IT.'

03.05

I liked being called a nice man! Although you don't actually
know it's true. Yesterday, for instance, I finished a sixteen-hour
shift, got on the number 30 bus and DID NOT give my seat up
to the old man who got on at the next stop. I'm still tortured by
it. He looked so disappointed. But I couldn't, Shelley. I was so
tired I could barely sit up straight. Sort of like now. But this
rather beguiling bird off the Internet is keeping me awake.
You sound very, very busy in your profile. Are you sure you have
time to date? I hope so because I'd love to meet up with you
some time. I wouldn't stick cables up your nose.

William x

I grinned excitedly and started typing.

03.16

Of course I have time to date! I think it's important to have lots
of extra-curriculars – I spend so much time at work that I see it
as a duty to myself to do other things too. I want to make sure
I'm properly rounded. (Dating is an extra-curricular.)

S

03.29

I agree. When you spend most of your life in the bowels of a
London hospital it's important to make sure your brain extends
beyond TMJs and craniofacial prostheses (or, I dunno, mergers

and global expansion in your case maybe?). I should try to be
more like you, really. Get some extra-curriculars going.
Anyway. You didn't reply about meeting up. Was it because I
told you about the man on the bus? (Or did I bring up dating too
soon? I have no idea how to handle myself in a situation where
I'm meant to be in charge. I feel safer when girls just ask me out.
It's simpler. Less opportunity to make a dick of myself.)
This is the least macho email I've ever sent. Things are going
wrong very quickly for me.

Wx

I hugged myself, unable to stop smiling. I loved un-macho
William and his craniofacial prostheses! I loved that he'd
asked me out twice in less than two hours!

'No,' I told myself, less sternly than last time.

03:42

That's OK. I don't like macho men. They're a bit distasteful.
And on the subject of distasteful: good God William the ENT
surgeon! The poor little old man on the bus? Appalling!
Um, I didn't respond to the bit about meeting up because we
have known each other for two hours. Can't we carry on this
emailing at least a couple more days? I'm rather enjoying it.
From Shelley, who is definitely going to bed now

Going to bed, my arse. I'd never been more awake.

04.02

No! Stay awake Shelley. This is much more fun! There is more to me
beyond the bad person who wouldn't give up their seat on the bus.

Although, actually, I sometimes wonder if I really am a bit of a shit. No obvious reasons, just a general feeling of Could Do Better. Do you get that?

I'm really pleased you're not too busy to go on a date. Judging by your last reply you're someone who will expect to be taken white-water rafting and hang-gliding, followed by high tea at a 1920s literary salon and a night at the Greenwich observatory learning complex astronomical rules.

I might just shake things up by suggesting we meet up and sit at a table with wine.

Don't even think of going to sleep. I like you. X

As if. I was sitting upright in bed, refreshing Shelley's inbox every twenty seconds.

04.23

Do I think I'm a bad person? No, actually, I don't. I donate money to charity and one of my weekly extra-curriculars involves charity work. Abandoned dogs and cats, specifically. Oh and I would always give up my seat to a little old man. Ha.

I suppose I could go on a sedentary date although I have my limits. The Action and Learning date you've outlined sounds far more appealing, Doctor William.

S

Damn Shelley and her instructions, I thought, fighting the urge to type a load of kisses after my casual 'S'. I *wanted* to kiss William. Both via email and in real life. *It appears*, I thought, looking over at the mirror and seeing my flushed cheeks and slightly wild eyes, *that I have completely lost control of myself.*

The sensation of having completely lost control was not something I'd ever felt particularly comfortable with, yet I was finding this ill-advised exchange deliciously, almost excruciatingly enjoyable.

You have a new message! advised the dialogue bubble floating up my screen. I felt a sensation of pure, rushing joy. The seconds it took for the message to load were torture. *Bloody hell, Charlotte Lambert, so-called Scottish Amazon, this is no good at all*, I told myself sternly. Then the message loaded and I forgot everything else.

04.41

Now then Shelley. That's not fair. I told you the truth about feeling like I could Maybe Do Better and you threw it back in my face with talk of charitable good deeds and some bollocks about volunteering. Talk to me! You may look beautiful but I do not believe you're perfect.
Come on . . . x
PS Is your skin really that smooth? It sort of looks like you've been carved from a piece of alabaster.
PPS Er, sorry. It's late. Might be getting a bit carried away. This Internet dating thing is dangerous, isn't it? Are these feelings real? Or are they just some sort of mad online fantasy? After all, you could be an old man.
PPPS I don't really think you're an old man.

I laughed out loud. 'I'll old-man you, William.' I giggled, hitting reply.

And then I paused. William had just been touchingly honest with me. Would I brush him off with some silly flirting or would I actually think about what he'd just said?

I moved my hands away from the keyboard. Was I perfect? (Clearly not.) Were there things about me that I'd change if I could? *Yes*, I thought, surprising myself. *Yes, actually*. Recognizing myself in Shelley a few hours earlier had made for some uncomfortable realizations. And William had somehow tapped right into them. How was he doing it?

Before I knew it, I was writing again.

05.01

Do I feel like I could do better?

I've never asked myself that question before. Well, I have, but I've always used 'doing better' in terms of working harder or achieving more. But, now you come to ask, I'm realizing (er, possibly right now) that I'm not very good at sitting with myself. You were bang on when you said I'd probably prefer a date where we do a million things in three hours. I can't stand being still – it sends me insane. That's not good, is it?

So now (where is this coming from?? Argh!) I'm also wondering if maybe I need to let go of my work a bit . . . It takes up most of my time and mental energy. But how does anyone do that without actually leaving their job?

Oh dear. Can of worms, William. Can of worms.

I pressed send, feeling a bit sick. 'You're writing on Shelley's behalf,' I told myself half-heartedly. 'This is for her, not you.' But none of the correspondence so far had had anything to do with Shelley and this was no different. This was 100 per cent me. Not just the surface me, either: I was writing things that I'd never said before. Never thought before. I read back over my last message and felt even more flummoxed. These observations about my life were not comfortable.

William emailed back almost immediately.

05.03

Do you think you're a perfectionist?

I exhaled slowly. This was all getting a bit heavy. And yet he was hitting home. Quite hard, in fact. Was I a perfectionist? Bloody hell, yes! I was more of a perfectionist than anyone I knew! I crippled myself trying to make the perfect risotto, to buy the perfect wine, to be the perfect employee. I got furious with myself if I lost so much as a *tenth of a second* from my ideal running time round Holyrood Park. A tenth of a second? Dear God! I passed my hand over my face, slightly dazed.

05.10

In a word, yes. Actually I'm a chronic perfectionist. And I don't quite understand why I'm only noticing that now?!
Honestly, William, I'm so cruel to myself. I'd like to be kinder if I knew how.
I think that deffo applies to relationships, too. I think I'd find them a lot easier if I could learn to just accept myself as I am – normal, imperfect. I wish I didn't spend all my time pretending to be better.

05.13

William, I'm sorry, it's late, I don't know what came over me. Please ignore that last message. It makes me sound like a loon and a lonely psychopath who's just completed a course in amateur psychology.

05.17

Rubbish. It makes you sound like a real human being. The sort of human being I would really like to meet. I understand what you're saying because in many ways, although for opposite reasons, I'm in the same situation. You'd love to take it easy: I'd love to get out there and make more of myself. You'd love to work less: I'd love to work more. I'd love career success. But I'm scared of failing.

I think you sound brilliant, Shelley the executive management consultant. Are you meant to have this sort of conversation after only four hours? Are you meant to like complete strangers? To the bollocks with it. That's how I feel. I do like you, and I'd love to meet up with you some time. Are you free this week?

05.24

What do you mean you want career success? You're an ENT surgeon!

05.41

Yes, I am. I forgot. Ignore me. I'm at the top of the game, baby. You should be begging for a date with me. I could stick my arm up your nose and all. Now, when are we going to meet? X

*

'Are you out of your fucking *mind?*' Hailey asked, staring in dismay at my laptop.

I looked helplessly at her. 'Oh, God, Hailey, do you think it's that bad?'

Hailey burst out laughing. 'Er, yes? Fucking hell, Chas,

you've just bared someone else's soul on their behalf! Without knowing the first cocking *thing* about them! What's Shelley going to say when she reads this?'

I shrugged.

Hailey's eyes narrowed. 'You're not planning to show her these messages, are you?'

I shut my eyes. 'Probably not.'

Hailey went silent. Then she cleared her throat and said, 'Charlotte Lambert, I think you're planning to throw Shelley off the trail and pursue William yourself.'

I opened my eyes. 'Maybe. Oh, God, Hailey this is awful. I don't know how to stop it.'

'I can tell you exactly how to stop it. You organize a date for them RIGHT NOW and then you give her the password for her OWN BLOODY DATING PRO-FILE so she can read these messages, just like it promises on your website. And then you back off and never make contact with either of them again.' She folded her arms across her hefty rack.

Horribly ashamed, I said nothing.

Hailey had come round after work to take me out for a fish supper: 'I want to get some solid junk food down you,' she said, loading me into The Tank and wheeling me up Broughton Street to the chip shop. My inability to sustain a conversation – so preoccupied was I with William – had not gone unnoticed. After a short bout of cross-questioning, I gave in and handed her my laptop, which I'd brought just in case the fish-and-chip shop had Wi-Fi. And William emailed.

Man, I'd lost it.

It hadn't helped that Hailey had immediately spied a

Word document that I'd minimized, containing details of twelve ENT surgeons called William, which I had compiled using the GMC database. And a doodle relating to how I could somehow poison Shelley Cartwright.

'CHAS.'

'Sorry. I know. I have to let them go on a date.'

'Damn bloody right you do, you psychopath! What's *happened* to you? Don't you turn into one of those stupid women who ruins her career over some juvenile obsession with a man,' she commanded. Turkish techno music boomed out of the speakers behind us and Hailey, demolishing a battered sausage under the strange glow of the chippy's pink neon lights, looked even more scary than usual. In spite of my best efforts not to be, I was feeling rather offended by her tone. Hailey had always been very bossy but this had begun to feel like a personal attack.

Seeing that I was upset, she softened a little. 'Come on, my love. You're a professional professional! Not a doorstep shitter-onner! Charley, *look after* this business of yours. It's brilliant.'

I sat back in The Tank, sighing. She was right. It would be an atrocious error of professional judgement to try to get involved with William myself. Apart from anything else, how would I ever meet him without telling him who I was and what I'd done? Inject some horrible malady into my eardrum and hope I'd get referred to him?

But the prospect of just letting him go was quite devastating. Yes, I had an electric sexual connection with John, but with William I felt like I was making my first ever emotional one. A real emotional connection, which had helped me examine my life in a way I never had before. Surely this was significant!

Stop it, I begged myself. *You had four hours of email. You have no emotional connection at all. You don't even know each other!* The merry-go-round tinkled on and on, going precisely nowhere.

'CHARLOTTE,' barked a voice I didn't expect to hear in my local chippie. I looked up and there she was: Granny Helen, sitting regally in a wheelchair of her own with Sam, slightly out of breath, behind her. He was wearing a grubby tracksuit from his university days and had broken a sweat from the short walk up the hill. In spite of this, he *still* looked attractive.

'Bowes? Granny Helen? I . . . What's going on?'

'I came to your flat to surprise you,' Granny Helen announced. 'Find out how this business of yours is going. I certainly did not expect to find you here eating sausage-shaped offal. Are you ill?'

'Quite surprised by this little scene myself, Chas.' Sam chuckled. 'You don't have a wholegrain wrap hidden under the table?' He wheeled Granny Helen round so she was parked next to me.

I was temporarily silenced. I had not expected to sit next to my grandmother – both of us in wheelchairs – in my local chippie. Together we must have made for an unusual sight. Granny Helen looked neat and stylish, her hair knotted into a bun that was pinned into the nape of her neck. (Mum did Granny Helen's hair for her every single morning.) Pearls hung from her earlobes and her make-up was immaculate. She smelt of powder and perfume and childhood. And, of course, I was dressed pretty smartly, as always. Yep. We looked odd.

Hailey, obviously of the same opinion, smiled. 'Don't you two look funny?' She leaned over to kiss Granny Helen's cheek, which had just been angled towards her. 'How did you get here?' she asked.

'Christian brought me,' Granny Helen replied. 'He wanted to come and see Charlotte too, but I forbade it. I don't get enough time with my granddaughter.' She sniffed. 'Even when she was recuperating at home in East Linton she was working on that dratted business of hers all the time!'

She peered ferociously at me over her glasses, inviting a challenge, but I offered none. Going to war with Granny Helen was absolutely pointless even when she was wrong. In this case, she was right. I sighed as Hailey smiled, clearly delighted to have found an ally. 'Hear hear!' she said as Sam wandered off to order a carton of orange juice, which was all Granny Helen was prepared to consume.

As Hailey and Granny Helen exchanged stories about how hard it was to get time with me, I watched him ordering his own meal – a deep-fried pie and chips, of course – while he jingled change in his jogging bottoms.

I was surprised he'd been physically capable of wheeling Granny Helen up the hill. He'd stumbled into the kitchen at lunchtime today, looking wrecked and muttering about an all-night shagathon with Yvonne, and had been in a state of dazed exhaustion ever since. While he'd sprawled on the sofa watching *Dr Who*, I'd tried to put Dr William out of my mind by writing some thirty client messages.

It hadn't worked.

As Sam paid for his chips, I made a huge mental effort to file William away for now. Granny Helen had arranged to come all the way here to see me, and both of my friends had nearly broken their backs wheeling Lambert women up the hill. I owed them, at the very least, the courtesy of my attention.

Sam arrived back at the table, handed Granny Helen her orange juice and opened a can of Coke for himself. 'Cheers,' he said absently, sinking his teeth into his deep-fried pie. Watching Sam eat was not dissimilar to watching Malcolm at his bowl and I studied him with the usual mixture of fondness and despair.

'You eat like Malcolm does,' Granny Helen told him. She had a habit of saying things that other people thought but tended not to voice. Sam shrugged: he knew. 'But you're extremely attractive,' she added. Sam blushed.

'Isn't he?' Hailey agreed. 'It's such a waste. Think what a decent man could do with those looks.'

Sam blinked, totally unconcerned. 'I am a decent man. Very decent. I've been faithful to Yvonne the whole time we've been together.'

'Six months is not a world record,' Hailey said. Granny Helen smiled slightly, watching Sam's face. She enjoyed hearing about his normally disgraceful love life. She said it reminded her of how lucky she was to have been married to Granddad Jack.

'No,' Sam agreed, 'but it's a personal best.' He cut a cheese-shaped wedge out of his bizarre pie and popped it into his mouth with comical delicacy.

There was a pause.

Then: 'I'll have one of these pies,' Granny Helen shouted over at the man behind the fryers. 'Enough,' she snapped, as Sam, Hailey and I burst out laughing. 'Now, Charlotte, how is the business going, my dear?'

I blushed, hoping Hailey wouldn't tell her about my disgraceful emails with William last night. 'It's going well,' I replied. 'Sam's been an amazing help with publicity and, thanks to his efforts, I've got nearly seventy clients! Isn't that fantastic?'

Granny Helen shook her head. 'I might have blasted-well known it would take off. Charlotte,' she said, in her most forbidding voice, 'I do hope you're not proposing to carry on with this thing when you start back at Salutech. Because let me be clear, my girl, you cannot do both.'

My friends nodded their agreement and Hailey raised an enquiring eyebrow at my fish. Sick already of the grease, I pushed the rest over to her.

It was a question with which I'd been grappling a lot over recent weeks. I'd set up First Date Aid because I would otherwise have lost my mind, but now it was up and running – and doing really rather well – the idea of abandoning it or, worse still, selling it, was appalling. I loved it! When I was feeling flat and frustrated with my leg, restless and edgy about doing so little, it breathed life back into me. And I couldn't deny that it thrilled me to see my business model rising out of nothing and giving Steve Sampson in Boston a serious run for his money. How could I hand that over to someone else? Just watch my hard work disappear in an online financial transaction?

But, equally, how could I carry on when I was back at

Salutech? I'd absolutely caned it with my physio to make sure I was able to be back in time for the Simitol launch: I couldn't just return to work and spend half my time writing dating emails. There wasn't so much as a spare second in a Salutech day.

First Date Aid took up a lot of time. It wasn't just the flirting, it was the admin too. The money, the marketing, the client relationships, the website.

Yesterday morning I'd checked my Salutech contract to see if there was anything in it that prevented me running my own business on the side. Technically, as long as I didn't use their computers or time, there was not. But my contract was kind of irrelevant. I'd be out the door if I was discovered; they'd find a way. Salutech loved me, right up to HQ level in Washington (although Bradley Chambers, the repulsive little man who was vice president of Salutech Global, probably loved me a bit too much), but only because they knew that they had my full and undivided attention.

I pondered. And then: *Don't care*, I thought obstinately. *I'm not letting go of my little company. I'll find time. And that's that.*

I would find time. I always did. Somehow.

'We'll see,' I told Granny Helen as her pie was delivered.

The chip-shop man, probably flummoxed by the presence of a pearl-earringed matriarch in his establishment, had found a little sprig of wilting parsley to lay on top and – with touching reverence – put down a plastic knife and fork for her with a piece of kitchen roll folded into a triangle. Granny Helen thanked him graciously, then turned back to me, eyes like bullets. 'Oh, we'll see all right,' she muttered ominously.

I looked at the clock. Probably another two hours before I'd be free to email William. Just to arrange a date between him and Shelley, of course. Nothing more.

10.45 p.m.

Hello William,

I sat back, flexing my fingers. 'Keep it brief,' I told myself, realizing that my heart was thumping again. 'He's not yours to flirt with.'

Sorry it's taken so long to reply to your last message. I had a difficult day at work and couldn't get online.
I would like to go for a date, yes. How does the twenty-sixth of September work? Shelley

I pushed my chair back and got up to make some tea. I didn't know what else to do with myself.

11.03 p.m.

Aha! Shelley! Evening greetings to you.
26th is fine, although I might die of anticipation between now and then.
Look, I wanted to say sorry if you feel that I came on a bit strong trying to get under your skin last night. The problem is that I like you just a bit too much for some bird from the bloody Internet. There's something about you.

But I don't want to frighten you so let's leave it at Wednesday
26 Sept and in the meantime I'll go and shag loads of slappers. x

Absolutely, categorically no, I told myself. Don't you *dare* bite.

But I was powerless.

11.05

What do you mean there's something about me?

Sx

I'd broken so many rules now that a kiss was neither here nor there. I felt quite insane.

11.12

AHA! Shelley is still ONLINE. Good. So, hmmm, what is it about
you . . .
It's not that I find you really attractive (although, for the record, I
do), it's more that I feel like there's something incredibly sweet
and girlish underneath this scary business exterior you have. *Are*
you really this scary corporate ball-breaker? Or is there someone
else underneath? I got the impression last night that there is.
Bugger. Sound like patronizing twat. We've never met. But . . . I
dunno. I feel like I know you. I feel like I can hear the things that
go on in your head. Even though we've never met, you just seem
so familiar.
This is too much. I need to shut the hell up.

'Oh no, oh no,' I said, staring in anguish at my computer
screen. 'Stop seeing me. I hate this.'

11.29 p.m.

It *is* a bit too much, Dr William. But it's strangely enjoyable.
Am I really this scary businesswoman?
Maybe not.
But I am! No, I'm not. I'm . . . argh, stop it.
I suppose what I know is this: I've recently had to take a break
from my normal (ball-breaking) career and have ended up doing
something a lot more jolly. And you know what? I've absolutely
loved it. There hasn't been so much as a whiff of corporate
toughness and I've not been stressed or exhausted. At all.
So perhaps I'm not a scary businesswoman. (But if I'm not, I'm at
a bit of a loss to know who I am.)
William, you can't just make me say that and not tell me
anything about you. You said last night you wished you'd made
something more of yourself. What did you mean?

Sx

11.40

What did I mean? Bloody hell, I don't know. I suppose I have a
massive, overwhelming feeling of underachievement. Like life is
passing me by and I'm not on board. Treading water. Wasting
opportunities. Having a great time but never really engaging
with anything or anyone. Girls come and go, meaning nothing –
not that I get around, I mean relationships – and my dreams just
get further and further away.
This is not a very romantic preamble to a date, is it? Sincere
apologies. You and your profile got me at a bit of a vulnerable
moment last night. And now I've opened a Pandora's box that

I'm having trouble closing. Worse still, I seem to have forced you to open yours.

Wow. I really do have all the moves, innit.

11.59

William. You may not have the classic moves, but I think you're the most honest, open person I've talked to in years. You get me. I'm not sure I like it!

00.05

Hmmmm. Same. Let's try something more pedestrian. Where are you from?

00.07

Small town outside the city [*true for both me and Shelley. Different cities though*. Different girls, *I told myself firmly*.] Where are you from?

00:17

I'm a city boy. The countryside looks so beautiful on postcards but in real life it annoys me. I don't know what to do with it.

00.22

I know what you mean! I plan 'trips to the country' and then have fuck-all idea what to do when I get there!

00.30

Maybe we could have a countryside date then. Exorcize some fears. Pretend we're just some couple who've gone away for a dirty weekend. (If it went really well, we could always turn it into one of those.)

Er, sorry. Too much.

Ah, just caught sight of your profile picture again. Are you aware of being beautiful? X

I felt madly happy and then madly sad. William was looking at a picture of Shelley, not me.

00.31

Inside and out [*he added*]. Even if you look nothing like your photo I still reckon you're beautiful.

I stopped feeling madly sad and felt madly happy again.

00.40

Why thank you, William.

Now. I like the sound of a countryside date but it will probably be impossible with my work schedule. It may have to be urban. Oh, and as the man it's your job to come up with somewhere imaginative and fabulous. No pressure.

And for the record I think doctors are amazing. So quite what you're on about with this feeling of not having achieved, of life passing you by, I have no idea. I've consistently overachieved and, as you appear to have worked out on my behalf, it's left me completely adrift.

Our conversation has rather blown me apart, William . . .

Not convinced this is very good Internet dating etiquette. Oops. *Giggles cheekily.*

Sx

00.53

I like that cheeky giggling. Oh, I like it very much, young lady.
I think you would benefit from doing a lot of cheeky giggling,
Shelley Businesswoman. I think you would benefit from running
around the house without any clothes on, giggling and singing
and whooping. And then maybe quitting your job for a bit and
giggling off to, I don't know, Berlin, where you'd go and get
stoned and hang out at strange discos by the river at 7.30 a.m.
eating hotdogs.

I looked wistfully at my plastered leg. It did indeed sound
rather wonderful.

But again, it sounds like I'm trying to do amateur psychoanalysis
on you. I'm not trying to say you're some uptight woman who
needs to set herself free . . . just that . . . I was just really touched
by you saying that you'd probably enjoy life more if you could let
go. It made so much sense to me.
And I don't care about email etiquette. This conversation has
rather blown me apart too, which is exactly what I needed to
happen. See you in seven days. X William

*

Promise me you just fixed up a date and left it at that, Hailey
texted me, just before midnight.

'Yep, date sorted,' I replied, staring at William's face on
my screen. That, at least, was true.

The date was in seven days. And as I turned my laptop
off and lay in the dark tingling all over, I realized that I
couldn't let Shelley go on it. Something real was happening here. I'd learned more about myself in two evenings

talking to William than I had in thirty-two years under my own steam. Wasn't this the sort of stuff that happened when you fell in love?

I pulled the pillow out from underneath my head and started thumping myself with it. 'You are forbidden EVER to use that word again,' I hissed. 'FORBIDDEN!'

Chapter Six

'So, you see, it's looking like I should be back really quite soon.' I stuck a crutch up in the air to signal how mobile I was.

Margot looked unimpressed. 'We'll be delighted to have you with us, Charley,' she said carefully – as if I was applying for a receptionist's job after recently doing work experience, 'but do you think you can cope here while you're on crutches? Salutech isn't particularly disability-friendly.'

'Well, that sounds to me like something Carly might want to look into,' I said smoothly. Carly from HR, delighted to have something to do, wrote down 'DISABILITY ACCESS' and underlined it twice, finishing off by circling the two words and adding an asterisk just to be certain. Margot looked at my crutches and shuddered.

I am calm six-foot woman, I told myself. *Not angry six-foot woman. I will not give her what she wants.* (Ness had once sat me down and told me that the only thing scarier than a six-foot woman was an angry six-foot woman.)

As if she were reading my mind, Margot took it to the next level, leaning back in her chair with all the expansive ease of a CEO. 'I wonder if you should be assessed by one of our doctors before you make any firm arrangements to come back.'

I took a deep breath. 'Margot, I've been keeping abreast of things and it's obvious that you've done an excellent job laying down foundations for the Simitol launch. Seriously –' I gritted my teeth '– I'm so impressed that you've won over the health minister and made such brilliant progress with the patient groups. But in two weeks we go public with the biggest brand launch in twenty years and the government and ABPI are going to be all over our every move. It's absolutely essential that I personally manage that process.'

'I couldn't agree more,' said a voice from the doorway behind me.

I froze. *Oh, please, no.*

John was meant to be in Paris at a conference set up by one of our competitors, who had a significant drug in phase three: I'd timed today's meeting especially to coincide with his absence. Of course I accepted I'd have to deal with him at some point, but I also knew that today was not the day. But there he was. All six foot four of him, suited, booted and beaming, still tanned from his honeymoon at that stupid *winery* in California with a stupid gold wedding ring on his finger. Stupid, stupid, stupid. And yet more impossibly handsome than ever.

I tried to stand up, but he bent down to kiss my cheek instead, saying it was nice to see me. I was so thrown by the situation that I could barely hear him, but I came to rapidly as he slid a hand discreetly along the curve of my neck. It lingered there for a split second before he straightened. I glanced round furtively but neither Margot nor Carly appeared to have noticed.

The dog. The flirty, dirty dog. Touching my neck with his *wedding*-ring hand?

And then I realized something very strange was happening. My neck was not tingling where he'd touched me. Well, not much. My privates were definitely not on fire. And actually, as the shock of unexpectedly seeing him wore off, I felt really quite calm.

Eh?

'Well, then, Charley!' he said. He only called me Lambert in private. 'How's the star of the company? Ready to take the helm on Monday?'

I nodded, noting that Margot looked furious.

John, meanwhile, was watching me keenly. 'Are you going to be OK, my dear?' he asked, in a more human voice. 'It won't be too much?'

'Course not,' I replied brightly. 'Margot can start emailing stuff today so I'll be up to speed.'

Why wasn't his compassion turning me to squelch?

John, perhaps wondering the same, squatted on his haunches and brazenly took my hand. I sensed Margot's frontal cortex exploding with envy and suspicion. 'Are you sure, Lambert?' he murmured quietly. 'Your health is far more important to me than Simitol.'

For a man as driven by his business as John, this was a fairly dubious claim. And yet, looking at his face, I got the impression that he was being absolutely straight. 'Of course I'm sure!' I said brightly, withdrawing my fingers. *I actually didn't want him holding my hand!* This was extraordinary. I wasn't falling apart and I wasn't hatching some deluded campaign to steal him back from Susan Faulkner.

That's because you're busy trying to destroy Shelley Cartwright's stab at happiness instead, my head informed me. *What a nice girl you are, Charley Lambert! Why bother looking for a man of your own when you could steal someone else's?*

John smiled, his eyes boring into mine. I smiled politely back at him and put my BlackBerry into my bag. 'Good to see you, Charley,' he said, after a pause.

Twenty minutes later, sitting in the back of a taxi on the A1, I tried to make sense of this. Was this thing with William the doctor – William the total stranger to whom I had no entitlement whatsoever – really enough to end seven years of unadulterated obsession with John MacAllister?

I thought about William and the way he had just effortlessly tunnelled inside my mind. He'd already been to places John had never got close to. I felt more confused than ever. Surely this was how you were meant to feel when you'd been with someone for a while and started to fall in love.

'STOP IT,' I shouted at myself, as the taxi pulled up outside my flat. 'THIS IS NOT LOVE.' I paid the bewildered driver and prepared to haul myself up the stairs, determined to take some positive action.

Failing to come up with a plan of positive action, I decided to call Hailey instead.

'Banqueting, good afternoon?'

'Hailey . . .'

'Hello, Charleypops! Please don't tell me you're calling to talk about the Internet doctor.'

'Um . . . I'm calling to talk about the Internet doctor.'

I leaned against the kitchen sink so I could look out of the window without the aid of crutches.

I heard Hailey pull the phone round the corner into the chefs' locker room. 'Chas,' she said. 'We've talked about this. He's not yours to obsess over, my love.'

'I know. But I saw John today and I felt nothing. All I could think about was how much William seems to understand me.'

'He doesn't understand you, Chas. He doesn't even know your name. When he thinks about you, he's visualizing some bird called Shelley. He's going on a date with *her*.' She sounded tired.

'Sorry, Hails. I'm really pissing you off now, aren't I?' I bit my lip, staring distractedly out of the window. Brightly coloured tankers cruised into Newhaven, calmly unaware of my romantic turmoil.

'No, my love, it's just . . . I just think you're in a fantasy world. If you're over John that's great but you can't really attribute that to this imaginary affair. Has Shelley seen the emails yet?'

'No. She hasn't even asked for them. She just doesn't care. She wants me to do all the dirty work so she can turn up and decide if William's *good enough*. He isn't right for her, Hailey! He's right for me!'

'So what are you going to do? Fly to London and spy on their date?'

Now there was an idea. 'Dunno,' I mumbled.

Hailey sighed, exasperated. 'Look, I can't stay on. But I'm telling you once and for all that this has to stop. It's immoral, it's selfish and it's insane. Understood?'

'Murgh.' I ended the call and looked at William's picture

on my laptop one more time. She was right: I was going to have to let him go. It was immoral, it was selfish and it was insane.

But as I looked at him, all handsome with his jumper and manly stubble, a bubble floated up the screen telling me I had a new message. Immoral, selfish and insane, I thought, throwing myself across the room without crutches and opening the message as quickly as I could.

Dearest Shelley. (Dearest? Too old-fashioned? Oh, never mind.) It's lunchtime and I've been thinking about you all morning. This is mad! I've decided to take up a load of hobbies to keep my mind busy until I meet you. Current favourites: poetry writing and harpsichord lessons.

I took myself out for dinner last night after my shift finished and imagined you sitting opposite me. You were tall and even prettier than you are in your photo. You arrived without glasses because you thought you looked better without them, but then you had to put them on to read the menu. I thought you looked lovely with them on. And off. I made an inappropriate joke about sodomy and then went bright red. You pretended to have a tiny little feminine appetite and then gnawed your way through a gigantic rump steak in ten minutes.

I watched you eat and wanted to stretch my hand out and hold yours. I didn't, though. I was being manly. But then you caught me looking at you and took my hand.

Then my real-life burger arrived and I stopped mooning over an imaginary woman.

I've bloked up now. Fuck harpsichords and poetry. I'm going to go and pump iron and watch football and drink lager. Maybe beat someone up. A patient, ideally.

How about a place called Polpo for our date? It's sort of Italian tapas, if such a thing could exist. Always noisy so if we don't get on we won't be sitting in silence. 7.30 p.m.? Surely you've finished work by then? If you haven't, make an exception.

X

I read the message three times, an uncontrollable grin stretching across my face. I wanted to be sitting across the table from William, eating Italian things and giggling as he made tasteless jokes about sodomy. I wanted to reach over and take his hand just like he'd imagined. I wanted this more than was healthy.

Was this Internet love? No way. It was bigger than that. *Real* love? 'Shhh,' I told myself, alarmed. But then I realized it didn't matter what it was. All I knew was that William was the most wonderful and brilliant man I'd ever met. And that I was going to have to disobey Hailey and find some way of getting him into my life.

Shortly after I'd sent a reply, Sam crashed through the front door with a face of thunder. No, worse than thunder. It was pure, sooty blackness. I slammed my laptop shut so he couldn't see what was going on but I needn't have bothered: he didn't even look in my direction. Instead he stormed over to the cupboard and took out a loaf of bread and the Nutella jar.

'Oh dear,' I said. 'What's happened, Bowes?'

He ignored me, shoving two slices of bread angrily into the toaster.

'Sam? What's wrong?'

'Yvonne,' he muttered.

'What about her?'

'It's over,' he said, abandoning the toast and marching off into his room. The door slammed behind him. I stared at it, open-mouthed.

Two seconds later, he wrenched his door open, marched back to the counter, grabbed the loaf, the Nutella and a knife, and took them with him. The door slammed again.

I was more shocked even than when they'd got engaged. Sam and Yvonne were . . . They were *lovely*! Delightful! Happy! How could this have happened?

This, Charlotte Lambert, is why you're far better off helping other people start relationships than trying to have one yourself, I thought, dazed. 'Fucking hell,' I said to the empty room. No one replied, but Sam's toast popped up forlornly.

Love is a nightmare, I thought. *Change of plan. Stop emailing William. Walk away before this ends in a miserable mess too.*

A great sadness welled up in me. Letting go was the right thing to do: nothing about the situation was healthy. William was due to meet Shelley in five days, the ball was now rolling and there was nothing I could do to stop it. Apart from anything else, I couldn't take another moment more of the bipolar it's on/it's off thoughts flying around my head.

There was no argument. I had to let go of William. And that absolutely sucked.

After a few seconds, I limped purposefully to Sam's cupboard, removed from it a loaf, his spare jar of Nutella, then took a knife out of the drawer and went to my own bedroom.

The door slammed behind me.

*

Margot marched out of my office in a vulva-skimming skirt, her inappropriate suede high heels stalking across the communications office with angry precision. She had always worn strange clothes but in my absence her wardrobe appeared to have undergone a metamorphosis from strange to plain old slutty. I wondered vaguely if it was an attempt to attract John, but doubted it. Margot didn't like John any more than she liked me. Or anyone else who was senior to her, for that matter.

This was going to be even harder than I'd thought. Margot had reorganized our entire system and was keeping any remotely important information close to her chest. Anything that would help me to do my job remained a mystery. But any information that was irrelevant or would annoy me was readily accessible.

'What about Suki Gilpin from the *Mail*?' I had asked her a few minutes earlier. 'She must have had something to say.' All of the papers had found out about Simitol and, inevitably, a few were trying to stir up trouble. Or, at least, a 'provocative angle'. Suki Gilpin was normally the worst for this.

'She called, yes,' Margot replied. Her face, which was curiously seahorsy, was closed.

'And? She needs careful managing.'

'And I dealt with it.' Margot sniffed.

'OK. Can you email me a written update of how they've all responded so far?' I said. 'I need to know what's coming my way.'

'I really don't have time to write update emails, Charley. I'm extremely busy.'

'With *what*? This is what I need to know, Margot. I haven't come back to drink tea and read *Vogue*.'

Margot rolled her eyes and consulted her watch. 'Charley, I'm sorry but I just don't have time to walk you through my in-tray right now. I'll try to find some time for you later, OK? Now, please excuse me, I've got a call to make.'

And off she marched.

I felt overwhelmed. Over the three months I'd been away I'd forgotten quite how demanding my job was, and indeed how crazed Margot was about status. In the coming weeks I couldn't afford to put a foot wrong and the weight of this responsibility, combined with Margot's complete refusal to hand my job back, was grim.

I tapped my fingers nervously, thinking about her recent trip to the Salutech HQ in Washington when she'd had the great pleasure of telling them how successfully she'd lobbied MPs in my absence. Even though she was refusing to tell me anything I needed to know about the trip, she'd had no problem telling me how much she'd impressed the board of directors. Apparently Bradley Chambers – vice president of Salutech Global and my most senior boss, generally found groping and leering at me when he was in Europe – had been stunned by her all-round amazingness. 'He didn't get my name wrong once,' Margot observed casually. Even though Bradley Chambers never missed an opportunity to sit too close to me in meetings, he'd always called me Sharon.

I turned wearily back to my computer screen where my messenger was glowing orange with an IM from John.

MacAllister, John: Morning Lambert. Margot behaving herself?

It was like the old days – a familiar and slightly inappropriate comment that put us in a flirty little club for two. And yet I felt none of my old pant-wetting enthusiasm.

> Lambert, Charlotte: No.
>
> MacAllister, John: Need any help?
>
> Lambert, Charlotte: No. I'll sort it out.
>
> MacAllister, John: This isn't very professional but I thought it would cheer you up . . . Becky my PA saw Margot on a date with a man two foot shorter than her the other night.

I snorted, then found myself laughing.

> Lambert, Charlotte: You're right. It has cheered me up. See you later for catch-up.
>
> MacAllister, John: Can we do it over lunch? Would be good to have some one-on-one Lambert time. Weren't we due a meal at the Tower?
>
> Lambert, Charlotte: Sadly I don't have time to go into town . . . Next week maybe. Oh, no, we're launching the biggest drug in the world. Maybe 2016?
>
> MacAllister, John: Hmmm. BTW, I've had to cancel my meeting with Arthur Holford in London on Wednesday. Can you cover? 11 a.m., his offices in Marble Arch.
>
> Lambert, Charlotte: Yes.
>
> MacAllister, John: That's my girl. You and me: dinner later this week. No arguments.

I was confused. This was sublimely weird. *I just wasn't bothered.* What on earth was wrong with me?

You've fallen in some sort of love with William, came the

reply. *You think about him approximately every thirty seconds and are dying inside at the thought of him meeting Shelley. But meet him she will, for he is not yours, Charlotte Lambert. On Wednesday night she will grope his testicles in a businesslike manner under a table in Polpo and you will lose him for ever. It is this tortuous thought that has reduced your interest in John MacAllister to almost nil. You loser! One fantasy after another! Never a real man! Never a real romance! Loser!*

Then I stopped short. Wednesday! I was going to be in London on Wednesday with work! Date day! That meant I could . . .

I could *what*?

I put my head into my hands and slumped over my desk. Being inside my mind was exhausting and embarrassing. What was wrong with me? Wearily I looked up at the clock to see if the day was nearly over.

It was not. It was eleven fifty-five a.m. and I'd only been there for four hours. But already I was considering abseiling off the fire escape. Trying to breathe deeply, I leaned forward to smell the bunch of flowers Ness had had delivered this morning. 'Take it easy!' her little recycled-cardboard notelet said. Fat chance of doing anything else, with Margot refusing to give my job back and me immobilized by fear, exhaustion and obsession with some doctor I'd never met.

I took another deep breath and picked up the phone. I'd call Alan Vicary at the *Guardian*. He had always been my first call back in the days when we'd been able to publicize our drugs. A nice, calm man with tufty ears who had once bought me a cigar to cheer me up after I'd been mauled in a press briefing. Our relationship with the press had had to change a lot over recent years but I still worked with him when I could.

'Alan Vicary.'

'Alan! It's Charley Lambert from Salutech. How are you?'

'Charley! How're all those fractures? Leg full of metal pins? We've all been thinking about you!'

This, of course, was a lie, but it was probably the first question today to which I knew the answer. 'Metal pins still there but I'm out of plaster and hobbling around,' I said. 'Could be worse.'

'Great! So, I hear the HIV miracle you've been working on all these years is about to arrive in the chemists.'

'Two weeks,' I said. 'And because of what it is I think we both know there's going to be a storm. So I wanted to let you know you can go back to calling my mobile twenty-four/seven if you need a comment or a scientist interview ... Patient group, key opinion leader – anything, anyone, Alan. I'll sort it.'

Alan sounded like he was puffing at a pipe. It wouldn't have surprised me; I'd once taken him for lunch near his office in King's Cross and he'd been wearing carpet slippers.

'Sure thing, Charley. Although your colleague – what's her name? Melissa? – called this morning to say her phone extension had changed but all press calls were still to come to her.'

There was an uncomfortable pause, which Alan filled with wheezy laughter. 'I'll take it you weren't expecting that. Oh dear. Well, Charley, you're the boss. I'll be sure to call you if I need anything.'

'Thanks, Alan,' I said, in as calm a voice as I could

muster. 'Yes, I'm still the boss. See you end of next week for the press conference.'

Before I stormed over to Margot's desk and swung for her, I called a random selection of other newspapers. All had had the same call from Margot. I dug my fingernails into my palms and boiled with anger. How dare she?

Furious, I pushed my chair back to get up. But without a decent left leg to counter the chair's movement, I shot backwards and found myself crashing onto the floor with a savage exclamation of pain.

'Shit, Charley!' Cassie, my PA, came running into my office. 'What happened?'

I was crimson. 'Oh, it's nothing,' I said, feigning laughter but managing only to make a hollow braying sound. Tears, over which I had absolutely no control, were gathering fast in my eyes. 'Just tried to get up too quickly! I'm fine!'

'No, you're not.' Cassie helped me up and popped me expertly back onto the chair, which she steadied with her leg. I felt excruciatingly stupid, embarrassed even to call myself her boss. 'Charley, please call me if you need help,' she said. 'You've come back pretty early.'

'Thanks,' I whispered, still scarlet. I looked at Margot who was on the phone, leaning back in her chair and watching the whole humiliating scene with pleasure written on her face.

When she came off the phone, I buzzed her. 'Could you come through, please?'

A few minutes later she wandered in with a cup of tea. Only one, of course.

'Margot, the medical press inform me that you have

contacted them in the last twenty-four hours to tell them that you are the first port of call for questions.'

'Correct.'

'The problem is, you're not. I am.'

'Since when did press calls go straight through to the director of comms?' she asked. 'There're ten people in this office who take calls before you do. You only get them if they're serious. That's your system, Charley.' She took a sip from her mug and stared at me, unsmiling.

Technically, she was right. But we both knew exactly what she was doing. The slippery little seahorse.

'Well,' I said, as calmly as I could, 'the usual rules do not apply at the moment. We're launching a huge product. Anything regarding Simitol comes to me first.'

Margot shrugged. 'Fine, however you want it.' She strolled out, completely unbothered, and I found myself, once again, on the brink of tears. I wanted to be in bed. My suit was chafing at the waist where I'd put on weight eating Sam's dinners and doing no exercise all these weeks, and my skin felt as if someone had held a blowtorch to it after just a few hours under the sterile breeze of the air-conditioning system.

'Good day?' Graham from Security had offered to drive me home. I rested my head against the window of his car, barely able to sit up straight.

'No,' I replied. 'Dreadful.'

Graham made a tutting noise. 'Margot's kept things well, though, aye? Worked hard, that one!'

I stared vacantly at the crowds crossing Leith Walk in

front of us. 'Yeah. Everything seems to be in good shape. I think she's done a great job. Great.'

'She's quite a little piece,' Graham said slyly.

I looked sideways at him. 'Piece?'

He grinned. 'Aye, piece. I find her rather attractive.'

I paused before I put the key into my front-door lock, unsure as to how to deal with the volatile wreck that Sam had become since splitting up with Yvonne. During the five days since his surprise announcement, he'd been drinking too much and now he was florid and unhealthy; his nightly meals had stopped and the Nutella and cheap bread were back. I'd grown to rather enjoy our chats over his grey macaroni cheese, his cabbage and Edam salads, and his wonderful attempts at home baking. But now the vibe in the flat was mostly silence or bad music.

Sam, in short, was absolutely devastated. All he'd told me was that Yvonne had caught him cheating. When, how or with whom I had yet to fathom but I'd been shocked, not just that he had cheated on her but that he had managed to do so without my noticing. How had he got away with it? *Easily*, I'd realized. *He's a pro!*

It felt impossibly sad that bubbly, silly, tiny Yvonne, with her excitable squeaks, was probably now reduced to a grieving heap on the floor. The poor girl. Had her tough little mum not threatened to 'beat tha livin' fuck' out of Sam if he came anywhere near her, I'd probably have tried to call her.

I put the key into the lock. *Please, God*, I prayed, *can Sam not be sitting around in a cloud of doom and stale fart. Please, God.*

I walked in. And for the first time that day my prayers

were answered. Sam was not sitting in a cloud of doom and stale fart. Rather than his bread and Nutella on the coffee-table, I saw, with pleasure, his complete works of Shakespeare. And from the direction of the bathroom I heard his voice, far deeper than usual, shouting something about lily-livered boys.

I broke into a grin. I knew that voice! It was his Actor Voice! Hailey and I had dubbed it the Bowes Actor Voice (BAV) after watching him playing Oedipus in a university production. We'd spent the night bent double with mirth at his boomy, two-octaves-deeper-and-ten-times-posher-than-normal delivery. I hobbled over to the microwave with my meal-for-two, giggling. I hadn't heard the BAV in a very, very long time.

'CHAS,' Sam boomed, emerging dramatically from the bathroom.

'Hello, Samuel the actor, hello, the BAV. What happened to Bowes the sulker?'

Sam hopped into the armchair, looking pleased but self-conscious. 'Samuel Bowes is putting himself back into circulation,' he said, a little less boomily.

I put our dinner in the microwave. I didn't approve of microwave meals, of course, but, given that Sam had abandoned his mad cookery sessions and I couldn't stand up for long, they were serving us rather well. 'So you're going to try to get some work?' I asked him tentatively. It was a minefield, Sam's acting career. He hated being probed about it, but if you didn't ask he complained that no one took him seriously as an actor.

'I'm going to try.' I looked over at him and, as I'd expected, his face had gone a little red. Sam found it very hard to talk about acting: it seemed to bring up all sorts of wild emotions that both of us were happy to avoid. 'If you can go back to work with a crazy half-healed leg I can get my arse off the sofa and try to get some auditions. Remember that showreel I made in 2010? I sent it to some agents a couple of weeks ago and one of them called this morning, saying he wanted to see me! It's bloody PFD, Charley. They're massive!'

I grinned and clapped. It was a huge relief to see Sam like this. 'Brilliant work, Bowes! When are you going down?'

'Tomorrow,' he said. 'I'll stay there till the weekend and see if I can hand-deliver the DVD to any casting directors. Maybe hook up with any friends who are acting. Just, you know, get the word out there.'

'The word that the Bowes is in town,' I said distractedly. This meant Sam would also be in London during William and Shelley's date on Wednesday. My mind began to race with absurd possibilities. Clearly I had to stay well away from it, but perhaps he could help. Perhaps I could ask him to . . . to intervene. Try to seduce Shelley and maybe hand William a picture of me by way of consolation? *Yes, great*, I thought angrily. *Perhaps you could hire a brass band and throw an erotic dancer into the mix.*

It had been three long days since I had last logged on to Shelley's profile. Three days since I'd taken a deep breath, emailed William to confirm Polpo at seven thirty on Wednesday and made up some cock-and-bull story about why Shelley couldn't email him again before the date. Afterwards, I'd gritted my teeth and called her.

'What do you mean it all got a bit personal?' she'd barked. 'Charlotte, if I find out that you've been divulging –'

'No, no! Not that sort of personal. I haven't given out your address or anything . . . It just got a bit, um, intense,' I said lamely. Knowing I had no choice, I then emailed Shelley the password to her love.com account so she could sign in and see just how 'intense' it had got. The thought of her wrath left me weak with fear but I had to wash my hands of the situation.

So it was not without amazement that I read her email a few moments later. 'I'm engrossed, Charlotte, this is good stuff. Do you normally go this far for clients? Quite frightening but it's all bang on. I actually think William will be well prepared for who I am.'

At first I'd been amazed; after a while I'd felt less surprised. Shelley and I were, after all, the same person. William had obviously hit as much of a nerve in her as he had in me. DAMN HER.

Sam was looking at me expectantly. Slightly nervously, in fact.

'Er . . . sorry?'

'I asked if you were OK. You suddenly disappeared,' he said.

'Er . . . yes, I'm OK, just shattered. Reckon I'm going to have some dinner, do a couple of hours' work and hit the hay,' I said vaguely.

'Don't be a fool. Just eat and go to bed,' he said. 'You can't work in this state.'

I shook my head. 'I haven't the choice. We've never been so busy.'

Sam looked as if he wanted to probe further but knew it wasn't worth it. 'OK. So, anyway, what do you think?'

'About what?'

'I knew you weren't bloody well listening! I . . .' Suddenly Sam seemed extremely awkward. 'I, er, wondered if I could maybe call Katy and ask if I could stay with her. She said I could sleep on her sofa any time . . . and I . . .' He trailed off.

'And you can't stay with any of your actor friends?'

'Well, Jamie's just got engaged, so they'll be shagging all the time. Howard's just had the bailiffs in and hasn't got so much as a chair to sit on. Helly hasn't spoken to me since we, er . . . and Tim's on holiday.'

'And you don't know anyone else in London? Apart from my pretty little sister?'

Sam slammed his fist on the sofa. 'I just broke up with Yvonne, Charley,' he said angrily. 'Do you really think I'm in the mood for trying to get off with someone else? My fucking housemate's little sister at that?'

'You're always up for getting off with someone, Sam. Come on.'

'Piss off,' he said, marching out of the room. His door slammed behind him. For the second time in the last few days, I stared at it in shock. 'Sam?'

Nothing.

'Sam!'

Tentacles of guilt wrapped themselves around me. Of course Sam wasn't going to London to try to seduce Katy. He was going down there to try to build up his fragile self-esteem, find a footing in the horrible world of acting and take his mind off his break-up. *You stinky bitch, Charley*, my head hissed. *Sam's been a great friend to you and you repay him like this? Shame on you!*

I hauled myself off the sofa, hobbled over to his bedroom door and walked in without knocking. Sam was on his bed, crying. He looked like a helpless child, balled up and rocking. My heart melted. 'Oh, Sam . . . oh, darling Sam, I'm so sorry,' I said, throwing myself awkwardly onto the bed next to him. 'Sam, Sam, Sam . . .' I put my arm round his waist and he crumpled onto my shoulder, sobbing.

'I miss her,' he howled. Rigid with shock, I stroked his back. I had never seen anything like this from Sam. Sobs tore through him. 'I feel so sad and confused and shit,' he yelled into my shoulder.

Five minutes later I served two bowls of microwave mush and called Katy. 'Katy Lambert, are you able to put up your big sister and her housemate?' I asked. Sam smiled, eyes still red, and promptly burned his tongue on a piece of red-hot parsnip. I shook my head despairingly.

'WOOOO, YEAH!' Katy shouted. I could hear a strange wind instrument playing in the background. 'WICKED!'

'Sam's coming down for some actorly networking and I've got a few meetings,' I said. 'I know you hate me going to hotels when I'm there with Salutech so I thought I'd stay with you for once.'

'TRIPLE 'MAZIN'!' she bellowed, ringing off.

Sam got up to fetch the HP sauce, which he squeezed liberally into his bowl. 'Thanks for this, Chasman,' he whispered, his face that of Mummy's Brave Little Soldier.

After dinner I put Sam to bed among his horrible lad mags, then slid helplessly back into the uncomfortable thoughts I was having about staying with Katy. The truth, of course, was not that I was staying with her because she complained when I stayed in hotels. Neither was it because I didn't trust Sam around her.

It was because I didn't trust myself.

A plan had begun to form in my mind, involving William and Shelley's date on Wednesday and some sly intervention from one Charley Lambert. It was a stupid plan that horrified my sensible side. But this sensible side (or what remained of it) believed that I wouldn't see the plan through if I was surrounded by Katy and Sam – people from my real world – rather than strangers in a hotel, where I was accountable to nobody and could sneak off on a stupid mission far too easily. Maybe, *just maybe*, if I stayed in Katy's Brixton house full of mad, creative people, there was a chance I wouldn't see this stupid plan through.

Maybe.

Chapter Seven

I woke up in Katy's spare room on Wednesday morning – the day of the date – and knew I was going to have to follow the plan through. All of the (many) reasons not to go to Polpo had strangely vanished from my consciousness: it was do or die. I couldn't face dying in an agony of 'what if'. I had to go.

The problem was, the plan was sketchy at best. Beyond a vague idea that I needed to be in Polpo looking glorious at seven thirty, I still had absolutely no idea how I was going to intervene while William and Shelley ate Italian tapas tonight. Start a brawl to attract his attention? (With Shelley maybe?) Sit near them looking tragic and beautiful in an amazing dress? Hmm. Perhaps I might faint so that a doctor (i.e. William) could soar over to administer urgent medical aid.

'Gah! GET A GRIP.' The fact of the matter was that Shelley Cartwright would march into a restaurant tonight and enchant William with her enigmatic coldness. Eventually she'd let go of her defences and they would fall madly in love and get married and she would move into his doctorish house in Bloomsbury and I would be stuck in Edinburgh with a peg-leg and a depressed housemate who yelled about gnarled harpies in the shower. Not to mention a pathological deputy at work.

Margot. I shuddered. It had been a huge relief to leave

Salutech for the airport yesterday afternoon. Nothing had changed in the office. Margot was on the phone most of the day, talking to *my* contacts and refusing to tell me what was going on, on the grounds that she was 'just too busy, Charley'. It had been a long time since I had sat in the comms office at Salutech and not been across every tiny thing that was happening. Powerlessness did not sit well with me.

I swung my legs out of bed and hobbled to Katy's kitchen. Sam was asleep in the sitting room, morning sun falling on his angelic fluffy hair, making him look like a big, slightly grubby kitten. Katy, he and I had been for noodles in Fujiyama last night, and as I watched him talk to her so stiffly and formally – to make absolutely clear to me that he was not on the pull – I had felt even worse about Monday's outburst. Sam was red raw at the moment. Not even half capable of seduction. I smiled fondly and crept into the kitchen, where an unidentifiable Young Person was asleep in a chair clutching a bottle of tomato juice. I tiptoed past him, glad that I wouldn't have to stay at Katy's again in the near future. I loved my trendy, enthusiastic little sister but her lifestyle baffled me. As if to confirm this, I opened her fridge – which had been almost empty when I'd gone to bed last night – and found about a thousand carrots loaded onto the shelves. 'DON'T EAT,' said a piece of paper taped to a carrot. 'VEGETABLE CARVING CLASS 2MORO.'

The milk I'd bought yesterday had disappeared to make way for carrots. No coffee for me, then.

Bollocks. I sighed, sitting down on the chair next to Juice Boy, wondering what William was doing right now.

Was he eating breakfast? What *was* his breakfast? I imagined it would be sturdy English classics such as kedgeree, kippers or black pudding. He would be a full-fat-milk-with-percolated-coffee man, not one for such fripperies as lattes or double-shot skinny soy moccaccinos.

What was he thinking about, as he spread marmalade on his no-nonsense toast a few miles north of where I was now? Shelley. Without doubt. Of course he was: he'd gone barmy for her and had had to endure five days without contact. He must be going out of his mind.

He wasn't the only one.

After my meeting with Arthur Holford I slunk off to Selfridges where I ate a muffin and bought a Lanvin dress while my back was turned. Later, I sat staring at it in Katy's sitting room, excited but ashamed. It was not a sensible expenditure but it was probably necessary: I had now begun to assemble some sort of plan for this evening that required an outstanding dress.

It was a fairly basic plan at present: simply that I would go to Polpo wearing my beautiful borderline-glamorous dress and that I would get there shortly before the date commenced. I would sit at the table directly opposite William and look nice, approachable and attractive. I figured that Shelley would arrive ten minutes late (because that's what I would do on a date) so I had precisely ten minutes in which to find an excuse to strike up conversation with him and dazzle him so much that by the time Shelley arrived he'd be wishing he was going on a date with me. I would eat a small and stylish meal, then pull on my fur coat (I didn't have one but there was still time) and glide out of the restaurant. William would be devastated but – and this was the great part – *I'd give my business card to a waiter and ask him to pass it on to William!* He'd come to the end of a horrible, dull meal with an uptight Shelley and his heart would leap as the waiter slid my card discreetly into his hand. Ta-da!

'You're an absolute twat,' Hailey said witheringly, when I called her and relayed the plan. 'I literally cannot believe you're doing this. Seriously, Charley, you need therapy.'

There was an uncomfortable silence. I'd called Hailey looking for approval (or, more realistically, a bit of girly camaraderie). Possibly I'd set my expectations too high.

'Get the hell on a plane and come back,' she said. She sounded actually quite angry and I realized I had scrunched myself defensively into the sofa where Sam had slept last night. His duvet was still there: I inched under it like a naughty dog.

'Come on, Hails,' I pleaded. 'Imagine I'd told you to stop seeing Matty after you'd begun to fall for him. Would you take any notice?'

'I fucking *knew* Matty before I fell in love with him, you freak! Charley, I'd been seeing him for three months! YOU'VE NEVER MET THIS MAN!'

I pulled the Sam duvet over my head but then threw it off me onto the floor. I wasn't having this. I was Charley Lambert, businesswoman and granddaughter of Granny Helen Lambert. I was not a weakling and I would not be spoken to like this. 'Hailey,' I said, with spirit. 'I've had enough of your criticism. You've been foul to me about this situation from the word go and you've not even attempted to understand. Why are you being so cruel?'

Hailey huffed like a teenager. 'Why am I being so *cruel*? More like, why are you acting like a wazzock, Charley? What the hell is wrong with you? How can you run a dating business and behave like this? And your fucking job, why do Salutech think you're in London?'

'I'm here on Salutech business!'

'Well, do your fucking business and come home, you moronic *teenager*,' she shouted. She was genuinely furious.

I, meanwhile, was feeling so ashamed I wanted to sew myself into Katy's minging sofa where I could be pummelled by lots of grubby artists' bottoms and have spliffs stubbed out on me. But I couldn't back down. Something bigger than me was in the driving seat now. 'It's great to know I can rely on you for support,' I said, as if I were somehow the victim here.

'You have no respect for others and their relationships,' Hailey said. Her voice was cold. 'Come home and bring Charley Lambert back with you. This freak masquerading as her is pissing me off.' She hung up.

Ignore her, said a voice in my head. *Sure, it's a bit lunatic to gatecrash William and Shelley's date but it's what anyone would do in your situation. Especially Hailey! She should be supporting you, not condemning you!*

The voice got indignant, reminding me about the time that Hailey had had an affair with a married Hibs footballer and nearly lost her job. Had I told her off? Had I hell. I'd gone to her flat at three twenty a.m. with a bottle of Scotch and listened patiently while she'd plotted to set fire to his penis.

I knew that my plan for tonight was silly. But it was also harmless. (Reasonably.) I was just going to present myself to William as Another Option, then sit back and see what happened. It was up to him whether or not he called me.

And then I was back in the madness again, fizzing over with excitement and nerves at the prospect of finally meeting Dr William. I balled myself up on the sofa and closed my eyes, imagining his sensible, intelligent face centimetres away from mine.

Ping, ping, ping, went my inbox, as emails poured in. It was now four o'clock and I was attempting – rather unsuccessfully – to take my mind off tonight by engaging in some stiff work. I was hooked up to Katy's piggybacked Wi-Fi, the contents of my in-tray stacked neatly beside my laptop on Katy's kitchen table. My beautiful Lanvin presided majestically over the scene, hanging from an abandoned light fitting in the ceiling. (I hadn't dared hang it in Katy's vintage-filled wardrobe because it smelt like old ladies in there.) I wrenched my eyes away from it and fixed my gaze on my screen. The screen immediately glazed over. *Honestly, William, I'm so cruel to myself,* I'd said last week. *I'd like to be kinder if I knew how.*

I stared at my phone, a terrible limbo crackling around me. The closer tonight got, the more desperately I needed support. Solidarity. Someone to tell me that my plan was brilliant. I'd thought about telling Katy but, given her Internet dating history, I strongly suspected she'd tell me to run for my life. Sam had been here earlier and I'd tried to pluck up the courage to broach it with him, but he'd been too preoccupied – terrified, even, about his five o'clock meeting with the agent, so I'd sent him off for a bath with a comforting carrot from Katy's fridge.

I looked back at my laptop, which, having given up any

hope of input from me, had wandered off into screen-saver mode. My eye followed a roving picture of me, Ness, Mum, Dad and Katy on the beach by Tantallon Castle with Malcolm last year. Ness was sitting on a rock behind me, her arm round my neck.

Ness! I sat up. Ness would support me! She was my twin: she never judged me. Ever. Even when I'd had to sack someone for wining and dining a journalist in an underhand bid to get (illegal) coverage for one of our drugs, Ness had bolstered me up and told me everything was OK. I needed Ness and I needed her right now. She'd understand!

'What's up, little Charley?'

Ness – a good nine inches shorter than me – was the only person in the world who called me 'little' Charley.

'Hello,' I said. My voice sounded croaky and strained.

'Oh, Charley, what's wrong, my love?' Ness ran the literary department at the Traverse Theatre and it sounded like she was in the brightest, loveliest room in the world.

I found myself too ashamed to speak, sitting in Katy's carrot-infested kitchen.

'It's not that bloody John, is it? Oh, Charley, I really –'

'No. Ness, I know this sounds mad but I think I'm in love with someone I've never met.'

There was a guarded silence. 'Are you online dating?' she asked.

'No. It's . . . it's a man that one of my clients is dating. Tonight's their first meeting, in fact. We started chatting and . . . I think he's amazing, Nessie. I don't know what to do. I can't think straight, knowing he's meeting up with someone else.'

Ness sighed. 'Oh, little Charley . . . Remember what Katy went through? She said she lost her mind when she was chatting to men online.'

'I KNOW. But, Ness, I've been flirting with men online for weeks. I have amazing banter with some of them! And I've felt nothing. But then this started and *bam*. I think I have to do something, Ness.'

'Such as what?' She sounded worried.

Ping, ping, ping, went my inbox. Four months ago I'd have ended the call, rolled up my sleeves and dived into the emails. I wouldn't even have *been* on the phone to my sister during work time, let alone planning some mad intervention on a school night. But things had changed. Somewhere in London a tall man in a polo neck was winding down his working day so that he could go and meet a woman who seemed 'so familiar' and whom he thought was 'beautiful'.

Ness was asking me something but I couldn't hear her. 'Are you near a computer?' I asked her.

'Er, yes?'

'Right. I'm sending you something,' I said. 'Call me back when you've read it.'

I emailed her the Word document into which I'd copied and pasted my correspondence with William. Then I stared blindly at a delegate list for our Simitol press conference and waited for her reply.

Ten minutes later my phone rang.

'See what I mean?' I demanded. 'You see, Ness?'

Ness said nothing for a few seconds. 'Actually, I do,' she said hesitantly. 'And it's kind of broken my heart seeing all of it. He's so much better for you than John or Nathan or any of those arrogant idiots you've gone for, Charley-pops. And all that stuff he said about you and your work . . . and about letting go . . . Wow! I couldn't have put it better myself!'

'You see?' I cried again, triumphantly. 'This is why I can't let the date happen! He's never even met me and he understands me like you do! And he's funny! And smart! And gorgeous!'

'He is, I agree. You seem well suited.'

'Exactly! I can't let the date go ahead, can I?'

'How would you stop it?'

'Well, I sort of might be in London . . .'

'*What?*'

'Hm, yes. I sort of thought I might get there just before the client arrives and maybe strike up a conversation. Possibly give him my business card? Just so he knows I exist, Ness.'

'But you can't!'

'I can! How will I ever track him down otherwise? Tonight is the first and last opportunity I have to meet him.'

Ness sighed. 'I can't stop you, can I?'

I felt a little flush of warmth spread over me. Ness was giving me her blessing. Sort of. 'No.'

'Well, call me tomorrow, and look after yourself,' she said.

I grinned. 'Love you so much, Nessie, thank you . . .'

Three hours later I walked down Beak Street, looking for Polpo. Delicious wafts of baking dough were coming from a pizza place on my right, and I wondered if it might be a better idea to cancel my mission and instead scoff a pizza in dignified solitude. Apart from anything else, I'd begun to feel rather uncomfortable about my appearance. My Lanvin dress was stunning in its simplicity and my heels (brought out on the rare occasions when I met a man taller than me) had made me feel special back at Katy's. But as I passed through a sea of jeans-wearing Soho types – most of whom for some reason appeared to be tiny pygmies – I felt like a massive over-dressed circus attraction.

But there was no way I was turning back. I might feel like a bit of a freak on the outside, but inside I was a madly overexcited lovestruck teenager. My heart was not so much fluttering as erupting, and all I could think of was that William and I might be minutes away from reopening our sublime connection. It didn't matter how stupid I felt: I just had to talk to him. I *had* to!

I'd check myself in for therapy at a later date.

I stopped briefly to check my reflection in the window of a Carnaby Street clothes shop and smiled shakily. I looked fine. Nice, even. All I needed to do was hold my nerve and be me. After all, it was *me* whom William had liked so much: he hadn't been interested in the all-powerful workaholic Charley whom John fancied, or the doctor-worshipping emotionally unavailable girl whom Dr Nathan Gillies had tolerated. No. William had gone for the plain old no-frills *real* Charley Lambert. Who knew?

A small crowd of people stood outside a doorway ahead of me. *Please let this not be Polpo,* I thought anxiously.

But of course it *was* Polpo. And Polpo was small. A solid mass of people lined the tiny bar and even tinier entrance, spilling out on to the street, clamouring for tables. I panicked. What the hell kind of restaurant was jammed at this time? How was I going to get a seat near William?

'At least two hours,' the waiter told me, harassed and hot. I peered over his shoulder and panicked. People were crammed in up to the rafters; the food looked amazing and the place was atmospheric and noisy. William was right: it was a good place for a date. If you could get a bloody table.

'I'm up for spending a lot of money,' I yelled desperately at the waiter. 'And I don't need much space. Could I sit in the corner?' I pointed to the end of the bar where staff deposited glasses.

'No,' he shouted. 'I told you, two hours.'

Dammit! I felt my fists ball with frustration. *I had to see him! This was my one and only chance!* I scanned the restaurant again.

And then I saw him. Sitting at the back at a high table, reading a book. He was even wearing the same polo-neck jumper. He was beautiful. I felt a strange sensation of inertia in my chest. Was I having a heart attack?

A large woman wedged herself in front of me, obscuring my view. I wanted to pound my fists on her bull-like back. 'Er, I was queuing,' I announced awkwardly. She ignored me and started badgering the waiter. I could only see William's elbow and felt faint with desperation. The woman moved back slightly and stood on my toe, causing white hot pain up the side of my leg, which could barely take my own weight.

'Excuse me!' I shouted, prodding her in the ribs. 'Excuse

me! I broke my leg in three places and you're now stand-ing on my foot. Can you move, please?'

The woman still ignored me but the waiter heard. 'Three places? OK, OK. You can go and sit at the bar when the gentleman in the red shirt leaves. Happy?'

Maybe he thought I was a disability campaigner. I didn't actually care. I practically hugged him.

I looked at the red-shirt man, who was now tucking his wallet into his pocket, and ducked behind bull-back woman to have one final check of my hair and make-up. What would I do? What would I say? How was I going to play this? Faced with the reality of actually being there, in a restaurant full of real people, eating food and talking loudly, I faltered. Bull-back woman shifted, opening up my view of the restaurant again but I ducked behind her, terrified.

'Off you go,' the waiter shouted, gesturing at the now vacant seat. I took a deep breath and started to pick my way to the bar, which led me directly into William's line of vision. I glanced at him just as he looked up at the door. He was nervous, I could see it in his face, which made me want him even more. Then his eyes scanned towards the bar and found mine.

Time stood still. I stared back at him. *It's me!* I called. *Me, the woman you don't know but probably should! Er . . . hello?* For a split second his eyes widened with recognition, but then his brow furrowed and he carried on looking around, confident I was not Shelley.

Feeling disproportionately disappointed, I realized that I was in urgent need of a plan. My original one had gone up in flames: there wasn't a free table in the restaurant, let alone one near him. In the light of this disaster, should I go over? Make something up? Blurt out the truth? Rapidly I weighed up my options and decided that a drink would be the best place to start. I was starting to sweat now. I sat down. '*Per favore*, five minutes,' the barman shouted, above the din. He was extraordinarily hairy.

'Broken leg,' I yelled. 'I don't care about the mess.'

Manoeuvring myself outwards, I turned to stare straight at William. He was reading his book again. I turned away and started tucking and untucking my hair behind my ear, a nervous habit for which Hailey had told me off about a thousand times.

'OK, *da bere*?' the waiter said, clearing up the remains of red-shirt man's cuttlefish.

'Er, wine please. Red. Large.'

'Which?'

'Er, the house? Or whatever has the highest alcohol content. I don't want to be sober,' I replied.

The waiter smiled. 'It is best to be you when you on a date, lady. The man rumble you later if you prepare to be someone else.'

'Eh?'

'If you prepare . . . prepare? No, *fingere* . . .'

'Oh, pretend.'

'You speak Italian?'

'Yes. I speak far too many bloody languages,' I muttered, thinking longingly of my conversations with William about my excessive extra-curriculars.

The waiter looked pleased. 'I give you the Valpolicella,' he said. 'It is much better than the house. You do not pay more. It is our little present!'

145

'Secret?'

'*Sì!* Secret! Similar word!'

He began to pour and I looked back at William. He was scanning the entrance again and, once more, our eyes met. A little smile crossed his lips as he looked at me – of recognition, attraction, confusion? I couldn't tell. I tried to smile at him but as I did so he turned away again and I was crushed. *He's not looking for you, remember*, I told myself. The waiter handed me a large glass of red. *He's waiting for someone else. If you want to talk to him, you're going to have to do just that.*

I swilled and sniffed. 'This smells spectacular!' I told the barman. He beamed through his forest of facial hair and kissed his fingers.

I drank a very large gulp and forced myself to stand up. It was now or never. The time was seven thirty-seven and, if my assumption about Shelley turned out to be correct, I had only a few minutes before she marched in bang on ten minutes late. *Should have bloody well marched straight over*, my head chided. *Fool!*

'Fucking fuck off,' I muttered. 'Give me a break here, I'm terrified.' Things were moving in slow motion now. 'I'm a Scottish Amazon,' I whispered hoarsely, picking up my wine glass and taking a tiny step in William's direction. Scottish Amazon, my arse. I was a terrified pixie.

And then everything went wrong. William suddenly broke into a dazzling smile. He stood up, did an awkward part-wave, then sat down, only to stand up again in a slightly chaotic fashion. Horrified, I looked over and there she was. Tall, tight-lipped but unmistakably nervous, pushing her way through the crowds towards him. I knew that walk well. It was the walk I did: a sideways crab designed for getting myself through tables. There was something about being tall that made me certain I'd send plates flying as I crossed a crowded restaurant floor.

I held my breath as William reached out a hand to shake Shelley's – or pull her in to kiss her cheek, I couldn't tell which – and then, without warning, my view was obscured. Utterly furious, I scowled at the stupidly dressed young couple who had blocked my view of William and Shelley. The bastards! The stupid, trendy, ridiculous –

'*Charley!*' Katy yelled. She was with Sam, who stared at me with a mixture of disbelief and fear.

I stared back at him. *What the fuck?*

They stood gawping at me. 'What the fuck?' Katy shouted, much to the amusement of the hairy barman.

'Um, hello!' I said, as she came to life and threw her arms around me. Shelley, I saw over Katy's jaunty vintage hat, was just sitting down, saying something humourless to William. He was nodding exaggeratedly to show that he *really* understood whatever it was she was complaining about. I felt sick. I had to intervene. But how?

'What are you *doing* here?' Katy cried, looking absolutely delighted. Sam, looking anything but delighted, arrived at the bar and kissed my cheek awkwardly. He was wearing a very Londonish cardigan and the buttons of his shirt were only half done up. A silver dog-tag hung round his neck, and although he looked yummy and trendy and young, I felt cross. Sam had always been a fashion victim but I couldn't help wondering if he'd ramped things up a level for Katy.

'What are you up to, Bowes?' I asked him.

'My agent meeting was just round the corner,' he said, 'and I wanted to take Katy for dinner to thank her for having me to stay.' I regarded him suspiciously, but eventually softened, remembering his desolate sobbing over Yvonne the other night. Even I, witness to fifteen years of dirty Bowes action, had to admit that he was unlikely to be trying it on with Katy tonight. I gave him a quick smile and he looked relieved.

'Oh, this is *wiiiiicked*,' Katy cried, ecstatic. 'We can all go out! After dinner! There's a wicked gig on in Brixton tonight. I was going to take Sam!'

I remembered my dress and heels, totally out of place here, and felt like a middle-aged woman on her way to the opera. 'I'm not sure I'm dressed for a gig . . .'

'Nonsense! No one gives a fuck what you're wearing!'

William, I could just about see, was laughing. Something inside me died. How could humourless Shelley possibly come up with a joke good enough to make him laugh? Sam shifted his weight on to his other leg and they were both obscured once more. I tried, slyly, to lean round him a bit.

'What are you looking at?' Sam asked. Katy was taking off her coat to reveal a powder blue sixties shift dress in which she looked disgustingly young, slim and pretty. Sam's eyes flickered over her before returning to me.

'Nothing. Just hoping there's a free table,' I said.

'We've got a ten-minute wait,' Sam said. 'You should join us.' He sounded about as enthusiastic as a wet haddock.

'YEAH!' Katy agreed. 'Oh, my God, Charley, that guy who was asleep in the kitchen this morning, Benoit, you've *got* to meet him properly. He's just totally amazing at playing the hang drum – do you know what a hang drum is?'

I glazed over, staring at William and Shelley. Shelley was sitting bolt upright, talking without smiling. William, to my surprise, had adopted an unexpectedly manly pose. He was angled sideways across his chair with his arm flung over the back, listening to Shelley in an extremely self-assured manner and occasionally running a hand over his stubble. While she let out what seemed to be an angry monologue he leaned forward casually, pouring white wine into her glass in the way men do when they want to appear masterful. I was slightly surprised by his self-assurance but I didn't care too much. The fact of the matter was that he was absolutely gorgeous.

I took my jacket off, even more hot and stressed than I had been when I arrived.

'Do you know those people?' Sam asked, following my gaze.

'No,' I said abruptly. 'Just thought the girl looked familiar.'

The main waiter came back. 'You are three now?' he asked, exasperated.

'Yes!' Katy said, breaking off her tale about Benoit the hang-drum player.

The waiter gestured behind him. 'We have a table here.'

It was in a sort of alcove but fortunately one of the chairs directly faced William's table. I'd be able to sit there, chat in a calm, adult way with my sister and housemate and spy in a mad, juvenile way on William and Shelley. And in so doing I'd make sure Sam and Katy weren't sitting together. Just to be sure.

But by the time I'd bent down to get my bag and blazer and hobbled over to the table, Sam had taken the chair. The little shit! He just wanted to sit next to Katy!

I slumped down opposite him, feeling exhausted and fairly despairing. I had just bought a six-hundred-pound dress for what? For a dinner that I was too uptight to eat, a forced conversation with Sam and Katy and, worst of all, an entire evening with my back to William and Shelley. This was ludicrous! It was shameful!

'Charley?' Sam was watching me curiously. 'Are you OK?'

Katy had gone off to the loo and I'd barely noticed. I nodded. 'Yeah, just tired.'

'Look,' he said, after a brief pause, 'I'm not trying to get off with Katy, OK? She's a great girl and she's been really kind. I just wanted to take her out to dinner.'

'Yes, yes,' I said. 'Fine. How's it going with the old acting thing, anyway? How'd it go with the agent at FTP – whatever it's called?'

Sam began to smile. 'PFD. I think it went well,' he said. 'Talking to the woman there reminded me how much I love acting. I've got to give it another shot, Chas. She loves my showreel.'

I tried hard to rouse some enthusiasm. 'Amazing, Bowes!'

Sam's smile had already faded and he was looking morose. This thing with Yvonne had obviously hit him very hard. But, as concerned I was, I had an overwhelming need to find out what was happening with the date. I looked over my shoulder as if to summon a waiter and saw William leaning forward, hands cupping his chin, listening to Shelley. He was smiling. Shelley, slightly flushed, seemed to have loosened up. Both were drinking wine very quickly. She was using hand gestures now and – I caught my breath – she was stroking her collar bone in a fake-absent-minded way. The bitch! That was one of my moves! I saw William's eyes dart down to look at it, just as she wanted him to. Oh, he was lovely and, oh, she was good.

Suddenly I hated Shelley Cartwright more than any other person on earth. How dare she stroke her collar bone? How dare she actually possess a personality? How dare she be over there when he should be sitting opposite *me*? Damn her to hell!

'Are you sure you don't know those people?' Sam asked, as Katy wove back towards us, grinning enthusiastically.

'Quite sure.'

'Well, stop staring at them, weirdo!'

'Piss off.'

'Piss off yourself, Charley. If you're going to sit there with a face like a slapped arse, go and sit in Burger King instead. They've got a Triple Whopper and fries for five twenty-nine today.'

'Ha!' Katy said, sitting down. 'I went on a detox last week and ended up getting a Whopper after two days. What kind of dick eats barley grass for breakfast?'

'Charley does,' Sam said helpfully. I gritted my teeth. 'Until the accident she kept huge packets of it in the fridge.'

Katy shrugged. 'Well, you look a lot better than I do, Chas. Fair fucks.'

I heard a man laugh behind me and knew it was William.

The sound stabbed me right through the middle and I took a long, deep breath. It was going to be a difficult night.

By the time we were on dessert, I'd more or less stopped speaking. Sam and Katy were drunk; I had not progressed past tipsy and now had that horrible dead feeling that did not improve however much wine I poured on it. They were talking about a Thursday-night open-mic session that Katy and Ruben the bassist had started in Camberwell. Sam had offered to be master of ceremonies tomorrow – 'I might try to get this PFD woman down to see my stuff' (*Stuff*? What stuff? Was Sam a stand-up fucking comic now? An organic vegetable salesman?), and Katy was in raptures over the headline act, a bowler-hatted Oxford-educated dandy who MCd in Middle English.

William and Shelley, I could see when I checked un-subtly over my shoulder, were still there. They were now chatting animatedly and William kept giving lovely rumbly laughs. Each one killed me.

When I returned to the conversation, Sam was talking about something called touch improvisation that he'd done at drama school. It sounded so unspeakably ridiculous that I went off to the loo, taking a good look at their table before I went downstairs. Shelley was sitting back with her legs crossed seductively and William was leaning forward. They had nearly finished their second bottle of wine and both appeared to have eaten dessert. Shelley had left some of hers on the plate, just to prove that although she might be six feet tall she was also dainty and feminine. I caught a blast of her brisk, unfriendly voice.

Then, just as I gave up and turned to go downstairs, William caught my eye. And he smiled at me. Broadly. He stretched his face into a proper smile for me. It lasted all of a second but I was bewitched.

Suddenly I was back again. I danced downstairs, thrilled. There was hope! In the mirror I pinched my cheeks. Maybe, somehow, William had sensed something when we'd stared at each other earlier. If I could just catch his eye again . . .

Then what? *Fantasist*, my head muttered. *All you've had is a few seconds' eye contact.*

'Er, not to mention two days of intense online conversation,' I corrected myself. The fight came back. I had to do something. What was the harm in leaving my card, like I'd originally planned? Worst-case scenario, he wouldn't have the foggiest idea who it was from and would never call. But the best-case scenario would be that he'd noticed me eyeballing him and, after a so-so date with Shelley Cartwright, was curious enough to contact me.

I scribbled something on a business card about being the tall girl who'd smiled, then paused, remembering what Hailey had said about respecting others' relationships. Was this in any way justifiable? *But you owe nothing to Shelley Cartwright*, my head told me obstinately. *She'd do the same in your shoes.* Not entirely convinced, I rearranged my breasts so that they formed some sort of cleavage and strode out again with my business card tucked into my palm. It was party time.

It was not party time. William and Shelley had left. Where they had sat, two napkins were strewn unceremoniously across their dessert plates. Their chairs were far from the table where they'd pushed them back in order to leave as soon as possible to . . .

I looked frantically out of the restaurant.

. . . to kiss.

William, the beautiful, perfect doctor, and Shelley, the snappy businesswoman, were standing in Beak Street kissing each other on the mouth. I walked slowly to the front of the restaurant. A deep, despairing jealousy washed over me. William pulled away and tucked a bit of hair behind Shelley's ear. She was flushed and excited, smiling like a teenage girl.

'Charley,' Sam said, appearing at my side. I ignored him. William smiled right into Shelley's face and asked her something. She nodded voraciously. Another date? I couldn't bear it. Then she tipped her face up and kissed him once again – a tentative, snatched affair – and skipped off into an Addison Lee minicab that was waiting on the corner of Lexington Street. William put his hands into his pockets and smiled after her, watching as the car pulled off.

'Chas?' Sam repeated. He was quite pissed off. 'You've behaved like a complete weirdo all night. What's happening?'

I stared at him blankly. 'Just a bad day,' I said eventually. 'A really, really bad day.'

Sam scrutinized me, glanced outside at the now-empty street and nodded, unconvinced.

Chapter Eight

A little later I allowed myself to be propelled out of the restaurant by a buoyant and chatty Katy, who had insisted I come to the gig in Brixton. We hurtled south in the high-pitched roar of a Victoria Line train, Katy and Sam giggling on one side of the aisle and me slumped in silence on the other. I realized I was still holding my business card, ready to give to the waiter for William. Tears of shame welled in my eyes.

You utter fool, I thought. *Running around after one man then the next, convincing yourself that they like you when of course they don't. Why would they? You're massive and unlovable!*

I was in despair. I'd escaped the toxic atmosphere of work to limp down to London where the supposed answer to my problems – William – had turned out to be as much of a disaster as anything else in my life. And tomorrow I'd have to abandon this mess and – what? Go back to the toxic atmosphere of work? You bet! What a great life!

I wallowed.

But then at Victoria I suddenly sat up. A group of suited businessmen were chortling away at the other end of the carriage, smart but drunk. Watching them, I finally remembered something that seemed to have eluded me for the last week.

My work used to keep me happy.

Really happy. Even when times were hard. I used to spend time chortling in my suit, just like those dudes.

What on earth had gone wrong? Until three days ago I'd loved my job! Salutech had been my haven, not a toxic hole! Was it the job that had changed? No! The job had never been so exciting! Margot? Pah, small fry! No, the problem was *me*. Somewhere along the way I had stopped being Business Charley, the Scottish Amazon, and had started being Pathetic Charley Lambert the self-pitying Labrador.

The fact of the matter, I realized, watching the suits segue effortlessly from banter to business talk, was that I had been drifting since I'd got back to Salutech. I'd been so certain that Margot would make my life hell that I'd basically rolled over and allowed her to do just that. I'd fixated on the unfairness of it all and had also spent way too much time on First Date Aid, allowing myself in the process to plummet into mad fantasy about William.

As a result I'd given my precious job no more than about 30 per cent. *Why?* Years of experience had proved that unless I gave 100 per cent I might as well not bother turning up! And, more importantly, years of experience had proved that giving 100 per cent made me feel happy, purposeful and in control. It was disgraceful to be ten days from the biggest brand launch ever yet have only a vague grasp of what was going on.

My head started ticking over. If I was prepared to pull my socks up at work, I could drag myself out of this cloud of doom very quickly. It seemed like a clear choice. Get back to my old ways: lots of hard work, healthy food, exercise and busyness – or carry on drifting around being sad and mad.

Enough of all this fantasy and time-wasting, Charley Lambert, I thought, in the style of Mr Motivator. *You go back to Edinburgh tomorrow and get your life back on track! OK, YEAH!*

I experienced my first ray of hope in a long time. Here was a solution that *worked*. And I knew that because I'd been road-testing it with outstanding success for several years.

First Date Aid had helped me evade madness during my recuperation but it had also taken my eye off the ball at Salutech and led me into behaviour so embarrassing I could hardly bear to think of it. First Date Aid had to go. I hated the thought of folding my lovely little company but not as much as I hated the idea of continuing to wallow around being a crazy, self-pitying low-achiever. Salutech came first. It deserved 100 per cent. It *paid* me to give 100 per cent. And, hopefully, if I jacked in First Date Aid I'd be able to forget about my shameful indiscretion tonight and head up the most exciting brand launch in recent medical history.

Done. Agreed. Signed.

Charley Lambert had a plan.

I felt a tiny bit more hopeful and sat up to listen to Katy and Sam's conversation about the importance of creativity in their lives. I didn't even make a vomity face.

Katy hopped excitedly up to the entrance of what looked like a penal dungeon in an alleyway off Coldharbour Lane. The sound of shit music inside was not appealing and

I had to work hard to muster up a show of enthusiasm. 'I'll pay the entrance fee!' Katy said, kissing a gigantic bouncer on the cheek. 'All right, Garfield?'

He winked at her, the rest of his face unmoving. 'Free for you and your friends, princess,' he growled.

We passed through, smiling dutifully. A vaulted room opened out in front of us, lit mostly by dim lights tacked on to the walls. The smoking ban didn't appear to exist here, and had there not been relentlessly thumping techno I might have fancied we were in a Harlem dive in the 1970s. Almost everyone looked fifteen years younger than me and absolutely everyone looked like they were taking drugs.

'Shall I get some pills?' Katy asked Sam. She said it in a slightly-less-loud-than-normal shout, as if I wouldn't hear her. Sam nodded excitedly.

I felt older than ever. Katy took my smart jacket and deposited it on a pile, then disappeared into the crowd to find someone called Pork. 'Since when did you take pills?' I asked Sam.

'Since always.'

'Bullshit! You haven't done drugs in years, Sam!'

'Charley,' he shouted above the music, 'butt out.' He looked pensive and fed up.

'Why are YOU in such a bad mood?' I shouted. He shook his head infuriatingly.

'*I*'m not!' He disappeared into the crowd too. I looked at my watch. Eleven forty-five. Perhaps if the band came on now we'd be able to leave in an hour. I went to the bar and ordered a glass of wine.

'Only vodka or rum,' the man yelled.

I bought a vodka, and then, on second thoughts, bought two more, for Katy and Sam. I went and sat on a speaker to wait for them. The crowd around me heaved and shrieked, the music pounding. I felt incredibly stupid, sitting in my sad expensive dress bought for a man called William who had never even heard of me. But as of tomorrow, things were changing. No stupid, no sad.

A short while later, Sam and Katy emerged from the crowd with beautiful grins on their beautiful faces. It was fairly obvious that they'd found what they were looking for. I appraised them. 'Are you two going to be mental all night?'

Sam giggled. 'Maybe!' He took off his fashion cardigan and threw it on top of my coat, nodding – slightly confusedly – to the music. One of Sam's principal draws for women was that he was a brilliant dancer but I was intrigued to see how he'd fare amid all this techno nonsense.

I gave them their vodkas as a lanky Asian man with heavy black glasses shuffled on to a platform and announced the band. Katy and Sam whooped and cheered, and I had to conceal a snigger. Sam was quite at home in this crowd, with his exposed chest and embarrassing man jewellery, but he wasn't fooling me. As the band started and he punched the air, I got out my phone to video him for Hailey. It was like our child was visiting his first school disco.

The band sounded like too many bands, these days: fast, catchy electro-rock with strangled vocals and attempted wry humour. I tried my best but longed for a bit of Belinda Carlisle and a glass of Merlot. In the absence of either,

I made myself comfortable on the speaker – which, mercifully, did not appear to be connected to anything – and leaned against the wall.

With a start, I awoke from a dream in which I'd been following William and Shelley into a forest rave. I had no idea where I was. I stared, afraid, at a sea of waving arms and felt loud music pulse through me.

Ah, Brixton. Yes. I was with Sam and Katy, who were taking stupid, dangerous teenage drugs. I scanned the crowd for them and found them almost immediately, leaning against a pillar to my left. Katy had her back against the pillar and Sam was kissing her hard on the mouth.

For a few seconds I froze in horror. But eventually – slowly and quite matter-of-factly – I levered myself off the speaker and walked over to them. I tapped Katy on the shoulder and she sprang out from underneath Sam, wasted and ashamed. 'House key,' I said to her.

'Sorry, Chas, we're off our tits.' She tittered.

I held out my hand. 'Key, please.'

Sam – I couldn't bring myself to look at him – grabbed my arm with the lack of respect for personal space that comes so easily to the inebriated. 'Just a bit of fun,' he yelled in my ear. A fleck of spit landed on the lobe and I threw his arm off me, glaring at him furiously now.

'You could have any girl in here,' I hissed at him. 'Any girl in Brixton, in London, in the bloody United Kingdom. I asked you to leave my little sister alone and you couldn't even do that for me.'

'Oh, fucking lighten up, Charley,' Sam slurred. 'Everyone likes a little kiss when they're up. You should try it yourself, let go a bit.'

'Charley, I'm seeing Ruben,' Katy squeaked. 'We're just fucked – it doesn't mean anything!'

'And I'm trying to get over a failed engagement, if you hadn't forgotten,' Sam added.

'Fuck you,' I said to him, ignoring Katy. 'She's twenty-two, Sam.'

'She's fit and she's up for it,' he shouted back.

Rage almost blinded me. 'Shut up, shut up, shut up,' I yelled. 'I'm going. Seriously, if you sleep with her tonight, I'll never speak to you again. Ever.'

'Whatever.' He turned back to Katy.

Twenty minutes later I was slumped on Katy's sofa, still feeling stunned. I concluded, reasonably, that tonight had not gone my way.

I stared at the room around me, marvelling at my choice of accommodation on the worst night I'd had since breaking my leg. Hundreds of inexplicable pictures of Katy wearing a maroon catsuit and top hat were spread all over the table, which also contained the remains of a fried egg in which someone had stubbed out a fag, a half-drunk bottle of organic cider and a plastic marijuana plant with 'Stuart' written on a label stuck to the side of the pot.

Enough.

I shuffled off upstairs to Katy's spare room – my temporary quarters – and discovered that Sam had dumped all of his things on the floor. Just looking at his stylish leather holdall I felt cross. Had he bought that to impress Katy? 'Fuck you,' I told his bag. And then: 'You'd better be sleeping on the sofa tonight, Bowes. If you sleep with Katy, I'll fucking kill you.'

I got into bed and pulled the duvet over my head. My flight was at six thirty-five a.m., which meant I had precisely forty-five minutes before it was time to get up again, a prospect that would normally have horrified me. Right now, however, I didn't care. The sooner tomorrow started, the sooner I could get back to what I did best, which was being Business Charley. Business Charley could deal with anything. She was a fearless Amazon. The toughest ever to come out of Scotland. Neither Sam nor Shelley could fuck with her. And Margot had better watch out.

I rolled over to attempt some sleep but became quickly aware that the room was not dark. Sam's laptop was glowing, with freaky cyber light, on the floor. 'Fuck off,' I told it crossly.

Nothing happened. I threw off my cover and stormed over to snap it shut.

But then something caught my eye. Something extraordinary.

On Sam's computer screen there was a brick-coloured webpage with CYBER LOVE ASSISTANTS emblazoned across the top. *Cyber Love Assistants?* And, taking up half of the page, the picture that had just caught my eye was of Shelley Cartwright.

Slowly, I sat down on my bed, my mind racing. A million explanations scrambled over each other but none made sense. I looked more closely. Not only was Shelley's photo there, so was her love.com dating profile. It looked sort of like a screen grab. To the right of the screen grab there was some writing:

Client: Dr William Thomas
Candidate: 'Shelley'
Candidate's dating website: www.love.com
Client's ranking for this candidate: *****
Emails to date with this candidate: 11.

I sat back, dumbfounded. And as I did so, a notebook next to Sam's laptop caught my eye. 'Polpo,' Sam had scrawled. 'Down Regent Street, turn left at Beak St then about 200 yards on the left - 7.30 p.m.' He had underlined the time so savagely that his pen had scored through at least two pages.

I looked back at his screen. Shelley stared at me, cold, confident and businesslike. 'What on earth is going on?' I whispered.

At the bottom of the screen I noticed a button marked 'User Account: Sam Bowes'. Slowly, gently – as if trying to avoid waking a poisonous snake – I reached out and clicked on the button. My head felt fuzzy and confused. Sam had a Cyber Love Assistants user account. And some connection with Shelley and William. Did this mean . . . ?

It did. There was a control panel, complete with a message from 'Cyber Love Assistants HQ'.

Sam, I've had an email from William Thomas saying he's not happy about the emails you've sent on his behalf to someone called Shelley. Far too intimate and personal apparently. Can you call me tomorrow, please. Regards, Steve Sampson

I snatched my hand back from Sam's computer. There was a clamouring in my head as I tried to process what I was seeing. *Sam* had written William's emails? Sam was a ghost-writer just like me? And of all the people in the universe he could be writing for . . . he was writing for *William*?

No! Sam was a bread-munching womanizing rotter, with the romantic capabilities of a chicken Kiev! There was no way! William had pulled me apart! Sam would *never* be capable of that!

I decided I must be hallucinating. Apart from anything else, Cyber Love Assistants was an American company. If they'd opened up for business in the UK, I'd have known.

At a loss, I clicked back to the previous page and stared at Shelley's picture again. Above the photo there was a button saying 'messages'. Too bewildered to remember about things like other people's privacy I clicked on through and gasped, for there it was: the entire chain of corres-pondence between Shelley and William.

I like you just a bit too much for some bird from the bloody Inter-net, William had written last Friday. *There's something about you.*

Then, at the end of the chain, I saw something that floored me.

Five days ago I'd messaged William on Shelley's behalf to finalize the date and explain why no further contact would be possible before they met. Here, in Sam Bowes's drafts folder, was a response he'd never sent. I read it with a hand clamped firmly over my mouth as if to prevent myself shouting.

Dear Shelley,

This is the strangest email you'll ever receive, probably. I begin it with an apology as the contents may be upsetting or offensive to you. Please be aware that this is absolutely not my wish.

My name is Sam and I am a dating ghost-writer. A company called Cyber Love Assistants pays me to write messages on behalf of clients who for whatever reason can't do it themselves. William, who you've been writing to, is one of their clients and it's me who's been writing his messages. It turns out that he's alarmed by how personal our exchange has become and I don't blame him. I would never normally enter into correspondence like this on behalf of someone else.

But I found myself unable to stop. I don't know what it is about you but I've been absolutely hooked on our exchange. I realize that it is incredibly unprofessional to break anonymity and contact you like this – particularly using the dating service – but having thought about it long and hard I decided I had no choice. Shelley, given that it's me you've been talking to, I wondered if there was any way you'd consider

FUCK NO BALLS SHIT COCK

The email ended and with it any hope I had of pretending this wasn't happening.

Sam, my flatmate, had written William's emails. *Sam* had got under my skin so badly that I'd turned into a lovestruck fool and tried – in a hideously embarrassing, immoral way – to intervene on the date. Furthermore it appeared that the exchange had made Sam go as mad as I had: we must have been in Polpo for exactly the same reason.

I put my head in my hands. What did this mean? Had I actually fallen in love with Sam? PLEASE, GOD, NO!

I tried to think about it calmly. I imagined Sam standing in front of me right now. He'd be wearing silly trendy clothes and he'd have the boldness and confidence that only the very attractive among us naturally possess. He would probably be munching a Nutella sandwich and apologizing, with a slightly frightened look on his face, for getting messed up on drugs and snogging my little sister.

No. I was not in love with Sam. If I was sure of anything, it was that. Absolutely, categorically no way.

But he's William! my head yelled.

I shut my eyes. This was a mess.

I had known within minutes of meeting Sam that I would never be interested in him, regardless of his looks. He was amusing, sweet and talented at acting, but he also embodied the type of man that left me cold: he was slovenly and childish and he organized his existence around sex, food and sport.

Yet the fact that he had written such honest, brave emails – which, I couldn't deny, had given me a hefty dose of self-awareness – made things very confusing.

But then: *No no NO!* I thought. *He just writes a good email! There's nothing there!*

My bipolar thoughts were interrupted by the front door banging.

'Night, then,' I heard Katy say. She sounded quite awkward and a few seconds later I heard her brogues scurrying past my door *en route* to her attic bedroom. Somewhere among the scattergun thoughts in my head I registered relief that she was going to bed alone. Which was lucky, because if he had slept with her I would have ended his life.

I could hear Sam shuffling around in the sitting room below me and tried to imagine him lurching as he turned the sofa into a bed. Did I have feelings for this drunk, pill-popping man?

No, came the instinctive response. It was pleasingly firm. *No, I don't. I never have done and I never will do. The emails can stay in cyberworld where they belong. They're nothing more than a fantasy! And I promised myself, no more fantasy. Ever again.*

And there it was. The answer. No more fantasy, ever again. Love and the Internet were too messy, period. I was getting out.

Satisfied, I rolled over and slept until my alarm clock went off thirty minutes later. Then, exhausted but hopeful at the prospect of a fresh start, I crept out of Katy's house into a cold, dripping street where I flagged down a taxi and fled for the airport. It was only a matter of hours until I could be back at my desk, ready to inject some order and control into my life.

Chapter Nine

I glanced over at Margot's desk. It was nine thirty-two a.m. and she still wasn't there. I shifted uncomfortably in my seat, trying to manage the vague sense of foreboding that was brewing inside me. I didn't want to delay The Conversation any longer. I wanted Margot to be listening to the speech I'd planned on the plane. And then I wanted her to give me my bloody job back. And, ideally, to stop wearing skirts that showed off her muff. But small steps.

I'd been at my desk just an hour but already I was feeling better. My inbox had been organized and prioritized and I was working steadily through the surplus that I'd been unable to address in the past few days. I was ready to take control again. Once I'd dealt with Margot, nothing could stop me. 'Raaaaaarrr,' I whispered to encourage myself. 'Raaaarrr!'

I glanced out of the window at the long, snaking driveway but there was still no sign of her. In spite of my frustration at Margot's absence I felt a growing sense of peace. It was a really beautiful autumn morning and a soft, low light played with the yellow leaves still clinging to the sycamores. Last night's painful events were locked away in a filing cabinet until further notice.

I buzzed through to Cassie. 'Have you heard from Margot?'

'She's out at BBC Radio Scotland,' Cassie replied. 'Remember?'

'Er, no?'

Cassie got up from her desk and came through. 'She told me she'd email you . . . They called asking for an interview so she's doing it. She should be on air in about ten minutes . . . Perhaps the email got lost.' There was a pause. 'She didn't email you, did she?' Cassie said.

I couldn't help but smile. Cassie was not only an awesome PA but she disliked Margot as much as I did. 'Right,' I said briskly. 'I'll call her now. In the meantime, can you tell John that Margot is about to do an interview for the BBC without my knowledge or consent?'

'Little slag,' John shouted, a few minutes later. 'She didn't even tell *me*!'

'I've been trying to get hold of her. Her phone's off but I've got a number for the breakfast-show producer, Chris.'

'What do they want her to talk about? Fuck, Lambert, she *must not* be seen to be promoting Simitol! We could end up having to withdraw the bloody product from the market before it's even launched!'

'I know. Look, I have to go.'

'Don't let her shaft us,' John said. He sounded very nervous.

Finally, on my fifth call, I got through to Chris the producer. Margot came on sounding extremely irritated. 'We're on air in two minutes,' she said officiously. 'It'll have to be quick.'

'I'll take as long as I need,' I said in a steely voice. 'We are not at liberty to do *any* media interviews until the launch next Friday. I need to know exactly what they –'

'You went to London,' Margot butted in curtly. 'What was I supposed to do? They needed a breakfast interview and, as your deputy, I had no option but to step in.'

'You had a million other options, such as calling me, or asking Cassie to get hold of me, or even talking to John. I won't tolerate any more of this sort of behaviour,' I added stoutly. She gasped but I held firm, surprising even myself. *No more fucking around. This is* MY *job!* 'For now, though, Margot, I need to know exactly what's going on at Radio Scotland.'

'I'm sorry, but I have to go and do this interview,' she said tightly. 'Perhaps you'd forgotten, during your jaunt to London, that we're in the middle of a really critical time right now.'

'I can assure you that I have forgotten *nothing*,' I replied. 'Now kindly stop talking in that pissy tone and tell me what the interview is about.'

I listened for a few seconds, then interrupted. 'No. Out of the question. The interview's pulled. You can't answer questions like that. You work in brand comms, Margot. You *know* that's out of the question.'

'What? The interview starts in thirty seconds – I simply cannot and will not –'

'You will. I am the director of communications and I am telling you *right now* to stand down. Conducting this interview would be a complete breach of protocol. It flies in the face of just about every regulation we're bound by.'

I put the phone down and breathed out. My hands were shaking and my heart was pounding. As I swung my chair round to face my desk, someone started clapping slowly. 'And she's back,' John said, from my doorway. He strode in, beaming at me in a way that still roasted my loins just a little bit. Rather than taking a chair, he sat on my desk, right in front of me.

'Yes. Lambert's back,' I confirmed, trying not to grin.

No more fantasizing over unsuitable men, I reminded myself. I cut short the half-grin and turned back to my screen as if to dismiss him. Unfortunately my mouse was right next to John's bottom so I was a bit stuck.

'How's that leg?' he asked, eyes pinned to my thigh.

'Painful.' I used a pen to get my mouse back and opened a document.

John was undeterred. 'Would a massage help? Or some *reiki*. I'm a *reiki* master in my spare time. I could bewitch your leg.'

I tried hard to control my smile. John still knew how to work me. 'No, John, I do not want you to perform *reiki* on my leg.'

'Could I maybe just run my hand along it, then? Solely for medical-research purposes.'

I felt the old urge to play the outraged schoolmistress and marvelled at how quickly it had come back now that I knew William was not real. But I had to resist any sort of flirting. *No more fantasy.* 'I don't think you'd enjoy my leg, John,' I said neutrally. 'It's full of metal pins.'

'Brilliant!' He jumped off the desk and crouched, placing his hand firmly on my ankle. 'Where are they?'

'John! What are you doing?!' I said, less forcefully. He was a nightmare. And I wasn't much better.

His large hand ran slowly up my shin, fingers feeling

171

gently around the bones. 'Blimey, Lambert, you've got a full-on toolkit in here.' His hand kept moving up but after a stern look from me he stopped at my knee.

'Off,' I said, quietly.

John stood up, feigning hurt. 'You're wearing stockings,' he remarked, as he walked back over to the doorway. 'Delightfully Victorian and sexy, Lambert. Makes up for the bionic leg. Keep it up.'

'I'll let you know how it goes with Margot after I've spoken to her,' I told him. I wanted him out of my office before I started enjoying his company too much.

'Margot's a pain in the arse,' John said. 'You can deal with her, no problem. Power-crazy little seahorse. She did well to hold the fort when you –'

'*What* did you just call her?' I asked, starting to laugh.

'Er, a power-crazy little seahorse. Oh, Lambert, don't go all boring and politically correct on me now. The girl looks like a seahorse! You know it!'

I couldn't stop laughing. I laughed and laughed and laughed, eventually leaning back in my chair and closing my eyes. The pain and disappointment of the last twenty-four hours evaporated as John beamed at me, delighted.

'Seahorse!' I howled, tears now coming out of my eyes. 'I call her that too!'

'A seahorse with dwarf-dating proclivities,' he chipped in.

At that I lost it completely, and only really stopped when Margot arrived in my office forty minutes later in a thick black cloud of rage. 'We need to talk,' she said, striding in and slamming the door behind her. She looked as if someone had inserted an unsolicited NASA rocket up her bottom. 'How dare you pull the interview just before –'

'You're quite right we need to talk,' I said. 'How dare *you* agree to a totally inappropriate and unauthorized interview at a time like this?'

Margot looked almost crazed. 'What do you expect me to do when you piss off to London to fanny around with John's cronies?' she spat back.

'Margot,' I said, sitting back in my chair, 'John asked me to meet Arthur Holford because he's talking about bringing us nearly a billion dollars in investment but he wants to know how strong our public profile is first. I wouldn't call that fannying around, would you? How about we discuss the real issue at hand?'

Margot's face was a complicated mixture of rage, frustration and shock. *She'd forgotten she works for Charley Lambert, Scottish Amazon,* I thought bravely. I battened down the hatches and sharpened my spear. 'Which is that you seem to be struggling to accept the hierarchy here. I really do appreciate what you did while I was away – it was brilliant work – but if you continue to operate behind my back, to conceal information from me and to attempt to control processes that are my direct responsibility, then I will have no option but to take formal action against you.'

She stared at me with undisguised hatred. 'You wouldn't,' she whispered.

'You're quite wrong, Margot. I absolutely would. So, you can cancel whichever of my projects you were planning to run yourself and spend this afternoon handing my job over to me – properly – or I can call Carly and get a formal warning under way. What's it to be?'

I took a deep breath. *Go, Lambert!* John walked through the office, grinning cheekily at me through the glass wall.

Margot turned on her heel. 'Very well. I'll start now,' she muttered, striding out in her microskirt. I was reasonably sure she added 'slag' as she slammed the door.

As I collected myself, Cassie walked into my office with a pile of newspapers. 'Er, press clippings for today, highlighted.' She giggled. 'And well done,' she added, in a stage whisper.

'Can you get me a superfood salad for lunch?' I asked. 'And don't buy me any junk again, even if I ask for it. I need a sharp brain, Cassie. Starting this afternoon. We're going to get this place sorted.'

'No problem,' she said. Her voice dropped to the stage whisper again: 'Well done for putting Margot back into her box!' she hissed. 'She's a witch! She told me yesterday that I looked really common in my trouser suit!'

I gasped but Cassie waved me off. 'From someone whose vagina is on display most days I didn't feel too upset.'

For the third time today I lost myself laughing. Things were on the up.

Later on, as I sifted through paperwork, picking through a salad, my phone buzzed. 'It's a man looking for his piglet,' Cassie said.

I grinned. 'Put him through!'

'Dad?'

'Hello, Piglet.'

I knew immediately something was wrong. 'Dad? Are you OK?'

He sighed. 'Yes, Charlotte my dear . . . but I fear my mother is not so well.'

I sat up, worried. Granny Helen was *never* ill. 'What's happened?'

'She . . . she had a bit of a stroke, Charley. We've been at the hospital the last twenty-four hours and she's much better now. But not . . .' Dad's voice caught. 'Just not quite herself.'

'Oh, Dad . . . Will she improve?'

'She might. But at her age the outlook's not great,' he said sadly.

I blanched, trying to imagine my spirited little matriarch of a grandmother being weak and ill. My earliest memories of Granny Helen were of her shouting orders from her throne and slamming the floor with her stick. Regardless of her age and physical strength, she had always been the head of our family.

'Are you OK, Dad?' I asked again gently. He sounded lost.

'Well, I'm quite shocked. I don't like seeing my mother in that state, Charlotte. But I have my fingers crossed that she'll improve.' He didn't sound convinced at all. 'Anyway, afternoon surgery's starting shortly and I have patients to see. Could you call Vanessa and Katy, Charlotte? I . . . don't have the heart to tell them.'

'Of course. Would you like me to come home tonight? Cook you some dinner? Go and see her in hospital?'

'No, no, we need to keep things as quiet as possible . . . I'll call tomorrow. *Au revoir*,' he said sadly.

'Um, *au revoir*,' I echoed.

No! I thought, dismayed. Granny Helen wasn't nearly old enough for this! And Dad loved his eccentric mother. However busy it was at the surgery, he'd still insist on having a full hour off at lunchtime so he could take her for her daily walk: in winter they had tea at the coffee house; in summer they sat by the fountain, chatting away while Malcolm padded around, sniffing out exciting things in the grass. They were proper friends.

Come on, Granny Helen, I thought, swallowing.

Ness was very upset, but in a typically undramatic, unselfish way. She made me promise to call her when I finished work, for an account of my night ruining William and Shelley's date.

'I won't call you,' I responded brusquely, 'because there's nothing to tell. A stupid waste of time. Best forgotten.'

Ness sounded quite relieved, if a tad disappointed.

Katy was still asleep from last night when I called. 'Hiya, Chas,' she mumbled. Then: 'Oh, fuck. Are you downstairs? Do you need me to let you out?'

I tried to interject but Katy started giggling, a rasping sound that soon subsided into chesty coughs. 'Oh, cunticles, I got off with Sam, didn't I? Gross! Sorry, Charley, bit of an error.'

After the conversation with Katy – who had been touchingly devastated about Granny Helen – I got back to work, trying to keep a lid on my fears for our grandmother. Katy had written off the snog as a five-minute wonder that was the sole product of brain-frying drugs. She was not in a hurry to repeat it. I'd believed her but had felt a renewed sense of outrage that Sam had not so much as texted an apology yet. It was yet another reminder of the fact that he really, *really* was not William.

I steeled myself and took work up another level.

*

'We're on fire!' Cassie said, from a pile of Simitol brochures on my office floor. It was six forty-five p.m.

'We bloody well are,' I agreed. 'High five!'

We waved palms across a sea of papers.

Swiping into the gym at five to nine I was assailed by the smell of chlorine, the synthetic pump of house music and the whir of machines. I knew it was probably a bit early to be back here but I was tired of having a thin, lanky peg-leg, and Caro, my trainer, specialized in 'wonky folk' like me. I'd been looking forward to tonight all week.

'Hiya, Charley!' yelled Heidi of the chunky bangles, the woman who ran the beauty parlour. 'Long time no wax!' She pointed at my crotch.

I ran into the changing rooms before she revealed anything else about the state of my privates. Emerging a few minutes later, I looked around for Caro. Instead, to my utter amazement, my eyes found Hailey.

'Er, what?' I said, walking up to her cross-trainer. Her face was streaming with sweat, and she started to laugh.

'Yo!' she yelled merrily, removing her headphones.

'Since when did you go the the gym? I won't kiss you,' I added.

'No, don't. I'm slimy.'

There was an awkward silence as we remembered our curt exchange of words yesterday.

'Look, about the –'

'I'm sorry I –'

I broke off, smiling. 'Forget it,' I said. 'I'm out of Fantasy Land now. Back in the real world. And I feel much better.'

'Good. You look great, actually. Much more like your old self. What happened?'

'Where to start? Well, William was gorgeous, Shelley was like a corporate plank, they snogged. Sam turned up and took a pill and snogged Katy. And then I discovered that Sam is a ghost-writer. And, of all the men in the world, it turns out he was ghost-writing for William. So, yeah, quite a night, really.'

Hailey gawped at me. 'Bowes snogged your little sister?' She whistled. 'Fuck, Charley, did you punch him?'

'No, but I should have.'

Hailey looked nervous. 'Did he . . . did they, er . . .'

'No, don't worry. He wouldn't be alive if they had.'

'Yeah, Katy's totally his type,' Hailey mused. 'Little and pretty and cool. Yuk, what a nightmare. And the thing with the Internet doctor, I . . . Hang on, *what*?' She stopped her cross-trainer. 'Sam was sending the Internet doctor's emails?'

I nodded. 'Uh-huh.'

'I . . . *WHAT*?'

I smiled sadly. 'It's extraordinary, no? No one's ever got me the way William did. I just can't believe it was Sam.'

'But Sam's . . . Yuk! He's a dog!'

'Yup. It's pretty embarrassing.'

Hailey slumped over the cross-trainer controls, looking like she was about to faint. 'Bowes,' she said dazedly. 'Bowes? And Charley?'

I jumped in smartish. 'No! No Bowes and Charley. Not now, not ever. It was just an incredible coincidence. As you said, anyone can be anyone when they can hide behind a computer.'

Hailey whistled. 'I'll say. Right, Chas, I think we need to schedule in some cocktails. Tomorrow night? We could get dressed up and go to Tiger Lily's.'

'I'd like that. But, Hailey, are you sure everything's cool between us? I was pretty upset about what you said to me yesterday.'

Hailey's face was suddenly thoughtful. 'Yes, my love,' she said. 'I really am sorry. It's just that . . . Well, Matty got back very late from a work party recently and I was so upset, thinking he'd been with another woman or something. I know he *wouldn't* but how do I know there isn't some girl out there trying to get her claws into him?'

I was bemused. 'What's that got to do with William?'

'Yeah, a bit tangential . . . I suppose I've just become a bit disapproving of any woman who goes after a man who's spoken for. I felt sorry for Shelley. He was meant to be hers, not yours.'

'Oh. Right.'

'Sorry. I know I'm being annoying and judgemental. It's just because I went and fell in love. It's turned me into a paranoid knob.'

I fiddled with the cord on my shorts, trying to decide if I was OK with this explanation.

I was.

''S OK, Hails. It was all a big mess.'

We smiled sheepishly at each other. 'Anyway, what are you doing here?' I asked.

'Decided it's time I lost some weight.'

'But you might lose your breasts! That'd be a national disaster!'

'The Boys aren't going anywhere,' she said, plumping

them up. She started the cross-trainer moving again, her massive boobs bouncing enthusiastically as if to prove the point. I'd never expected to see Hailey at a gym.

By the time I arrived home it was nearly eleven. My left leg was throbbing and I now felt incredibly guilty, unable to dodge how cruel it was to take myself off to the gym after thirty minutes' sleep and a demanding twelve-hour work day.

I wondered what William would say about my overdoing it yet again.

And then groaned. Not William, *Sam.*

Had Sam understood Shelley so well because he'd lived with me for years? Was he thinking about my work–life balance when he'd started unpicking Shelley's? As far as I was aware, Sam was far too absorbed in his own schedule of television, Nutella and women to take any notice of my day-to-day activities, never mind judging them. But maybe he'd been watching all along. Maybe, when he wondered if Shelley was quite sweet and vulnerable behind her scary business exterior, he was taking his cue from me. I swelled indignantly. I would not have Samuel bloody Bowes thinking I was some freak who'd be quite sweet if she calmed the hell down. No way!

After an angry pause I sighed, climbing reluctantly off my high horse. The fact of the matter was that I had no idea whether or not Sam had been thinking of me when he'd probed Shelley and, furthermore, I'd probably never find out. There was no way I was going to tell him I'd written Shelley's emails.

And, in fairness to Sam, he'd made himself vulnerable

too. It certainly wasn't just me who'd been exposed. Hadn't he talked openly about how he felt life was passing him by? About how he was desperate for career success but trapped by fear?

I felt an unprecedented moment of tenderness for him. The poor thing, stuck in a world of mindless promo work and occasional bar jobs. Why on earth had I assumed he was happy with that when he was a talented actor? Nothing about his lifestyle made sense, really, yet I hadn't so much as bothered to question it.

Sam and William, it occurred to me, were probably very different. William had been surprisingly manly and posturing in Polpo – and there was also the complaint he'd made to Sam's boss that Sam's emails were 'too intense'. What a terrible irony if it turned out that William was just like Dr Nathan Gillies, i.e. an arrogant cock, and that Sam turned out to be the interesting, sensitive, intelligent man who had turned my world upside down.

I lay back on my sofa and closed my eyes. It felt uncomfortable to have such thoughts about Sam, however innocent they might be. No matter how hard I'd worked today, thoughts of 'William's' emails had popped up repeatedly and I couldn't help but worry that it Meant Something.

'Arrrgh. Stop it!'

Work, my head reminded me feebly. *Work gets you out of mad thinking!*

Wearily, I got up and turned the kettle on. I couldn't deny that work worked for me. I needed to get the ball rolling for closing down First Date Aid and there was no harm in having another go at my Salutech press speech for next week.

One of Sam's mini features on First Date Aid had gone to print yesterday and my inbox was full. Looking at all the new business, I longed to keep it alive – but I remembered last night's pact with myself and knew it had to go. Salutech came first. As long as Salutech was at number one I was sane. I sighed, wishing I'd had a little more time and energy to grow my rather brilliant little company.

I started going through the emails one by one, moving them into different 'Closing Business' email folders. New clients would get a standard letter but my long-termers would get something a bit more personal, I thought.

Hi there, I am far too busy to spend time Internet dating so I thought perhaps you could help me, began the first message. I moved it into a new-client folder and clicked on to the next. *Hi Charlotte, It's Ingrid here, remember me?!!!!* Of course I remembered Ingrid. A hefty silicone chest and one of the busiest dating inboxes I'd managed. Ingrid was popular. But she had wanted 'something a bit more intelligent, like maybe someone who works in middle management???' and had asked for help 'cos my messages are really stupid!!!!!'.

She'd had four dates in a week with 'middle-management' types and by all accounts things were going well: '*I've slept with three men this week!! All well clever too!!! Going to see two of them again, thanks Charlotte it was a real laugh working with u will definetly recomend you to my desperate mates!!!*'

I smiled. I'd rather liked Ingrid and her silicone baps. I was sad to lose her and her 'desperate mates'.

And then my heart sank.

Dear Charlotte,

I just wanted to thank you for helping to organize my date last night. I met William in central London and it went well. I can't pretend I wasn't slightly shocked by the scope of the emails you sent on my behalf but as it turns out you represented me very well (how did you do it?) and, resultantly, the date was a great success.

However, I need your help. Please call me as soon as you read this and don't worry if you get a foreign ring tone.

Thanks,
Shelley Cartwright

I looked at my watch. It was now twenty past eleven. It would be best if I jumped in straight away and told her I was closing the business, but did I really want to talk to her at this time of night? Indeed, ever?

Shelley answered the question for me by ringing my First Date Aid mobile. The ring tone blasted angrily through my silent living room until I had no choice but to pick up. 'Er, hi Shelley,' I said nervously.

'CHARLOTTE,' she yelled, from what sounded like a hurricane. 'DID YOU NOT GET MY EMAIL?' I tried to respond but she interrupted, 'I can't hear you, bloody howling wind here. I'm in Battery Park. Hang on.' I heard the click-click-click of her heels and then the buzz of café life as a door swung open. 'Sorry. Can you hear me?'

'Yes.'

'Good. Battery Park, New York, too much bloody

wind. Give me Central Park any day, lovely at this time of year,' she barked.

'Shelley, how can I help you?' I asked wearily.

'Right. Well, Charlotte, I need you to carry on emailing William for me.'

I looked around as if she was speaking to someone else. 'Excuse me?'

Shelley ordered a flat white and a slice of shortbread. 'My biggest client has suffered an emergency in the last twenty-four hours and I was flown over to their head offices early this morning. It's – Oh, it doesn't matter. Anyway, I'll be here for the next week and my only contact with William therefore is by email.' She cleared her throat. 'Er, we exchanged a couple of emails today,' she said, sounding embarrassed, 'but it's not going very well.'

'I see,' I said. I didn't.

When she spoke again, her voice was quieter. 'I'm afraid I'll lose him if I carry on emailing him,' she said. 'This is all very embarrassing, Charlotte, but I want to hire you to email him during the next week. I . . . like him. And I can't write emails.'

Thank God I was closing the company. 'Shelley,' I said gently, 'I'm afraid I can't help. My service is designed for pre-date conversation. I think anything beyond that would amount to a deception that I'd feel uncomfortable –'

'Please,' Shelley said, cutting in. 'Please,' she repeated, more softly. 'He's special, Charlotte. I'd be devastated if I messed this up. I'll pay you anything you want. And I'll write an endorsement for your website. Anything.'

I was taken aback. Shelley Cartwright had become a human being. How sad to have to let her down now. 'No,

I'm afraid it's just not possible,' I said eventually. 'I'm actually having to close my business. For various reasons, I –'

'But I can't do this myself,' Shelley interrupted. 'I'm not clever enough, funny enough. And what do you *mean* you're closing your business? You're utterly brilliant! What you did for me was extraordinary!'

And that was that. My work ego marched in and took control. Quite simply, her words had made me feel good and I wanted more. And even though a small part of me – the part that 'William' had opened up – knew that it wasn't healthy to boost my self-esteem like this, I knew I'd lost the battle. I had no power. I was in her hands again.

'OK,' I heard myself saying. 'OK, I'll do it.'

'WONDERFUL!' she roared, suddenly Shelley Cartwright again. I could picture her face, all flushed and angry, just like mine was on the rare occasions when I was truthful with others about my feelings. 'Now,' she continued, 'I'd like you to start by reading the emails we've sent each other today – they're fairly poor. Let me give you my email login so you can read them and I'll call you back in a few minutes . . .'

I ended the call and flopped back on the sofa, scratching my head. How had I been swayed so easily? *Don't panic*, I told myself. *It's your last assignment. You can close down all the other client relationships and just do this one last job.* I meant it.

One last job.

It had now been so long since I'd slept that I was beginning to lose track of what was real and what was hallucination. I was pretty sure Sam was staring at me, saying something about carrying me. But Sam was still in London. 'What?' I muttered. My vision swam.

'Chas, wake up or I'm going to have to carry you to bed.' Sam took my glasses off and squeezed my hand.

'What? Where?'

Sam laughed softly. 'I just got in. I've spent the last couple of minutes prodding you but you were completely unconscious. Please tell me you didn't work a full day?'

I shut my eyes again. 'Go away. I'm not talking to you.'

I felt Sam sit down next to me on the sofa. 'I'm sorry,' he said quietly. 'I came back early to apologize in person.'

I opened one eye. He certainly looked sorry, but I said nothing for now.

'Whatever you may think, I've never had designs on Katy. I was just temporarily off my face.'

I pulled myself up a bit. 'We've got wasted and snogged some random people, Sam. But did you really need to do it with my sister?'

He looked mortified. 'That stuff hit me like a steam train. Come on, Chas, you've taken drugs!' There was a silence. 'Oh, no, you haven't, have you? Don't like the sensation of being out of control, right?' His face fell. 'Sorry, I didn't mean to insult you on top of everything else. I just can't believe I took that filthy shit. What a moron. I slightly hate myself.'

'Sam,' I said tiredly, 'of all people . . . I asked you not to go there.'

'I know.'

There was a long silence. I watched thoughts flashing across his face – such a young, pretty face still, the bastard – and knew what he must be thinking. He'd snogged Katy because he was miserable after seeing

William and Shelley kissing in the street. Just like I had been. We'd seen our hopes dashed and had turned to the things we knew best – me to work, him to the nearest available girl.

I'd been so busy thinking about myself and my own feelings since last night's discovery that I'd somehow forgotten Sam had fallen hard as well. What was it he'd said in that draft email? He didn't want to break anonymity with Shelley but he basically had no choice?

Sam didn't do stuff like that. Writing love letters. Telling girls how he felt. I'd had years of observing him and I knew his patterns. The idea that it was *me* who had cast this spell on him was . . . weird. Indescribably weird. I wasn't sure I liked it.

'How's First Date Aid going?' he asked suddenly.

I froze. 'Why?'

Sam looked suddenly shifty, which alarmed me. He was after something. 'No interesting clients at the moment?'

Shit. What was he getting at?

'No one in particular.' I shrugged.

Sam shrugged too. Both of our shrugs were crap.

Silently I begged him to let it go, but it seemed he had other plans. 'Just wondered if you had a client called Shelley?' he said, in a slightly strangled voice. 'She, erm . . . She's a friend of a friend. Someone said she was going to contact you.'

Oh, God! I thought, panicking. *He's beginning to put two and two together! He's wondering why I was in Polpo!* There was another awkward silence as I fought the urge to get up and run, possibly straight out of my third-floor window.

Should I just tell him? Then: *No! NEVER!* Our friendship wouldn't survive that kind of awkwardness. It was only because we rarely went deeper than a puddle that our cohabitation had worked so well.

'No, I don't have a Shelley on the books,' I said vaguely. 'Doesn't ring any bells.'

Sam seemed extremely relieved. 'Oh!' He beamed, with another crap shrug.

I needed to get the hell out of there. 'I think I'll go to bed, then,' I announced. Sam moved over so I could swing my legs off the sofa. 'Night, Bowes.'

'Night,' he said. He was already miles away.

'Oh, and actually, just so you know, I'm closing First Date Aid down.'

Sam was back in the room. 'You *what*?'

'I'm closing it down. I can't do it alongside Salutech. Work has to come first.'

'But you *can't!* It's brilliant! And it's going from strength to strength!'

I felt guilty. Sam had thrown all his energy into helping me. But I stood firm. I'd made a pact with myself. I had to be happy and busy with Salutech. I couldn't be mad and unfocused any longer.

'I'm really sorry, Bowes,' I said gently. 'I know how much effort you put in. And I'd like to pay you for it –'

Sam waved me off angrily. 'I don't want to be paid. I just want you to keep going. It's a lovely business. Far nicer than that wank-shit company you work for.'

'I have no choice, Bowes. I'm truly sorry. Night.'

As I brushed my teeth, I pondered what Sam would have thought if he'd known the truth. Obviously, he'd be upset that his dreams of Shelley Cartwright were shattered and that it was none other than his lanky corporate housemate who'd stolen his heart. But I suspected that for him it would end there. Boys were different: for him it would go along the lines of

1. Disappointment
2. Have a beer
3. Find someone else.

I wound some dental floss between my fingers, yawning. I should try to do some work but I was half dead.

Then my reverie was broken by the sound of phones ringing and men yelling.

'OH, MY GOD . . .' Sam was standing in the bathroom doorway. He was holding my phone, which was ringing, and he was as white as a sheet. 'NO!' he yelled.

Oh, God! Shelley! I hadn't got back to her! I grabbed the phone. My heart sank. SHELLEY CARTWRIGHT CALLING. I was sunk.

Sam looked as if he were about to pass out. 'No!' he repeated, this time in a sort of guttural groan.

'I don't know who this –'

'DON'T YOU DARE,' Sam rasped, as if he was dying. 'IT WAS YOU . . . I FUCKING . . . OH, GOD!'

The phone stopped ringing. We stood staring manically at each other, neither with any idea what to say.

'Make this go away,' Sam said, in a small voice. I wished desperately that I could.

The phone started ringing again and Sam sat down on the toilet lid, arms hanging limply by his sides. 'Fuck,' he said, as if his world was ending.

I answered my phone. 'Um, hello?' I whispered.

'CHARLOTTE,' Shelley roared. 'Are you going to email William for me or not?'

In my deathly silent bathroom, her yells boomed way beyond the confines of my phone. Out of the corner of my eye I saw Sam's head drop into his hands. 'Um, yes,' I muttered. 'I'll get on to it as soon as possible. I have to go, Shelley, bye.' I ended the call and sat down on the side of the bath. I fiddled with my blouse, immobilized. What should I say? What would Sam say?

After what seemed like eternity, I looked at him. 'Yes. It was me,' I said. 'Sorry,' I added.

Nothing.

I continued: 'If it helps, I fell for William. Just like you fell for Shelley. That's why I was in Polpo.'

Sam's eyes widened in shock and he opened his mouth to say something but nothing came out.

I realized that my only option would be to try to see the funny side, and smiled. Poor Sam. I at least had had eighteen hours to process this most uncomfortable of truths. 'We were emailing each other, Sam. I'm sorry.'

Sam's head fell back into his hands.

'Oh, Bowes, please don't faint on me.'

A ghost of a smile crossed his face as he looked up. 'You?' he said eventually.

I nodded, smiling ruefully. I was absolutely determined to avoid getting all serious and intense. If we kept it light, there was just a chance we'd survive. "Fraid so.'

Sam's face clouded over as he finally believed me. 'No!' he said, rather shrilly.

'Yes,' I told him firmly. 'And I know you've been working for Cyber Love Assistants, you little shit. Do you believe me now?'

After a pause, Sam nodded. 'Chas. I . . . This is fucked up, brother.'

'Not as fucked up as you working for Cyber bloody Love Assistants!'

Sam ignored me. 'So we were emailing each other from the next room?'

'Yes!' Then something occurred to me. 'Sam,' I asked, more gently. 'Is this why you and Yvonne . . .?'

'She found an email I'd sent to Shelley,' Sam said flatly, looking down at his trendy jeans. 'Or you, I suppose. Oh, my God, this is such a disappointment, Chas. Why didn't I *check* that you weren't working with her? Anyway . . . Yvonne found the email and got really upset and I was trying to prove to her that it was a work thing and suddenly I just sort of realized that . . . that it wasn't. There were real feelings involved. So I had to let her go.'

'And you didn't cheat on her?'

'Well, not physically. But mentally, for sure.' He sighed. 'It can't have been right with Yvonne if I fell for someone else but I miss her, Chas.'

There was a silence, during which Sam began to look very awkward. It was obviously occurring to him that he had fallen for none other than me.

'Um,' I said, clearing my throat. 'I think we need to get something out of the way. It doesn't affect anything.'

Sam was confused.

'I mean, no feelings between *us*, right?'

'Of course not,' he said, as if I were mad. 'Fucking hell, Chas!'

I felt a bit hurt. Seeing him slumped on my toilet, looking like a wounded puppy, I knew for certain that I didn't want Sam but it would have been nice if he hadn't sounded quite so disgusted. But I made sure nothing registered on my face. There must be absolutely no oddness or confusion between Sam and me. I took a deep breath. 'So. Cyber Love Assistants! Bowes! How could you!'

'Oh, yeah. Steve Sampson wants to expand into Europe so he's running some trials. He put an ad in the *Stage* asking for witty writers and I thought, bugger it.'

'Steve Sampson can fuck off! This is my pitch!'

Sam grinned for the first time since he'd arrived in the bathroom looking like someone had just bitten his balls off.

'Oh,' I said. 'No, it's not my pitch any more. Damn. He'll probably take all my customers now. Which is fine,' I added unconvincingly, trying to be the bigger man.

Sam seemed annoyed briefly. But was then lost in his thoughts again.

'Why didn't you tell me you were working for him?' I persisted. 'I don't understand.'

'Just felt embarrassed,' he said.

'But why?'

'Just cos . . . cos it's your thing. I felt like I'd muscled in way too much when you set the company up and that this would be the final straw. Me queering your pitch, y'know.'

I felt like an exasperated mother. 'Oh, Bowes, you silly sausage! I was unbelievably grateful for the help you gave me. I couldn't have done it without you!'

Sam drummed his fingers on his thighs, and I thought

I'd probably have paid a lot of money to find out what he was thinking now. 'Fucking hell,' he remarked.

'I have to go to bed, Bowes.' I needed to get out of there. I needed peace and quiet to pore over it all in my head.

Sam nodded distractedly. 'Sure. Night.'

But then, as I began to haul myself up, his hand shot out and grabbed my wrist. 'Wait. Chas, is Shelley asking you to email William while she's in America?'

'Um, actually, yes. How do you know?'

Sam slapped his leg excitedly. 'Wicked! Mega! Bo!'

I sat down again, yawning. I was ruined. 'Wicked mega bo what?'

Sam jiggled up and down on the toilet. 'I had my first direct contact from William today, offering me any amount of money to help him! He said their emails are awful!'

Not knowing why this was so exciting, and realizing I couldn't sit up straight a moment longer, I limped off to bed, with Sam in hot pursuit. 'Think about it, Chas! William and I are now in *direct* contact! So are you and Shelley! We know what they're both thinking! We can pool resources! If we worked together on this, we could have that relationship sewn up in a matter of days, brother!'

I pulled the duvet over myself, still fully clothed. 'Now that's an idea,' I conceded.

'No, Chas. You have to take your clothes off.' Sam turned around. 'Strip.'

'Fascist,' I said, sliding exhaustedly out of my clothes. 'Keep your back turned.' I got into bed.

Sam hopped on to it like a cat. 'What do you think? Shall we get these two love birds together or what?'

I yawned again. 'Oh, why not? It'd be a nice note to end

on before I close the company. But I don't like the idea of you working for Cyber Love Assistants.'

'I'm not. I was only on a month's contract, which finished last week. But William was so keen on Shelley that he forced Steve Sampson to hand over my phone number. I'm a free agent.'

I raised a sleepy thumbs-up.

Sam grinned down at me. 'There's one last thing,' he said suddenly. His expression had changed, which alarmed me.

'Go for it,' I said cautiously.

'I can't let you shut First Date Aid down, Chas. It's too fucking cool to lose.'

'You have to. The decision's made.'

'Well, I'm unmaking it.'

My eyes were heavy. I let one close and kept the other one open a crack. Sam certainly looked serious. 'Sam, I hear you, but I can't keep it going. I have no time. Look at me. I'm spent.'

Sam was balling his fists and jiggling on the spot, like he'd been doing since I'd met him aged eighteen. 'I know! You can't do it alone! So, um, how's about we become partners? I can run it for now and you can get involved again when you've got time. Maybe you could write the odd client email every now and then. But I could do the rest. And we could start offering ghost-writing services to men! They're far shitter than women at writing messages. What your female clients don't know, Chas, is that men don't care what women say in their emails. But women rate email banter higher than everything else.

Remember that survey last week? A lot of men out there need help!'

I lay like a corpse. 'You want to be my partner? And open it up to men? Is that right?'

He punched my bed excitedly and, in spite of my crushing exhaustion, I had to laugh. He was such an entertaining child at times. 'Yes! I could run it, do the admin . . . It's not like I've got much else to do at the moment. I could help us spread all over the country, chat up PR girls and advertising execs . . . Think how much coverage I got you in the summer!'

I thought about it. I really did *not* want to shut the business down. And if Sam took charge I could concentrate on writing dating emails – perhaps with a limit as to how many women I had on my books at any one time. The emails, after all, were the part I loved best. And I certainly had no problem sharing the small profit I'd begun to make: First Date Aid had never been about money.

Yet the idea of handing over to anyone – let alone Sam – still worried me.

'Chas,' he said, interrupting my thoughts. 'Don't you remember what I said in William's emails? I want to do more with my life. I've got money left over from that clinical trial I did for your company. I could invest it. And you know I'm good at marketing *and* flirting. We'd be proper awesome business partners!' He held out his hand.

I shook it. 'OK, Bowes,' I said slowly. 'You're on.'

He punched the air. 'Whoo! To us, business partners!'

I smiled weakly from my pillow. 'To us, um . . . business partners!' I replied.

Sam suddenly leaned down and kissed my forehead. 'Go to sleep,' he said, and all but sprinted out of the room.

It had been an odd day, all things considered. I rolled over and felt myself fall into a coma. With Sam taking over First Date Aid, I really would be able to throw everything into Salutech and get back to being the Charley Lambert of old. I'd enjoyed getting closer to her today: I'd felt more in control of my life than I had done in the last four months.

Chapter Ten

On Saturday morning I was awoken by a loud roaring and the sensation of a furry animal having taken residence in my mouth. Hailey and I had got in from our cocktail adventure at two forty a.m., and although last night I'd been rather proud of this, I now regretted it severely.

The roaring continued. Confused and irritable, I straggled through to the kitchen where a rather remarkable sight awaited me.

'Good morning!' Sam boomed. His voice hovered dangerously close to the BAV and he was pouring a bright green smoothie out of the blender into two glasses. For no obvious reason, Phil Collins's *Serious Hits LIVE* was pumping loudly out of the iPod dock.

'Eh?'

Sam grinned. 'I said, "good morning".'

'What . . . What are you doing, Sam?' My voice was beautifully croaky.

'Just looking after myself, Chas. One has to work hard to look this good.'

He *did* look good. I'd never seen Sam awake at this time of day but normally when he did emerge – some time around midday – he was clothed in a rotting towelling dressing-gown and would spend most of the day lying on the sofa watching DVDs. But today he was conspicuously vertical and was wearing a pair of – excuse me? – *running shorts?* 'Are you OK?' I asked him suspiciously.

'Never better! Pear and rocket – try it.'

I took a tiny sip. 'Bloody hell! That's delicious!'

'Ha. Now, we need to get cracking with William and Shelley. William called me at bloody seven o'clock asking what was going on. And after that we can have a proper chat about First Date Aid. Forward planning, financial stuff, marketing.'

I stared at him in amazement. 'Er, sure thing, Bowes. But I smell like a badger's dump. Can I have a shower first?'

He saluted.

'By the way,' I croaked, 'what's with the sportswear and healthy breakfast? Where's your dressing-gown?'

'Oh, I burned it last night.'

'You what? Where?'

'In the fire,' Sam replied, emptying the last dregs of smoothie out of the blender.

I looked. There in my grate, amid a large pile of ash and charred logs, was a forlorn little section of dressing-gown belt. 'Bowes, you're a psychopath.'

The opening bars of 'Take A Look At Me Now' started playing, accompanied by screaming and whistling from Phil's live audience. As I dragged myself off for my shower, I was still laughing. Sam was ridiculous.

'Hey, Chas,' he called, as I left the room. I stopped and turned. 'Ten years ago they said I'd never get over my Phil Collins addiction. But take a look at me now!'

Over a breakfast of porridge and green smoothie, Sam opened his notebook and started to talk Shelley/

William strategy. 'Right, so when is she back from New York?' he asked, scrawling a makeshift calendar into his notepad.

'Not sure. When she called on Thursday, she said she'd be away for a week. So let's say Thursday, the seventeenth of October.'

Sam drew an arrow through the days until then. 'OK. Now, William's given me direct access to his email. Do you have the same?'

I nodded. 'Yeah. She's set up a special account for me to use. Trust me, she'll be checking it every five seconds and phoning me with feedback on my efforts.'

'Is she quite anal and controlling?'

'No, she just likes William.'

Sam was clearly amused. 'Is she anal and controlling?' he repeated, just a bit too pointedly for my liking.

'Well, yes, a bit,' I said grudgingly. I didn't want to be tarred with Shelley's anal brush. I ignored Sam's grin and fired up my laptop. 'Have you looked at their correspondence so far?' I asked him.

Sam squeezed honey on to his porridge. 'Yes. It's terrible. Read it now so we can develop a battle plan.'

'Given Shelley's email skills, a battle plan is a very good idea. Every time she contacts me it's like she's punching me in the face.' *No new messages*, the page said when I logged into Shelley's email. Disappointment momentarily overwhelmed me and I sighed.

Sam looked up. 'What?'

'Nothing,' I said hastily. I didn't want him to know that there was still a part of me that got upset when there wasn't a new message from William in my inbox. This was going to take some getting used to. I gulped the remainder of the smoothie and opened the most recent email, scrolling down to the bottom of the chain.

Hi, William had begun. He'd emailed at seven twenty-eight the morning after their date. *You free Saturday night? Cheers, William.*

I was horrified. 'Cheers? *Cheers?* Sam, they *snogged!* He can't sign off with bloody "cheers"!'

Sam nodded at my computer to indicate there was plenty more where that had come from. His eyes danced with mirth.

Shelley had replied fifty-five seconds after William's message. I winced.

> I have to go to New York. Work emergency. We'll have to meet
> another time. Sincere apologies, Shelley

'She is one cold fish,' Sam remarked, reading over my shoulder.

Hey, William had responded. *That sounds like the worst excuse for cancelling a date I've ever heard!! When you back?*

'Double exclamation marks? You're a doctor!' I was outraged.

> I don't know. I'll advise you as and when I have more information.
> Cheers, Shelley.

'No! "Cheers"? Not her too!'

'Yup,' Sam replied. 'No bloody wonder they called us in.'

> Hi Shelley . . . So what's going on out there? Global
> meltdown? W

Hi William, it's complex, a work thing. I can't discuss it with you.

Hey I heard a funny joke the other day. A man walks into a bar.

(ha ha) Cheers, Shelley

Right. Well, keep me posted on your return. : -) William

I got stuck into my porridge. 'Awful, Sam,' I muttered. '*Awful*. Smileys? Opening with "Hey"? Signing off with "Cheers"? I can't bear it! Good porridge, though. I'm impressed.'

'Thanks. I mixed in some honey and cinnamon and sultanas and a tiny bit of single cream,' Sam replied nonchalantly, as if whipping up a tasty low-GI breakfast was part of his daily routine. 'Now, Chas. I think the problem is Shelley's so bloody brisk that William's got scared. So he's knocking out really crap, defensive one-liners. I say we warm Shelley up first.'

'Hang on. William started this. His email was *terrible*! It was him who started the "cheers" epidemic . . .'

'But he emailed her at seven thirty the morning after a date! It doesn't matter what words he used – that shows how keen he is!'

'CHEERS?' I shouted. 'Cheers?'

We had a face-off.

Sam was laughing first and after a few seconds I joined in.

'Oh, bums,' I said.

'Oh, balls,' Sam said. 'That's not a good start to our working relationship.'

I shook my head.

'OK, Chas, I agree. They're both rubbish. Let's warm *both* of them up. It's Shelley's turn to write but perhaps

William should kick off with a good-morning email so Shelley feels, I dunno, more wanted. Might relax her.'

I thought about it and had to smile. During my correspondence with 'William', he had emailed early in the morning twice and I'd floated around on a pink fluffy cloud for hours. What woman in her right mind wouldn't love being a man's first thought on waking?

Sam brought his own laptop over to the table and started typing.

I thought about what Shelley had said to me in the last forty-eight hours. What would make this email super-special? 'I know!' I said suddenly. 'Shelley told me she loves Central Park in the autumn. Say you love it too! Then she'll be all like *oh, my God, we're like sooooo compatible.*'

'Good work, partner, good work,' Sam muttered, and I went off to brush my teeth. When I returned five minutes later, I was rather surprised to discover him limbering up in a pair of brand-new trainers.

'Bowes?' I asked, confused. 'What's wrong?'

'Thought I'd go for a jog,' he said. 'I'm serious about this business, Chasman. I think it's possible we could take over the world and I need to be in good shape if that happens.'

I just stared at him.

'Shut up and read the email I sent,' he said, smiling.

I sat down at my laptop but couldn't resist eyeing up his running outfit while Shelley's email refreshed.

'Don't get any ideas,' Sam said. 'You won't be ready to go running for months with that peg-leg.'

I grimaced. Dr Nathan Gillies had hinted that I might

never run again, a fact I had filed away in the back of my head for now.

'You were serious in those emails, weren't you?' I said, watching him. 'You *do* want to do more with your life. That had nothing to do with William.'

Sam had apparently developed a strong interest in a shelving unit. 'Mmm.'

Shelley's inbox loaded and I read his handiwork.

Good morning Ms Cartwright!

How is New York today? One of my favourite ever things is running through Central Park on an autumn morning. It's so crisp and lovely and yummy that I often find myself able to run a substantial marathon as opposed to my normal hundred or so metres. Some fairly funny squirrels hanging out there too.

So, a humdrum day yesterday. I had a tinker around in someone's ear but didn't find much. (NB Once I discovered a little woodlouse and her baby nestled in a patient's eardrum. I got photographed for the *ENT Journal* for that one.)

So. Are things improving out there or is the global economy about to actually collapse? Could I take you for one last dinner before it does? In fact, I'm not asking, I'm insisting. How long until you're back?

Wx

I clapped my hands. 'Lovely, Bowes! Brilliant Central Park stuff too. However did you know she's a runner? I'm sure I didn't tell you.'

'Because she's just like you, Chas,' he said. 'Course she bloody well runs.'

He was saved from a swinging fist by the loud ring of my First Date Aid mobile.

'Hello, Charlotte speaki –'

'CHARLOTTE!' Shelley bellowed.

I held the phone away from my head. 'Er, hi, Shelley.'

'He's sent me a *divine* email. Have you seen it? Have you?'

'Er, not yet,' I lied. The machine gun was well and truly back.

'He even likes Central Park in the autumn! I mean, my God!' she yelled. Sam, who at a distance of five metres could hear her as clearly as I could, gave me a thumbs-up and slid out of the front door in his running outfit.

'I should probably wait a while before responding,' I told her. 'Always good to remain a bit mysterious.' I thought of the fifty-five-second delay she had left before replying to William's email on Thursday.

'No, I want you to reply right now,' Shelley barked. 'I'm having brunch at my desk. If you reply to him immediately I'll be able to read it.'

'OK, well I –'

'Please book him in for Thursday the eighteenth – that's the night I get back,' she screeched. 'And in response to his question say I'm busy but not having a breakdown.'

'OK . . . *Are* you having a breakdown?'

'No,' she said, after a pause. 'No, but it's stressful. A lot of responsibility. I could do with a massage and some sleep. Or, at least, a bit of a break.' She sounded oddly vulnerable.

'Well, take care of yourself,' I said. 'I'll write to William now.' I ended the call before she got the machine gun out again, and ran over to the window.

'BOWES,' I shouted.

Sam, who was just exiting the front door below me, looked up. 'She wants you to write back now?'

'Yes! I agree, she *is* obsessive and she *is* anal. The most anal woman in the history of anal.'

A well-heeled mummy, emerging from the Urban Angels café with a wholesome-looking child, shook her head angrily and glared up at me as if I were a turd.

Sam burst out laughing. 'Coming back up, Chas.'

Good morning, Dr William,

Ah, a dinner invitation before I've even finished my brunch. Bliss! I'll say yes please.

Sam strode in and sat down next to me, reading as I typed. He smelt of Persil.

So here I am at my desk, wrestling with a super-sized American brunch delivery. The meals here are so huge I'll barely finish a quarter of what was in front of m

'No,' Sam said. 'Don't give him all of that "Oooh I don't eat much, oooh, I'm just a little dinky flower." Men hate that shit.'

'Really?'

'Really!'

Fair enough. 'OK.'

Sam pinched some of my coffee. 'Forget Shelley, Chas. Just be yourself. It's worked so far. William's hooked.'

A warm glow. I resumed writing.

> So here I am at my desk, eating a hearty brunch. I love a good
> sausage of a morning.

Sam giggled.

> I can't believe you love running around Central Park in autumn
> too – that's an amazing coincidence. It's my absolute favourite!
> I find running – particularly there – really quite life-affirming.
> It transports me away from my work for an hour, which is no
> mean feat.
> Yes, things are quite serious here. But I'm doing my best.
> Speaking of work, congratulations on the woodlouse: that's a
> truly profound achievement.

'Get her to say something a bit less jokey about the wood-louse,' Sam said.

I was bewildered. 'But . . . you made up a story about a freaking woodlouse! What isn't to joke about? C'mon, Bowes, I really have to get on with work . . .'

Sam ignored me. 'Remember that joke I cracked back at the beginning – about having my hand up someone's nose? William went mental! He'll be even less impressed with this one. But, anyway, I'm serious. Feed his ego a tiny bit. Us men *love* being complimented on our careers. Makes us feel all big and manly.'

I shot a sideways look at him, wondering how long it had been since anyone had complimented him on his.

> Seriously, though [*I wrote – rather grudgingly*], any sort of
> mention in a trade journal is pretty impressive, woodlouse or
> not. What a fantastic job you do.

I could do dinner on Thursday next week. I might be a bit wild-
haired and hallucinatory as I land at six thirty that morning . . .
and may possibly speak in an American accent all night . . . but
if that works for you, we're on.

X X X

Sam laughed. 'I'm amazed I didn't work out that it was
you,' he said. 'You ridiculous workaholic nutjob.'

I frowned. 'Er, you can pipe down, Mr Snot-green-
smoothie-and-running-shoes-at-nine-on-a-Saturday-
morning.'

Sam shrugged. 'I'm a member of the UK workforce
now. Anyway,' he said, leaning forward, a rather subversive expression on his face, 'before you press send, I'd like
you to consider disobeying Shelley and suggesting Friday
night to William.'

'Out of the question,' I replied, without hesitation.

'Why?'

I sighed. Men and women really were so very different.
To me, a weekend date was extremely significant – I hadn't
broken my leg over a Tuesday date after all – but I was
damned if I knew how to explain that to him.

'Urgh. Bowes, it's complicated, but basically she's a girl
and she can't offer him Friday night. And that's that. But
if William suggests it, she can say yes.'

Sam looked pained. 'I cannot cope with women.'

I didn't budge.

'Well, I can see I'm not going to win this one, Chas. Go
ahead with your Thursday offer. And I'll write back and
suggest Friday instead.'

Then I smelt a rat. When a man emailed one of my clients wanting a Friday-night date he was normally after sex. 'What's with Friday, Bowes?' I asked suspiciously.

'I know what you're thinking. But you're wrong. It's just that if they meet on Thursday she'll be exhausted. But if they do Friday she'll have had some sleep and will have the weekend ahead of her.'

I eyeballed him, unconvinced.

'Chas, come *on*! Women like this are always free at the weekend! They cram their weeks to buggery and then have nothing to do on a Friday or Saturday night. It's their dirty secret!'

I blushed. It was true. Friday night was my 'friend' night but as often as not I just hid in my room, planning the weekend's activities. It was mortifying that Sam had noticed. 'Fine, fine, let's do it. Now I HAVE to get on with work.'

After he'd gone running I had a little embarrassed sulk. I didn't like Sam being aware of my weaknesses, and the fact that he'd noticed I rarely went out on a Friday night made me feel stupid. I closed down my email, relieved to be able to get back to work. But as I pulled a document wallet out of my satchel I heard a key in the door and in walked a gigantic bunch of flowers with Sam concealed somewhere under them.

'Bowes?' I said uncertainly. The smoothies and the running kit had been hard enough. I couldn't take it if Sam had also become a flower-buyer overnight.

'For you,' he said, staggering to the table. He put them down and sank into a chair to catch his breath. The flowers completely dwarfed him.

'What? Why are you buying me flowers?' I felt mildly panicky. 'Sam, we're business partners, you shouldn't –'

'Someone just delivered them in a van, you knob.'

I coloured even more. Fool! Why indeed would Sam buy me flowers? Flushed and awkward, I pulled a card out of the bouquet and tore it open.

So sorry to hear your grandmother is ill. Please just call if you need help with hospitals/doctors/treatments. I know people and can help. Jx

I sat down suddenly. John had never bought me a coffee, let alone a bunch of flowers the size of a car. What was he up to? I felt torn. Part of me knew I'd been here before, John sending out quite strong signals that turned out to be nothing of the sort. And when I'd been in London I'd promised myself an end to all of the fantasy about men who weren't interested.

But since I'd been back he *had* seemed interested. Very interested, actually. There had been all the usual flirting, leg-groping and X-ray smiles, but I had also caught him watching me a few times in a way that seemed – dare I say it? – tender. Yesterday I'd gone outside to sit on a bench among the yellow sycamore leaves and call for an update on Granny Helen. As I'd chatted to Mum, I'd suddenly sensed I was being watched. And there he was, standing in a window on the third floor, smiling at me in a kindly way. As I'd walked back through Reception a few minutes later, the lift doors had opened and out he'd strode.

'Come for a walk!' he'd said, taking me by the elbow and guiding me outside. This was surprising behaviour.

John worked as hard and obsessively as I did; he was not one for autumnal strolls. I glanced up at him and he smiled back in his usual naughty fashion. We set off along the drive under the trees.

'Lambert . . . you looked very romantic out there on the bench in your autumn woollens.' He beamed. 'Everything OK?'

'Fine,' I said shortly. I didn't know what he was up to but I knew I had to try not to flirt.

John put his hands into his pockets and his cheeky X-ray smile faded. 'Have you found a boyfriend, Lambert?' he asked suddenly.

I was shocked. He had never asked about my love life. He'd always just carried on as if I was single. Once again, my head started ticking. Why was he asking? Was this significant? Should I say 'yes' to see what happened? *Shut up*, I told myself. *Shut up*.

But it was too late. I was already intoxicated by the possibility of John being jealous and so, rather than denying it, I made a noncommittal face. 'Why do you ask?'

It was his turn to look surprised. He'd obviously expected me to say no.

'Oh. Well, you looked very *into* the phone call you were having,' he said. For the first time in the history of John MacAllister, he'd sounded a bit awkward.

I began to smile. He really might be jealous! This was extraordinary! 'John,' I said gently, 'it was my mother. My grandmother's had a stroke and just got out of hospital today. I was ringing to find out how she was.'

John raised an eyebrow and, for a second, I saw something that looked suspiciously like relief. But it was fleeting.

'I'm sorry to hear it, Lambert. Why, in the name of God, didn't you tell me? What can I do?'

I was touched. 'Nothing. It's a stroke. You know the score.'

John had stopped walking. 'Please, Lambert,' he'd said softly. 'Allow me to help you sometimes.'

Now Sam was watching me curiously.

'Er, they're from John, actually,' I said. My face coloured.

Sam looked surprised. 'That still rumbling on?'

I still felt embarrassed that I'd accused him of buying me flowers. What if Sam thought I *wanted* him to buy me flowers? Arrgh! At this moment John felt like a very useful decoy. 'John and I will always be rumbling on.' I smiled secretively.

Sam shook his head, grinning. 'You dirty dog,' he said, and for the third time that morning, he left the house to go for a run.

I sat down, got out my Salutech folder and worked for six hours without a break. Ness and I were going home to see Granny Helen tonight: I didn't want any confusing thoughts about men to be present in my head. And, as usual, work put paid to any such nonsense. By the time I met Ness I was clear and focused once more. I was Charley Lambert.

We sat on the back seat of the 44D bus, like we had as teenagers on the way home from school. Ness was on the phone to her girlfriend, Sarah, and I was slumped against the window, watching East Lothian slide past: darkening potato plantations, the odd ruined castle and now-grey hills rolling away in every direction. Although I was itching to drive again I was quite enjoying all of the bus journeys. It had been years since I'd stopped to notice the view.

I was tired but I felt great. Positively tingling, in fact. I'd caught up on a lot of Salutech stuff today and was rather chuffed that my swansong for First Date Aid was Project William and Shelley. It felt good to be helping someone for once.

Sam, as discussed, had written back to Shelley, suggesting they meet on Friday night instead of Thursday and I was awaiting her next manic and excitable call from New York. I grinned as we trundled through Haddington, wondering if I *could* set aside a little bit of time for First Date Aid each day. Just so I could keep my hand in . . .

'What are you thinking about?' Ness asked, ending her call. She was wearing Aztec-patterned culottes with thick tights and looked delectable.

'About the fact that I'm a workaholic, actually.'

'Oh. Blimey. And?'

'And I feel good about it. It makes me feel alive.'

Ness nodded, although it was clear she didn't approve. 'Workaholics end up grinding to a halt eventually,' she said, after a pause. 'I don't want that to happen to you.'

I didn't say anything.

'How are your working hours at the moment?'

'They're exactly as you'd expect a week before we launch the biggest product ever. Ness, please don't lecture me. I'm tired.'

Ness didn't say, 'Exactly.' I felt grateful for her ability to refrain from interfering. It was not a trait that was readily available in our family. We lapsed into a companionable silence.

We were travelling fast towards East Linton now and my phone signal was down to three blocks. Shelley Cartwright, running around New York, must have known because she chose that moment to call me.

'CHARLOTTE,' she roared, in her normal welcoming tones.

'Shelley.'

'He's REJECTED MEEEEEEEEE,' she cried. *Dammit.* What had Bowes done now?

'Er, how?' I asked.

The bus stopped in the centre of town and Ness guided me off as I juggled my bags and John's flowers without dropping the phone. We walked at a snail's pace along the street as Shelley wailed. 'ARRGHH!' she screamed down the phone. Ness looked alarmed. 'I suggested Thursday and he suggested Friday instead! SHIIIIIIIIIT!'

'I . . . I don't understand what the problem is,' I said gently. 'Friday's a great date night!'

'Yes, but he REJECTED ME for Thursday! I put myself out on a limb and he said no! If he was interested he'd cancel whatever he's doing! He's going on another date! I know it!'

I found myself momentarily speechless: Shelley was actually insane. I felt markedly better about the shady activities I'd indulged in recently. Apparently love could turn even the steeliest of businesswomen into mad, howling wretches. 'I don't think that's true,' I replied, as levelly as I could. 'William could be doing all number of things on Thursday. He could be at a funeral for all we know!' I added brightly.

'He's on a date,' she insisted. 'I *knew* it wouldn't last. It was those awful emails I sent before I hired you!'

'Nonsense, Shelley. It's very obvious that he likes you. *Are* you free next Friday?'

'Er, yes,' she said sheepishly. 'But that's not the point. The point is he –'

'No, that *is* the point,' I said firmly. 'If you're free, meet him.'

I heard Shelley take a glug of something. Great, she was drunk too. 'OK,' she said meekly. 'But can you tell him no at first? And then email back an hour later saying yes? Tell him my original plans were cancelled or something. He mustn't think I'm free on a Friday night.'

I sighed. 'Sure. I have to go, Shelley. Have a nice afternoon.'

'What in the name of Jiminy Cricket was that?' Ness asked. She looked like an outraged pixie. I loved my sister.

We'd been standing outside our parents' front door for nearly five minutes now. A few late roses were clinging grimly to the wall by the front door and the smell of fish pie was wafting out of the open kitchen window. 'Ah, nothing,' I said. I didn't even know where to begin.

Ness laughed. 'Whatever it was, it was not nothing. Come on, spill the beans.'

I'd been sitting with the knowledge that William was Sam for three days now; I was desperate to confide in someone. I looked at Ness and knew I could tell her anything. So I spilled.

'You think I've lost it, don't you?' I said, a few minutes later.

Ness looked puzzled. 'No,' she said slowly. 'But I – The thing with Sam, Charley, what's with that?'

'There is no thing with Sam,' I said. 'We were ghost-writing to each other without knowing it. And now we know. It was embarrassing for five minutes and then we decided to help get these two people together. The end.'

'But . . . but there was so much chemistry, Charley. I saw those emails. You don't think you and Sam could –'

'*No,*' I replied firmly. 'Never. In a trillion years, never.'

Ness shook her head, as if recovering from a trance. 'You're right,' she said. 'Sam is a dirty tramp.' Hearing Nessie's little voice calling Sam a 'dirty tramp' gave me the giggles, which turned into belly laughs.

'What's going on out there?' Granny Helen's voice shrilled, out of the kitchen window. 'Is that the bloody Jehovah's Witnesses or is it my granddaughters?'

We grinned at each other and walked inside.

'She's doing better than we expected,' Mum whispered, as she poured us some wine in the warm, steamy kitchen. 'She slept for ten hours last night and woke up demanding a kipper sandwich served with kiwis.'

Mum and Dad had taken Granny Helen to California some years ago during one of their 'new age' holidays that involved comfortable hotels and luxury transfers. Granny Helen had fallen in love with kiwis there and ever since – long before kiwis had become voguish in the UK – she had sent Mum and Dad to a supermarket twenty-five miles away every week to buy them. When Mum forgot to buy kiwis one Christmas, Granny Helen went on strike and set up a picket line outside the kitchen. 'Don't go in there,' she'd said loudly. 'That woman is stuck in the past. Won't even serve a bloody kiwi for breakfast.'

'Sounds positive?' I said uncertainly.

'Definitely,' Mum agreed. 'She whacked your father round the backside with her stick when he told her she couldn't let Malcolm sleep on the bed with her. Said that if he couldn't allow a dying woman one last wish then he deserved to have his ears boxed.'

I felt a bit happier. 'She doesn't sound like a dying woman to me.'

'No,' Mum said wryly. 'No, I don't think she's a dying woman right now. But . . . Well, a stroke at her age can't just pass without consequence.'

Granny Helen was as sharp as a nail one minute, tired and vague the next. Dad, meanwhile, was doing his best to behave as if nothing had happened. He wore an expression of forced jollity all evening and cracked lots of bad jokes in Granny Helen's direction, most of which she met with her customary scorn. '*See?*' his face said, when she cut him down to size. '*See? She's fine!*' After the fish pie Mum served a special kiwi pavlova in Granny Helen's honour ('I don't have much of a sweet tooth,' Granny Helen sniffed, eating four slices in a row) and Dad treated us to a spectacular rendition of 'Ring of Fire' on his banjo. His playing had improved significantly but it was still very far from good. Malcolm, clearly in agreement, went off to bed and put a big brown paw over his ear. Granny Helen fell asleep in her chair.

When I watched Dad scoop up Granny Helen's tiny body and carry her next door to her cottage, my breath caught in my throat. 'She's totally back to normal,' he remarked, to no one in particular.

After the door shut behind them, there was a long silence. 'Dad's in denial,' Ness announced.

Mum shrugged. 'He is a doctor, Nessie,' she said. 'He knows better than us.'

'Oh, Mum, come on. Granny Helen's ninety-one. You know what a stroke means at her age,' Ness said.

I was surprised. Ness was rarely so blunt.

'The reason I'm saying this,' Ness said, as if reading my mind, 'is that I'm properly worried about Dad.'

'Me too,' Mum replied, after a pause. 'He's incredibly attached to her. I don't know what we'll do when she . . .' She trailed off.

We looked at her sharply. Mum *always* knew what to do. She avoided our eyes and started clearing plates. 'We'll just all have to keep our fingers crossed for her,' she said briskly. She put the kettle on and Ness and I knew the subject was closed.

As I drifted off to sleep in my higgledy-piggledy bedroom, I became aware of a vibrating sensation in the region of my left leg. 'Fuck off,' I muttered, trying to find my phone.

'Oh, no, *really* fuck off,' I said, seeing Shelley's name on my caller ID.

YOU HAVEN'T REPLIED TO WILLIAM YET???? she texted, a few seconds later. I ignored her. Some things were bigger than finding love for a stranger.

My phone started ringing again and I sat up, enraged. 'Shelley, it's eleven fifty-two p.m. and I am with my family. I will reply tomorrow, OK?'

'Um . . . Hi, Chas?'

I looked at my phone. Oh, balls. There was Sam's name

with an accompanying picture of him wearing a condom on his head. 'Sorry, Bowes.'

'Good customer-relations chat you've got there,' he remarked mildly.

'Sorry, I just – she – urgh.'

Sam chuckled softly. 'I know. William's as bad. They're driving me mad already.'

'Is that why you're calling me? Has William been on your back?'

'Of course not!' Sam sounded hurt. 'I just wanted to check you're all OK. I've been worried about Granny Helen.' There was a silence. 'I like to keep an eye on you weird bunch of Lamberts,' he said.

I was touched. 'That's really sweet.' I smiled. 'Thank you. Well, Granny Helen's sort of not great, Dad's in denial, Mum's stressed about Dad, I'm tired . . . Ness is as gorgeous as ever, though.'

'Chasmonger, sounds tough. Get some sleep . . .' This was probably getting a bit too close to a soft 'n' gentle chat for Sam and he stopped talking.

'Thanks for calling, Bowes. I'm surprised you're not out chatting up laydeez, it being Saturday night and all.'

'Ah. Well, actually I am. I'm having a drink with some-one. But I wanted to check you're OK.'

'That's very kind. Now get back to work.'

'Aye-aye. Night, Chas.'

I smiled and rolled over. Sam was a dirty dog but he was also the sweetest man on earth at times. It still sur-prised me.

Chapter Eleven

The sound of a distant train whirring across to Dunbar and the rhythmic thump of Malcolm's tail against the kitchen dresser woke me the next morning. A lie-in was tempting but I had a mountain of work to do for next Friday's Simitol launch and, of course, a dating email to write. It was Shelley's turn to message William, and overnight she had sent me three increasingly crazed emails begging me to reply to him *right now* because if I didn't reply soon he'd decide she'd gone off him and back off. Apparently. I'd read them this morning, amazed. Shelley might be a kick-ass businesswoman with the demeanour of a police truncheon but her self-esteem was on the floor.

'We're far better off out of all of that relationship bollocks,' I told Malcolm a little later. 'Turns us all into mentals.' I'd tried to sneak off to Edinburgh early but had been unable to resist his beseeching face. 'Love me,' it had said. 'Feed me. Walk me.'

Coming home early, I texted Sam, as Malcolm jumped gleefully into the River Linn, paddling around like a big brown smiling seal. *Pls evict any loose women from the flat so we can sort out W&S.*

Malcolm climbed out of the river and shook himself dry all over me.

'You stinker!' I laughed, clipping on his lead. He beamed

up at me, as loving as ever. No human being made me laugh as much as Malcolm could. There was a lot to worry about at the moment but Malcolm was definitely helping.

By the time I got back, Mum and Ness were looking confusedly at what appeared to be a large sunken teacake. Mum shrugged helplessly as Dad burst in whistling. 'I've made a special breakfast loaf, girls! I'm calling it Barbados Roll,' he added, as if this somehow explained things.

Just over an hour later I hobbled down Broughton Street where van drivers were still loading cheeses and complicated-looking bread into delis and cafés. The air was sharp and the wind from the east made my cheeks smart. As I rounded the corner of Forth Street, I spied a petite young girl in full Saturday-night attire letting herself out of my front door. She barely noticed me as she staggered past on her spiky heels. I grimaced, genuinely disgusted. It had been a while since I'd seen this, and for that reason it felt even more tawdry than it used to in the days before Yvonne.

'Good night?' I asked Sam, as I arrived in the living room. To my surprise, I found him sitting at the table, typing away on his laptop.

'Surprise!' he said, showing me an area of bookshelf that he'd cleared and filled with lever arch files complete with proper printed First Date Aid labels. Enjoying my astonishment, he then pointed at two stacks of business cards, which sat in a Perspex box. I was gobsmacked. How had he done all of that? And so quickly? Sam's interactions with technology seldom stretched beyond the cheese toaster!

'So . . . we got our first male client overnight!' he reported.

'Wow! Less than twelve hours after you updated the website?'

'Yes! Marcus. Banter skills of a jolly frog. Well-meaning but excitable and ridiculous. I'm looking forward to helping him, actually.'

I sat down and beamed at Sam. He was surprising me at every turn: I had a sudden urge to run over and squeeze him. But, for obvious reasons, I resisted. There could be no confusion between us at the moment.

'Anyway,' he continued, 'I wanted to talk to you about our rates. I think we can and should increase them. Oh, and William and Shelley, why haven't you replied yet? William texted me at midnight asking if I thought Shelley had forgotten about him and was banging some Manhattanite in a bar!'

'Wow,' I said, flopping backwards on the sofa. 'Those two are properly smitten. And a bit mad. Shelley called me last night screeching about being rejected. Then she emailed me overnight saying she thought she should just abandon it. She said she's lost her nerve.'

'What? He asked her out! How is that a rejection?'

I waved him away. 'Don't even ask.'

'Nutters,' Sam remarked.

'Nutters,' I agreed. 'Coffee?'

'Yes. Make it strong.'

I got up and switched on the espresso machine. 'I think the only thing that'll persuade Shelley to stop being such a silly sausage is if William turns this Friday-night date into something really extravagant.'

'Why should he?'

'Because she was devastated that he wouldn't cancel whatever he was doing on Thursday. It's going to take a big gesture to convince her that he's serious.'

Sam gasped. 'Is she out of her *mind*? He wants to spend Friday night with her! Why the fucking fuck should Thursday matter?' He looked genuinely exasperated.

I shrugged. It was mad, of course. Bonkers. But, rather embarrassingly, Shelley's skewed reading of the situation did make some sense to me. Sam turned back to his computer, realizing that he wasn't going to find as much solidarity in me as he might have liked.

'What's her all-time favourite thing?' he asked eventually. 'I can suggest they do whatever it is on Friday night, maybe.'

I didn't know and, moreover, I didn't really want to think about it. I was feeling really twitchy about not having started my Salutech stuff yet. 'Dunno. Look, Bowes, I'm afraid I need to get on with work. Just propose something that'll make her feel special.'

Sam eyed me levelly for a few seconds and I could see he was disappointed. After all, we'd made a deal – we sorted out William and Shelley together, pooling our resources and information.

And that was that. I couldn't have anyone disappointed in me: I was going to have to help him, in spite of my need to work. I'd just finish at midnight tonight rather than ten p.m.

Not without relish, I opened up Shelley's early emails. 'Ummmm . . . Well, she likes going to the gym –'

'You'll have to do better than that,' Sam interrupted. 'What sort of a date would I suggest around that? A protein shake in the members' lounge followed by a rogering in the sauna?'

'Shhh, Bowes . . . I'm reading . . . Aha! She loves opera. Specifically, *The Pearl Fishers*.'

I think the Pearl Fishers' duet is quite incredibly beautiful, Shelley had written in her autobiography back in mid September. The force of her sentiment had surprised me. *It makes me cry every time I hear it. So tragic.*

Sam turned away and opened up a Google page. 'That's the right sort of thing,' he said. 'But they never show *The Pearl Fishers* – I have no idea why. Shelley's quite right.'

I was surprised. I hadn't known Sam was into opera, and told him as much.

'I do have a cultural life, Chas,' he said. 'I'm not all about beer and birds, you know.'

I raised an eyebrow. 'Interesting. I could have sworn I'd just crossed paths with a girl in a Friday-night skirt,' I said casually. Sam carried on looking at his computer screen but I could see his cheeks go red. 'Blushing, Bowes?' I asked him. 'Everything OK?'

'She was my first since Yvonne,' he muttered. 'Leave it.'

I busied myself with the coffee, feeling a little ashamed of myself. Sam's business was Sam's business, not mine.

'OH, MY GOD!'

I whipped round. 'What?'

'It's only bloody on at the Coliseum in London!'

'What? Eh?'

'*The Pearl Fishers!*'

'No WAY!'

'Yes way. Right, we have to get tickets,' he said, loading up a new webpage. A few seconds later he thumped a fist on the table. 'Sold out.' He pondered the situation for a few seconds, then stood up, fishing his mobile out of his pocket. 'Leave it with me,' he said, avoiding my eye. He slunk past me and into his room.

I sat down on the sofa to do some of my peg-leg exercises, sipping coffee. I looked over at our new 'office' and smiled. I was rather enjoying working with Sam. As long as he maintained his new wholesome and productive existence, and kept Friday-night Friends to a minimum, I felt living with him was becoming a rather good thing.

'Oh, I am the bomb,' he said, emerging triumphantly from his bedroom. 'The BOMB!'

I sipped my coffee, confident that he'd explicate. He did.

'Two tickets, front of the royal circle, Friday night,' he said. 'Do I or do I not rule the *world*, Chas?'

'You most certainly do. How the hell did you pull that off?'

'A girl I know . . .' Sam said, winking. 'Say no more.'

It was weird. Certain as I was that my feelings for William had not been transferred to Sam, I was definitely finding myself more bothered about his myriad romantic trysts. Somewhere along the way they had stopped being funny and had started to seem a bit horrible; a bit tawdry.

I dragged myself back to the matter in hand. 'Right, then, Bowes, drop Shelley a line to tell her about the tickets. She'll go mental!'

Sam wasn't keen. 'I don't think I can. William sent the

last email . . . If a woman doesn't reply you've got to sit and wait until she does. You can't just send another. Double-messaging. Bad.'

I shook my head. He had to email her, end of story. 'Desperate times, Bowes.'

'OK.' He started typing. 'Double message it is.'

Now then Shelley, I'm presuming your silence means you are rendered immobile with adoration for me rather than that you've flown into a fit of pique about me being busy on Thursday.

'Careful, Bowes,' I said, reading over Sam's shoulder.

What I didn't mention earlier was that I have two tickets for Bizet's *The Pearl Fishers* on Friday next week. It's a wonderful opera; that duet frankly makes me weep. You cannot say no. So ideally I suggest you say yes.
Yes?
I wonder how it's going out there. You seem so incredibly driven, Ms Cartwright; I am quite sure you will be saving that company's ass. You're actually a bit amazing. X

'Nice,' I said, handing Sam his coffee. 'Very nice. She can't say no to that.' As we chinked our cups, I felt a wave of excitement. 'I love this!' I told him. 'I know it's naughty, but isn't it fun?'

Shelley did not say no. Ten minutes later, she rang me and fog-horned down the phone so loudly that Sam, who was in the bath, could hear. '*THE PEARL FISHERS!* IT'S MEANT TO BE! SAY YES FOR ME! WHAT ON EARTH WILL I WEAR?' she roared. I grinned. If these two worked out, they would make the best success story our website would ever hold. *Psychotic workaholic tamed by doctor with exclamation-mark addiction*, I imagined. Sam and I were flying.

Sam's phone started to ring on the coffee-table and I leaned over to look at it. 'Shit, Sam, it's William!' I called.

'Bring it in!' he yelled. 'Door's unlocked.'

I covered my eyes and launched myself into the bathroom with Sam's phone held in front of me like a shield. I heard the water swell as Sam leaned forward. 'You're such an uptight Victorian, Chasmonger,' he remarked, taking it from me.

'I just don't want to see your knob,' I replied primly. I sat down on the toilet lid, facing away from Sam with my hand over my eyes just for safety.

'Hi, William,' Sam said calmly. 'What's up?'

A loud tinny voice filled the bathroom and I realized Sam had put William on speakerphone. 'What's up? That's a very good question,' William replied. I wasn't sure I liked his voice. He sounded extremely self-important, the sort of person who made knowledgeable comments about champagne vintages.

'Eh?' Sam said. His casual manner alarmed me.

'Are you in a toilet?' William asked suspiciously.

'Yeah,' Sam replied. 'I'm in the bath.'

William exhaled irritably and I tried to do a throat-slashing gesture in Sam's general direction. He ignored me.

'Well,' William continued, 'I was calling to ask exactly what you think you're doing, inviting Shelley to the opera on my behalf. I do not have tickets. Furthermore I've looked online and they are not even available to buy. What the hell are you up to?'

'Chill,' Sam said.

I was flailing an arm in his direction. He couldn't talk to a client like that!

'Chill, William, I got you some tickets. The best in the house, actually. And you don't even need to pay for them.'

William was momentarily silenced. 'Oh,' he said gruffly. 'Oh, well.'

'I didn't have time to email you before I sent that message,' Sam continued, 'but basically you're taking her to her very favourite opera in the world ever. The duet bit makes her cry.'

There was a pause. Appalled, I turned to look at Sam, who put a hand over his privates. *You IDIOT!* I mouthed at him.

'Er – and how do you know that?' William asked eventually.

'It says so in her dating profile,' Sam bluffed easily. 'She changed it last night.' He waved frantically to get me to go and update Shelley's dating profile. I glared and ran through to the living room.

'Sorry,' he said, emerging a few minutes later. His lower half was wrapped in an ancient Teenage Mutant Hero Turtles towel but his upper half still looked as stupidly toned and tanned as it had done when he used to wander round in fisherman's pants quoting Noël Coward at university. 'Sorry, Chas. Bit of a slip there.'

''S OK,' I replied. 'I changed her profile just in the nick of time. And I'll change it back later so she doesn't notice. But – seriously. Concentrate.'

'Chas,' he said, after a pause. 'Will you please grant me

227

a bit of respect? Just because I don't operate like you doesn't mean I don't know how to deal with clients. If I'm taking over this company, you'll have to trust me.'

I didn't know how to respond to this. Was he right? *Of course not*, my head said. *There is only* one *way to deal with clients*. But I had a sneaking suspicion Sam might be right. Slightly unsettled, I sat down and opened up my Salutech folder.

Five minutes later I was in an uncharacteristic Sunday coma, fast asleep on the sofa.

When I came to, I found myself staring at a very large penis. 'Wargh!' I shouted, covering my head with a cushion.

'Oh, sorry,' Sam said conversationally, turning the TV off. 'You were asleep.'

'So what, you just thought you'd watch some porn? Jesus, Sam! You'd better not have been cracking one off . . .'

'I wasn't. This is a multiple-award-winning film,' he said mildly. 'In fact, it's really quite beautiful.'

'Well, perhaps you could enjoy its beauty another time,' I suggested, shuffling off to the loo. I settled down on the seat and screamed again.

'What?' Sam shouted. 'Chas?'

'IT'S SEVEN O'CLOCK! I've been asleep for hours!'

I heard him laughing in the living room. 'Indeed. You were very sweet. You even sucked your thumb at one point. You needed the rest.'

I washed my hands and went back through, feeling

concerned and jumpy. The day had nearly passed and I'd achieved nothing whatsoever. I couldn't afford to laze around on the sofa like a normal person. I had far too much to do. But Sam had other plans.

'We're going to the pub,' he announced. 'Come on.'

I was immediately flustered. On the one hand I now knew Sam's views on my work–life balance and felt like I should prove to him that I could just do casual, spur-of-the-moment pub trips. But on the other there was no denying how desperately I needed to do the work I'd planned. I stood on one leg, slightly anguished, and tried to work out what to do. But Sam took the matter into his own hands by bringing my coat over and plonking a Cossack hat on my head.

'Um, give me ten minutes to get changed, Bowes.' It appeared that I was going.

'No way,' Sam replied, pulling me out of the front door. 'We'll go like this. Just round the corner to the Barony.'

I followed him obediently. I'd never before been to the pub in a pair of tracksuit bottoms.

I sat watching Sam chatting easily to the barman as he ordered our drinks. He was partly obscured by clouds of steam pouring out of the glass-washer and had an old drunk man slapping him enthusiastically on the shoulder. A woman, who looked like she was the wife of one of the band members, came up and pinched his cheek, delighted to see him. I smiled. I had lived here for what? ten years? and didn't know a single soul in this pub. In fact, I'd only been in here about three times.

I liked it. It felt safe and comforting with its smoke-stained ceiling, noisy band and colourful bar. Everyone was tapping their feet to the band's Van Morrison covers, except for a couple who'd obviously had a row and were studiously ignoring each other, he staring at his pint and she reading a Dryden quote on the wall over and over again. *You're better off out of that*, I thought, pondering the mentalists that William and Shelley had become. Evidently it was impossible to be in love and avoid drama. And I was not interested in drama, thank you.

'What are you thinking about?' Sam said, putting a glass of wine in front of me. He had a pint of something dark and cloudy.

'I was thinking how lucky we are to have such a nice local.'

Sam grinned. 'You can't call it a local when you never come in here, Chas.'

I blushed. 'I was just thinking that. But you know what? I rather like it!'

'Ha! You should find space in your mad schedule for us to have a regular drink here. You, me, our tracksuits. Is that a date?'

I half nodded.

'No, no,' he said hastily. 'I don't mean *date* date, obviously, I just . . .'

We retreated into our drinks and watched the band in silence. After a few minutes I found myself bobbing along quite merrily to the music, and realized that Sam was watching me, not without amusement.

'What?'

'Nothing. It's just nice to see you properly chilling.'

'I chill a lot!'

Sam raised an eyebrow. 'Chas, I don't want to embarrass you,' he began awkwardly.

'Then don't,' I butted in.

'Ahem . . . I just . . . I was just thinking about some of the stuff you said in your emails. About your work taking over your life, and shit . . .' He stopped talking and gulped down a lot of pint. He looked anywhere but at me.

'I was just pretending to be Shelley,' I said huffily. I drank some more wine.

Sam looked even more awkward. It seemed like he'd planned this chat forgetting that he was completely incapable of having deep-and-meaningfuls. 'You don't want to make any changes, then?'

'No,' I replied firmly. 'No. On Friday next week we're announcing Simitol to the world. Can you even imagine how huge that is? Countries all over the world will want to buy it and, what's more, even the poorest will be able to afford it because of the sliding scale we've –'

'Yeah, yeah,' Sam interrupted. 'Charley, this is what I mean. Yes, it's huge. Yes, it's amazing. But what about you? Where does your *life* fit into all of this?' He went puce. This was easily the most profound thing Sam had ever said to me. As if to compensate, he stuck a finger in his ear and poked about a bit.

I finished my wine and stared at the glass, feeling stupid and patronized. What business was it of Sam's how I conducted my affairs? I felt my hatches slamming down. 'I am happy, busy and successful,' I said stiffly. 'I'm living the life I always wanted to live. Do you hear me? This is what I want.' I got up to go to the loo.

By the time I got back, Sam was engrossed in conversation with a pretty little girl on the table behind us. 'I work between London and Scotland,' he boomed, in the Bowes Actor Voice.

I got my BlackBerry out and started replying to my work emails.

Chapter Twelve

MacAllister, John: I must say, I'm enjoying your outfit today,
   Lambert. The way that crisp white shirt tucks into that little
   teenage skirt . . .
Lambert, Charlotte: You got that straight out of Bridget Jones.
MacAllister, John: Oh Lambert be nice. I'm having a horrible time.
Lambert, Charlotte: Washington office?

John MacAllister is writing, the dialogue box said. Then it cleared. John MacAllister had stopped writing. I pursed my lips. What was he up to?
   John MacAllister is writing, it told me again, after a lengthy pause.

MacAllister, John: No. Just personal stuff.

I sat back from my computer, surprised. This was not John's style. He could do sexual, he could do powerful. But *feelings*? No. Never!
   Was it something to do with Susan? A tendril of nervous excitement started to uncoil somewhere deep inside me, but I wrestled it back down. After all, I'd been here several times before. And, most importantly, he was married now. I was not, under ANY circumstances, interested in reigniting our old flirtation now he had a ring on his

finger. It had been wrong then; it would be twenty shades of wrong now.

MacAllister, John: Can I take you to dinner please. Wednesday, Oloroso XXX

I stared at the screen, even more shocked now. *Tread very carefully*, I told myself.

Lambert, Charlotte: OK John [I typed gingerly]. Could do with a catch-up about Friday's press launch anyway.

I closed the dialogue box and marked myself as offline. A catch-up prior to our big (enormous) launch day on Friday. That was all.

My head snapped up to the door where Margot had appeared, a saccharine smile plastered to her face. 'Any chance of a chat?' she simpered.

Margot had been suspiciously pleasant since I'd threatened her with disciplinary action last Thursday. I knew she was up to something – and this worried me – but the more I threw myself into my work the less I cared. I was back at the helm and we both knew it.

'I've got ten minutes,' I said carefully, looking at my watch.

'Great,' Margot said. 'I just wanted to update you with the schedule for Friday as it stands at the moment.'

Margot, I had to concede as I flicked through her paperwork, had done a good job with the schedule. I told her as much and was met with a frightening seahorsy smile.

'Thanks for your time,' she said, ten minutes later. 'Isn't it great to be working together again?'

I watched her and her nasty short skirt slink out. And felt a little chill.

Wednesday arrived, the day of my dinner with John. And at seven that evening I simply got up and walked out of my office, explaining to Cassie that John and I had a last-minute meeting in the city centre. 'I'll call you a car,' she said. Margot, who was walking past with exaggerated slowness, stopped completely. 'Who's the meeting with?' she asked pleasantly. I hadn't left the office before ten p.m. all week.

I ignored her. 'No need,' I said to Cassie. 'John's PA's already organized a car for him and I'm going to drive. See you tomorrow, guys!' I all but Olympic-sprinted out of the door.

As I turned out onto the A1 and started heading towards town, I realized my hands were actually clammy on the leather steering-wheel. 'Sort it out, Lambert!' I snapped. It was only John, after all. I'd known him for seven years! *And wanted to hump him pretty much every day for that seven years*, my brain added. I shook my head as if to dislodge the thought. It was a dinner. Nothing more. I'd promised myself no more fantasy about men who weren't interested and that was that. Especially men who weren't interested and had a history of playing games with me *and* were now married.

I forced my thoughts towards First Date Aid. Shelley had accepted William's opera tickets with a nonchalant email ('Don't you dare tell him how excited I am,' she had boomed) and, date number two now sorted, Sam and I had agreed we should take it back to light banter until Shelley was home from New York. This morning, on my recommendation, 'William' had emailed to ask her about her family. 'Men talk about themselves far too much,' I'd told him, as I ran around the kitchen eating Weetabix while sending emails, trying to find my notes for this morning's meeting and ironing a cardigan. 'Girls always notice when a man doesn't ask questions.'

I straightened my new Stella McCartney dress as I slid out of my car in the New Town. I had spent a long time choosing it: smart enough for work but, once I'd shed my cardigan, tight and, well, sexyish enough for a date later on. It did not look like I'd bought a new slutty dress with which to impress John.

'Lambert! You've bought a new slutty dress to impress me!' John said delightedly, as the waiter seated me opposite him. We were sitting by a floor-to-ceiling window at Oloroso with a candle burning seductively in an orange glass tube between us, a Manhattan-like sea of red leather spreading away towards views of the castle. Through the window at which we were seated it seemed as if night had fallen, but off to the north I could still see a distant pinkness clinging to the firth. I gazed across at it for a few seconds, trying to filter some of that relaxed twilight energy into my otherwise racing brain.

'It's not slutty and it's not designed to impress you,' I said, as calmly as I could. 'I've had it a while.'

'Nonsense, Lambert. It's new. And you look ravishing in it, my dear.'

I looked him squarely in the eye. 'John, stop it. I am your director of communications.'

There was a charged silence while we both processed this statement. Did I see myself *only* as his comms director? Probably not, if I were honest. John smiled. And to my fairly experienced eye it was a smile that was born out of more than just pleasantry. I got the distinct impression that he didn't see tonight as a dinner with his head of comms. I breathed slowly and deeply, scrabbling for control. *He's married, he's married, he's married.*

'Sorry, Lambert,' he said. 'The problem is, I have a fatal weakness for powerful women.'

A waiter came over and poured Bollinger into my glass.

I smiled lightly. 'Well, it's lucky you just married one,' I remarked.

'Ouch,' John murmured. His eyes bored into me with the impossibly attractive and knowing smile that had made me fall for him in the first place.

'So,' I said brightly, opening my menu. 'To what do I owe this rather unexpected pleasure? You're not about to resign or anything, are you?'

John looked surprised. 'Of course not! I plan to become a fat cat, Lambert. An enormous hairy tabby with a cigar habit and a Bentley. At present I'm only a slightly overweight farm cat. Long way off.'

I tried to keep a straight face, but it was impossible. 'Oh, John, the tubby farm cat,' I said, laughter spilling out of me. 'Poor you.'

John also failed to keep a straight face. I fancied him most when he became overwhelmed by his own hilarity. 'Yes. Just a feral farm cat still,' he said, chinking my glass. He reached up and loosened his tie a little and, try as I might, I couldn't tear my eyes away from his neck. Damn him.

'No, Lambert,' he said eventually. 'I wanted to have dinner with you tonight because I wanted to have dinner with you. We're far too bloody busy and I miss having you to myself.'

'You've never had me to yourself,' I said, to my fork. I never knew what to do when John stopped being naughty and started being affectionate.

'You know what I mean, Lambert. I miss being able to have lunch with you in the canteen. I was very fond of our lasagne dates,' he added, in a sad voice.

I refused to take the bait. *He's married, he's married, he's married.* 'But we've been planning this launch for ages . . . Of course we're busy. The big moment's arrived!'

John snapped his menu shut. 'Lambert,' he said. 'Stop it.'

'Excuse me?'

'I said, stop it,' he repeated, with that impossible smile. 'I don't want to talk about work.'

I began to panic internally. *What else is there to talk about?* I thought. *I don't have anything to talk about beyond work! I'm dull! He'll be disappointed!*

'OK,' I said, as confidently as I could. I buried myself in the menu and prayed for inspiration.

While we ate a complicated asparagus starter, John quizzed me about Granny Helen. 'I can pull strings, Lambert,' he said earnestly. 'If she needs the best private medical care, I can make that happen.' He looked searchingly at me, perhaps keen that I take him seriously for once.

'Thanks. But she's ninety-one and she's had a stroke. I don't think there's much that anyone can do.'

'I'm sure your father doesn't see it that way,' John said mildly. 'Sounds like the poor chap is devoted to his mother. The offer of help is there, Lambert. You can call me twenty-four hours a day.'

I paused, an asparagus tip halfway to my mouth. 'Thank you,' I said, genuinely touched. I felt a slight shiver. It would be dangerously easy to let John get close to me if that was what he was trying to do. I looked at him: tall, immaculately dressed, unbearably handsome and suddenly quite . . . real. Not the smoothly caricatured Sexy Boss but a person, a normal, decent person with feelings of his own.

Be careful, I reminded myself.

Over main courses the conversation steered towards John. I discovered he had a brother; a fact of which I had been wholly unaware. *Dear God*, I thought. Two naughty MacAllisters roving Scotland? *Lock up your daughters.*

I was just cutting into a piece of turbot, beginning to unwind, when he dropped the bomb. 'You haven't asked me about Susan,' he said.

'I . . . Sorry,' I replied, going instantly crimson. 'Er, how is she?'

'Having an affair,' he announced. 'She left me last week. She's packing up her stuff and flying out to the States this weekend.' He sliced off a piece of fish and chewed, watching my face.

With a huge effort, I managed to look unfazed. 'Oh, John, I'm sorry,' I said calmly. 'Are you OK?'

'Fine,' he said, shrugging and spreading his hands wide. 'Really, I'm fine. She left her rich American husband for this tubby farm cat sitting in front of you and clearly she must have missed the platinum cards she used to have access to . . . because she's now run off with an even richer American.'

I watched him, mute. I hadn't the faintest idea what to say but fortunately he didn't seem to need me to talk. 'It began while we were on our little honeymoon in California, actually,' he said, with a wry smile. 'We were invited to dinner by the owner of a wine estate and she met him there. He's a funny shape, Lambert. Normal except for a huge beach ball shoved under his shirt. I sort of wanted to prick him with a pin to see if his stomach deflated.'

I snorted into my napkin.

'I didn't prick him with a pin, of course. I felt fairly resigned about it. I married Susan because I thought that having a ring on my finger would help me get over you, but it turned out that the ring did not have the desired effect.'

'Is everything OK with your meal?' our waiter asked, appearing suddenly at my elbow. He had the shiniest shoes I'd ever seen, which I stared at as if my life depended on it.

'GREAT!' I screamed. 'AMAZING!' Had John just said that? Had he? It was the sort of thing I'd wanted to hear him say for a very long time but now it was out there I was paralysed.

John, who'd been looking a tiny bit vulnerable for the

first time in our seven years' working together, relaxed and smiled affectionately at me. 'Steady on, old girl,' he murmured.

I looked at him, and then at my lap. My heart was hammering; I was enthralled and terrified by what John would say next.

'I long for you,' he said quietly. 'As much now as I did before I became a married man.'

After a pause, during which I felt both euphoric and disbelieving, I muttered something.

'Sorry?' John said, leaning in.

'I said, you long to sleep with me, John. That's all.'

John laughed. 'Yes, well, that's a given,' he said. 'And you want to sleep with me.' I started to protest but he held up his hand and carried on. 'Sex is irrelevant,' he said thoughtfully. 'You and I have never been just about sex. We're a meeting of minds, Lambert, and you know it.'

I thought about this. I wanted to see us as a meeting of minds; I loved that idea. But were we? We'd never even properly talked! Until a few minutes ago I hadn't even known he had a brother. In a rather unsteady voice, I pointed this out.

John shook his head. 'I'd argue that we avoid "talking", as you call it, Lambert, because it would lead us quickly into dangerous territory. Like this territory right here.'

I didn't know what to say, so I ate a tiny forkful of designer champ. Was he right? I was too shocked by what he was saying to know.

'We *are* a meeting of minds, Lambert. Sorry, I should call you Charley. We're cut from the same cloth. We want the same things and we go after them the same way.'

'But . . . you don't really know me, John. You don't know what my values are, or how much I –'

'Oh, let's not wank on about values. We like to work hard so that we can live well, Charley. End of story. I bet I could describe your kitchen, my dear, because I bet it's the same as mine. I watch you at work and it's like I'm watching myself, only with a better pair of legs. You're me, I'm you.'

I thought back to our first meeting, seven years ago. Me, terrified in a cerise blouse; him, cool as a cucumber in a perfectly pressed white shirt open at the collar.

'I remember that day, too,' John said, watching me. 'I saw how scared you were but I also saw the tremendous strength and courage you have, and that was it. I was gone. I've wanted you every day since then.'

I opened my mouth to say something but nothing came out. 'At least swallow your champ before gaping at me,' John said mildly.

For crying out loud, I told myself. *This is what you've been waiting for for seven long years! Pull your bloody finger out!* But something didn't ring true. I put my cutlery down. 'John, we met more than seven years ago. If this is honestly how you've felt ever since – and I'm not convinced I believe you, by the way – then why are you telling me now?'

'For the same reason you've never done anything about it,' John replied simply. 'I'm a businessman. I'm determined and ambitious. And us being together would cause trouble at Salutech. Bradley Chambers would probably sack the pair of us out of spite. He's always fancied you, the dirty old bastard.'

I batted this away. I did my best to ignore Chambers's slimy advances.

John's face softened. 'There were so many risks attached,' he said. 'And I just wasn't prepared to lose you from my team. You've transformed our public profile. Literally transformed it. You're a miracle.'

I rather loved this but there was still a problem with what he was saying. 'Your feelings can't have been particularly intense if you were happy to put Salutech first, John. People risk their careers all the time for The One.'

I expected a wisecrack, but John nodded pensively. 'I've often asked myself the same thing,' he said. 'Am I insane? Am I a cold, half-dead monster who puts my company before the woman of my dreams?'

I choked slightly.

'Oh, Lambert, no drama,' John said. He was actually beginning to blush. 'The point is, I'm the CEO of this company. All bucks stop with me. The pressure those bastards in Washington put me under is quite intolerable at times and I suppose . . . I suppose I let that get in the way. But you can't sit on your feelings for ever, Charley.' He looked suddenly tired and drained. 'I can't ignore it any more. I'm prepared to risk my job.'

I was dumbstruck. He seemed 100 per cent genuine.

'For the record,' he continued, 'I think about our little sojourn in the broom cupboard every single day. It was glorious, until that bloody granny turned up. Dirty woman.'

In spite of myself, I giggled. 'That granny didn't shove a mop up your arse and force you to start an affair with Susan,' I pointed out. 'You did that all on your own.'

John slammed down his wine glass too fast; a splash escaped over the top and spread silently into the table-cloth. 'Dammit, Charley, I've *told* you why I got together with her. I'd not even sat down to breakfast the next morning when I had Bradley cunting Chambers on my mobile screaming at me about something. It was like he knew I was about to start an affair with the star of the company. So I just grabbed the nearest woman.'

'Star of the company?' I asked, surprised.

John burst out laughing. 'See?' he said. 'See? We're the same! I've just poured my heart out to you and yet the only thing you can hear is that Bradley Chambers calls you the star of the company. We're cut from the same cloth, Charlotte Lambert!'

I looked at him, still uncertain. I so wanted to believe him. Trust him. Get close to him. The longer I'd spent back in the saddle at Salutech, the more him-and-me had started to make sense again. But I didn't have one more broken heart in me. I had to know he was serious. And I certainly needed to be sure that his marriage was over.

A ringing sound was coming from my handbag. I scrabbled round for my phone, mortified. 'Bugger, sorry, John . . .'

John smiled. 'Be my guest,' he said. 'Answer it!'

So I did, just like I did everything else John told me to do.

'HELLO?' I probably sounded like Shelley.

'Er, Chas?'

It was Sam. Dammit! Why had I answered the phone?

I shimmied out from under the table and strode off towards the bar. 'I can't really talk, I –'

'No problem.' He yawned. 'I'll ask you later.'

'Ask me what?' I could hear him smiling.

'I thought you couldn't talk.'

'Go on.' I was enjoying watching John as he stared across at the Forth, looking impossibly handsome.

'Oh, it's just about William and Shelley. You asked about William's family in the last mail and I wanted to know more about Shelley's family before I replied. Just in case there's any similarities that I can impress her with.'

I watched John top up our champagne glasses. 'The only thing I can think of is that Shelley's brother also works at St Mary's where William works. He's some sort of researcher.'

'OK. Brother . . . researcher . . . St Mary's . . .' Then he stopped. 'Hang on. How do you know William works at St Mary's? I never wrote that!'

I blushed. I knew, of course, because I had stalked William.

'You stalked William, didn't you?' He chuckled. 'Chasmonger!'

I was too embarrassed to speak. Sam was laughing properly now. 'Ha ha! You properly *loved* William!' He giggled. 'You loved *me*, Chas! Ha ha ha!'

I couldn't take any more. 'I'm on a date with John,' I cut in.

Sam stopped laughing. 'Seriously?'

'Yes. I have to go.'

Sam whistled. 'I wondered about that foxy dress. Well, enjoy yourself. And don't let him sleep with you on the first date.'

I smiled. 'Roger.'

'Definitely none of that! You're a fox! Make him wait! And hang on a second. Isn't he married?'

'It seems not. His wife is flying to America this weekend to start a new life with some bloke she met on their honeymoon.'

Sam whistled. 'Mental.'

As I approached the table again I began to feel excited. I was a fox in a foxy dress and the man I'd wanted for seven years was begging me to give him a go. What wasn't to love?

'OK,' I said, as I sat down. 'First, can you prove to me that Susan's left you? I need to be sure about that.'

John watched me for a few seconds and then pulled his phone out of his pocket with a resigned expression.

'Do you want to call her?' he asked. 'Or to read the text message she sent to tell me it was over? Because that's how she ended it. With a text message. Very modern, don't you think? She's already gone, Lambert. She's coming this weekend to get her stuff and then I'll probably never see her again.'

There was little amusement in his tone and I shook my head until he put his phone back into his pocket. Christ, he had finished with Susan. He was single and he wanted me.

'OK,' I continued, less firmly than before. 'I believe what you're telling me about Susan. And, for the record, I'm sorry. But my question is, why now? What's made you change policy about not messing around with a colleague, John MacAllister?'

'I just couldn't take any more,' he said simply. 'My life was beginning to feel smaller and sadder by the day without you in it.'

To my intense embarrassment, I felt my lip wobble. I was strangely moved by this. By John, in fact, who had somehow become smaller. More humble. More human.

'Charley, I've never felt like I did when I watched you sleep in that hospital bed.'

The lip wobbled harder.

'And as soon as I told you I was going to get married, I felt you just shut down.'

'Hardly surprising,' I replied.

John nodded. 'Then when you came back to Salutech you seemed different. As brilliant as ever but your attention was elsewhere. I began to fear you'd met someone.'

You weren't wrong, I thought sadly, remembering the mad excitement of my correspondence with William.

'The thought of you being with someone else was ghastly,' John admitted, looking up in surprise when I burst out laughing. 'What's funny, Lambert?'

' "Ghastly"! That's such a middle-aged word!'

'Well, I'm a middle-aged man. Asking a beautiful younger girl, of whom I am undeserving, if she will give me a chance.'

And there they were. The words I'd dreamed of. In fact, they were *better* than my dream. Never in a thousand years would I have imagined John laying out his heart for inspection on a starched white tablecloth. I'd always just thought that when the moment came – if the moment came – the circumstances would be quite grubby and sordid.

I looked at him, all six foot four of him, and he looked right back at me.

'Charley? Will you give me a chance?'

I picked up my glass and downed my champagne, noticing that my hands were shaking really quite violently. For some reason the word 'yes' had stuck in my throat. What was holding me back?

'Have a think. I'm going to the loo,' John said abruptly. He trailed a tentative finger along my bare shoulder and then all but ran off.

I stared out of the window at the lights twinkling on the Forth. John's *pied à terre* was down there somewhere; he owned a bonded warehouse conversion near the high-end boozers and posh oyster joints around the Water of Leith mouth. I imagined waking up in bed to find him padding up to the bed with a cafetière and some sort of aspirational pastry basket, complicated jazz spilling out of the speakers of his multi-zillion-pound Bang & Olufsen. Being with John was what I'd always wanted. For years I had fantasized about us driving to work together, laughing about office politics, sharing our hopes and fears for Salutech. We would spend weekends in his architecturally significant home on the far side of Loch Lomond. And we could maybe even have that troop of super-talented, multilingual but slightly naughty children I'd dreamed of.

It could all be yours, I thought. *The life you've always wanted. Your perfect job, home, partner, everything.*

But there was one little problem. And having known John as long as I had, I had a feeling that it would be our final stumbling block. Elation suddenly turned to sadness.

He came back and sat down. 'Well?' he ventured, when I remained silent.

I shook my head.

'What do you want?' he asked. 'I'll see a divorce lawyer in the morning. I'll call Bradley Chambers and just tell him we're together. Face the music. Anything, Lambert. Just tell me what you want.'

I stared at him, now truly stumped. This was the trump card. The promise I'd thought he couldn't make. John MacAllister was finally telling me he would do anything to be with me. Risk his job, take on Bradley Chambers.

'And Susan's leaving England this weekend?'

'Susan is leaving this weekend.'

'Um . . . Well, yes!' I heard myself saying. 'Yes! Call me when she's gone and then we'll . . . We . . . Wow! More champagne, John, more champagne!'

Two hours later, happy and drunk, I walked into the lift and leaned against the wall as John directed it to the ground floor. It had been quite an evening.

'I'm excited,' I told him timidly.

John looked at me for a few seconds, then moved over to stand in front of me. 'I'm sorry,' he said conversationally. 'I know we agreed to wait until next week in the interests of decorum but I'm going to have to grab you and ravish you.' And with that he leaned down and kissed me, hard.

For a second I struggled but I knew I had no chance. I kissed him back, running my hands up and down his shirt inside his jacket, pressing against him.

The lift doors suddenly pinged open and we sprang apart, only to find ourselves in an empty corporate vestibule. John straightened his suit jacket and offered me his arm. 'I'm going to walk you two metres round the corner to George Street,' he said, 'where I will flag down a taxi.'

'But I only live on –' I started to argue.

John put a finger over my lips. 'I don't give a monkey's vagina where you live, Charley Lambert. You are coming home with me and that is a direct order.'

'Fuck me . . .' I breathed, staring around me in wonder. John smiled, hanging his blazer on a rusted iron hauling hook.

'I do rather hope to,' he said pleasantly, taking my cardigan off. His hands on my shoulders made me shiver and he dropped an expertly placed kiss on the nerve endings at the bottom of my neck. I breathed in sharply, feeling myself fall apart. I knew I should wait until Susan was at least out of the country and living on her new wine estate but – realistically – the likelihood of that happening was minimal. I was here. John was here. We'd waited seven years.

John's apartment took up the whole top floor of his building and featured three huge walls of plate glass. An exterior balcony ran the entire length of the room, dotted with pieces of beautiful driftwood furniture and rich yellow globes of light hanging down from the edge of the roof. The interior was subtly lit with a combination of larger, red globes and very technical-looking spotlights on tiered racks, plus a few softly glowing globes arranged around the wooden floor. Enormous, slightly worn Inca rugs lay under some very expensive furniture and a pristine black kitchen ran across the bricked wall at the back. Separating it from the room was a long marble breakfast bar, just like mine. I suppressed a grin. John was right about most things, rather annoyingly.

'Where's your bedroom?' I asked suddenly.

'Oh, Lambert, where's the romance?' John asked, a mock-peeved expression on his face.

I grinned. 'I'm interested from a design point of view,' I informed him.

John turned to a metal door. 'In here,' he said, flicking a switch. I gasped – it was magnificent. More globes of light were arranged on the floor. The bed was gigantic and an entire wall was made of glass. I grinned with pleasure. 'Wow.'

And then: 'ARRGH!' The lights had suddenly gone out and an automatic blind was sliding fast down the floor-to-ceiling window. 'John! I can't see! Put the lights on!' I heard an evil giggling from somewhere over my right shoulder. 'Now!'

'Make me,' he breathed, somewhere over my left shoulder.

I felt afraid and excited, not to mention madly aroused. 'Where are you?' I said softly.

A low chuckle, this time somewhere in front of me.

I tingled in ways that were not related to alcohol. 'John . . .' I said. I was breathing rapidly now, almost unable to believe that I was only minutes away from a dirty tryst with John MacAllister. If I figured out where the bastard was hiding.

I screamed as a finger trailed up my ankle and then was whipped away. I grabbed out in the direction I thought he was in, and got nothing but a handful of thin air. Another low chuckle came from what sounded like completely the other side of the room, near the bed.

'John!'

'Lambert, I should tell you I've got the most enormous erection I've ever had. You're going to have to find it and deal with it very quickly.'

I breathed in slowly, enjoying this prospect.

I started to move over to where his voice had come from and heard a rumble of laughter to my left. 'It's not getting any smaller,' he said softly.

I lunged in the direction of his voice but still found nothing. This was excruciating. There was a pulse beating between my legs. 'I can't take much more of this,' I said. 'If you don't come and find me, John MacAllister, I'm going to take my clothes off and make myself come and you won't be invited.'

I heard a soft groan, very near me now. 'I would like that very, very much . . . but I'd have to watch, Lambert. And my dratted night-vision goggles went missing.'

I began to shake with laughter. 'You're a mad pervert! Damn you, scampering around with your massive erection, torturing me. I'm getting naked!' I unzipped the Stella McCartney, which fell to the floor with a soft, clothy thump.

'Oh, good God,' John muttered, from what sounded like just in front of me. 'Charlotte Lambert is shedding her clothes in my bedroom.'

I took my bra and knickers off and stood there, feeling my whole body pulsating. 'Correct,' I told him. 'Naked and very, very ready.'

I screamed again as a hand reached out from nowhere and grazed past my nipples. 'Bullseye,' John murmured, his breath sounding raggedy. I made a sudden lunge to my right and then I had him.

My hand closed around his arm and I swung myself over, clamping my body against his. He slid his hands up into my hair, tilted my head back and kissed me very, very hard. We both gasped as he slid his erection along the gap between the top of my thighs. It was, as promised, pretty enormous. It grazed my clitoris as he moved, kissing my neck and shoulders. I held on to his torso for all I was worth and he moved himself against me, still kissing me hard. I slid my hand down his back and grabbed his rewardingly muscular backside, pulling him in.

'Lambert, I . . .' he muttered hoarsely '. . . I don't know what to do. I want to taste you, I want to be inside you, I want to see you, I want to feel that wonderful mouth of yours around my cock . . .'

'Right,' I said, digging my hands up through his hair. I pushed him downwards on to what felt like a very expensive hide rug beneath us. 'I suggest we try all of the above in that order. Item one on your agenda: tasting me.'

I lay back against the end of the bed as John kissed his way down my chest and stomach and arrived between my legs. At first, he just breathed hot breath on me, until I was writhing and begging. A slightly unwelcome memory of Hailey popped into my head, of her eyes sparkling as she said, 'I bet he'd just make you *scream* in bed!'

As John's tongue finally made firm contact with me, and his fingers slid into places where I'd never expected John MacAllister's fingers to be, I started to do just that. 'Oh, GOD!' I shrieked. 'John!'

Chapter Thirteen

'I don't know what you find so funny, Lambert,' John said. He was wearing his favourite peeved expression, a mixture of furrowed brow and wickedly twinkling eye.

I pulled a section of pricey feather duvet over my face but carried on laughing. 'It's just –' I broke off, laughing even harder.

John looked down at his naked body. 'Are you laughing at my physique?' he asked. 'Because really, Lambert, I don't see anything to laugh at here.'

'No!' I giggled. 'It's just . . . It's just that when you ran off to the loo in the restaurant last night I was looking down at Leith and imagining spending the night with you and this is exactly how the day started! You padding towards me with a wanky cafetière and a basket full of aspirational pastries!'

John grinned. 'You're every bit as much of a wanker as I am,' he said. 'I ordered these at great expense to impress you. The least you could do would be to eat one and shut up. There's even a brown one made of horrible health-food things in case you decide to be difficult,' he added.

'They're lovely,' I replied. 'And you're naughty, assuming that I'd come home with you.' John smiled and got into bed next to me.

'Well, of course you were going to come.' He grinned,

leaning down to kiss my left nipple. 'You've waited seven years, Lambert.'

As we shot through the early-morning streets of Leith twenty-five minutes later, BBC Gaelic gabbling away softly in the background and smatterings of rain driving into John's windscreen, I began to sober up mentally.

I turned my head and watched him driving. He looked strong, relaxed and undeniably happy. 'Stop perving at me, Lambert,' he said, without glancing round.

'I thought you'd ditched Lambert in favour of Charley,' I said, 'as part of your attempt to convey the depth of your sincerity about us.'

'I'll call you Charley if you want,' he said, placing a large warm hand on my thigh.

'We have to be really, really careful,' I said quietly.

John turned the radio off and the sound of the rain hitting the windscreen increased. 'I know. At a time like this . . . I'm sure you won't be discussing it with anyone.'

'Most certainly not,' I said. Someone who looked very much like Hailey was jogging across the road ahead of us at the traffic lights. I leaned forward, rubbing the windscreen with my sleeve, but the rain was too heavy for me to be sure. Hailey didn't run anyway. In Leith or anywhere. I settled back and tried to come to terms with the enormity of what had happened. Oh, my God! Arrgh!

Fifteen minutes later I was sitting at my desk, eyes down, convinced that everyone knew what John had done to me that morning after I'd eaten the 'horrible' wholegrain pastry. The memory of it both delighted and terrified me. John was right: we'd both be dead if Bradley Chambers found out.

I turned my chair to the window to take a deep breath and compose myself. Tomorrow was the launch day for Simitol and tonight we were all flying to London, ready for a day of press interviews. It was the biggest day of my career: I simply couldn't have a head spinning with mad thoughts – indeed with anything that didn't involve Salutech.

I felt rather irritated when, a few minutes later, an email entitled 'William/Shelley' dropped into my inbox from Sam.

> Good morning, you dirty woman, I thought we agreed there was to be no rogering your boss last night? Anyway, I know you're up against it today but any chance you could reply to William's email? I really think we need to keep these two simmering: they both seem to go mad when there's any gap in communications. Sorry to ask but knowing you it'll only take twenty seconds. Have a good day. Bowes, Acting Director, First Date Aid X.

'Piss OFF, William and Shelley,' I muttered, under my breath. 'I'm busy!'

But I had never been good at saying no to people when they asked me to do things. As fast as I could, I opened up Shelley's email and read Sam's latest offering. As usual he'd done a good job and – as planned – 'William' was now asking about Shelley's family.

Without fully realizing what I was doing, I went a little off-piste with my response.

My family . . . well, my father is credited with having invented vibrating anal eggs. He now runs a naturist resort in Ibiza. My mother is an art thief and was last seen skulking in a bush outside Drumlanrig Castle in 2003. The world's press reported the theft of Leonardo's *Madonna of the Yarnwinder* the next day and I haven't heard from her since. But a large sum of money is deposited anonymously into my bank account annually so she must be alive. Oh, and my brother is having an affair with the milkman. Pedestrian stuff.

Bugger, work calls. I'd better go. Thank God I'm leaving tomorrow. And I just cannot believe we're seeing *The Pearl Fishers*, you have no idea how much this means to me. It is the best second date ever.

Shelley x

John walked past the glass walls of the comms office, throwing a gigantic grin in my direction. *Oh, fuck it*, I thought happily, adding a whole row of kisses.

As I closed down Shelley's email and got to work, an instant message pinged onto my screen.

MacAllister, John: I know we have to be careful

MacAllister, John: BUT

MacAllister, John: Dear GOD Lambert! I cannot stop smiling.

MacAllister, John: You have the most divine body I have ever had the pleasure of servicing.

MacAllister, John: I am a walking erection today.

I blushed deeply, checking over my computer to see if anyone was watching me. Then I put my head down and worked. John having fallen into place somehow helped me shut out everything else and concentrate solely on tomorrow's launch. I worked without stopping until eight p.m. when a car arrived to take me to the airport. All the boxes were ticked, the people briefed, the problems ironed out. By the time we took off, I knew we were ready.

Maybe I'm getting another crack at a perfect life, I thought, as our plane banked down into the glittering light maze of London. I was truly back on top of work; Margot had somehow faded away; the madness of my William phase had vanished. John wanted to start a life with me; Sam was running my brilliant little business for me; and, even though Granny Helen was ill, my family were still as close and loving as ever.

I wasn't really sure what I wanted beyond this.

Three hours later, wrapped in a combination of luxurious sheets and a slumbering John, I decided I *didn't* want anything else. Which must surely mean that I had arrived. Perfection.

The next day was caffeinated, stressful and difficult. Unlike just about every other pharmaceutical company in the UK, we did not have our offices out near Heathrow so we couldn't very easily invite the press to come to us. Today we were running around between various media studios in the morning and giving interviews at Claridges in the afternoon. A mini press launch had been organized at the last minute and was taking place at the end of the day. This didn't happen for drug launches any more. Today was big. The pressure was on.

But I had an answer and a back-up plan for every problem and was able to face off every glitch before it could hurt us. Sporadically, I would catch John watching me proudly and feel a warm, rather naughty glow. Last night had been even more spectacular than Wednesday. John's fascination with my body gave me a confidence I'd never realized I had. 'Dear God, Lambert,' he'd gasped at one point. 'You've set my testicles on fire, young lady! *Why did we wait so long for this?*'

I'd had four orgasms between one and three o'clock this morning. It was an all-time personal best.

In the lobby at Broadcasting House we bumped into Margot and the leader of a patient group, fresh from an interview with Radio 2. 'Went absolutely brilliantly,' Margot told us happily. 'No problems at *all*.' She smiled warmly at me and I shuddered. I still didn't trust her.

We agreed to share a taxi to Shepherd's Bush where we would split up to cover various BBC assignments. John sat between Margot and me in the back of the taxi, two of our researchers chattering away on the fold-down seats. His thigh was pressed firmly against mine. I tingled all over with excitement. At last, at last, at last!

As we passed through Notting Hill, I pulled out my phone to listen to my backlog of voicemails. There were five messages from the media, two from Cassie and one, rather annoyingly, from Sam. 'Hey, Chas, hope it's going well. I had a message from a new client last night asking you to call her urgently. She insisted on talking to a woman . . . She didn't give her name but here's her number . . .'

Not without irritation, I copied the number down as my phone started to ring again.

'Charley Lambert?' I answered.

'Hi, Charley, it's Cassie. The *Mail* wondered if someone could do a phone chat later today. Here's the number. The journalist is on a mobile.'

I scribbled it down and gave John an unobtrusive pinch on the bottom. He responded with a schoolmasterly shake of his head and a look that made me feel even naughtier.

Stop flirting and get back to the Mail, I told myself sternly.

I dialled the journalist's number and leaned my head against the taxi window while it connected.

'Hello?' a woman's voice answered. Margot was talking to someone on her phone too and I covered my ear to drown her out.

'Hi, it's Charley Lambert, you wanted me to call about the piece in the *Mail*?'

There was a pause.

'I beg your pardon?' the woman said. She sounded oddly familiar; I wondered if I'd spoken to her before. 'What's going on?'

'Er . . .' I stopped, confused. Oh, *shit*, I thought suddenly. I pulled my book back out and realized I'd made a fairly substantial error: I'd called the new First Date Aid client rather than the *Mail* journalist.

I lowered my voice to something barely more audible than a whisper. 'I'm so sorry,' I said. 'I got my businesses a little mixed up. It's Charlotte from First Date Aid. I was given a message to call you. Although actually now isn't a great time to –'

'*What?*' the woman said.

'*What?*' Margot barked into her phone.

260

And then my heart stopped. Slowly, I looked up from my phone call, just as Margot looked up from hers. I looked at my phone screen, which said, *Margot: active call.*

'I'll have to leave you here. The rest of Wood Lane's closed,' the taxi driver said.

Margot stared at me and fear rolled in.

It was Margot who'd contacted First Date Aid. And it was Margot I'd called back.

In a state of shock I got out of the taxi and stood on the pavement outside Wood Lane tube, frozen. John followed me, digging out his own phone, which was ringing. 'Two minutes,' he said, walking a little way up the road. The researchers were deep in conversation, leaving me with Margot, who was emerging from the taxi with a face of pure evil.

She walked up to me with a glint in her eye. 'I might have known it,' she said softly. 'With an ego like yours . . . Of course you'd set up a pathetic little business on the side. One big job not enough for you, eh, Charley?'

'What are you talking about?' I faltered.

'Shut up, Charley. Don't you *dare* patronize me now.' The eerie smile Margot had worn for the last week had gone. In its place was someone who terrified me. If she told anyone about this, I would be in more than a compromising position. I'd be totally rogered.

'Well, this is a nice little surprise,' she remarked, folding her arms. 'There I am, innocently seeking some help with my love life – because I'm humble, unlike you, Charley. I *know* there're some things I'm not so good at – and look what I found.'

'Please don't do this,' I said quietly. 'I don't even work

on the company any more. I handed it over to a friend . . . Can we not just let it go?'

Margot started to laugh again. 'Oh, no, Charley, I'm afraid we can't. After all, you're a stickler for putting Salutech first, aren't you? Isn't it you who likes the communications department to be run with one hundred per cent dedication? Eh?'

I gaped at her.

Margot folded her arms across her chest. 'So. The press conference later,' she continued. '*I* should run it. I don't think you're in a position to be representing the company on such an important day.'

I shook my head dumbly. 'No,' I began. 'No, Margot, you know I can't –'

She held up a hand. 'Oh, but you can, Charley. Because not only do I now have proof that you're not giving Salutech your full attention, but I also have proof that . . .'

She stopped talking as John arrived. 'Right, ladies, time to go.' He strode off ahead with the researchers, throwing me a fleeting smile.

Margot snorted derisively. 'That's the second thing for which I have proof,' she said lightly.

'What?' I asked.

'Your affair with John,' she explained, as if talking a child through an arithmetic problem. I stopped walking.

'You slept with him finally on Wednesday night after your "business meeting" in town. Now, Charley, I'm not sure that's a sackable offence but we both know Bradley Chambers in Washington has a soft spot for you. And we both know he'd be none too pleased if he found out that John was fucking you.'

My phone started to ring. 'Sorry, Charley, but there's problems with Sky News,' Cassie said. 'Can you call them?'

'OK,' I said dully. 'I'll see what I can do.'

'Thanks. And I'm afraid that animal-rights group launched a huge viral campaign against us this morning. I need you to get online ASAP.'

'Right,' I said. 'Will do.' I ended the call and felt my precious world crumbling around me once again.

I had not made it. Nothing was perfect. Last night's euphoria felt suddenly absurd and embarrassing, a pathetic little self-indulgent celebration. Margot despised me and now had me in her power and, depending on how evil she was feeling, I could lose Salutech, John and even First Date Aid by the end of today. There would be no mercy.

'OK, take the press conference,' I said desperately. We were nearing the entrance to Television Centre, a place that normally filled me with excitement but now filled me with despair. Would this placate her for now?

She smiled politely. 'I also want to do all major interviews. And the round-up video conference with Washington at the end of the day.' I stared at her. 'I want your job,' she explained kindly. 'And I'll get your job. But I won't get it by behaving like a whore around John MacAllister. I'll get it because now you're going to get the fuck out of my way and let me demonstrate how well I can do it.'

'OK?' she added, when I failed to respond.

I looked ahead at John and the researchers, marching into Reception full of excitement and bravado. Our best patient advocate, who'd been waiting on a sofa, jumped up and shook their hands warmly. Everyone was laughing and smiling.

This was their day, not mine. 'John,' I called. He turned round.

'Be very fucking careful,' Margot whispered, her plastic smile unmoving. We walked into Reception together.

'John, I, er, feel very faint. I don't know what's wrong with me. I'm going to have to hand over to Margot for the next hour or so,' I said. I sat down sharply on a coloured bench, realizing that, as far as the nearly fainting bit went, I was actually telling the truth. 'I'll come and find you when I feel better,' I added weakly.

'Lambert?' John said, crouching in front of me. 'What's wrong? Shall I get a doctor?'

Out of the corner of my eye I saw Margot scowling. 'No, no,' I said. 'I'll be fine. Probably just all that caffeine on an empty stomach. Margot'll look after it.'

John looked over his shoulder at Margot, who flashed him her most capable, businesslike smile. He looked back at me. 'OK,' he said eventually. As he strode off into the bowels of Television Centre with Margot, he glanced back, confused and concerned.

I slumped on my bench and despaired.

An hour later, having responded to all the messages on my BlackBerry, I signed in to go and find something to eat in the canteen. 'She can't do this,' I muttered to myself, as I gnawed listlessly at a starchy bagel. *Oh, but she can*, my head replied quickly. *She's got enough on you to have your desk cleared in twenty minutes.*

Hailey, I thought. Hailey was my first port of call during a crisis. But as soon as she picked up the phone I knew it was a mistake: for whatever reason she'd gone back to being weird and slightly distant. 'Just tell Margot to shove her BlackBerry up her arse,' she said distractedly.

I was on my own.

I sat down again on the bench just as Margot swept into Reception, chatting and laughing with John and the others. She swung a BBC pass between her fingers and I was rigid with fear once more. I stood up and straightened my suit jacket nervously as John led me away from the group.

'Are you better, Lambert?' he asked, genuinely concerned. But as I tried to formulate the response, Margot arrived at his side.

'The press interviews start at Claridges in twenty-five minutes,' she said. 'Our car's waiting. We have to go.'

'I'll come when I'm ready,' John said, not breaking eye contact with me. Then the chief researcher plucked at his sleeve and John had to turn away, leaving me with Margot.

'One email to Bradley Chambers telling him where your attention's been recently,' Margot whispered brightly to me. 'Just one, that's all I need. I think it'd be best if you throw the towel in for today, Charley.'

John turned back to us. 'Well, Charley? Are you OK?'

I hung my head. 'No,' I said. 'I . . . need to go back to the hotel, I think. I'm so sorry.'

There was a stunned silence. 'But,' John began, 'we have the *press conference* in two hours. I – Charley, we need you!' His eyes searched mine for the usual spark, for the die-hard director of comms who was always ready for battle, but he found nothing.

He walked me over to the bench and made me sit down. His thumb moved over my forearm gently. 'Lambert?'

I had no more fight in me. Tears were sliding out of my eyes; the sight clearly stunned him.

'Oh, my God,' he said. 'You really are sick.'

I nodded, not even trusting myself to speak. 'Go on,' I whispered. 'Go get 'em. Margot's got it covered. She'll do a grand job.'

Chapter Fourteen

I woke up the next morning with no idea what day of the week it was and, for a few blissful seconds, I existed in a pleasant no man's land: no blackmail, no fear, no shame.

But it didn't take long for it all to come flooding back. I felt my whole body tense as I relived yesterday. Every awful moment, from that phone call to Margot through to my early flight back to Edinburgh. *What would Margot do next?* However I tried to talk it up in my head, the fact of the matter was that I had plummeted from senior director to sitting duck in a mere twenty-four hours. I was entirely at her mercy.

John had emailed late last night to say that everyone at the press conference was disappointed that I was ill. Margot had done 'a reasonable job' but he had rejected her plans to do the round-up chat with Bradley Chambers in Washington, opting instead to do it himself. I wasn't surprised: John let very few people near the super-holy Chambers. *PS*, he wrote. *I struggled to think about anything today beyond the sight of you wrapped around me like a smooth peachy monkey. I am enthralled by you, Lambert. Enslaved. Enchanted. X*

I managed a grim smile. At least I had the boss onside.

But the smile faded as soon as I remembered that that was part of the problem. And if John found out I'd been running a business he'd probably despatch me quicker than you could say 'smooth peachy monkey'.

My thoughts were interrupted by the sound of a bass-baritone voice starting up in the shower with a rousing chorus of (rather surprisingly) 'Onward Christian Soldiers'. I couldn't help but grin. Apart from that girl last weekend – who appeared to have been a one-off – Sam had changed beyond all recognition. Gone was the slob I'd lived with for so many years and in his place was a hard-working, confident and inspiring chap, who was shaving regularly, remembering to put the bins out and making some quite outstanding middle-class salads.

The shower stopped and with it Sam's singing, much to my disappointment. 'CHAS?' he yelled, exiting the bathroom and marching into the kitchen. 'You awake yet? I'm making breakfast!'

'Hello, weird-healthy-morning Bowes,' I said, shuffling into the kitchen a few minutes later.

Sam was getting fresh berries and some very posh yoghurt out of the fridge. 'Organic,' he announced casually.

I signalled my approval and sat down at the breakfast bar. He served me fruit and yoghurt and then got some amazing granola out of a glass jar. 'Coffee? I've got some lovely Colombian.'

I put my spoon down. I couldn't take any more of this. 'Sam, what has *happened* to you?'

He laughed. 'I feel great, that's what's happened!'

I watched him as he bustled round the kitchen with bowls of healthy fayre. 'I've *loved* the last week, getting stuck in to our company. It's going so well, Chas, and I think we could make it really big . . .' He trailed off, sticking some yoghurt into his mouth. 'Isn't life *great*?' he asked happily.

And without further ado I burst into tears.

'Urgh,' was Sam's response to my tales of woe. 'Messy.'

I nodded miserably and Sam covered my hand for a moment. 'Don't beat yourself up,' he said. 'I know what you're like. There *will* be a solution.'

'What, though? Even if I'd managed to remove my name from the First Date Aid website after handing it over to you – which I didn't – she knows that I've been sleeping with John.'

Sam winced. 'Well, it's not great. But you're not actually breaking your contract doing either of those things, are you?'

'Oh, come on, Bowes! You know what Salutech's like!'

There was an uncomfortable silence.

'Maybe just try to forget about it for today, brother,' he said uncertainly. 'See how it all pans out on Monday.'

I stared morosely into my granola. Sam was useless in difficult situations. Why couldn't he *talk* to me? Like, really talk, the way he did as William?

'How's about we cheer you up by calling William or Shelley to find out how the big date went?' he said. 'It was last night!'

After a pause I shrugged. I'd give anything a try. I got out my phone so that we could call Shelley first.

'CHARLOTTE!' Shelley hissed. 'I'M IN HIS BED-ROOM! HE'S MAKING KIPPERS!'

I smiled, in spite of myself. 'It went well, then?'

'YESSSSS. THE OPERA WAS BEAUTIFUL. THEN HE GOT ME DRUNK AND I . . . OOPS!'

Sam started laughing and had to put his hand over his mouth. I was grateful to Shelley for bringing comedy into my doom-filled morning.

'I'm so pleased,' I told her. 'I'll leave you to your breakfast. Enjoy!'

'WOULD YOU LIKE A TESTIMONIAL FOR YOUR WEBSITE? I OWE YOU SO MUCH, CHARLOTTE.'

Sam nodded voraciously.

'Actually, yes. That would be great.'

'I'LL EMAIL IT TODAY. I CANNOT BELIEVE IT, CHARLOTTE, I WAS WEARING A DRESS THAT MADE ME LOOK REALLY FLAT-CHESTED BUT HE STILL SEEMED TO BE ATTRACTED TO ME!' she hissed.

'Went amazingly,' William whispered, a few minutes later. We heard him pull the grill out to inspect the kippers. 'She was wearing a stunning dress, Sam – made her cleave look bloody enormous!'

I shook my head despairingly.

'Bonza.' Sam chuckled. 'So, what next?'

'Well, mate, I was hoping you'd have some ideas. Is it OK to ask her round here for dinner?'

Sam looked surprised. 'Of course! Nothing'd feel quite so special as having dinner cooked for me by someone I cared about.'

I, too, was surprised. I hadn't expected to hear Sam say something like that. I'd thought his ideal date would be a naked sumo wrestle for two on his bed.

'OK . . .' William mused.

'So, William, happy with services rendered?' Sam had switched back to the new work voice I'd been hearing recently.

'Couldn't be happier, mate,' William said. 'Thank you.'

'Well, feel free to email me a testimonial for the website. Just first name, obviously.'

'You know what? I'll do that,' William whispered. He started rattling cutlery around.

'I'll let you get back to your kippers,' Sam said. 'Enjoy your morning. Cheers!' He hung up and gave me a victory salute.

I didn't return it. 'Bowes, not again!'

Sam looked blankly at me. 'What?'

'Kippers! He didn't tell you he was doing kippers, you twat!'

Sam was crestfallen. 'I'm not very good at this, am I?' he muttered.

Why, on top of all of my many other faults, was I horrible too? WHY?

'Don't be silly,' I said, chastened. 'You're amazing at it. Better than me, even,' I added. I meant it as well.

'Nonsense.' Sam suddenly put his coffee down and, without warning, marched over and pulled me into a hug. I sat like a lump of wood, a bit stunned. Sam and I didn't hug much. 'Thank you,' he said.

I was confused. 'For what?'

He pulled away. 'For getting my arse into gear. I know you were pretending to be Shelley at the time but whatever. Thanks to your emails I've . . . um, come out of a coma.' He moved back to his seat, looking embarrassed.

I blushed. I loved the idea of having had this effect on someone's life. Particularly Sam's, which had always seemed so full of potential and yet so wasted.

The ensuing silence was broken by the doorbell. Sam jumped up. 'Aha! I invited Ness and Hailey round for brunch,' he explained, buzzing them in. 'You've been so damned busy since you went back to Salutech I thought you could do with some bruvvahood.'

I felt a big swell of gratitude. Sam was right. Throwing myself into work had definitely made me feel sane and in control again (Margot and her blackmail excepted) but there had been a notable deficit in normal human company. Sam was so very thoughtful these days. If only we –

I cut myself short. If only we nothing.

Hailey had brought about ten thousand sausages and was looking rather unlike herself in a floaty floral dress. Given that she had been wearing tight-fitting slutty ensembles since long before I met her, I wondered if this meant Matty had tried his hand at buying her clothes. 'These are the best sausages you will ever eat,' she announced. 'I had six yesterday. Don't judge me until you've tried them,' she added. Ness, who was the sort of annoying person who probably only ate half a sausage a year, laughed nervously. She had brought fruit.

Hailey swept Sam to one side and took over the kitchen. 'Bowes, this is not your place,' she informed him. She rolled a good fifteen or so sausages into the grill pan and got a gigantic loaf of bread out of her bag. She started slicing it and spreading it thickly with butter, barking commands to Ness, who was apparently her sous-chef. Watching her, I couldn't help but notice how ironic it was that *I* was the one with the reputation for being a hard-nosed businesswoman yet I had only a scrap of her self-confidence. I had had to fire just two people in the course of my career and both times had cried in the toilet afterwards; Hailey despatched naughty chefs and skiving waiters as calmly as Sam flicked off bogies.

As Hailey bossed Ness around, my thoughts drifted back to Salutech and I began to wonder if this was the way Margot would start treating me in the office. Margot was as bullish as Hailey but with none of the wit, charm or empathy that made Hailey such a likeable girl to be around. I shuddered. That seahorse had wanted to wipe the floor with me from the moment she'd arrived in our office. I'd long since stopped trying to work out why. But wipe the floor with me she could now, unless I came up with something really clever and brilliant in the next forty-eight hours. It was a grim prospect.

'Are you portioning for dwarfs?' Hailey asked Ness, who was chopping fruit into bowls.

Ness giggled. 'Sorry. I'm used to Sarah. She eats almost nothing,' she said. It was true: Sarah was even tinier than Ness. (Granny Helen had named them 'the lesbian pixies of Edinburgh' the first time Sarah had been introduced to her. Fortunately Sarah had found this funny.)

Hailey snorted, tipped two of Ness's fruit salads into one bowl and presented it to Ness. 'This is a real portion,' she announced. 'Unlike you, Ness, I have a hale and hearty man to feed. Please take note.'

The dynamics in Hailey's household must be hilarious. I could only imagine how meal preparation would look: Hailey throwing gigantic meals together with noise and smut while Matty opened tins with a laser-beam sword. 'How are things with Matty?' I asked her.

Hailey didn't turn round. 'Really good,' she said slowly. 'Really, really good. I actually think . . .' She trailed off.

'What?' Ness asked.

'I think we could be heading for dud duh-duh-duhhhh, duh duh duh-duh.' I nearly passed out.

Sam, who was less talented at the art of diplomacy than the rest of us, gaped. 'YOU?' he gasped. '*Married?*'

Hailey shot him a finger. 'No one could be less suited to marriage than you, Bowes,' she informed him. 'Imagine what it was like for us when you pulled that one out of the bag!'

A fleeting moment of pain shot across Sam's face and I felt suddenly protective. 'Leave him alone, Tits,' I said to her.

Sam waved me away. 'Ack, she's right,' he insisted. 'But seriously, Hailey. Engaged soon? Have you been talking about it together?'

Hailey turned away, smiling enigmatically, and as she did so her floaty dress caught on the side of her belly, which seemed to be rather rounder than normal.

Oh, my God, I thought. *She's pregnant!* I clutched the side of my chair for support. Sam getting engaged – admittedly not for long – and now Hailey getting PREGNANT? I couldn't take much more of this! Sam, Hailey and I had all been single for ever!

Sam was interrogating Hailey about her possible engagement (Matty had been spied in a jeweller's in Stockbridge apparently) and I tried to reconcile myself to the idea of her having a baby. It seemed too fantastical and mad for me to get excited. *Hailey a mother?* How had we got so old? Would the same thing happen to me soon?

My thoughts turned quickly to John. The range of feelings attached to our 'relationship' – if I could call it a relationship yet – was bewildering. Above everything else, of course, I was ecstatic to be here after all these years. Kissing him was a knee-trembling affair and his naughty messages left me dizzy and girlish; it was almost impossible to keep him at arm's length at work. I wanted to beat my chest and screech that he was *mine*! But it was still mortifying that – even though Susan had left *him* – I was basically shagging a man who'd been single for twenty seconds.

But there was no such thing as a perfect relationship, I reminded myself. I slid my phone out of my dressing-gown pocket and re-read the message he'd sent me this morning: *She's moving her stuff out now and soon I will be entirely yours, Charlotte Lambert. Please remove clothes in preparation.* X

I smiled. I still couldn't believe this was happening.

'Chas?' Hailey barked. I looked up. She was putting the sausages between the slices of bread without even halving them.

'Yes?'

'What's this?'

Sam slunk over to the fridge to get his ketchup, looking like a guilty dog.

'Bowes tells us you went on a date with John,' Hailey said, her eyes narrowing. 'This true?'

I braced myself. Already I could feel her energy change. I didn't want another lecture: I felt shitty enough. 'Yes,' I said. It just popped out; I couldn't help myself. A big, warm guilty grin stretched across my face. 'And, before you give me a hard time, I'm not just being a slag. He's left his wife and he wants to be with me. Permanently.'

Three amazed faces stared across the mound of sausage sandwiches at me. 'Seriously?' Ness asked. She looked alarmed.

'Yes, seriously,' I said, slightly hurt. For the last seven years my friends had actively encouraged flirtation with John. *They'd better not change their tune now*, I thought. This was my time. My man. I'd waited half a lifetime and finally he'd arrived in my lap. I wasn't taking any shit.

Hailey opened her mouth, probably to trumpet some righteous stuff about it being far too soon, but Ness broke in: 'Whoopeee!' she shouted, running over and jumping on me. 'At last! At long last!'

Sam looked amazed for a few more seconds but then scampered over and made it a three-way hug. 'That's fucking magic, Chas!' he said. 'You waited long enough, brother.' He pinched me on the cheek as if he were in some Cockney drama. Hailey had her hands on her hips.

'Stop it,' I said to her. 'He's felt the same way as me for seven years. He should never have married Susan in the first place and he knows that. If you'd heard what he said, you'd be pleased for me,' I added.

Hailey seemed unconvinced. 'Well, if you're sure,' she said.

I nodded. 'Very.'

Something must have cleared in Hailey's head because she picked up a sausage sandwich and toasted me with it. More modestly than Ness and Sam, but it was definitely a vote of confidence. 'Well, cheers, Chas. To you and John.

Wowzers! Now, tell me. How are things in the bedroom department? Oh, my God, does he make you scream?' Ness blanched and Sam fled to the bathroom. I started laughing and began to fill her in. For the first time in the last twenty-four hours, I was feeling a bit perky. *Maybe there will be a way around all this mess*, I thought hopefully. After all, I wasn't a bad person. I was just doing my best in what had turned out to be a fairly imperfect life.

Morning turned into afternoon and the sky cleared as we sat around my living room, eating and chatting. Ness had had us in stitches with tales of a mad playwright she was developing a script with: he had turned up at the theatre dressed as a woman in the hope that Ness would 'renounce her lesbian ways' and love him. She wasn't even sure that it had been a joke: he had now written an opera and four poems dedicated to her. Sam, meanwhile, had been showing off our sparkly new website and was now wetting himself over the testimonials William and Shelley had written. Shelley had produced a hilarious polemic and William had come up with an uncharacteristically hyperbolic review of Sam's emailing skills. 'Those two!' He chortled. 'Bet they were sitting side by side writing these on their BlackBerrys without the faintest idea!'

'Should we put both recommendations up?' I asked him. 'It would be such a shame if they saw each other's names up there and realized what had happened.'

'Shame? It'd be fucking hilarious, Chas!' He giggled. 'And William and Shelley aren't exactly unusual names.'

We eventually uploaded both comments, agreeing that if they were serious about each other they'd have to come clean about their ghost-writers eventually. We toasted tea mugs happily. 'To our bloody BRILLIANT little business, Chas!' Sam beamed. He was flushed and excitable.

'*Your* business,' I prompted, not without sadness.

Hailey, meanwhile, was emerging from the bathroom with a very red face. 'Phone sex?' Sam asked her. She went even redder.

Sam looked amused. 'Was it violent?'

'Eh?'

'Well, you don't look post-orgasm,' he said.

Hailey batted him off. 'Mind your own, Bowes.'

An expression of discomfort settled on her face and I knew she needed help.

'So. My job is fucked,' I announced loudly. All heads turned to me and I felt Hailey's gratitude.

As I told Hailey and Ness about my Salutech woes, I felt Hailey relax – although not fully. I hoped everything was OK with this baby. Assuming there was one. I made a mental note to schedule in a night for just the two of us as soon as possible.

Everyone agreed that I would somehow find a way to triumph over Margot. 'You hold that place together,' Ness said earnestly. 'Without you, Salutech would implode and all the scientists would atomize.'

'That's exactly the sort of thing Dad would say, Vanessa Lambert!'

Ness looked pensive. 'Dad's a bit nuts at the moment, Charley. I called yesterday to find out how Granny Helen was doing, and you know what he said? "She's fine, Nessie. Nothing that a good few Scotches and a nice pipe won't sort out." I was like, "Dad, you're a *doctor*!" '

Sam chuckled. 'Your dad really is something else,' he remarked.

I realized that, irrespective of my fears about work, I felt happy. I loved the three people in this room. Whatever was going on elsewhere in my life, I had companionship, laughter and some nice tea today.

My phone began to ring. 'Oh, speak of the devil,' Sam said, handing me my phone. 'Dr Lambert on the line.'

'Daddy!'

There was a silence.

'Dad?'

And then I heard Dad's voice, quiet and uncertain, telling me that Granny Helen had died.

The afternoon turned strange and sad. Autumn sun shifted across the floor as the afternoon progressed and, out of a primal need for comfort and safety, I lit a fire, around which we sat in blankets. Mum had taken over the call eventually, explaining that she and Dad were still at the hospital and that they would prefer it if we came to see them tomorrow.

Ness sat and cried quietly for two hours. Hailey tried to lighten the atmosphere with a succession of wonderful Granny Helen impressions and, when they stopped working, she cooked more sausages. Sam, still not very comfortable with emotions belonging to anyone who wasn't a performing actor, gave me a long, awkward hug before scampering off to the bathroom for 'a long evening soak' even though it was only four o'clock.

I sat mostly in silence, listening to everyone around me. I felt only shock and disbelief; the sadness had not yet reached me. It was impossible that Granny Helen was no longer here. She was the head of our family. The leader of the Lamberts. Leaders didn't just disappear.

Eventually, Ness drifted off to find Sarah, and Hailey had to go home to cook for Matty, who was having to work weekends in the run-up to December when his gardens were to become a Christmas Wonderland.

And then it was just me and Sam. We sat in companionable silence, watching *Finding Nemo* and then *Bridget Jones*, Sam getting up every now and then to put more wood on the fire and to make tea. Twice he received calls from female voices but twice he cut them short and explained that he was with a friend who needed company. Twice I squeezed his hand, grateful to him for not leaving me on my own. He cooked risotto at some point in the evening, and I smiled as I watched the intense concentration in his face as he chopped mushrooms. He was still a child, really, but he was trying. He was changing. He was committed to being better.

At some point during the third film in our DVD marathon Sam drifted off to sleep, curling down sideways into a foetal position on the sofa. And within minutes I was alone again, battling all of the thoughts and fears that a day of company had kept at bay. Shock about Granny Helen, serious worry for Dad and a lingering sense of dread over what this would mean for our family. Fear about Margot combined with spiralling panic about how much work I had to do over the coming weeks. If I had a job at all. Thoughts of John, of how our relationship would work (and why he hadn't yet called me), thoughts of Hailey maybe having a baby and worry for Ness who had been quite inconsolable about Granny Helen. *Tick*

tick tick. My head whirred, exhausting me, and, sick of all the noise, I tried to put a lid on it all.

But the more I tried to squash everything down, the more anxious and upset I felt. What had I actually *done* today? Nothing! Sitting around eating sausages and drinking tea was all very nice but I had achieved bugger-all, which, considering I was at war with Margot, was inexcusable. If I was to have any defence against her I had to be more on top of work than ever before. I began to feel angry and ashamed. Who the hell did I think I was, moaning to my friends about Margot trying to steal my job when I was doing nothing to protect it? We had just launched our biggest ever drug! Why had I not spent the day monitoring the press? Why had I not been calling my colleagues in Europe to find out how they were getting on? Why was I not collating figures and preparing reports?

Because you need a break, a small voice in my head suggested. I batted it down. I could take a break once the campaign was running smoothly and Margot was under control. Careful not to disturb Sam, I reached over the side of the sofa for my satchel, pulled out my laptop and work files and got stuck in. I needed to fight for my job.

'What the arsing hell are you doing?'

I jumped in the air. 'Shit, sorry, Sam, did I wake you up? I'm just catching up with a bit of work.'

'No,' Sam said, pulling himself up. He looked properly annoyed. 'No,' he said, more kindly this time. He plumped a cushion and sat up next to me. 'You've just lost your granny. Give yourself a break. For once.'

I winced. Somewhere deep inside I knew there was

some sense in this, but not as much sense as there was in me working. 'This stuff needs doing before tomorrow,' I said obstinately.

'Tomorrow's Sunday,' Sam said, swinging his legs out on to the floor. Gently but firmly he confiscated my computer and put it on the table. 'And currently it's two fifty-four a.m. No one in the world cares enough about Simitol to need you right now. You've been bereaved, Charley.'

I stared at him as if he'd punched me in the face. *Bereaved.* Now I believed that Granny Helen had died. Out of nowhere I had a vision of her sitting on a chair outside her cottage when Ness and I were five years old, feeding us her home-made plum jam on slices of cheese. 'You are the two bonniest girls this side of the Forth,' she whispered fiercely. 'If anyone tells you otherwise, I'll take my stick to their backside.' I hadn't thought about that day in years, but now the memory was dizzyingly strong; a bittersweet taste of my past now seeded with loss. 'Sam,' I said, tears welling. 'Granny Helen's gone.'

'I'm sorry,' he muttered. 'She was fucking amazing.'

I gulped.

'Will you stop working now?' he asked. 'You need a good cry and then bed.'

A tear fell slowly down my nose. 'I want to work,' I whispered.

Sam sat down slowly on the sofa next to me. I moved my thigh over to accommodate him as another tear squeezed itself out.

'Work is not the answer,' he said uncomfortably. 'To this or to anything.'

I picked at a hangnail on my thumb, hoping he'd stop. I didn't want to hear this now.

'Look, Chas, you *told* me you hide in your work,' he said. I was alarmed. It had been an unspoken rule that we would not quote anything that either of us had said as William and Shelley. I got up and wobbled off towards my bedroom, Sam in hot pursuit. 'You *told* me you couldn't let go,' he persisted. I looked at him as I got into bed. He didn't appear to be enjoying this much but it kept on coming. 'Don't you want to do something about that?'

I knew how happy he had been lately and – just for a fleeting second – it occurred to me that maybe I *did* want to do something. Deep inside I knew that it wasn't healthy to have a job that ruled your life. I knew that it wasn't right to work manically when your grandmother had died. Sam was now working every day yet he had . . . freedom. And a lightness about him that I knew I didn't have.

But the window of possibility soon closed. My situation was the opposite of his. It was all very well for Sam to throw himself into First Date Aid and clean living and auditions and exercise because he fancied a change. But he had started with a baseline of boredom, laziness and low income. He had nothing to lose. I was starting with a baseline of money, achievement and responsibility. I had everything to lose.

So I shook my head. 'My work is too important. I know you can't understand, Sam, but please don't give me a hard time about it. It's essential to me and that's just how it is.'

I pulled the duvet over my head and Sam left my room. I heard him sit down on the sofa and imagined him, chin resting in his hands, trying to work out what to do with me. I hated that thought. *Hated* it.

I resolved to keep my work activities more private from now on. Sam knew too much about me, these days; he had too many opinions on my lifestyle. I didn't like it.

Chapter Fifteen

'Morning, Charley,' Graham from Security shouted as I passed through the gates.

I hadn't been struck off the staff list yet, then.

'Stay calm, stay calm,' I said, under my breath, as I parked. Being at home with my family yesterday had been devastatingly sad, and now I felt even more vulnerable to Margot's hate campaign than I had on Friday. It hadn't helped that John hadn't called me all weekend. According to him, Susan had been moving out on Saturday. So why no call on Sunday? Had she changed her mind? Had *he*?

As I walked into the lift I felt panic and dread ratchet themselves up to the next level. I had no battle plan, no defence, nothing. There was nothing I could do to stop Margot revealing my secret and there was nothing I could do if John had decided that we weren't meant to be. The feeling of powerlessness was quite devastating.

'Morning,' Margot said, marching into my office a few minutes later. She closed the door behind her. 'So, what are your thoughts about the week ahead?'

I studied her nervously. 'What do you mean, what are my thoughts?'

'I'm referring back to our little chat, Charley. But if you need your memory refreshing, here's a recap: I want you out of the way. I want you to stop taking a shit on me so I can show this company what I can do.'

'I have never "taken a shit" on you,' I replied slowly. 'In fact, the only time I've been anything other than supportive of you was when you refused to give my job back.'

'Whatever,' Margot said, looking bored. 'You know what's going to happen if you don't co-operate. I'll call Bradley Chambers and he'll sack you. Sound good?'

I imagined Chambers's call to me after he'd learned of my misdeeds: 'You mean, Sharon, that you've been given the opportunity to control the public face of the UK's largest biotech pharma and you choose to write online love letters instead? I'm sorry, Sharon, I just don't believe it! You're our brightest star!'

But, either way, you're out of the door, would come next.

'What's on your agenda?' I asked Margot, unable to disguise my fear.

She sat down. 'Well, I'd like to take over communicating with the other European offices,' she said. 'I want to be their main liaison.'

I shrugged in as noncommittal a fashion as I could muster. 'Anything else?'

'The doctors' conference next week. I want to do it.'

I breathed out, relieved. This was something that an inexperienced person simply could not run. John would never agree to it.

Margot continued to list jobs that she would never be allowed to do. But she must have read my thoughts because she broke off with a murderous look on her face. 'If you're thinking John'll never let me do these things, Charley, you'd better think again. It's your job to find a way of getting me in on them.'

Fear returned. *She'll stop at nothing. If I don't come up with a plan very bloody quickly I'll be on the dole.* And that prospect – which seemed more real and possible as each minute passed – made me feel quite desperate. Seriously, what would I do if I lost my job? How would it feel to have to stand in front of John and nod meekly when he told me he had no option but to let me go? And how would our relationship ever survive that? It wouldn't. It would be impossible to overcome. My lover, who'd sacked me. No way.

'Right,' I said to Margot, trying to sound decisive and calm. I sounded neither. 'Is that it?'

Margot smiled, sliding her pen into her mouth in a way that I found rather disgusting. 'Actually, no,' she said. 'I was thinking I might just take a free trial of the services on offer at First Date Aid.'

I went cold. 'As I said to you, I don't work on First Date Aid any more. I set it up while I was off sick and now I've handed it over. You'd have to deal with Sam.'

'Oh, but I want *you*, Charley.' She gave a tinkling little laugh, perhaps the most evil noise I'd ever heard. 'Tell you what,' she added conspiratorially. 'There's a man I liked the look of. I'll show you his profile and you can get going, eh?'

'No,' I said obstinately. 'You could use this to frame me. Forget it.'

Margot laughed again, louder this time. 'Oh, Charley, I have enough evidence to frame you a thousand times over. I've got all those disgusting, pathetic messages between you and John, for starters. And in legal proceedings I think you'd struggle to prove that you are not the "Charlotte" whose name is on the website, eh?'

'How did you get my personal messages?'

'I gave Keith from IT a hand job,' she said conversationally. 'Now, if you pull up love.com, I'll find the man in question for you. Shouldn't take long – he's online all the time, he –'

'What? You gave someone a *hand job* for access to my account?'

Margot laughed the toxic laugh again. 'I like sex, Charley,' she said. 'And, what's more, I like it with as many different men as possible. Oh dear, what a pervert, eh? How will uptight Charley Lambert, who probably only gets naked once a year, take orders from someone who actually likes sex? Hey?'

I was absolutely astounded.

'Let's have a look at this chap, then,' Margot said, leaning across me to open up love.com. 'I can write messages to men on adult friend finder in my sleep,' she said, typing in her login details. 'But it's the normals I struggle with, Charley. The boring twats on run-of-the-mill dating sites. People like you.'

I laughed hollowly. I was under the control of a psychopath.

But then Margot's latest object of desire loaded up on the screen and I stopped finding it funny.

Because there, smiling out at me, was Matty. 'Online now!' his profile announced merrily. I felt the world close around me just a bit tighter.

'He looks a bit enthusiastic for me,' she continued. 'I prefer them with a little hint of darkness. But he's dirty. I can spot it a mile off.'

'How?' I whispered incredulously.

'Oh, I've slept with hundreds like him. This guy is the

sort that fucks strangers and then runs off to wifey for his lasagne.'

I felt even sicker. My beloved Hailey . . . who was possibly pregnant. Oh, God.

I needed more information. 'Is he the one you were talking about when you said he's online all the time?'

'Correct. He's always there.'

I wanted to cry.

'Send him a few lines this morning, won't you?' Margot said lightly. 'I'm free on Wednesday night.' And, with that, she swept out of my office.

I stared, trance-like, at my computer. I hadn't the faintest idea what to do. All I could think of was Hailey's ecstatic face when she'd told us she was moving in with Matty. Could Margot ruin my life *and* Hailey's?

Yes, I thought. I put my head into my hands, wishing that I could somehow unplug myself and hibernate for a while.

My bag vibrated and I fished out my phone, grateful for any sort of a distraction from the present.

It was Shelley.

'Hi, Shelley,' I mumbled.

'Ah, hello,' she said. She was not roaring and I knew instantly that something was wrong. It turned out that since she had left William's house on Saturday morning she had not heard from him. 'I don't quite know what to do,' she said uncomfortably. 'I wondered if you had any tips.'

Her voice was loaded with embarrassment and I felt a great empathy. Poor Shelley, so desperate for reassurance that she was prepared to risk the humiliation of calling me. I imagined her in her office, paralysed, unable to concentrate on anything beyond her mobile phone. And, once again, I realized that Shelley Cartwright and I were in the same boat: sitting at our desks, frozen with fear, waiting for something to happen.

'Actually, Shelley, I'm in the same situation,' I said, surprising myself. 'I'm still waiting for a man to call. He should have called me on Saturday night. But call he will, if he's the right man. I've just got to sit it out and not let my life grind to a halt in the meantime.'

I sat back, surprised by my wisdom. Maybe I *would* work as a dating coach if I got booted out of Salutech.

Shelley sounded taken aback. 'Oh, sorry to hear it.' Her attempt at camaraderie was comically gruff. 'I'm sure he'll call you.'

'Likewise, Shelley,' I said gently. 'William really liked you. If I know anything, I know that.'

I heard her breathe out nervously. 'I hope so, Charlotte,' she said. 'I hope so.'

And within seconds of ending the call, I got what I'd been waiting for all weekend: *Lambert. Office. Now. XXX*

The relief was like a deluge. So heavy, in fact, that I began to feel slightly uncomfortable that John had so much power over me. *Oh, come on, it's normal to be in this place*, I told myself, thinking of Shelley. *We're all the same. Mental.*

Before I went to see John I called Sam and asked him to find out why William hadn't called Shelley. For whatever reason, William and Shelley had begun to matter to me rather a lot. But as I swung round the corner towards John's office, I forgot all about them. All I wanted to know at this point was that Susan had now left the country. I wanted talk of futures. Then at least I'd have something good on the boil.

'Ah, Charley, good morning,' John said, in a business voice. The door was in the process of closing behind me and his PA Becky would be able to hear everything we said until it shut. Until the catch clicked behind me I couldn't even look at him.

'She's gone,' he said quietly. 'And divorce proceedings are well under way. I'm yours, Lambert. Yours to do with what you will.

'It's true!' he continued, when I found myself dumb. 'I've been thinking about you all weekend, Lambert. Barely been able to stop wanking,' he added, as if commenting on the weather.

I tried not to grin but it happened anyway. 'Why didn't you call me, then?' I asked, immediately hating myself. I'd always been his warrior, the fearless Amazon of Salutech. I couldn't stand being needy.

John merely smiled wider. 'Because, Lambert, Susan had several tonnes of stupid clothes and her move took longer than it should have done.'

'Well, I'm sorry it . . . er, ended,' I said lamely. I was nothing of the sort.

'Oh, shhh, Lambert,' John said. 'Marrying her was the stupidest thing I've ever done. Schoolboy reasoning. Marry one woman to forget about another? Insane! But it all worked out as it should have done in the end.' He got up from his desk and guided me round to his sofa area, which wasn't visible from Becky's desk. I shivered at the feel of his hand on the small of my back. In spite of all the darkness, I felt suddenly compelled to rip my suit off, yelling, 'RUMP ME NOW!' I resisted this temptation.

John sat down and ran his hands through his hair. 'It's a bit messy,' he acknowledged, 'but she wants a quick divorce. Soon it'll be just you and me, Lambert, stomping around that bloody loch and having furious sex all the time. Sound good?'

I was enthralled by this idea. It felt like a fairy tale. A slightly dysfunctional one, but a fairy tale all the same. Charley Lambert was getting her handsome prince.

'Could I possibly have a quick feel of your magnificent breasts?' John asked. His eyes were twinkling with mischief.

'Can't you allow a girl even a few seconds of romance, John?'

John looked impish and naughty. 'It's your fault, Lambert. You shouldn't be so bloody divine to look at and clever at your job.'

I beamed foolishly, in spite of my best efforts not to.

'Could we quickly fuck in a cupboard?' he asked hopefully.

My warm glow diminished a little. 'No!'

'Toilets?'

'No.'

'Could I maybe just have a quick feel of your bottom?'

'John!'

He looked comically guilty and then something far more sincere came over him. He leaned forward and gave me a long, lingering kiss. 'Sorry,' he muttered. 'Seven years' waiting turns a man to madness.'

I felt a bit safer and smiled my forgiveness.

'Could I interest you in some egg on toast in the canteen?' he asked.

We spent our first thirty-five minutes as a couple eating hard scrambled eggs with cold toast in an empty canteen with a view of the A1. I told him about Granny Helen and how worried I was about Dad, and he told me how stupid he felt about having married the wrong woman.

I went back to my desk with a tiny bit more confidence. Maybe there was a solution to this mess with Margot. I just didn't know what it was yet.

Sam called mid-morning to tell me he had spoken to William, who was on the phone *right now* ordering Interflora's most extravagant bouquet for Shelley. 'Someone told him you're meant to wait until Tuesday to call,' Sam said, exasperated. 'Where the fuck do they get their ideas from? I think we should write a handbook, Chas.'

I smiled weakly. 'It's nice to be helping them, though.'

He agreed, but said that it was all a bit time-consuming in his opinion.

He had a point. 'You're right, actually, Bowes,' I said. 'Why are we putting so much effort into William and Shelley? Why does it matter so much that they get together?'

Sam hesitated, and when he answered, he rather knocked the wind out of me. 'Because we can't be, I suppose. Together.'

A big silence opened on the line between us. Sam was absolutely right. We couldn't be together. Ever. It was biologically impossible. Yet we both knew that something big and important had passed between us, and we were willing to channel it into the correct place. *How touching,*

I thought. *And how true. Shelley and William had to fall in love because Sam and I can't.*

It was simple and it was lovely.

'You're right, Bowes,' I said slowly. 'I hadn't thought about it like that.'

I heard him smile. 'Have a good afternoon, Chas,' he said gently. 'Don't let those bastards get you down. You're better than them.'

I ended the call. Samuel Bowes was full of surprises.

Then Margot marched into my office and the moment was gone.

'I want to schedule a meeting this afternoon,' she announced, 'in which you can start handing over the projects I want.'

I took a deep breath. I had worked out which projects I could give to her without compromising my job but the doctors' conference was impossible. I'd tried suggesting to John that Margot ran it 'as a gesture for her recent hard work', but he'd just laughed. 'Of course she fucking can't!' he said. 'I'd sooner leave your parents' Labrador in charge of the fucking thing, Lambert!'

I tried to relay a watered-down version of this to Margot but she wasn't interested. 'Sort it out,' she said.

There was an uncomfortable silence.

'So, have you emailed that man for me yet?' she asked, switching the nasty smile back on.

I felt even more depressed. Matty.

I had checked his profile a few times and each time he was online, his round, earnest little face beaming out at me from the computer. I'd been driven insane trying to work out what was going on. Apart from anything else, he was working in a wild garden in the wilds of Fife where, even if he sat on top of a telegraph pole, he wouldn't stand a chance of finding phone signal. It made no sense. *Why are you doing this?* I'd raged silently at his picture.

'I didn't email him, no,' I told Margot. 'You said he looked married. I just . . . needed to be sure that you definitely want to go there.'

Margot laughed, a nasty sound. 'You don't just have a rod up your arse,' she told me. 'You have a fucking *truncheon*. Just send him a first approach – now,' she added, 'and forget about the rest. None of your business.'

But it was my business. It was very much my business. Margot raised her eyebrows. 'One call to Chambers!' she whispered. 'Just do it!'

So I did.

The afternoon passed in an unpleasant blur. I handed over the less important jobs to Margot, reasoning with myself that if I wasn't a control freak I'd have given them to her anyway. The major projects I held back and panicked over.

The high point of the afternoon was when an ecstatic (but still bellowingly loud) Shelley called to tell me that William had sent her flowers. 'SOME ABSOLUTELY FANTASTIC PEONIES IN THIS BOUQUET!' she yelled.

But then she threw something at me that I hadn't been expecting. During her uncomfortable hours waiting for a sign of life from William, she had logged on to our First Date Aid website, as if this might bring the object of her desire closer.

'I wanted to ask about your partner,' Shelley barked. 'The one who's taken over from you. Now, I presume, from what you said about waiting to hear from a man over the weekend, that Sam is a partner only in the business sense.'

I confirmed that was so. Shelley continued to interrogate me about the business. And then, just as the phone call seemed to be coming to an end, she asked something even stranger. 'Do you have a history with this Sam, Charlotte?'

'No!' I said, shocked.

'Not even a flirtation?'

'Not even a flirtation.'

'Shame,' she said reflectively, and then, in Shelley Cartwright-style, she ended the call.

The lowest point of the afternoon had been emailing Matty. And receiving an enthusiastic response within ten minutes. And then another, and another. Matty had agreed very readily to a Wednesday-night rendezvous and I was now at a very low ebb.

'You're rather good at this email bullshit, Charley,' Margot said, as she left the office. 'Your little dating company will probably do quite well when you crawl out of Salutech on your belly.' She shimmied off, whistling.

Please God, I prayed. *Help me. Send me a sign.*

God remained silent.

'Bowes?' I called, shutting the front door behind me. I'd looked forward to seeing him all the way home and was kind of hoping he'd be able to make me laugh about how rubbish my life was and feed me whisky.

The flat was silent.

Disappointed, I made myself some mushrooms on toast and then, still jumpy and miserable, sent a text message to John, asking him if he wanted to go for a drink. He'd been in a board meeting all afternoon and we'd not had time to arrange anything. *Alas,* he texted back, *I've got some French friends staying. Making dinner now.* Just told them about me and Susan, might be a bit early to introduce you . . . *But you mark my words, the sooner I can be bashing a big piece of boeuf into submission for my dear Lambert, the better.*

I felt a girlish rush of excitement at the thought of John standing at his marble-topped work surface being manly with a meat hammer.

I spent an hour on the phone to Ness, who told me to confront Matty rather than tell Hailey, and then I drafted twenty different emails to Matty, deleting every single one. The moment I pressed send, I would set in motion a process that surely had no possible outcome other than Hailey ending up heartbroken and single. Potentially carrying his child.

I couldn't do it. Not today. And so, hating myself for being so weak when I should be strong for my friend, I did some work, exchanged some cheeky messages with John about *saucisson* and slunk off to bed with my tail between my legs.

I was just curling up into an exhausted ball when my phone began to ring once again. 'Fuck off,' I muttered, peering at it. My heart sank. It was Shelley again. My enthusiasm for helping her was not high at this moment in time: William had sent flowers, for God's sake!

But Shelley hadn't called with a crisis: she had called to announce – rather grandly, I thought – her intention to 'help' Sam and me with our business.

Slightly defensively, I began to remind her that I was a businesswoman myself and felt confident that the company was in good shape. 'And, besides, it's no longer mine to worry about –'

'No, no,' she interrupted, in her most terrifying boom. 'Listen here, Charlotte. I turn good companies into hyper-successful multi-billion-pound businesses. With minimal effort I could bring you huge investment and help you turn First Date Aid into something that would set you up for life.'

'But . . . we don't *want* to turn it into something huge,' I said lamely. This was a lie, of course. 'It's really nice of you but –'

'I want to thank you for what you've done for me,' Shelley said loudly. 'William and I spoke for three hours tonight. I think he's perfect for me. I've never felt so sure about a man, especially after such a short time.'

In spite of myself I smiled. 'Oh, that's marvell–'

'The fact of the matter, Charlotte, is that you have an excellent business model, which could be developed aggressively and expanded into overseas territories. You have only one competitor in the United States – are you going to let him come and pinch Europe from under your nose?'

'Erm . . .'

'No,' she answered for me. 'You won't. And for that reason I've secured you and Sam two last-minute places at an extremely important investment dinner on Thursday.

Go to the Balmoral Hotel at seven p.m. and ask at Reception for the RBA event.'

I agreed, if nothing else to get her off the line. That would be my final, final, final thing. After that I'd walk away from First Date Aid completely and concentrate one thousand per cent on Salutech. I needed to.

Chapter Sixteen

On Thursday night I scuttled along Forth Street towards my front door, clutching a baguette and some deli ham. My plan for the evening was quite simple: eat baguette, eat ham, mutter darkly about John's French friends – who were still bloody well staying with him – and go to bed.

It had been a challenging week. Margot had now taken over several of my smaller projects and the lessening of my workload had actually been quite pleasant, even though the circumstances were all wrong. Also, much to my relief, Bradley Chambers had decided to come over from Washington next week so there was no question of me giving her my bigger gigs. Even Margot knew better than to try to mess with Chambers, who would short-circuit and possibly explode if I was not visibly in charge.

Things at home were still bleak. Dad was lost, according to Mum, and twelve more patients had transferred themselves to the medical centre in Dunbar while he was off work. 'We're a bit buggered,' Mum said tightly to me. Mum didn't swear. I was worried.

But there was, at least, a tall, handsome, funny man brightening up my days. The chemistry was intense and rather naughty but, much to my chagrin, his friends had been staying with him all week and were not leaving until tomorrow. We had had minimal physical contact, apart from a rather shameful twenty minutes in the deserted third-floor boardroom on Wednesday morning. *I am being eaten alive by the thwarted desires of my penis!* he had texted me earlier, while sitting directly across the table from me in a management meeting. When I declined to respond but instead voiced my reservations about a TV documentary that had been pitched to us, he stared at me in anguish and sent a barrage of further messages. *LAMBERT! My penis is waiting to hear back from you! Kindly show him some respect!*

I smiled as I walked up the stairs. Penis and I would get together very soon. And in the meantime I had a nice French baguette and some ham for dinner.

As I fumbled for my key, the door was pulled open by Sam.

'Oh!' he said. He seemed to be in some sort of a hurry. 'Turn round!'

'Bowes?' I exclaimed. 'Is that a *suit*, Bowes?'

Sam smiled self-consciously. 'Thought I should make an effort.'

He looked lovely. The suit, which was tailored right into his frame, was an unusual shade of grey, which, with his narrow-striped fashion shirt made his eyes look greener and brighter than ever. He was even wearing hair product and man perfume. Feeling suddenly proud of my beautiful flatmate, I tucked his smart scarf – which had gone a bit haywire – into his suit jacket and straightened his wool coat. 'Whoever she is, she's a lucky girl, Samuel Bowes. You look gorgeous!'

Sam shook his head. 'I bloody knew you'd forget. It's our investment thingy at the Balmoral, Chas.'

'Oh, no!' I smacked myself on the forehead with my baguette.

Sam consulted his watch. 'But thankfully you're home much earlier than normal. Come on, let's dump your stuff and go.'

I was stricken. 'But my baguette!'

'We could meet someone who wants to invest in us all the way into Europe!' Sam exclaimed. 'Fuck the baguette!'

'But – but what about Margot? I've told her I'm not involved with First Date Aid any more. What if one of Salutech's investors is there tonight and he mentions it to someone? She'll find out I'm there, Sam, I know she will!'

Sam turned round and gave a big V-sign to Edinburgh. 'FUCK YOU, MARGOT,' he shouted. 'Chas, it's fine. We'll call it my company. You're already off the website. You can just be there as my date or something. But will you fucking *come on*? I know nothing about business investors!'

With one final wistful glance at my baguette I gave in and ran off to my room. I changed my work blouse to a deep purple silk slip, which John had expressed a particular liking for, and threw my suit jacket back on, joining Sam on the stairs. 'Right then, Bowes,' I said, clattering down the stairs in my work shoes. 'Let's go and get our company some investment! Oh – I mean *your* company.'

Sam chuckled, offered me his arm and we chatted companionably all the way up the hill to the Balmoral.

'We're here for the RBA event?' Sam said to the receptionist. 'Samuel Bowes, First Date Aid,' he added shyly.

She looked at a piece of paper and nodded. 'This way, please.'

We followed her through the grand foyer and two

opulent lounges, grinning self-consciously at each other. It felt odd to be in grown-up business mode when the 'business' in question was a flirting service run from our sofa.

The receptionist walked us into Number One, a very smart Michelin-starred affair where I'd eaten once before with some colleagues. 'Please,' she said, gliding towards a table in the corner. I looked at Sam, who seemed as confused as I was.

The receptionist offered to take my coat. 'Sorry,' I said. 'I think there's been a mistake. We're here for an investment event, not dinner.'

The woman nodded. 'All delegates dine first,' she explained. 'The presentations and mingling begin at nine p.m. next door.'

Sam was ecstatic. 'That's great!' he squeaked. 'Thanks!' It wasn't every day that Samuel Bowes ate in Michelin-starred restaurants.

The receptionist, caught in the firing line of a Sam's smile, was immediately helpless. 'No problem, sir,' she simpered. After a few seconds she scuttled off with a big red scald on the back of her neck.

I sat down, laughing merrily. 'Oh, Bowes! Do you ever get tired of it?'

Sam shook his head solemnly. 'Never, my brother.'

A waiter appeared at my arm and handed us menus. 'Champagne?' he asked. We looked at each other like two excitable school children. 'YES, PLEASE!'

After ordering, we eyeballed the diners around us, speculating over potential investors. To my intense relief I didn't recognize any of them. 'I reckon the dude with the moustache is good news,' Sam said. 'He'd love you, Chas.

A big tall businesswoman who uses all those crazy corporate words. Flash him your tits, go on.'

I wanted to laugh but I was momentarily stung. Even though I knew he wasn't making a dig at my height I couldn't stand Sam calling me 'big' and 'tall'. His predilection for tiny willowy women had always made me feel bulky and unfeminine. But I pulled myself together and sipped some champagne. It didn't actually matter what he thought: we were business partners and housemates.

'How are you at the moment, Chas?' Sam asked.

'Erm . . .' I didn't actually know. 'Well . . . up and down, I suppose. But OK. John's certainly helping matters.'

Sam was thoughtful. 'I've got a lot of respect for you, brother,' he said. 'You've had a rough year. But you're fighting on. Which is full-on awesome.'

His approval was welcome. I'd never really thought that Sam took much notice of my life; it was, after all, so different from his.

'I hope John gives you all you want,' he said, after a pause.

I nodded enthusiastically.

Sam was obviously waiting for a fuller response.

'It's going really well,' I told him, unsure as to what he was after. 'I'm happy. He's been really sweet about Granny Helen and . . . I dunno, we're just having a nice time.'

Sam smiled, rather politely, I thought, as the waiter put down some tuna carpaccio in front of us. It looked quite incredible, sitting on what appeared to be a topiary garden of oriental vegetables.

I got stuck in with gusto, but was rudely interrupted.

'YEEUUGH!' Sam shouted, bringing the restaurant to a standstill.

'*What?*' I hissed.

'They didn't cook the fucking fish!' Sam whispered. 'Look! It's raw!'

I burst out laughing. 'Oh, Bowes. It's meant to be! It's carpaccio.'

'Oh,' he said, mortified. I laughed even harder. It really was like having a little brother at times.

'Stop laughing,' he said, obviously hurt. 'We don't all dine at posh restaurants all the time, Chas.'

I was instantly remorseful. 'Oh, Bowes . . . I only go to places like this because of my silly work,' I lied. 'Otherwise I'd be stealing napkins and spitting raw tuna out of my mouth like a normal person.'

Sam brightened up and I made a mental note to avoid any further ridicule. He wasn't a trumping teenager on my couch any more; he was very precious and brilliant and he deserved respect.

The conversation somehow turned back to John.

'Are you in love with him?' Sam asked interestedly.

I thought about it and realized, to my surprise, that I didn't know yet. I wondered if this was weird but decided it wasn't. After all, we'd only just got together. 'I'm very happy,' I said firmly.

'OK. Well, then, is John in love with *you*?'

I began to feel cornered. What was he getting at? Since when had Sam Bowes, who never went on more than one date, cared so much about love? 'Er . . . I don't know. He's been exceptionally keen. Don't forget he married Susan in the hope that he'd get over me, and then left her when it didn't work out,' I pointed out. 'That's got to be pretty significant.'

Sam looked pensive. 'Significant or insane, depending on how you see it.'

I flushed. I couldn't stand the idea of my friends disapproving of John after I'd waited for him so long. 'Sam,' I said awkwardly, 'I told you, John was trying to avoid a difficult work relationship. Yes, he went about it in an odd way but the point is that he *had* to put Salutech first. He's the bloody CEO.'

Sam gazed levelly at me. Eventually he shrugged. 'OK,' he said.

I didn't like Sam's tone one bit. 'Piss off,' I muttered. I poured myself some more wine, much to the consternation of the waiter hovering nearby. There was an awkward scuffle as he tried to take the bottle off me and I fumed, knowing that Sam was watching me with a patronizing expression. What was his problem?

He touched my hand when the waiter went away. 'Sorry, Chas,' he said quietly. 'I didn't mean to insult you or John. I just want you to be happy.'

I looked at him suspiciously. He certainly seemed genuine, but I hadn't missed the implication that being with John would make me *un*happy.

'And I'm sure you will be happy!' he added, obviously spotting the same flaw.

With a considerable effort I pulled myself together again. I didn't know why Sam and I were having so many spiky moments these days but I wanted them to stop. We weren't just old friends now – we were business partners and we had a duty to put up a united front.

I made myself smile. 'To First Date Aid!' I said, raising

my glass. 'May we bleed the rich dry tonight, Samuel Bowes.'

We clinked glasses. Things returned to normal.

Over the main course, which Sam declared 'the best fucking meal EVER', he dropped into the conversation – rather casually, I thought – that, following a trip to London yesterday, he was on final recall for a 'massive' part in a 'massive' play. 'Is that or is that not MASSIVELY EXCITING?' he asked, his face alight.

'Very! So does that mean the play's in London?' I asked, rather hoping it wouldn't be. I was enjoying living with the all-new functional, hygienic Sam.

'Yep. The Garrick. Er, Charing Cross Road, major West End theatre,' he added, when I looked blank. 'It would be *amazing* if I got this gig.'

'Wow, Bowes! Amazing indeed! High five?'

Sam grinned. 'Not yet. Final audition is Monday.'

The booze was seemingly limitless and Sam and I got embarrassingly drunk. We also, unfortunately, got the giggles. Neither of us seemed equipped to eat in a Michelin-starred restaurant. Twice I loaded my fork, only for everything to drop off as I lifted it to my mouth. Then followed a desperate and unladylike scramble to restore everything to my plate; a scramble that attracted pin-striped disapproval and made us laugh even harder. Strangled snorts escaped across the otherwise calm and civilized restaurant; the waiter smiled glassily. And just to prove to Sam that I only went Michelin in a work capacity I pilfered a Balmoral napkin. (A few minutes later I put it back when he wasn't looking.)

Sam took things to a whole new level when dessert arrived: he tried to stab his way into the brandy snap construction that was encasing his mango ice cream. It proved tougher than predicted and his spoon ricocheted sharply, flying out of his hand. It shot across the table and pinged loudly against the wall, coming to rest in the middle of the floor where he and I stared gravely at it before starting to snigger again.

'Fucking stop it!' I whispered at him, trying to cover my face.

'You stop it!' he hissed back. He had his napkin held in front of his mouth, not that that helped in any way.

A honk slipped out of my mouth and I turned my back to the restaurant, mortified but even more helpless with laughter. 'You are destroying our chances of investment,' Sam whispered. 'PUT A FUCKING SOCK IN IT!' Then he clutched his stomach and laughed until he cried. I leaned against the wall and howled as silently as possible. The well-dressed investors watched us with silent disgust and I knew our chances of getting so much as a ha'penny out of them were rogered.

'Shelley will never speak to us again,' I gasped a few moments later. I was exhausted with the effort of laughing so much. Sam, who looked similarly destroyed, was slumped over the table, loading sugar cubes into his coffee. I raised an eyebrow.

'It's free sugar,' he said defensively.

We chinked coffee cups. 'I'm basically very drunk,' I confessed. 'Bit worried about sounding serious or capable.'

Sam sipped his coffee. 'Likewise, Chas.' We giggled.

The suited men were engaged in a heated debate about something financial and I stared at them, impressed and intimidated by their vocabulary and assertiveness. The confidence that came with wealth always threw me.

'I think we've fucked up any chance of impressing them,' Sam observed. 'I certainly wouldn't invest in two knobs throwing spoons around in the corner.'

Teenage rebelliousness took hold of me. Fuck those suits! I liked being a knob throwing spoons in the corner! I didn't want to go next door and be all grown-up. At Salutech I had to be grown-up all day; I missed the giggling and trumping and knob gags from when we'd set up First Date Aid together in the summer. All I actually wanted to do right now was to get into my pyjamas and watch crap films with Sam. Be a knob. Not worry or care what anyone else was thinking.

I looked unenthusiastically at the suits. They seemed to be winding things up: presentation and mingling time must be drawing near.

'Are you thinking what I'm thinking?' Sam asked, interrupting my thoughts. There was a very naughty, very teenage look in his eyes.

'I'm thinking I want to skive!' I whispered.

Sam's eyes sparkled. 'Me too!'

I glanced furtively at the door. 'They can't make us stay, can they?'

'Chas, they'd probably pay us to leave, my brother.'

One of the suits looked wearily over at me. *Oh, for the love of Jesus*, his face said. I hoped to God Shelley didn't actually know any of these people.

'We won't be letting Shelley down, will we?' Sam asked, reading my mind. 'I'm worried she'll have paid for us to be here.'

'No way. This'll be funded by stinking-rich venture capitalists.'

Sam brightened. 'Well, then, I say we do one, Chas. Let's crack open some Scotch and watch *Dirty Dancing*.'

Sam was the best business partner in the world.

We finished our coffee, gave the waiter time to disappear, then left at a brisk trot, chortling like naughty children.

I bowled drunkenly through the lounges and lobbies, Sam striding confidently ahead of me in his sharp suit. I felt a great fondness as I watched him. The Samuel Bowes walking in front of me might be a bit squiffy but he was an eligible, impressive and very likeable young man, these days, unrecognizable as the slob who had colonized my sofa for the last ten years.

I remembered how he'd lamented the stagnation of his life a few months ago when he was pretending to be William. It had been a cry from the heart, a deep longing for purpose and worth. *I have a massive overwhelming feeling of underachievement*, he'd said, *like life is passing me by*. It certainly wasn't passing him by any more. *You're a clever sausage, Bowes*, I thought fondly. *I'll really miss you if you go to London.*

Outside, not quite ready to go home, we wandered aimlessly around the concrete slopes of the underground shopping centre, exchanging fantasies about what we would do with First Date Aid if we did somehow land a big investment deal. I was a bit unclear as to how I'd find time to start working on it again but I knew there'd be a way.

'We must be doing OK if Shelley's so keen to help,' I said, sitting down on a cold bench.

'Greatest company on earth,' Sam said, without hesitation. He sat down next to me and we gazed at the Balmoral. In a room towards the back of the hotel a corporate party was in full swing: overweight men in shirts danced to a tune we couldn't hear while the women tried to writhe seductively in their special sparkly dresses and heels that thrust them uncomfortably forward. We watched in silence as they thrashed around without inhibition under a disco ball.

'I like my life,' Sam remarked out of nowhere.

'Good,' I said, feeling a little worried. Comments like this always generated in me an urgent need to like my own. *Do* I like my life? I wondered. I grimaced. What with Margot and her blackmail, Dad's depression and work problems, and the horrible knowledge that Hailey's partner was cheating on her, things were about as far from perfect as they could be. I slapped myself on the forehead. There it was again: 'perfect'. Hadn't I told William that I needed to ditch perfectionism? That I'd probably feel a hell of a lot happier if I could just let go? 'Perfect' was not a helpful word!

Further unease set in as I remembered those emails with 'William'. The basic fact of the matter was that I had discovered some big things about myself during that time and had done nothing about any of them. Whereas Sam had chosen to tackle his stuff head-on. Four months ago he had been unemployed, lazy, bored and unhealthy; now he was running a company, actively auditioning, taking exercise and feeding himself well. *Why haven't I changed?* I thought. *Am I failing?*

But what was I meant to change? Was I meant to quit

my job just because I couldn't find a healthy work–life balance?

Of course not! My job was my life!

And therein lies the problem, an annoying little voice said.

After a few seconds I put a lid on it. It was like the world's crappest merry-go-round.

Sam was looking at me. 'What the hell was that, Chas?'

'What?'

'You just went through some epic mental battle,' he said mildly. 'Including slapping yourself on the forehead.'

I waved him off. 'Just worried. Dad, work, Hailey, you know.'

Sam nodded sceptically. 'Can I interest you in half a Snickers?' he asked, pulling a misshapen bar out of his pocket and splitting it in two. 'Mm, nice chocolate bar . . .'

I shook my head. 'No thanks.'

'You're being snotty because it's junk food,' Sam told me, taking a big bite.

'No,' I lied. 'I'm just full.'

'Liar.'

'I'm not lying! I'm full!' I sounded very lame.

'You knob. Nobody's ever full after a posh meal. Eat some dirty chocolate, knob!'

I giggled. Encouraged, he waved the chocolate in my face.

'Stop it!' I ordered. Sam did not stop it: instead he grabbed me and put me in a headlock. 'KNOB! Eat chocolate!' he shouted, in his best Cookie Monster voice. He shoved the chocolate in my face. I squirmed against him but it was no use. The harder I pulled, the more I laughed. Sam, too, was laughing now. I tried one final attempt to wrench myself free and, as I did so, heard a terrible noise. I gasped. The Bowes had trumped!

'NOOOOOOO!' I screamed, scrabbling even harder. 'Get off me! Get your evil backside away from me!'

Sam collapsed with laughter, letting go of me and fanning the air. I ran off to sulk a good distance away from him. 'Sorry!' he cried, completely hysterical.

'Actually, you can give me that chocolate,' I said crossly. 'It's the least you can do to make up for your behaviour. Savage!'

Sam finally recovered and threw it over. He held his half up high as if proposing a toast. 'To us,' he said. 'The best business partners ever. I'm a pikey who knows nothing about tuna arpeggio; you're a work-fiend who knows nothing about chocolate . . . Man, that fart smells.'

I was laughing again. 'Tuna carpaccio!' I cried. Sam was sitting like a little gnome on the bench, still wafting his trump away from him, blithely unaware of his error.

'Tuna, eh?' he asked, blinking.

I folded my hands over my stomach. 'Stop it. Stop talking. We have to talk about serious things. I'll wet my knickers if I have to laugh any more.'

Sam patted the bench next to him, declaring it a trump-free zone. 'Right, serious things,' he said, trying to look serious. He didn't pull it off. 'Hmm . . . OK, tell me what's going on with Hailey.'

My face fell. 'Oh, Bowes, it's a mess,' I said sadly, and told him the whole sorry tale.

'Oh, *no*,' Sam said, when I'd finished. 'No!' He looked really quite stricken. 'How could he do that to our lovely Tits? Hailey's amazing!'

I nodded gloomily.

'What a CUNT!' Sam exclaimed.

'God knows how many girls he's dated behind her back,' I said.

'CUNT!' Sam repeated, even more angrily.

His anger was infectious and I felt my temper rise. How dare Matty move Hailey into his house and then make a fool of her? In public, too. He knew I ran a dating business! Did he not think I'd see him there? Did he not even *care*? Was it true, what Margot had said, that he was the sort of man who met some strange woman for a sordid fuck and then went home for his lasagne with wifey? My blood boiled. He couldn't get away with this. It was disgusting! He was living with my *best friend*!

'I have to confront him,' I said suddenly. 'Now! This can't go on a moment longer!'

Sam agreed. 'Yeah. The CUNT,' he shouted. 'Give him what-for, Chas!'

He looked at his watch. 'Ten forty-nine. That's not too late. *What a cunt!*'

I steeled myself and dialled Matty's number.

As soon as the phone began to ring, I knew I'd made a mistake. 'No,' I whispered to Sam. 'No, this is wrong. I'm drunk.'

I went to cancel the call but it was too late. Hailey had answered Matty's phone almost immediately. 'Chas?'

She sounded confused. *You stupid idiot, Charley*, I thought furiously.

'Oh . . .' I said. 'Hi!' My voice was far too high-pitched.

There was a silence. 'Why are you calling Matty?' she asked suspiciously.

I baulked. 'I wanted to talk to him about the Christmas Wonderland he's working on,' I said. I could hear myself slurring slightly and felt even angrier with myself. This had been a stupid plan. 'Feeling festive . . .'

Then Hailey said something extremely odd: 'Are you sleeping with my boyfriend, Charley?'

I did a double-take. '*What?*'

'You heard.'

I was astonished. 'No! I am definitely not sleeping with Matty!'

'What the *fuck*?' Sam whispered.

There was another pause. When Hailey spoke again, she sounded horrible. 'Why the hell did you call him at this time of night, then? Tell the truth, Charley.'

I didn't know what was happening but I knew that I needed to end this call immediately. 'There's nothing to tell. I'm with Sam, we're drunk and we started talking about the Christmas Wonder—'

'Don't LIE TO ME!' Hailey roared.

I was utterly shocked. I didn't know what I'd just walked into but I wanted to get out of it quickly.

'You tell me right now why you were calling Matty,' Hailey hissed. 'Are you sleeping with him?'

'No!' I cried. And, because I didn't know what else to do, I took a deep breath and told her exactly why I had called Matty tonight. My voice was wobbly and frightened, but I held firm and told her everything I knew. What else could I do? Sam stared at his shoes, listening and nodding. 'Cunt,' he whispered, when I got to the bit about Matty replying to Margot within minutes.

'Fuck off,' Hailey said eventually. 'Fuck off, you drunk,

delusional fantasist. If I find you've been sniffing around after my boyfriend, Charley, my God I swear I'll . . .' She paused. 'Just fuck off.'

The line went dead.

I put my phone down. 'Didn't go very well,' I said shakily. I was really quite traumatized. What the hell had just happened? Why on earth was Hailey suspicious of *me*? I felt my lip begin to quiver. Drunken crying was something I'd always found rather distasteful but right now it seemed rather appealing: I was (a) very upset, (b) very wasted and (c) in the company of someone who (albeit by accident) knew more about me than anyone else in the world. *Sam really understands me now*, I thought drunkenly. *If I can't cry in front of Sam, I can't cry in front of anyone.* I let a little tear wobble off down my cheek. 'She said I'm a drunk, delusional fantasist, Sam. And she thinks I'm sleeping with Matty. MATTY!'

Sam shuffled over to sit closer to me. 'Come on,' he said. 'She was just lashing out. You gave her some really bad news.'

'No!' I cried. 'It was like she'd been suspicious of me for ages, Sam. WHY?' The crying was really gaining momentum now. I felt sick. Hailey was my right-hand man! Sam didn't understand the bond between women. It was sacred. 'Sacred,' I muttered to him. 'Me and Hailey have a sacred connection, man . . . I can't lose her, Sam. Without Hailey I have nothing!'

'Great song,' Sam said reflectively, patting me on the back.

'Eh?'

'Whitney Houston, "I Have Nothing",' he said. 'Beautiful.'

Somewhere deep inside me I knew this was extremely funny but I was deep in fear now. Hailey, my best and most precious friend, hated me and seemed to think I was having it off with her partner. While I couldn't understand that, I knew that it had been a huge and unforgivable error to call Matty at ten fifty on a Thursday evening. Why couldn't I have waited until tomorrow?

'I'm a terrible, stupid person,' I wept.

Sam put his arm round me. 'Cry it out, cry it out,' he mumbled. 'Own that emotion. Feel it. Experience it.'

Once more I knew that Sam was saying something very funny, as he so often did when drunk. Somewhere among my tears I found a smile. 'Where did you get that kind of chat from?' I asked him, holding my scarf against my cheek to stem the flow of tears.

'Drama school,' he replied, nodding wisely. 'It's OK, Charley. Just allow yourself to feel the pain.'

So I cried a bit more.

Eventually I stopped and we agreed that it had been extremely stupid to call Matty while I was drunk and that I had to apologize first thing tomorrow. But I was still angry with myself. What kind of a horrible drunken fool behaved so carelessly? And, while we were at it, why was I generally so out of control tonight? Skiving off from the investment meeting and sneaking out of the Balmoral? Attempting to steal *napkins*? What *was* that? I went to nice restaurants all the time! I was on a strange high tonight; it was definitely more than just drunkenness. There was a breathlessness, an absence of balance. Sometimes, when my clients emailed to tell me how a date had gone, they had described exactly this. But I was not on a date. I was in the middle of a business evening with my housemate.

Sam removed his arm from my shoulders and I felt the cold air bite my neck. 'Do I look like a fiend?' I asked him, trying to pull myself together. 'Mascara everywhere?'

Sam leaned over and peered at me, trying hard to focus. I stared at his skin, marvelling at its youthfulness. How, when I used expensive creams in a sub-military facial regime, did I have far more wrinkles than Sam? I asked him as much.

Sam smiled. 'Hang on and I'll check your wrinkles too.' He leaned closer. 'Hmm,' he said. I could smell his breath on my face, sweet with wine and mango. 'Hard to see,' he murmured. 'Smile a bit?' I obliged.

'OK,' he said. 'Now make that face you make when you're trying to solve a problem.'

I thought about Margot and felt my features change. I laughed. 'Do I do this face a lot?'

'Yes. Well, I'm afraid you do have a few wrinkles, Chas. But they're rather charming. Smile again?'

I smiled. Sam smiled back at me. We sat there for a few seconds, smiling at each other and I felt the weird out-of-control thing start again. I wanted us to run down into Princes Gardens and make dens and climb trees.

'What are you thinking?' he asked.

'Um, that I want to go and climb trees in Princes Gardens,' I admitted. Sam chuckled. 'What were you thinking?'

'Bit odd,' he said, after a pause. 'I was thinking about

those emails we sent each other. And how it's been a bit confusing since then.'

Edinburgh suddenly seemed to go silent. I stared in alarm at Sam. I had gone to some lengths to make sure there was no confusion. Why did he have to bring this up now? 'Confused how?' I asked him nervously.

Sam had that determined expression he wore when there was something he had to say, however unwelcome it might be. The first time I'd seen it was when a girl had come up to him in the student union and asked him when they were going to meet up again. His face had set in the same way and he'd informed her, in a scared but determined voice, that they weren't. She had thrown a pint of Snakebite at him.

'Confusion over the fact that we, y'know, basically fell in love and then just forgot about it,' he said firmly.

I began to blush and stammer. 'But . . . we didn't know . . . we didn't realize . . . It's been fine since then, no problem at all, no awkwardness, we're both in relationships, well I am, you probably will be again soon, it's fine, Sam,' I gabbled.

Sam watched me, perplexed. 'I agree,' he said slowly. 'But I've never felt like I did then. With those emails. I think we should make sure.'

I felt like I was going to faint. Why couldn't he just shut up? 'Make sure of what?' I mumbled.

'Make sure that we're not meant to be together,' he announced. 'That there's nothing beyond the emails.' I could see how nervous he was but his jaw was set. He meant it.

'Er . . . And how would we do that?' This was horrible.

Sam looked down, and in that moment I knew he wasn't just nervous, he was petrified.

'I think we should kiss. Just to prove that there's nothing. A sort of scientific experiment.'

There was a terrible silence while Sam dug his fingernails into his thighs and I weighed up the pros and cons of getting up and making a run for it.

Then: 'Maybe,' I heard myself say.

Panic. *WHAT?* I should *not* be kissing my housemate! And my housemate should not think that I wanted to kiss him!

Calm down, I begged myself. *Try to look cool.* Given that Sam appeared to be serious, and was looking quite grown-up for once, I forced myself to consider it seriously too.

After a few seconds of frantic deliberation, I had to concede that it was not an absolutely terrible idea. There *had* been awkwardness and confusion for me since London, however much I'd tried to squash it down. Nonetheless I was quite certain that there were no real feelings involved. I'd asked myself several times if I liked Sam and the answer had been consistent: NO WAY! So what was the problem with one kiss if there was nothing in it? I was the sort of person who liked a good piece of solid scientific evidence. A short, passionless kiss would probably draw a nice firm line under the whole thing.

I relayed this to Sam. He thought about it and then nodded. And I realized I had just agreed to kiss him.

Panic descended once again.

'How should we go about it?' I asked, in my best scientific-experiment voice.

'Not sure. Do you want to get all upset again?' he asked.

'And then I could put my arm round you and you'd look at me and then we lean in slowly?'

I considered this proposal. 'Nope,' I said eventually. 'That sounds too romantic.'

'True. Well, let's just count to three and then do a peck on the lips. No messing around, get it over with quickly.'

'OK,' I said. 'Sounds like a plan.'

Nobody moved.

'Bowes?' I said. 'Are you going to do it?'

'We just agreed we'd count to three.'

'Oh. Right. Well, you count.' As drunk as I was, I was feeling very frightened. *It's a scientific experiment! Get a grip!* I shouted at myself.

'OK,' Sam said, leaning towards me. 'One, two, three . . .' I froze. He stopped about six inches from my face. 'You look terrified, Chas.'

I was. My hands were shaking. But something was telling me that it was imperative to carry out this experiment. I shook my head and said that I was absolutely fine, thanks.

'Right, one, two, THREE,' Sam said. He closed his eyes, I did the same, and a few seconds later I felt his lips touch mine.

Sam's lips were warm and actually felt very nice. There was a brief pause while we both had a think about what to do next. I felt that our lips should probably part a tiny bit just so we could say we'd done a proper kiss. Sam clearly felt the same because he started to kiss my top lip. Very softly, very slowly. An unexpected electric charge passed down my spine and I shivered suddenly.

Sam sprang away. 'What?'

'Nothing. Just a drunken spasm.'

We looked at each other warily for a few seconds.

That felt nice, I thought, dismayed. To my great consternation, I realized that I definitely wouldn't object to trying again.

'Well?' I said nervously.

'Well?' Sam repeated. His troubled eyes were searching mine for something, so I gave him what he obviously wanted.

'Just as we thought,' I said loudly. 'Nothing.'

Sam nodded vigorously, clearly relieved. 'Yes. I think I might go home, actually. I'm wasted.'

'Me too,' I said, jumping up. I definitely wanted to be the first to leave.

We walked home very fast for two people who were as drunk as we were. Not much was said.

Chapter Seventeen

I woke up to find a pair of eyes staring at me from a range of about four inches. I stretched and smiled, snuggling forward into his body. I might be so tired that I felt like I'd been attacked by a pack of mallet-wielding cavemen but at least I was in bed with a heavenly man.

'Yippee!' John said, immediately rolling on top of me. 'Lambert's awake!' He slid his hand down my stomach.

'No,' I told him, grabbing the hand before it reached tropical climes. 'No, John, I'm too tired.'

I *was* tired. Beyond tired, in fact. John and I had been up working until three thirty a.m. and the alarm had gone off at six. I was so tired that I wondered if I was actually dead.

Today was Wednesday, the day of our doctors' conference, one of the most important events in our Simitol launch schedule. It was also the day of Granny Helen's funeral and I was therefore going to miss it. It had been given to a gloating Margot, although John was very concerned about how Bradley Chambers – who had been scuttling around all week like an angry little rodent – was going to react when he discovered I wasn't in charge. But John was going to tell him at the last minute so he couldn't object and, to ensure Margot had as smooth a ride as possible, we had prepped it up to the eyeballs last night.

'Gruuuuhh,' I said, as John's hand began to wander again.

He paused. 'Lambert? Are you constipated?'

'Have to get up. Need to check the paperwork one last time before I drive to East Linton.' I had told Mum and Dad I'd be at the table by nine so that we could all have breakfast together.

John chuckled and pinched my nipple. 'Hmm. Well, I'll overlook your disobedience just this once,' he said, rolling out of bed.

I dragged myself into the shower, ignoring the fact that my facial skin had the quality of translucent cabbage this morning.

'Now, Lambert,' John said, arriving suddenly beside me. 'I really do think today would go better if we were to have a short burst of invigorating intercourse.'

'You're an animal,' I told him, handing him the soap.

He washed his face grudgingly, then put the soap down, a subversive look in his eye. 'You're right,' he said. 'I *am* an animal. Controlled entirely by my instinct. And I'm afraid my instinct demands that I mate with you right now.'

Without any further ado, he picked me up and carried me back to bed. 'I *can't*,' I cried. 'I have to get my papers in order and I have to go home, John, John get *off* . . . *oh*. Oh! Oh, my goodness . . .'

And that was that.

A little later, I drove along the A1, mired in guilt. There was something disgusting and disrespectful about my having given in to John this morning. Why hadn't I said no to him? Why could I never say no to bloody *anyone*?

'Sorry, Granny Helen,' I whispered. I imagined her shaking her head, muttering darkly about the youth of today, and managed to smile bravely. I was dreading the day ahead. I wanted my parents to look after me and make me feel safe, whereas in reality it was my job to do that for them. Of all the times I could find myself looking after my parents this had to be the worst: Dad was all but mute and even Mum – the strongest and most capable woman in the universe – seemed frail and uncertain. I could see their age and their limitations all of a sudden and it made me feel uprooted and vulnerable.

Hailey had told Ness in an abrupt text message that she wasn't going to come today. I had called her incessantly since Thursday night but she had cancelled every single call, eventually sending me a brisk and deadly *Fuck off* text message. Hailey had adored Granny Helen and it dismayed me that she hated me enough to boycott the funeral. Eventually I had written her a long email, apologizing for my oaf-like insensitivity in calling when drunk but making quite clear that what I had said about Matty was real.

As Ness had pointed out, Hailey must surely have checked love.com by now to verify my story, so it was confusing to both of us that she was blanking me. Why was this my fault? And why, in the name of Geronimo, had she thought *I* was sleeping with Matty?

I arrived in my parents' kitchen just before nine o'clock and all thoughts of Hailey – and indeed anything else – evaporated into the sad, stale air. None of the usual hustle and bustle was in progress: Dad was leaning against the Rayburn, staring blankly at Malcolm, Malcolm was sitting in his bed staring blankly at Dad, and Mum was serving up a very un-Mum like breakfast of Frosties and UHT milk. Katy and Ness, who'd arrived last night, looked beautiful but sombre. Katy was wearing a black vintage slip with a chunky cardigan and an elaborate 1980s alice band; Ness was small and sprightly with a lovely shirt dress and boots. As usual I felt large, dull and corporate in a plain black shift dress I normally wore to work.

Malcolm, fortunately, greeted me with wild enthusiasm, shoving my bag out of the way with his nose and wagging not just his tail but his whole body. He even jumped up and tried to dog-cuddle me and I knew things must be really bad when Mum didn't tell him off.

After giving everyone a quick hug, I sat down to eat some Frosties and listened while Ness acquainted me with the running order for today. We were interrupted by the incessant ringing of my phone, which I eventually dug out to silence, embarrassed and annoyed. 'Stupid bastard phone,' I muttered, just as it started to ring again. It was John, and after a few seconds' deliberation, I decided that I should probably answer. I slid off into the lounge.

'Hello, Lambert. Are you surviving, my poor girl?' John said.

Feeling cared-for was very nice. 'I'm OK,' I said quietly. 'But it's pretty dark here.' I heard Dad shuffle up the stairs. He sounded like an old man.

'Oh, Lambert,' John said, in tones so kindly that I felt my lip wobble. 'If there's anything I can do, please let me know.'

I nodded, not trusting myself to speak.

'Now, Lambert,' he said. 'I'm so very, very sorry to do

this to you, my dear, but I, well . . . I need to ask you to come into work for a short while.'

There was a silence as I tried to work out if he was joking.

'Lambert?'

'Er . . . are you serious?'

'I'm so sorry, but yes. It's an emergency. The funeral's at two this afternoon, right? You'll definitely be back in time.'

'What's happened? Can't someone else cover it?'

'I'll explain when you get here. But Chambers has categorically demanded you come.'

'I – I *can't*, John, it's my granny's funeral!'

John sighed. 'Lambert, I don't know how to say this, but I think it's that or . . . Well, he said it would constitute serious misconduct if you didn't come in.'

I was dumbstruck.

John continued: 'I appreciate it's terrible timing but . . .'

'Please, don't do this to me,' I whispered.

I heard a door open and Bradley Chambers's voice in the background. 'Is she on her way?' he barked. 'If not, tell her she needs to be. It's an order.'

An hour later I sat slumped on John's office sofa while he paced up and down, wringing his hands and explaining that Bradley Chambers had refused to allow Margot to run the conference. I could hear what he was saying but I couldn't actually believe it.

'Sorry, John,' I said carefully, putting up a hand to silence him. 'Can I get this straight? You tricked me into coming in "for an hour or two" so that you could make me go off and do the conference? Is that right?'

John looked agonized. 'Not exactly tricked, Charley. I just . . . Chambers ordered me to get you in and then explain once you were here.'

I gawped. 'And you *agreed* to that? On the day of my grandmother's funeral?'

The door swung open and Chambers marched in. John jumped, almost as if to attention, and without even thinking I did the same. Why did this fat little bastard have so much power over us?

'Sharon,' he leered unpleasantly. 'Sorry to inconvenience you.' I almost laughed. 'Inconvenience' was not the word I'd have used. 'But this is a big deal,' he continued. 'We've had a lot of trouble at the other conferences in Europe. I need you in charge, Sharon,' he said.

'It's Charley,' I snapped. 'You know it's Charley.'

Bradley Chambers looked stunned. 'I thought it was our little joke,' he said stiffly. 'I told you, you remind me of a girl I used to know called Sharon.'

'Well, I'm not her,' I said. 'Can you just confirm this? Does my job hang on whether or not I do the conference?'

Chambers narrowed his eyes and looked like the filthy gutter rat he was. 'Well, it's a shame to put it like that,' he said softly, 'but I would struggle to keep on a comms director who refuses to direct comms.' He stared straight at me with his repulsive, glassy little eyes, and bile rose in my throat. I looked beseechingly at John, who was standing behind him, but he avoided my gaze.

I was on my own. And so, backed into a corner and

slightly paralysed with shock, I felt myself give in. 'Right,' I said stiffly. John couldn't even look at me. I got up and did up the button of my blazer. 'I'd better go and tell Margot I'm running the event after all.'

'Sure thing, Charley.' Margot smiled frostily. 'You just can't let go, can you?' I was standing woodenly in front of her desk.

I shook my head at her, begging her not to carry on. But it was like a red rag to a raging bull.

'Nothing on earth would persuade me to miss my grandmother's funeral,' she said, handing over the conference folder. 'You strange, cold girl, you.'

You strange, cold girl, you, I repeated bitterly, as I fired up my computer. I must be dead inside.

I pulled out my phone, trying to work out what on earth I was going to say to Dad.

While I pondered this awful dilemma, a text message arrived from Hailey: *I've changed my mind*, it said. *We can sort out our differences another time, I'm not going to miss Granny Helen's funeral just because of a row. Some things are too important. X*

I stared at my phone, feeling like I'd been punched in the face. Never had a truer word been spoken.

'What the fuck was I thinking?' I asked the room. 'What the *fuck*?' Of course I had to go to my grandmother's funeral! How could I have doubted that even for a second? I looked at my watch. I had given in to Chambers's blackmail precisely six minutes ago, but they were already the most shameful six minutes of my life.

I got up and put on my blazer just as John slid into my office.

I could barely look at him. This big, strong man, after whom I'd lusted for seven years, was a spineless coward. 'Yes?' I said, walking over to the coat rack.

'Just came to check you were OK, Lambert,' John said awkwardly. 'I see you're off to the conference already. Well done, old girl. I know it's awful but you did the right thing. I'll make it up to you . . .'

This was amazing.

'Chambers has been very difficult lately,' John continued.

'John,' I cut in. 'The situation is clear – you don't need to explain. But I am not missing my grandmother's funeral.'

John looked shocked. 'Lambert,' he said uncertainly. 'You can't go . . .'

'I have to,' I said briskly. I started to pull my coat on. 'Neither you nor Chambers has any right to force me do the conference.'

John was looking quite afraid. 'Lambert, I'm sorry, you really do have to –'

'I do NOT!' I interrupted furiously. 'I do not have to do anything! I booked a day off! I stayed up till three fucking thirty! I AM GOING TO MY GRANDMOTHER'S FUNERAL!'

I picked up my bag and made towards the door but John moved over and actually blocked my way. I gasped. 'John!'

At close range I could see quite clearly that he was afraid. Of who? Me? Chambers? What was wrong with him? John was a corporate ballbreaker! 'Margot will manage it perfectly well,' I said tightly. 'Please move out of my way.'

John didn't move but he took my arm. His hand rested lightly on it but behind the hand I could feel a huge force. 'Margot *won't* manage it perfectly well,' John said, raising his voice. He'd never raised his voice at me and yet at this moment I couldn't have cared less. This man was not fit to be my boss, let alone my lover. 'She won't be a patch on you, Charley. She's wearing yet another vulva skirt and Chambers will probably –'

'What the hell do you mean I won't manage it well?' Margot said, marching in. The glass walls of my office weren't designed for one hundred per cent privacy. 'Well?' She stood with her hands on her hips, staring at John.

'Margot, please,' John said angrily. He looked wild.

'For your *information,* John, I'm better equipped to do this conference than Charley,' Margot continued. Her voice was rising to a rather un-seahorsy screech.

'Enough!' John shouted. His face had taken on a red tone that I'd never seen before. A little pulse had started up next to his eye. 'Margot, please leave this office immediately. I need to talk to Charley.'

Margot didn't move. 'Have I walked in on a professional argument or a lovers' tiff?' she sneered. 'Is poor little Charley-warley sulking that John didn't leave his wife?'

There was a terrible silence.

'*What* did you say?' I asked her. My voice was deadly quiet.

Margot grinned. 'Oh, wow,' she said softly. 'Oh, wow. You think he's left her! Well, he hasn't, Charley! He had dinner with Susan and Bradley Chambers last Thursday, making sure his precious boss didn't smell a rat. *Pathetic.*'

'Shut the fuck up,' John shouted, wheeling round at her. Flecks of spit flew from his mouth. 'How *dare* you bring up my private life?'

Margot must be making it up – John had had his French friends staying last week! Then I leaned back against my desk. Maybe he hadn't had French friends staying last week. Maybe Susan hadn't run off with the rich owner of a wine estate. I felt suddenly faint. The world had gone mad.

John was shouting at Margot now, properly shouting, and she was shouting back at him, threatening to tell Chambers about me and him. Or something like that – I wasn't sure. My brain had suddenly gone foggy. Various thoughts slopped through my head, all weirdly shaped and accompanied by strange underwater noises. *John hadn't left his wife.* Furthermore, he was so afraid of rocking the boat that he was trying to prevent me – physically – from leaving the office.

Is this what I want for myself? A job like this, a man like this?

Waves of exhaustion rolled over me. I'd had little more than a couple of hours' sleep and my eyes were still slitty from last night's hard work. *What is it all for? All this hard work? All the achievement? Salutech doesn't care about you! John doesn't care about you!*

No, I thought, staring blindly at a spot on the floor between Margot and John. No, the only people who really cared about me were my family, whom I'd been prepared to ditch at the slightest hint of pressure from my boss.

And then: *Enough*, my head told me. *You can't do this any more.*

I paused, surprised. But another thought came, stronger than the last: *I don't want this.*

And so, as if in slow motion, I stood up, took my family photos off my desk and stuffed them into my handbag, which I put back on my shoulder.

I don't want this, I repeated to myself, with mounting amazement. And I knew it was true.

I straightened up. 'I resign,' I said.

'Yeah?' Margot was shouting. 'Well, how about this, John? Your little slut has been running a company on the side since she broke her leg. A *dating* company, of all things.' She spat the word out as if there was excrement in her mouth.

John turned to me, astonished. 'Bullshit,' he shot back, turning away from me again. 'That's impossible. She works all the hours God sends.'

Too bloody true.

'I resign,' I said again.

John ignored me. 'Prove it,' he hissed at Margot.

Finally, my brain started to work.

'I resign,' I said loudly. 'Is anyone actually listening to me? I'm leaving now and I won't be coming back. If you want to sue me for my notice period then go right ahead. I want my life back.'

Two faces looked blankly at me.

'What?' John said.

'You heard,' I replied. 'We can discuss this all via email, or phone, or I can come in to do it formally, but right now I'm going to my grandmother's funeral.'

John was flabbergasted. 'You can't leave,' he said incredulously. 'You can't just – just *leave*.'

'I have to,' I said slowly. 'I'm thirty-two, nearly thirty-three, and I have no life. And my dad needs me.' The words caught in my throat and I walked around John and out of my office.

'How the hell will I explain this to Chambers?' John sounded almost childish. He was hot on my heels.

'I'm sure you'll work it out,' I said softly. 'You're used to putting him before anyone else.'

As if on cue, Chambers scurried towards the office, his mean little face sniffing the air for trouble.

'Off to the road show, then, Sharon?' he asked suspiciously.

I looked him up and down, this disgusting little prick of a man who had taken it upon himself to touch my backside more often than I cared to remember. 'Fuck you, Runty,' I said to him.

And then I turned my back on John MacAllister for the first and last time. I handed my security pass to Cassie and walked out of the comms office, my car keys jangling loudly in the silence.

As I exited the lift downstairs, legs almost buckling with shock, a heavily made-up woman with immaculate and extremely massive hair stormed through the main entrance. 'Where will I find John MacAllister?' she asked the security guard. She was American. She had serious nails. Talons of scarlet. She wasn't speaking very loudly but there was something utterly terrifying about her. So terrifying, in fact, that I found myself momentarily rooted to the spot, watching her.

And then I realized she was Susan Faulkner. Susan MacAllister now. Oh, I'd stared at her photo for hours.

The security guard tried to explain that she would probably need an appointment to see the CEO but Susan cut in with a deadly smile and a voice of steel: 'If you try to stop me, I may get violent,' she said quietly. 'John MacAllister is my husband. And I've just found out that the filthy pig has been sleeping with his press woman. If you let me up there, I will murder only him. If you detain me, I will murder you *and* him. OK?'

'You'll find him on the third floor,' I interrupted, suddenly coming to life. I put my foot into the lift to keep the doors open for her. 'And, yes, he has been sleeping with his "press woman", I'm afraid. He told her his marriage was over and that you'd run off with another man to America. I'd definitely go and murder him if I were you.'

She stared at me for a moment and I watched her face change. Then she let out a bloodcurdling war cry and charged into the lift.

I smiled and walked out into the world.

Fifteen minutes later I was stomping up a very pedestrian-unfriendly verge alongside the A1, feeling slightly silly. During my filmic departure from work I hadn't spared much thought for logistics; in particular the fact that Salutech owned my car. The sudden absence of wheels, and indeed of anything resembling a bus stop, had not facilitated my great escape but I reckoned another twenty minutes would bring me to a bus that would take me home. That was all that mattered to me right now.

I'd been unable to get hold of Ness and had eventually

called Sam, who said he'd try to come and pick me up. However, I wasn't expecting to see him any time soon. He didn't own a car.

I was dumbfounded by the events of the last hour. So dumbfounded, really, that I kind of didn't have any idea how I was feeling. When Sam had asked me, I'd just sort of shouted, 'Raaaaaarr!' then tripped over a pothole and dropped my phone. There was an incredible feeling of lightness around my chest, but I was aware that this could be the breathlessness of shock as opposed to some meta-physical sense of freedom.

But among all the thoughts that were flying around my head – panic, disbelief, astonishment, anger, joy, to name but a few – there was one thing about which I was very certain. And that was the fact that John was not the man I'd thought him to be.

He was weak.

I was deeply shocked. John had always been the strong-est, most confident man I'd known and it was this confidence that had mesmerized me for seven years.

And yet John was so scared of Bradley Chambers that he had tricked me into coming into work so he could, what? *Kidnap* me? What was he going to do? Bundle me into his car boot and roll me out at the conference? It was actually laughable. And to think he was so scared of his boss he'd tried physically to stop me leaving the building . . . It was quite sick, really.

'John is weak,' I said out loud. 'A weakling!'

But an idea was forming somewhere in my head. A rather radical one. *I'm not all that strong either*, I thought slowly, hopping across a drainage ditch. Had I not flayed myself alive for Salutech? Had I not, a mere hour ago, agreed to abandon my family on one of the hardest days we'd ever had together just because Bradley Chambers had decreed it must be so?

'*I*'m a weakling,' I muttered, extricating my tights from a clump of brambles.

And then: 'I'M A WEAKLING!' I tried it a bit louder and it felt glorious. I was not a Scottish Amazon or anything of the sort. I was just another weak, imperfect person, a girl who'd thrown her life into her work because she had no idea how else to live.

'I'M NOT TOUGH AT ALL!' I shouted, grinning. 'WOOOO!'

A lorry driver honked at me, clearly perplexed by the sight of a six-foot woman shouting to herself as she crashed along the grass verge in a suit and heels. I waved in acknowledgement. 'YEAH!' I yelled, feeling something release in my shoulder blades. 'I'm a knob!'

Another horn sounded behind me. Not even bothering to look round, I waved my hand in acknowledgement. 'WHATEVS!'

'Charley,' a man's voice yelled. 'Get in the fucking car, you lunatic!'

I whipped round. 'SAAAAAAAM! Sammeeeee!'

Sam grinned, leaning over to open the passenger door of the car he was driving. 'Oh, my God,' he said, as I threw my bag into the back and hopped in beside him. 'Oh, fucking hell, you've gone mental!'

'Whoop!' I responded. 'YEAH!'

Sam pulled away from the kerb, foot hard on the accelerator to avoid another lorry speeding up behind us. He was laughing. 'Oh, Chas, this is a glorious day,' he said. 'WHOOOOOOOOOOP!' he whooped.

We both whooped for a bit and then I settled back in the seat, trying to find a comfortable position. 'Hang on,' I said. I took my heels off and threw them out of the window on to the verge. 'There!' I stuck my feet up on the dashboard, laughing at the number of ladders running up my tights.

'We'll pick them up on the way back,' Sam said.

'Yup,' I agreed. We both laughed and I felt free. I'd been hiding at John's house since Sam and I had conducted our scientific experiment last Thursday, terrified that he had noticed how much I'd enjoyed it, but Sam hadn't let me get away with it. He'd called me most days with First Date Aid queries and updates and had seemed so completely normal that I'd begun to relax. Clearly, for him, it hadn't been an issue at all.

And the lovely thing was that, right at this moment, I didn't care.

'I am a free woman, Sam!' I cried suddenly. 'I'm FREEEEEEE!'

Sam grabbed my shoulder enthusiastically, his eyes on the road. 'I'm so fucking proud of you, Charley,' he said, suddenly emotional. 'You got out of that shithole. You have no idea how much this means to the people who care about you.'

I glanced sideways at him. Even though it was November, Sam was wearing sunglasses and, with his hair blowing in the breeze from the still-open window, he looked like some sort of film star. 'Thanks for coming to get me, Bowes,' I said gratefully. 'Did you steal a car?'

He grinned. 'No. It's Sheryl's.'

'Sheryl who? Tell me this isn't some sex-friend's car, Bowes?'

'No,' he said, slightly hurt. 'Sheryl from downstairs.'

'Oh!' I was surprised. 'But you don't know the Greens.'

'Doesn't matter,' he replied. 'You needed picking up. I'm sure you'd do the same for me.'

I would. I had a whole world of possibility opening up before me. I was going to have time to borrow a car and help a friend. To go for a walk. I could make someone dinner. 'I feel like a newborn,' I said.

Sam smiled.

'It's like I'm starting again, Sam. I'm totally shitting myself, and I'll probably have a panic attack soon, but right now I feel like I might burst. With excitement and hope and stuff. Do you know what I mean?'

'Yeah,' he said. 'I do.'

As I peered sideways at him, I saw how happy he was for me and I wanted to cry. *We'd done it!* We'd taken action! We'd fought through all the fear and started our lives again! I positively glowed. If it weren't for Sam, I wouldn't have been here, fighting my way down the A1. I would never have taken my life back.

'We did it, Bowes,' I said. 'We did it together.'

Sam was looking dangerously emotional himself. 'Right on, brother.'

I watched him driving for a while and pondered how

much I loved being with Sam. Not only was he silly and kind but he was *safe*. I felt no urge to be someone else when I was with him: not clever, not strong, not witty. It was OK to be a moron or a bore and I loved him for that.

'So, John's a wanker,' he said, after a few minutes.

I snorted, although not without sadness. 'Yep. And he's probably dead, too. His wife arrived just as I was leaving. She was made of ice. She's going to kill him. Absolutely no doubt about it.'

Sam punched me on the shoulder. 'Bo,' he remarked. 'And do you have any sort of a plan?'

I thought about it. 'No,' I said truthfully.

'Good girl.' He reached over and squeezed my leg. Oddly, I wanted to hold on to him but he moved his hand to the gear stick and, in true Bowes fashion, started singing along enthusiastically to a Backstreet Boys song on Sheryl Green's car stereo.

I closed my eyes and fell asleep.

At two o'clock that afternoon, I walked slowly down the aisle of the crematorium chapel behind Mum and Dad, who had their arms around each other. Nessie, Katy and I had copied them and I felt strong and protected with my beautiful sisters on either side of me.

We sat down on the pew and I felt someone squeeze my shoulder from behind. It was Hailey. 'Love you,' she muttered, a tear rolling down her face.

Sam, who was sitting next to her, smiled kindly at me. 'I'm so proud of you Chasmonger,' he whispered. And it was then, looking at his lovely green eyes – so full of understanding and compassion – that I let go and started to cry. I cried and cried and cried.

Today was one of the saddest days of my life but it also felt like one of the happiest. However uncertain the future felt right now, I knew I was ready for the challenge. Ready for the unknown. Ready, finally, to find out who Charlotte Lambert really was.

Chapter Eighteen

'What the hell are you doing here?' I mumbled, sleepy but very amused. Malcolm looked round to check that no one had detected him, then wagged his tail. 'Malcolm, if they find you upstairs, you're in a world of trouble.' He wagged even harder, grinning at me as if I were the most beautiful and amazing woman on earth. 'Go downstairs before we get rumbled,' I told him. 'Go on, you great big fool.'

Malcolm rejected this plan, opting instead to trot over to my bed where he stuck his nose joyously into my duvet.

'No!' I jumped out of bed and, scanning the landing for signs of human life, ran him down the stairs. 'You are a very bad boy,' I told him, as he head-butted the door to the cupboard where his food was kept. I measured out his meal and added a bit of water, trying but failing to get the bowl on to the floor before he shoved his head into it.

I sat at the kitchen table and watched him eat, smiling fondly. It was cold and beautiful outside. Sharp winter light punched through the bare branches, illuminating tiny cobwebs and old dust on the kitchen window. A cat sat on our gatepost, watching a solitary bird chirping from Dad's apple tree. There was a lovely stillness, broken only by a column of steam coming from the boiler vent. It snaked up into the air and quickly fluffed out into nothing.

I walked over to the kettle where last night's glasses

were still piled, grainy red stains sitting in the bottom of well-fingered wine glasses and Scotch tumblers full of melted ice. It had been a good send-off. After an awkward, sombre start, we had all relaxed and shared our Granny Helen tales, most of them very funny. My aunts, uncles and cousins, a small handful of neighbours and also Hailey, Sam and Sarah had stayed until the bitter end and now they were all asleep, dotted around our house and Granny Helen's cottage next door. Malcolm and I might be the only ones up but I still had the sense of security I'd felt yesterday, of being surrounded by people who made me safe.

'I don't have a job,' I told Malcolm, as the kettle boiled. He cocked his head comically to one side, licking the remains of his breakfast from his nose. 'Oh, Malcolm, I do love you,' I told him. Needing no further encouragement, he jumped up and stuck his face into my belly.

'Morning,' a sleepy voice said in the doorway. It was Sam. His hair had taken on a very amusing triangular wedge shape after a night on the sofa and he had one of our old blankets wrapped around him. 'I wouldn't say no to a tea,' he announced. He pulled out a chair from the kitchen table and yawned, running his hands through his hair.

I lined up two mugs, thinking how nice it was to have Sam at my parents' house. I'd been looking forward to bringing John here some time but had also felt that I'd probably have to come in first and clean up a bit. There were no such worries with Sam, who, until recently, had had the domestic habits of a farmyard pig. And with whom I felt very relaxed.

It occurred to me that I was comparing my housemate to my ex-lover, so I moved my focus elsewhere. 'Why are you up so early, Bowes?' I asked.

There was a pause.

'I have to get back to Edinburgh pronto,' Sam said eventually. He appeared to be concentrating hard on the bird on the gatepost outside.

I sat down and slid a mug of tea in front of him. 'What's going on?'

Sam didn't reply for a while, but when he did his voice sounded different. 'Chas,' he said. I looked up sharply. 'Yes?'

'I got the job.'

For a moment, I had no idea what he was talking about but it came eventually. The acting job, of course. The *London* job. The definitely-not-Edinburgh job.

I knew I should feel happy but I didn't. Why was Sam being taken away from me now of all times? I'd just quit my job, for crying out loud – now was the time for us to start out together as a business! Scrap that: now was the time for us to start out together as human beings!

I forced myself to remember what he'd said about the acting job being pretty much the gig of a lifetime. 'Congratulations!' I said shrilly. 'Did you get the part you wanted?' I tried to look happy.

He nodded, barely able to contain his smile. 'For real. I got one of the main bloody parts, Charley!'

I was gutted. 'Oh, my God!' I said emptily. 'Wow! That's amazing! I'm SO pleased for you!' I clasped his arm miserably. 'So happy, Bowes! And proud,' I added. I *was* proud. But with this came sadness of a severity that confused me.

'Thanks,' Sam said bashfully. 'It's probably the best news I've ever had. Eleven years of nothing and then – boom!'

I made a face that was meant to show awe and delight.

But I was not delighted. I was sad and also quite afraid. Part of the reason I had felt relatively secure about marching out of Salutech and into a new life was that I knew Sam would be there with me, doing exactly the same thing. It was unsettling to think that I now had to do it alone, particularly if Sam was going to be moving on with his life down in trendy London, surrounded by beautiful people.

'Does that mean you're leaving soon?' I asked. *At least give me a few days, just to get myself started. I need you!*

But I knew it wasn't going to happen. It was written all over his face. 'Actually, I'm leaving today,' he said awkwardly. 'Sorry, Chas. I got the call yesterday and we start rehearsals on Monday. I was going to stay another day but that'd only give me Sunday to find somewhere to live in London.'

I nodded in what I hoped was an understanding manner as Sam explained that they would run from mid-December until February. My heart sank further when he admitted that he wouldn't make it back to Edinburgh at all because it played on weekends – and that there was even a chance of the play extending into the summer if it went well.

'You may decide to move to London properly,' I blurted out, hoping he'd deny it.

He didn't. He just nodded reflectively. 'If things go well, then, yes, I suppose I might.'

There was a silence during which Malcolm started munching loudly on his balls.

I sipped some tea and smiled brightly. 'Well, Bowes, I'm absolutely thrilled. Cheers!' I shoved my cup rather forcefully at him, slopping a lot of tea on to his nice shawl-collar jumper. 'Oh, fuck! Sorry!'

'Ah, whatever,' he said easily, mopping it up with a tea-towel. 'It's exciting, isn't it?' He paused. 'I'm so grateful to you, brother.'

I watched him guardedly, waiting for him to expand.

'I'd never have done this without your emails,' Sam said. 'I'd have just carried on lying around eating junk and doing nothing. I owe this job to you.'

Exactly! I thought. *We're a team! Don't do this!*

Sam finished his tea and stood up. 'We should say goodbye,' he said to the window. 'It might be a while. Although with all your free time maybe you could come down to London for a weekend and we could party?'

'Sounds good,' I replied. We both knew this would never happen.

I got up. 'Well, bye, then,' I said, giving him a quick hug. 'And congrats.'

'I hope your dad's OK,' he said, making for the door. 'And that you take some proper time off, Chas. I know you're planning to get back into First Date Aid but, bruv, you need rest. Even with a broken leg and pelvis and whatnot you didn't take it easy.'

'I will. But I'm looking forward to taking First Date Aid forward with you,' I added hopefully. I prayed Sam wouldn't ditch that too.

To my great relief he nodded emphatically. 'Absolutely!

Actors have an easy life, Chas. I'll have plenty of time to do it. We'll probably speak every day!'

I was feeling really miserable now. Of course we wouldn't speak every day. He'd soon get dragged into his new life and I'd spend my days sitting around in silence emailing total strangers on behalf of total strangers.

'I *hope* we speak every day,' Sam added, after a pause. His face had clouded over and I saw that he was actually quite sad himself. A proper lump swelled in my throat. This shouldn't be happening.

'What play is it?' I asked, as Sam hugged Malcolm goodbye.

Sam smiled. '*The Tempest.*'

I gasped. I knew nothing about Shakespeare but I knew *The Tempest* all right. Sam's time-honoured chat-up line, the one he'd been using since the first day I'd met him at Glasgow University, was from *The Tempest*. I didn't know why but I began to experience a strange emotional shift as I looked at the boy standing before me. 'Wow, Sam! Who are you playing?'

Sam grinned even harder. 'Ferdinand!'

'Don't tell me he's the one who uses that line?'

'Yeah! Jackpot!'

'Brilliant,' I said, now genuinely entertained. 'Well, let's hope the girl playing Miranda will be fit and then you'll really mean it when you say that line!'

Sam laughed uncomfortably. 'Er, yeah, let's hope so.'

We were standing in the doorway now, cold air seeping hungrily into the kitchen. Sam smiled a final farewell. 'I'm so glad everything happened as it did,' he said. A small blush was appearing on his neck. 'You've basically changed my life, Chas.'

And then he went, disappearing round the corner towards the square with his hands in his pockets and the collar of his coat up against the stiff wind.

'CHARLEYPOPS?' I came to with a start. Hailey was standing behind me in the kitchen with Malcolm exploding excitedly around her. She looked worried.

'Hi,' I said. My voice sounded woolly.

'Are you dead? I just said your name three times before you heard me.'

I smiled. 'Not dead. Just . . .' I trailed off. *Just absolutely gutted*, I thought.

Hailey gazed suspiciously at me. 'Why are you standing in the doorway? You're not seeing ghosts, are you?' I couldn't help but laugh. She looked not dissimilar to Sam, rucked up and spiky after a night sleeping on the other sofa with three sleeping bags piled on top of her.

'No. I was letting Sam out. He had to go back to Edinburgh.'

Hailey nodded sagely. 'Yes. We had a good old chinwag when everyone went off to bed last night. Fucking amazing he got that part, eh?'

I nodded and a silence sprang up between us. We'd behaved ourselves yesterday but the situation had demanded it. Now, though, there was nothing between us and last week's awful phone call. Even though I wanted to get angry that she'd accused me of sleeping with Matty, it was hard to feel anything other than fondness for Hailey as she stood in front of me, hair sticking out in a bad halo round her head, my old pyjamas struggling to meet round her newly rounded belly.

'I'm not pregnant,' she said, following my eyes. 'I'm fat.'

I hovered by the front door, unsure what to say. Fortunately Hailey had decided to run this conversation. 'I've been comfort eating,' she announced. 'Or comfort bingeing, more like. I've suspected Matty of playing around for a long time.' She stared at me defiantly, daring me to contradict her. I said nothing, but sat down slowly at the table and gestured to her to do the same.

She pulled a sleeping bag over her stomach, something I'd never seen her do. Hailey had an amazing body, all padded curves and wobbly bosoms, and she'd always been justly proud of it. Now she was not. She was hiding herself. The day of twenty sausages made a lot more sense.

'And before you ask,' she said, 'it had never even crossed my mind that Matty and you were messing around. But I *knew* he'd been somewhere on Wednesday night and I was going through his phone when you called . . . In my mad state I thought he must be shagging you if you were calling at nearly eleven the next night.' She pulled the sleeping bag round her more tightly. 'I'm sorry,' she said, embarrassed. 'You were trying to help me and I acted like a psychopath.'

I couldn't bear to see Hailey so broken and ashamed. 'No,' I said softly. '*I'm* sorry. I was drunk. It was inexcusable to call at that time of night.'

'But you were calling Matty, not me!' she said, eyes flashing. 'You were doing the right thing! How could I ever have suspected you? I . . . urgh,' she said, obviously disgusted.

'Stop it, Hails,' I said. 'Stop beating yourself up. You're the innocent party here. It's Matty who's in the wrong.'

She nodded thoughtfully. 'Can I make some tea?' she asked eventually. Her voice was wobbling.

'Of course.'

A tear fell down her cheek. 'Actually,' she said, 'can I have a hug?'

After a very long hug, during which both of us cried a little, we got dressed, took Malcolm out for a walk and Hailey told me what had been going on.

From the moment she'd moved in to Gore-Tex Towers – and thus been with Matty a lot more – she had noticed that his behaviour was often rather erratic, coming home late with a series of weird excuses and spending far too much time on his iPhone. 'Remember how we thought it was amazing that he was online when he was working in a remote garden?' Hailey asked. 'He fucking well wasn't. He works in a bloody *office*, Charley!'

The day after I'd told Hailey about Matty and Margot she had followed him to work and had been amazed when he'd parked outside the offices of a debt-collection agency out towards Musselburgh. At five thirty p.m. he had driven back into town and met up with a woman he obviously didn't know in the lobby of a tatty hotel near the railway station. They had had two drinks each 'and a plate of PRAWN SKEWERS, Chas. PRAWN FUCKING SKEWERS? What kind of a courtship is that?' and had then disappeared upstairs. He had returned home at eight forty-five and given Hailey her customary cuddle, eaten his dinner and then run a bath. 'He took his fucking iPhone with him,' Hailey muttered darkly. 'No doubt organizing the next slag.' Hailey had moved out the next day and was staying with her mother in Falkirk.

'I just can't believe what I'm hearing,' I said. Malcolm galloped head-first into a flock of pigeons, barking excitedly as they took flight.

'That's why I got so shitty with you,' Hailey said, 'about William the Internet doctor. I'd been suspicious of Matty for ages and sort of convinced myself that all women were evil husband-stealers.'

She threw a stick for Malcolm. 'You can only steal a husband when he wants to be stolen, though,' she said sadly. 'I feel like such a fool.'

I grabbed her gloved hand. 'You're nothing of the sort, Tits.'

After a short battle I persuaded Hailey to move into Sam's room. She resisted for a while, informing me that I needed peace and quiet, not another lodger, but once I'd filled her in about Salutech and the very scary uncertain future stretching ahead of me, she agreed. 'I'll keep an eye on you,' she said affectionately. 'Make sure you're not storming off, trying to take on the world.'

I smiled gratefully. 'I may well need help with that.'

We walked round Smeaton Lake in contemplative silence, Hailey lost in thoughts about Matty and me lost in thoughts about Sam. I didn't want him to go. I wanted him to stay and hang around with me in the flat and take me to the Barony, to make me funny dinners and put on funny films.

I resolved not to talk about Sam for the rest of the day. There were bigger fish to fry.

'Me and Sam had a kiss to make sure those emails meant nothing,' I heard myself remark. I could have slapped myself! Hadn't I just resolved *not to talk about him again*? Could I rely on myself to do bloody *anything* any more?

With a visible effort, Hailey dragged herself out of wherever her head had been. I watched her process what I'd just said. 'Oh, my God!' She looked like she was about to faint. 'You WHAT? What was it *like*?'

I shrugged in what I hoped was a dispassionate manner. 'Scientific. It was an experiment. Science.'

'WHEN? WHERE?'

'Late one night last week. We were drunk; it was nothing.' I thought I'd sounded reasonably off-hand.

Hailey stopped walking and stared at me. 'Have you had sex with the Bowes?' she whispered.

'Of course not!' Why couldn't I keep my mouth shut?

'Thank holy God for that,' Hailey said eventually. 'That would be absolutely disgusting. You and Bowes? Urgh! Worst couple ever!'

'Too right.' I laughed, rather loudly. She was right. It would be awful, me and Sam.

There was a weird silence as we walked on, which Malcolm took the edge off by plopping into the near-freezing lake and thrashing around for a few seconds before exploding out again.

'Actually, Charleypops,' Hailey said thoughtfully, 'you should probably ignore me. I mean, what the fuck do I know about men? I moved in with someone who likes to be tied to the end of the bed with a dog collar.'

I snorted and, after a few seconds, Hailey joined in. A few minutes later we were doing what we did best: clinging to each other, howling with laughter.

*

When we arrived back home, the relatives had gone and there was a smell of eggs, bacon and change in the air. Dad was buzzing around in a way he hadn't done in weeks, toasting bread at the Aga, chatting to Ness and Katy and – for reasons that were unclear to me – wearing a fez. I raised my eyebrows inquisitively at Ness but she just shrugged, smiling. Dad was a law unto himself.

'Piglet!' Dad exclaimed, as we came in. 'And Hailey! Sit down and have some breakfast!' Malcolm leaped excitedly around the kitchen, a big wet monster who loved us madly. Dad gave him a piece of toast and tried to look remorseful when Mum told him off. 'Here's to an exciting new chapter,' he announced, as we sat down to eat. Mum smiled secretively and we listened, now interested.

'I've been suffering a bit of a malfunction in the happiness department,' Dad said reflectively. 'But I woke up this morning and felt certain that my mother would be pelting me with kiwis if she knew I was moping around.' He sniggered. 'She was an absolute bloody tyrant, my mother,' he admitted.

Everyone laughed and toasted Granny Helen.

'So I've decided to have some fun,' he continued. 'Those hippies have it sewn up with all their chanting and essential oils.'

Katy nodded knowledgeably; Ness and I exchanged confused glances.

Dad carried on: 'We got up this morning and wrote letters of resignation,' he said proudly, putting his arm round Mum's shoulders. 'East Linton clearly doesn't seem to need a surgery any more and we're feeling the call of the wild!'

'Oh, God,' Hailey muttered.

'We're off to India again!' Dad shouted. 'But this time we're going for a long time! Until Christmas!'

I gasped and Ness clapped. 'Fucking amazing!' Katy yelled.

'Katherine . . .' Mum started, but Katy had enveloped her in a hug.

I began to say that I should probably pay for this holiday, given that my broken leg had ruined their last Indian adventure, but Dad interrupted, 'No more four-star hotels for us, Piglet. We're going backpacking.'

'Brilliant,' Hailey cried. 'Oh, how I love the Lamberts.'

Dad went on to tell his gobsmacked audience that they wanted to start off in an ashram, for some 'spiritual enlightenment', and then take on India's rusty old train network. 'I want some curry,' Dad enthused. 'And mangoes. And some God!'

As we ate breakfast, plotting, planning and laughing, I found myself thinking what a shame it was that Sam had had to leave so early. He'd have loved the atmosphere and the nonsense and the bacon. And Dad, too. That was the good thing about Sam. He thought my family were great.

'What about you, Charlotte?' Dad asked gently. 'What will you do next?'

I thought about it. The truth of the matter, of course, was that I had no idea. My life was stretching before me looking alarmingly empty – apart from First Date Aid – and while I was happy I'd escaped Salutech, I couldn't pretend I felt very confident.

Perhaps sensing my fear, Dad patted me on the back. 'It doesn't matter what you do, my piglet. You're free!

Roam the country at leisure! Jump in a bog! Roll in a field! Dump on a tump!'

'Dad, you're insane!'

I told my parents for the first time about First Date Aid and was surprised by the extent of their enthusiasm for it.

'My, oh, my,' Dad exclaimed. 'You cheeky little Cupid . . . If Jane leaves me for a handsome young Indian, I'll be sure to sign up.'

Mum ignored him. 'Will you be able to earn a living from it, Charley?' she asked anxiously.

I told them about the huge boost that Sam had given the business since we'd become partners, getting us important media coverage, opening up our services to men and transforming the website from something nice and functional to something so fabulous you'd want to pay us just to look at it. 'He's been absolutely incredible!' I enthused.

'Charleypops's business is brilliant,' Hailey told my parents firmly. 'You should be very proud. There was this woman who looked like a decomposing vegetable, and Charley got her a date with the best-looking man in Brighton! That's how good she is!'

'Oh, Sonia,' I recalled. 'Yeah, I worked really hard for her. When she wrote back the day after to tell me how it went, I nearly took the train to London to give her a hug! The poor girl had absolutely no confidence in herself and it was great to be able to help.'

'You love this,' Ness said, watching my face. 'You never talked about Salutech like that.'

Katy agreed. 'Yeah, you just went all corporate and wankerish when you talked about work.'

'Hear hear!' Dad shouted. 'Our clever, brave little pig-let, striking out on her own! Cheers!'

We all chinked orange juices and I beamed. But under-neath the warmth of the moment sadness tugged insidiously at me. The sadness was called Sam. Sam Bowes – without whom First Date Aid would have been no more than a hobby – was probably letting himself out of my flat for what might be the last time. He was moving on to bigger, better things, his lazy green eyes now full of purpose and ambition. It was the end of an era. And that sucked.

Much later, once Ness, Katy and Hailey had left and I'd given Mum and Dad's house a good clean, rearranged the pictures in my old bedroom, walked Malcolm again and written a formal letter of resignation to Salutech, I lay on my bed and tried to chill.

I discovered within about thirty seconds that Taking It Easy was a very difficult business.

After a few minutes I went downstairs and made some herbal tea, forcing myself back to the sofa to drink it. I tried to breathe slowly and deeply, like enlightened people did. *In . . . and out. In . . . and out.*

DO SOME FIRST DATE AID EMAILS, my brain screeched. *OR GO AND BUY A NEWSPAPER. OR CLEAN THE OVEN. MAYBE DO ALL THREE. PREFERABLY NOW.*

I opened an eye and saw Malcolm sitting in front of me, looking puzzled. 'I'm trying to chill,' I told him. 'Try-ing to just, you know, be.'

He looked doubtful.

When my phone rang a few minutes later, I jumped to it as if my life depended on it. Quite how I was going to maintain good mental health without work was a mystery.

It was Shelley, calling to tell me about another investors' event she'd got Sam and me into next week. Strangely, when I'd emailed her last week, thanking her for getting us into the Balmoral conference but explaining – honestly, I supposed – that we had been unable to secure funding, she hadn't seemed too bothered. *No problem, there'll be other opps*, she'd written back, her mind obviously elsewhere. Shelley didn't normally talk like this. Now she was back on it again. 'It's another dinner,' she barked. 'At the Kitchin. Private hire, the whole place will be closed for this event. You two MUST go. Great opportunity for the business.'

I smiled. Somewhere along the line I had grown to like Shelley Cartwright, in spite of her steam-train approach to communication. And I was very touched that she was so keen to help First Date Aid. 'I'll go,' I said. 'But it'll be just one person for the guest list. Sam's moved to London.'

There was a brief silence. 'Oh,' Shelley said eventually, obviously disgruntled.

Immediately I felt insulted. Did she think I was incapable of doing it without Sam? 'Shelley, I'll be absolutely fine on my own,' I said, probably a little too defensively. 'I was running this company alone for quite a while before Sam joined me and I've been working in the corporate world for more than ten years.'

'Have you now?' Shelley mused. She was clearly somewhere else.

'Yes. I started –'

'Right,' she interrupted. 'Well, I will put you on the guest list. When will your partner return to Edinburgh?'

Did she fancy Sam or something? There was a lovely photo of him on the website (we had had more than a few emails asking if Sam was available for dates) and I was beginning to wonder if Shelley had seen it and wanted a piece of Bowes too. Trying not to sound huffy, I told her I had no idea when Sam was returning – if he returned at all – and then she went all vague and preoccupied and ended the call. It was obvious that she had lost interest in what I was saying.

I let it go. Our business was doing very well without her, thank you very much.

I decided to allow myself twenty minutes to do some First Date Aid emails, perhaps to prove to Shelley that we didn't need help. Chilling was rescheduled for later in the afternoon.

I powered up my laptop and logged on.

There were several emails, one of which was from a bile-spitting client about a date with a man who'd turned out to be married (this was my fault, apparently) but I was far more interested by the most recent, sent only fifteen minutes ago.

'A message for Charley Lambert,' it said in the subject line. It was from Sam. I smiled, pleased. I liked the thought of him pausing to write to me before he left the flat. It was comforting.

I have a friend called Charley Lambert, the email began.

Eh? Half frowning, half smiling, I read on.

> She's a few hours into her new life of freedom. She's said
> goodbye to some harmful things from the past – and some
> harmful people, too – and is about to start out on her own.

Malcolm sat next to the sofa. 'Sam's sent me a lovely email,' I informed him. I'd already stopped frowning and was now grinning.

> She's afraid. She doesn't know if she'll make it, but I know she
> will. She has no idea how to just sit still (I would bet ten
> thousand pounds that she reads this within an hour of me
> sending it) but I know she'll learn. She's capable of anything, this
> girl. She's one of the most legendary legends in, well, legend.
> Life without her will be just that bit colder and crapper. I will
> miss Charley Lambert, a lot, and I'm sad I won't be there while
> she starts out on this new journey.

I hugged myself. It was lovely to hear this from Sam. Spine-tinglingly lovely. No, scrap that: it was thrilling. He just didn't say things like this to me in real life. It was like having William back again.

> Please tell her she'll be OK. Because she will be. There isn't
> anyone out there like her and I'm well fucking happy to have her
> in my life.
>
> Sam X

I read the email three times, happy and alive in a way I hadn't been since I'd been emailing William. *Here* was the man who'd got under my skin. Here was the man who'd turned my life upside down. Right here in my inbox. That amazing man who could read my mind and make me feel vulnerable and special and sparkly and breathless all at once.

I realized I was crying. I realized that it didn't matter if William, Sam or Barack sodding Obama had sent those messages. The fact of the matter was that I'd fallen in love with the man who'd written them. And, however inconvenient and improbable it might feel, that man was Sam.

I was in love with Samuel Bowes. 'What am I going to do, Malcolm?' I wept. 'I love Sam! And he's just moved to London!'

But Malcolm was asleep.

Chapter Nineteen

As my train pulled out of Waverley Station, The Fear set in. I should never have agreed to this. It had been nearly a week since I'd said goodbye to Sam and I'd thought about very little else since. It had been a rather intense time and all the evidence was pointing towards my having turned into an obsessive moron.

I hadn't tried to put myself off him. I couldn't have done it if I *had* tried. The feelings that gripped me every time I thought about him (approximately twice a minute) were too big; they were not within my control. I'd been swept off down a river I'd never expected to navigate and the best I could hope for would be a short and relatively merciful ride.

For a few days, I'd been cross about it all. Why Sam, of all the men in the universe? Sam and I were fundamentally incompatible, we were –

But every time I'd gone down this road I'd stopped short. Because, actually, Sam and I were the people who had written those emails. Which meant that we were probably a lot more compatible than I'd cared to believe.

After a while I'd dared to try imagining us as a couple; a prospect that, until only a few weeks ago, would have made me soil my pants laughing. But it was worryingly easy to imagine. Sam belonged in my life. I didn't need to make adjustments: he was already there at the centre of my universe. I pictured us walking together in a cold, blowy field near my parents' house, Sam throwing sticks for Malcolm. Sitting in the pub, Sam giggling about an audition and me holding his hand proudly. Most shocking of all was the ease with which I could imagine us waking up in bed together and smiling at each other like goons. That was my favourite image. The thought of him being that close to me brought on an intense longing, not the helpless horn I'd had for John but something ten times more lovely.

And then I would feel deeply sad because I knew it would never happen. This was a one-sided fantasy. Sam was already talking about his fit co-star and he'd also commented on how hot one of my new First Date Aid clients was. And most of all, as I reminded myself throughout the day, <u>I was not Sam's thing and never had been</u>. That part was underlined for emphasis. <u>I was not Sam's thing</u>. He liked small girls he could throw around the bedroom. He had told me this several times over the course of our fourteen-year friendship.

This cycle – scrummy snoggy sugary thoughts followed by sharp and crushing disappointment – was killing me. I'd escaped my Salutech prison only to check into an even more merciless jail. It was torment.

And aside from this – beyond the obsessive cycle – I missed Sam being in my flat. I missed him like a crumble misses its custard. Arriving back to help Hailey move in last week, I'd found a pile of Sam's boxes in the hallway and, poking out of one of them, was his teddy bear. Without stopping to think I'd whipped the bear away, named him Bowes Junior and hidden him in my bed. I let him sleep on the pillow and propped him up when I made my bed every morning. I had possibly kissed his nose once or twice.

The fact that Sam shamelessly owned a teddy bear made me love him even more. I was bursting with it. It was awful. I prayed that it would pass soon and that I wouldn't have to see him before it did.

It was fairly alarming, therefore, that I found myself on a train to London ready for an entire day in his company.

It was Shelley's fault. She'd called a few days ago, trumpeting with excitement that she'd persuaded a friend of hers to write a feature about First Date Aid in the *Sunday Times*. 'THIS IS THE CHANCE OF A LIFETIME,' she had yelled, going on to make clear that nothing short of nuclear fall-out would be an acceptable excuse for me not to come down. 'You'll be doing a chummy photo-shoot with Sam,' she added briskly, without the slightest idea how simultaneously terrifying and wonderful this sounded to me. She told me again how determined she was to help move our business along and this time I didn't bother arguing. I was mute anyway.

Two minutes after I'd croaked, 'Yes,' to Shelley, Sam called me, shrieking like a child. 'FUUUUUUUCK!' he'd screamed. 'FUCKING *SUNDAY TIMES*!'

'Fucking *Sunday Times*,' I'd repeated unenthusiastically.

I hadn't slept last night. I was a wreck.

Desperate to take my mind off it all, I lurched to the buffet car for a calming cup of tea – which actually just made me even more buzzy and mad – then sat down to open my post, which I'd shoved into my bag as I'd left earlier this morning. So far the old sitting-still business had proved a bit troublesome, but maybe (after opening these envelopes, dealing with anything that came up, filing my nails and then retouching my make-up) I might be able to do nothing for an hour or so. Or at least fifteen minutes.

Breaking the habit of a lifetime was not proving easy. This week I had twice caught myself getting into the shower at six thirty a.m., an act that had not gone unnoticed by my new housemate. Yesterday morning Hailey had marched into the bathroom while I was mid-shower, roaring, 'GET BACK INTO BED, YOU GREAT BIG MENTAL!' I scrabbled around trying to cover myself up while she stood, bouncer-like, at the door, waiting for me to leave. I whimpered and left.

First in my pile of mail: a bank statement that I didn't look at. The prospect of life without a sturdy pay cheque was too frightening to contemplate right now. There were three letters for Sam, which I added to the pile in my bag. And then came something that made my heart stop momentarily: a letter from Salutech.

But it was no more than an acknowledgement from HR of my resignation, finishing off with a note to say that, because of my senior role within the company, my case would be dealt with 'by the Chief Executive Officer'.

I swallowed nervously. What would that actually mean? Would I have to go in and talk to John?

It was very strange, after all these years, to feel cold at the prospect of seeing him. I didn't miss him, I didn't want him, I didn't even feel sorry for him when I imagined him having to deal with my departure. I just wanted to draw a line under it and forget about him as quickly as possible. It was becoming clearer by the day that he and I hadn't stood a rat's chance in hell. Not because he had failed to leave Susan, not because he was terrified of Chambers, not because I'd stormed out of Salutech. No, we had been doomed because I'd already fallen for someone else.

'Dammit.' I sighed. I'd lasted a whole minute without thinking about Sam.

I filed the letter in my bag and tried to file my thoughts with it. It was super-important that Sam and I looked like the perfect business partnership during our interview and photo-shoot; Sam had promised to abstain from trumping for the afternoon and I'd promised (myself) to abstain from strange and moony behaviour around him.

I opened the final letter, which looked a lot more interesting. It was a handwritten, very expensive envelope with something quite rigid inside. Was it an invitation to some sort of exclusive spa day? A nice big cheque? A Valentine maybe! Sent three months early just to be sure!

It was none of these things. It was a thick, shiny card, featuring a black-and-white picture of two beautiful people holding hands on a moonlit beach, gazing into each other's eyes. They looked like they were about to remove their clothes and hump in a very beautiful way. Behind them, a full moon cast a beautiful train of rippled light along the sea. It was all very beautiful. I looked again at the two beautiful people standing at the centre of it all. The beautiful man was Samuel Bowes and the beautiful woman was some pesky slag called Katia Johnson. *THE TEMPEST*: SPECIAL INVITATION was stamped in the corner of the picture in a beautiful cerise.

I stared at the invitation and felt my heart break a tiny bit. Katia Johnson must be Miranda, Sam's onstage lover. The one he'd mentioned in THREE EMAILS this week. And, needless to say, she was everything Sam liked. She was small and pretty and was wearing some wispy little dress that was being blown by the wind from the sea. 'Stop looking at him like that,' I snapped at her, disconcerted by the absolute adoration in her eyes. Sam's face was open and vulnerable; he gazed back at her with an intensity that made me want to cry. Somehow in the course of my obsession I had forgotten that Sam was probably spending a lot of time pashing an actress at the moment. Was the pashing going beyond the confines of the rehearsal room?

Arrgh! Stop it! I screwed my eyes shut. *Please, God, help me fall in love with someone – anyone – who is not Samuel Bowes.*

'Hi,' said yet another beautiful girl, wearing an assortment of furry things, 'I'm Alice, your stylist.' She looked no older than eighteen. I shook her hand and tried to be jolly. Why was there a stylist here? I'd spent most of the last week trying to find an outfit! I'd been into every bloody shop in Edinburgh! And Glasgow too, for that matter!

'Kaveh wants you two to look really contemporary and fresh,' she said smoothly. 'I've got some great ideas for you, Charley.' She turned to Sam, who looked extremely lovely in a pair of slim jeans, weird leather shoes and a classic tailored shirt. 'You're probably OK as you are,' she told him. 'Fab shoes.'

I stomped off to get changed. This morning was definitely not what I'd hoped for. The 'art director', Kaveh, a spectacled man wearing deck shoes and ankle-length tweed trousers (in winter?), had told us that he wanted us to be spontaneous, youthful and fun. This had been a bad start. I didn't know how to do any of these things. *I'm a bloody businesswoman*, I thought darkly. *Not a teenage pyjama party model.* Worse still, the photographer had said within seconds of my arrival that he wanted me to take my glasses off – something I never did: I looked like a mole without them – and Anna, the *Sunday Times* journalist, was flirting openly with Sam.

Alice held up a very short, chiffony full-sleeved dress in a faecal colour. 'Perfect,' she announced. 'We'll put berry-coloured tights and some ankle wedges with it . . . Maybe I'll get the hair-stylist to fuck up your hair a bit too,' she mused. I fumed. I'd got up an hour early this morning to make sure my hair was as unfucked-up as possible.

Forty-five minutes later I stared at my reflection in absolute dismay. 'I can't!' I said to her, anguished. 'I'm nearly seven foot tall!' The ankle wedges were gigantic. I'd tower over Sam like this. The dress was nice enough but on me it barely covered my bum cheeks, and my 'fucked-up' hair involved a stupid bow. I looked, quite indisputably, like a massive seven-foot toddler.

She smiled. 'Don't worry about your height. You're both going to be lying down. Great legs, by the way.'

I didn't give a toss if we were lying down or swinging from the ceiling: I simply couldn't go out looking like this. Sam and I were already eye to eye height-wise: I couldn't become taller than him! I tried to talk her into giving me a pair of flats but she wouldn't. 'It'll look lovely,' she breezed. 'Your nice long legs with the chunkiness of the heel . . .

It'll look all clean and angular . . . With lots of soft chiffony lines up top . . . Delish!'

I wanted to cry.

When I finally shuffled out, eyes fixed to the floor, Sam was already draped over a *chaise-longue* in the middle of a brightly lit white cube. 'Great,' I muttered. He seemed as natural and relaxed as Malcolm was when he snored in front of the fire.

I tried to shuffle over to him without him seeing me – probably a rather unrealistic feat – but no sooner had the ankle wedges traversed thirty centimetres than he looked up and whistled. 'Wow, Chas! Brother! You are WELL HOT!'

I went bright red and immediately sensed Kaveh the art director getting angry. Bright red faces didn't work well on stark white sets. I scuttled over and sat down at the far end of the *chaise-longue*, lest Sam notice how gigantic I was. 'Look like a knob,' I muttered to him.

Sam's brow creased. 'You do not look like a knob in the slightest,' he said firmly. 'You look lovely. But you also look really uncomfortable.'

I nodded miserably. 'They won't even let me wear my glasses.'

Sam was puzzled. 'But your glasses are you, Chas.'

I shrugged. 'They don't want "me".'

Sam got up. 'I do,' he said. 'This is a feature, not a fantasy.'

I watched in amazement as he ambled over to Kaveh and gestured in my direction. After a couple of seconds Kaveh interrupted him, presumably to defend his styling, but Sam put his hand in the air to take back control. Even when the photographer got involved he just continued to shake his head, politely but firmly. They all turned to me, and then Sam was talking again, extremely confident and clever. And, try as I might, I felt a lovely sensation of warmth envelop me. Sam was up there defending me. As in the real me, not the me that Kaveh and Alice and the other trendies wanted me to be. The longing I'd felt inside me for the last week took on a whole new dimension. I was really, really, *really* in love with Samuel Bowes.

I bet Katia bloody Slagface the actress has got there first, I thought sadly, remembering the look of love on that invite. No actor was good enough to fake something like that.

The shoot eventually took place, with me in the lovely tight plum-coloured trousers I'd bought, worn with a compromise top, which sat halfway between my tasteful jumper and Kate's chiffony dress shocker. My hair had been returned to normal – save for a Kirby-grip that swept my fringe off to the side – a look I rather liked, in fact – and I was back in the flat brogues I'd rocked up in.

Sam and I were draped artfully over each other on the couch and were instructed – repeatedly – to throw our heads back and laugh youthfully. At first, this had been excruciating and we'd looked about as youthful and care-free as a pair of Victorian state officials. But after a few attempts Sam had whispered to me that Kaveh had turned up this morning in a purple cape, and I whispered back that I'd found his teddy bear and named him Bowes Junior, and we'd got the giggles, Kaveh had got what he wanted, and the whole agonizing affair was brought to a timely end. After an 'afternoon tea' of tiny morsels of sushi ('Don't they fucking *eat* anything in this city?' I muttered to Sam) we sat down for what turned out to be quite a nice interview with Anna the journalist. The more we talked about our business, the more we glowed. Watching Sam, I knew he was as proud of it as I was, and I felt even sadder that he was in the process of throwing himself back into acting. We were a brilliant team! He should be up in Edinburgh with me, making terrible omelettes and emailing mad people!

Towards the end of our interview, a very smart woman arrived in the studio. It took a few seconds for me to work out who she was or where I knew her from but, as she whipped out her BlackBerry and started hammering out an impatient email, I remembered exactly who she was. I broke into a grin.

'Shelley!' I said, walking over to her after the interview. 'At last!'

Shelley looked up from her BlackBerry and once again I had the sensation of looking straight at myself. Only this time something was different. I might not have mastered the art of relaxation yet but, as we eyed each other, I knew that we were no longer in the same world. I was not on that BlackBerry, or in that suit, or indeed in that head any more. I was not a Power Woman. I was just a Normal Woman. Who now got a stonking eight hours' sleep every night and was learning that there was a life beyond the office.

'Charlotte Lambert,' she barked, shooting a hand out. 'My God! What a bloody pleasure, at long last!'

Without any self-consciousness she stood back to

appraise me. 'You look quite good,' she announced eventually. I nodded a thank-you and wondered if I would ever get used to the way she behaved. Sam snorted and tried to turn it into a cough, and Shelley's eyes swivelled to him. 'Well,' she said, again standing back to look him up and down. 'Sam, Shelley Cartwright. I'm one of Charlotte's clients. Or, at least, I was,' she added, with a fleeting, blissful grin. The grin quickly closed down and Margaret Thatcher came back. After a quick appraisal of Sam, she nodded. 'Were you satisfied with the interview?'

'Yes,' Sam started. 'Actually, it was great that she was so interested in –'

'Excellent,' Shelley boomed, cutting him off. 'I believe it will be in the paper this Sunday.'

'Thank you very much for this, Shelley,' I said. 'It'll really help us.'

She waved a hand. 'Yes, yes. How long are you down here, Charlotte? Do you two have time for dinner?'

I wished fervently that I did. I was still on a high from Sam marching off and demanding that I wear my glasses and some marginally less stupid clothes; I was desperate to be with him for longer. 'My train's in ninety minutes,' I said sadly.

Shelley nodded vaguely and I realized her head was elsewhere once again. What was going on with her at the moment? Sam's phone went and he retreated to answer it with a very happy look on his face. *Arrgh!* I thought. *Fucking Katia!*

Shelley watched him go and I wondered once again if she, too, was after Sam. It seemed pretty improbable but, there again, every woman on earth fell in love with Sam at some point. I just hoped that my turn would prove brief and merciful.

'I hear they're very excited about him over in rehearsals,' she remarked.

I was surprised. 'How do you know that?'

'Oh,' she said airily, 'David, the director, is my cousin. Couldn't believe it when he told me he'd cast Sam. I thought, I know that bloody name! Anyway, David's been raving about young Master Bowes.'

I swelled with pride. Of course he bloody was! My clever Sam!

Then Shelley dropped a bomb. 'The chemistry between him and the girl playing Miranda is extraordinary,' she said knowledgeably. 'Part of the reason that Anna, the *Times* journalist, wanted to do this piece was that she'd recently read an article in the *Stage* describing them as the most beautiful couple in Theatreland.'

Shock and disappointment smashed into me like an iron weight. The most beautiful couple in Theatreland?

Oh, God! Of course they were! Had I not looked at Katia Slagface and thought she was the very embodiment of Sam's perfect woman? 'Yes,' I said bravely. 'I reckon they're a couple offstage as well as on.'

Shelley nodded confirmation and I decided that I'd like to die.

The cruelty of this timing was intense. The *day* I'd grasped how I felt about Sam he'd gone to London and fallen for someone else. It was beyond cruel.

I tried, with limited success, to pull myself together, aware that Shelley was watching me curiously. 'It's a shame you're not here tonight,' she said thoughtfully. 'A contact of mine wants to channel some funds into a UK venture and he's specifically looking for something with popular appeal. He's trying to increase his portfolio of fluffy investments.'

I winced.

'Not that First Date Aid is fluffy,' Shelley continued smoothly, 'but in comparison to Middle Eastern oilfields it's fairly homely.' Sam wandered back over to us. 'Just telling Charlotte about a contact who's keen to invest in a company like yours,' Shelley explained. 'He loved the sound of First Date Aid. Was keen to meet you while you were down here.'

Sam looked at me, but I couldn't meet his eye. *You're shagging Katia Slagface*, I thought miserably. *Just go away and leave me alone.*

'I'd love to meet him!' Sam said, just as I said, 'I'm really sorry but I can't.'

Shelley was annoyed: 'Are you absolutely *sure*, Charlotte? Could you not go back in the morning?'

I glowered. All I wanted now was to get the hell out of there, away from Shelley, Sam and all the beautiful people in that studio. 'No,' I said shortly. 'Sorry, but I have a dog to look after. My parents are abroad.'

Sam looked surprised. 'You're looking after Malcolm?'

I was not. I had put in a bid but my mum had rejected it, opting to accommodate Malcolm with the Joneses in East Linton so he wouldn't miss out on his daily splash in the River Linn. 'Yes,' I lied.

'But Hailey could look after him?' Sam sounded

confused and I wanted to punch him. *Fuck OFF!* I thought angrily. *Leave me alone and run off to your pretty little girlfriend!*

Shelley folded her arms. 'I'm offering you something very special here,' she announced unsympathetically. 'Most small businesses never get within a hundred miles of an opportunity like this.'

Sam was staring at me. I knew the face he'd be making, kind but a little frustrated. And then I realized I was going to start crying. *No!* I thought. *NO! Please, please no!* Without looking up I tried to locate the door so I could make a run for it. I didn't care how odd a galloping exit would be: all that mattered was that I didn't let them see that I was crying. But just as I worked out where the door was, I felt a hand close round mine.

'Charley?' Sam said gently. My face was hot and red, and I knew I was sunk. Two large, helpless tears slid out of my eyes and on to the floor. 'Charley!' Sam repeated. 'What's wrong, dude?'

I shook my head, hoping I'd disappear in a puff of smoke. I felt Shelley shift uncomfortably in front of me.

'Sorry,' Sam said. 'Can you just give us a sec?' He held on to my hand and led me outside, where I bawled on to his shoulder for two whole minutes. Huge sobs racked me and I clung to him for dear life. I knew that this was just about the worst shoulder to be crying on but I had little choice in the matter: these sobs were coming whether it was convenient or not. When they finally subsided into snotty sniffs and little spasms, Sam took my handbag and pulled out the packet of tissues that he knew would be there. He held one over my nose and instructed me to blow, which I did, expelling a vast river of snot. Sam sniggered. 'Nice,' he said, dropping it delicately into a bin.

I tried a smile. I could see my red nose and couldn't even begin to imagine how mad I must look with mascara and thick studio make-up running down my face.

Sam put a hand on each of my arms. 'Please tell me what's going on, brother,' he said quietly. 'You've been on edge all day.'

Just for a second I considered telling him. What did I have to lose? Sam was going out with a beautiful actress; I'd lost already. But I couldn't. I couldn't bear to watch his face cloud over with pity and listen to his gentle explanation that he 'really valued me as a friend but . . .' And, anyway, I'd begun to understand that Sam and I just couldn't communicate in real life the way we could on email.

There was no point. No point trying to talk to him.

'Just having a really hard time coping with everything,' I said eventually. 'You know those days when you wake up and everything's too much?'

Sam nodded sympathetically. 'You've been through some huge shit,' he said. 'Like, multiple cowpats. Of course you're feeling bad.'

We stood looking at each other, Sam smiling in a kindly way and me gazing at him through sad, swollen eyes. I looked away first. It was too painful. I needed to get out of there, on a train and back up to Scotland where I belonged.

But Sam had other plans. 'Stay,' he said. 'Let's hang out tonight. We don't have to meet the investor, we can just bimble around if you want. You can come and see my horrible flat in the ghetto! I'll even make you some healthy shit!'

I wanted to. I wanted to be spontaneous and, more to the point, to hang out with Sam, but I felt too raw. What would I say to him? What would I have to talk about beyond the fact that I'd gone and fallen in love with him?

'Please, Chas,' Sam said. 'I miss you.'

I sniffed loudly. 'You won't be hanging out with Katia?'

'Actually, I was meant to be. We were going to rehearse at mine.' A smile crossed his face quickly, which stabbed me in the heart and then in the womb for good measure. 'But I spend all my time with Katia. I'd like to hang out with you tonight, my brother.'

And then I had no option but to sniff, attempt a smile and say yes.

'If you don't fancy the ghetto we can just find a pub and have a pie,' Sam said. 'Or a salad,' he added quickly.

I smiled. 'Thanks, Bowes,' I snotted. 'You're the best.'

When we went back in, Shelley resumed bullying us about meeting her contact. 'A drink! An hour of your time, for God's sake!' she foghorned. 'There'll be plenty of meetings further down the line . . . For now he just wants to meet you. Come on!'

Sam tried to hold her off for my sake, but I gave in. It was clear that we would not be leaving the studio until we said yes and, in spite of my fragile state, I did know this was a once-in-a-lifetime offer. Shelley marched off, delighted, to call him.

'Seven o'clock, Mandarin Oriental in Knightsbridge,' she snapped on her return. Her face softened briefly.

'With your help I met the man of my dreams, Charlotte,' she said. Her voice was suddenly quite human and sweet. 'I really wanted to return the favour and this was the only thing I could think of. Good luck.'

And then off she swept, shouting into her BlackBerry, the click-click-click of her heels ringing out around the studio.

'I wish she'd stop sending us to posh hotels,' Sam said wistfully. 'I have fuck-all idea how to behave in those places, Chas.'

I looked at him and – forgetting my anguish over the Most Beautiful Couple in Theatreland – I laughed. 'Do you know what, Bowes? Me neither. Let's have one drink with him and then get the hell out of Knightsbridge.'

We shook hands.

Sam went off for the final two hours of his rehearsal and I went for a mini pedicure and a coffee in Harvey Nichols, sitting in gay denial about Sam being part of the Most Beautiful Couple in Theatreland. I fantasized about him ending his romance with Katia Slagface because she was uncomplicated and carefree (he preferred difficult, uptight workaholics). And I prayed that his kindness towards me today had been a sign of a deep and all-consuming love.

When six forty-five came, I felt reluctant to leave. I didn't want to go back into reality. Reality involved pretty much none of these things being true.

We met outside the hotel and, even though I'd seen him two hours before, my heart still leaped. *LOVE ME!* I implored him. *NOT KATIA!* He looked madly handsome and also a little bit tired, which just made me want to put him in my pocket and take care of him.

We gazed up at the imposing edifice of the hotel, straightened ourselves out and marched in.

Almost immediately, we found ourselves in a strange situation. The bar was almost empty, save for a rich-looking couple from the Middle East, so Sam and I sat down and ordered drinks. But before they even arrived the receptionist appeared at my elbow, asking if I was Charlotte Lambert, here to meet someone from Holden Steiner. 'Er, yes?' I said. It sounded about right.

'Your contact called to say he was running a little late.' She smiled at Sam, ignoring me completely. 'But if you'd like, you can check into your room while you wait?'

I explained that we were not guests, but she smiled and handed me a smart white envelope. Inside was a printed message: *I felt bad about bullying you into staying in London. Have a room on me. Shelley.*

Speechless, I showed it to Sam. 'Sweet Mother of Jesus,' he said, face white. 'CHAS! You lucky fucker!'

The receptionist was clearly in love with Sam already, but she tore her eyes away from him and smiled at me. 'Welcome to the hotel, Ms Lambert,' she said kindly. 'I'll get someone to show you up to your room right now.'

The room was incredible. The bed was larger than my flat and the views over Hyde Park were stunning. Were I with the man of my dreams, this would have been the best hotel room I could have asked for. And, sadly, I *was* with the man of my dreams, but he was whispering sweet Shake-spearean nothings into the elfin ear of a wispy-dressed slag.

'Can I bounce on your bed?' he asked, breaking my thoughts.

'Yes,' I replied. And then: 'Christ, Bowes! *Look* at it!'

Sam bounced on my bed while I wrote Shelley a grateful message of thanks and then went through an elaborate pretence of calling the Joneses and asking them to look after Malcolm for me. Perhaps after a luxurious sleep and the greatest breakfast ever, I'd feel sufficiently fortified to leave this Sam stuff behind in London.

Perhaps.

'Let's go and meet the investor,' I said tiredly. Life could be very cruel at times.

Down in the super-sleek bar we made idiots of ourselves by asking three different businessmen if they were here to invest in us. None, embarrassingly, was.

I called Shelley when it got to seven thirty. 'HANG ON,' she roared, even though she appeared to be in a silent room. 'I'LL CALL HIM.'

A few minutes later she called back and informed us, somewhat awkwardly, that Mr Investor from Holden Steiner was terminally delayed. He would be in his offices in St James's until at least midnight. He was sorry. 'Jolly bad luck,' she muttered loudly. 'Have dinner on me. Put it on your room bill. I feel very bad about this, Charlotte.'

I hesitated. Sam and I had snuck out of the Edinburgh investment event without so much as a handshake with an investor. All we had done was throw food around the room, giggle like knobs and nearly steal a napkin. I felt uncomfortable accepting such an extravagant gift. The restaurant was run by Heston Blumenthal, for Pete's sake! It'd cost a fortune!

'No, we'll sort ourselves out,' I started to say.

'DINNER IS ON ME,' Shelley roared. 'YOU STAYED IN LONDON BECAUSE I TOLD YOU TO.'

I caved in quickly. I'd have had to be very odd to turn down a Heston dinner and I had a strong feeling that Sam would never forgive me if I said no.

By some stroke of outrageous fortune there was a cancellation in the restaurant, and soon after Sam and I found ourselves sitting in a spare, beautiful dining room, staring at menus that sounded like they'd been invented by a nutty nineteenth-century professor.

'Seriously?' Sam said, after a few minutes' silence. 'Pigs' ears? Cockle ketchup?' He looked at me, bewildered. 'What the *fuck*?'

I shrugged. 'It's Heston Blumenthal,' I said. 'People go mad for this stuff.'

Sam looked depressed. 'I'm tired,' he said childishly. 'I want a vindaloo with naan bread and poppadoms.'

For no obvious reason I felt convinced that this was all my fault. 'Well, then, get a curry,' I snapped defensively. 'I'll enjoy this world-class, award-winning food and you can eat a bucket of takeaway rubbish on a bench. Deal?'

We had a face-off, which Sam broke first. 'Sorry,' he said. 'I'm being a twat.'

I smiled back. 'Sorry. I'm being bossy.'

Sam's eyes narrowed and I knew he was scheming. I loved his scheming face: it had the subtlety of a jumbo jet. 'Are you tired, Chas?' he asked me, after a short pause.

I nodded. I'd got up at six to get the train to London.

'So do you *really* want to sit in a formal restaurant and eat dinner you don't understand?'

Damn him! Of course I didn't. Reluctantly, I shook my head.

'And when you called the majestic curry a "bucket of takeaway rubbish", were you just being petulant?'

I nodded even more reluctantly.

Sam slapped his leg triumphantly. 'That's my girl! Right, we're going to get an Indian takeaway and eat it in your fucking ginormous palace of a bedroom with surround-sound TV and shit.'

It was a very appealing thought – I was exhausted just from sitting at this table – but I felt very anxious about leaving. 'You can't just walk out of a Heston Blumenthal restaurant!' I whispered.

Sam studied me. 'Swear on your mother's life that you wouldn't prefer a cuzzer,' he said, 'and I'll stay.'

I glared at him.

'Cuzzer or cockle ketchup,' he said softly, on the edge of a giggle.

'Go on, then.' I sighed. Sam grabbed my hand and squeezed it. 'Sterling work, Chasmonger!' he said. 'You go up and I'll nip out and find a takeaway. See you in a bit.'

And with that he sped off, leaving me to explain to an astonished waiter that actually we weren't going to dine after all. 'Are you quite sure, madam?' He looked like he was going to faint. I just grinned apologetically and fled.

As soon as I arrived back in my room, I realized that the prospect of spending one-on-one time with Sam was ter-rifying, particularly in a room designed to encourage luxurious lovemaking. It didn't matter that we'd had a million meals together in my flat over the years. Things had changed. So I ordered a bottle of room service wine at my own expense. I didn't care about being unemployed: being sober was not an option. And while I waited for Sam to return, I had a couple of pre-mixed vodka tonics from the minibar, which meant that, when the phone rang twenty minutes later, I was able to see the funny side in what was happening downstairs.

'Hi, it's Catrina in Reception,' said an incredibly well-spoken woman. 'I have . . . a man here saying he wants to come to your room. He's carrying a plastic bag containing takeaway curry. Is this correct, Miss Lambert?'

I sniggered, covering the mouthpiece with my hand. I could just imagine Bowes strolling in, whistling casually, and the surprise on his face as he was apprehended.

'Er . . .' I began, then had to laugh again. I pulled myself together, not without effort. 'Yes, he's my friend,' I said. 'And he's not staying over. We're just, um, dining.'

There was a silence. 'Very well,' Catrina said. 'Please feel free to call us to remove your empty wrappers so that you do not have to sleep in the smell of takeaway curry.'

I winced to my very core and promised Catrina I'd do just that.

'Bad times!' Sam said merrily, as he arrived. 'They think we're chavs!'

'We are, Bowes. We're eating takeaway curry in the Mandarin Oriental.' He got busy laying out boxes of beautiful-smelling curry on a shiny table, which he pulled over to the window so we could sit on the floor and eat while watching the horses on a floodlit Rotten Row. Sam was very relieved to see my wine. 'Thank God, brother,' he said. 'I bought a bottle but it cost two ninety-nine. It's probably just meths.'

I poured us both a large glass.

Thankfully, soon after, I began to relax properly and also to remember why I enjoyed Sam's company so much. It was just so *easy*.

Providing we kept things light.

The conversation turned to my parents' middle-aged backpacking adventure and Sam seemed enthralled by their tales. 'They're volunteering at a tiger sanctuary at the moment,' I said. 'Mum said in her last email that Dad keeps trying to take baby tigers home with him.'

Sam chuckled. 'Oh, Christian. I'm so glad he's OK again. He's a proper legend, your old man.' He stuck his naan bread into my masala.

I was pleased that Sam loved my mad dad. Dr Nathan Gillies had pointedly misunderstood Dad on the two occasions he'd deigned to meet my family. And even though I'd only been with John for five minutes I knew I'd have been uncomfortable taking him to the ramshackle madness of my childhood home.

Later on Sam – as if reading my mind – asked how I was feeling about John. For a second my heart leaped. *Yessssss!* I thought wildly. *He's jealous!* But then I remembered that Sam was in the Most Beautiful Couple in Theatreland. He was asking about John because he was my friend. *My friend, my friend, my friend*, I chanted to myself.

Maybe in a few months (years?) I'd start seeing Sam as my friend again. Because I certainly didn't see him as a friend at the moment. What sound-of-mind woman wanted to passionately kiss her friend the way I wanted to passionately kiss Sam? I couldn't bear how relaxed and beautiful he was, sprawled against a heavy armchair, one finger absently poking about in his ear, his eyes following the horses below us.

'John,' I said slowly, trying to work out how I felt. John was not in a great place, according to Cassie. When his wife had marched into the office and started screaming at him for sleeping with me (I still felt ill to think that I'd slept with a married man, knowingly or otherwise), Chambers had apparently gone completely insane and threatened to sack him. Had he not just lost his director of comms he probably would have done. Now, I heard, Washington were freezing him out and I presumed that his fat-cat plans were in serious jeopardy.

'I almost feel sorry for him,' I told Sam truthfully. 'He's messed up on a monumental scale.'

'But you'd still do him,' Sam stated confidently.

'No. No way. Not even because he's married. It's just . . . that chapter is closed, I guess. He's part of a life I don't want any more.'

'Wow,' Sam said. He seemed genuinely surprised. 'I never thought I'd hear you say that!'

I smiled ruefully. 'Me neither. But the longer I spend away from work, the more I realize how much I'd been wasting my life there. John, Salutech, everything. It was all wrong.' I speared a piece of overcooked lamb on my plastic fork and munched contemplatively. 'I've been quite a fool,' I admitted. 'A mad, suit-wearing fool.'

'That's my brother The Chasman you're talking about. Go easy on her. She just needed to sort her shit out.'

By the time we'd finished the food, Sam was obviously drunk because he opened the bottle of wine he'd got at the takeaway, which smelt – as predicted – like methylated spirits that had once had a brief fling with a few low-quality grapes. 'Cheers,' he said, whipping out two Curly Wurlys from his coat pocket for dessert. I shook my head despairingly – it was only ever with Sam that I ate stuff like this – but decided what the hell.

Funnily enough it was only around Sam that I didn't care so much about things like my figure.

After dinner we hauled ourselves, tubby and drunk, on to the sofa where we sat staring out of the window at the night sky. I was pleased with how tonight had gone. Things had felt quite normal. There had been no flirting – and, sadly, no snogging – but some of the awkwardness that had crippled me earlier today had gone.

So I was very unsettled when Sam suddenly announced that he was feeling weird.

'Oh?' I said, instantly on guard.

'Don't you?' he asked. He was staring fixedly out of the window.

I felt a bit cheated. Had I not just congratulated myself on managing to get through tonight without any awkward moments? *I've been feeling weird enough!* I wanted to shout. *Don't you dare throw any more weirdness into the mix!*

'Weird about what?' I asked him. I tried to sound nonchalant in the hope that he'd take my lead.

He didn't. He just looked frustrated.

'Chas, we bloody well kissed each other two weeks ago. Don't you feel weirded out by that? I do.'

I was floored. A million thoughts exploded. Weirded out in a bad way or a good way? Had Sam been thinking about our kiss? Oh, God! How much? How did he rate it? And how did he rate me, for that matter? Was it good or bad that he looked so uncomfortable he might have been giving birth to a marrow?

I was frozen to the spot and needed to say something. Tell the truth? Lie? Respond in a different language? Arrgh!

'A *bit* weird, I suppose,' I said brightly, as if this were all a big silly joke. 'I mean, it's a bit odd to kiss someone to prove you *don't* like them!' Then I panicked. Was that too much? Did it sound like a hint? Oh God, oh God.

'Very odd,' Sam said. I poured all of the Scotch in my minibar into two glasses and shoved one at him. 'But, as far as experiments go, it was pretty conclusive,' he continued, putting down his glass of awful wine. 'Don't you think?'

Damn you, Bowes, I thought darkly. Don't you throw this back at me and make it my responsibility. 'Myugh,' I replied helpfully. It was as noncommittal a sound as I could make.

Sam forced out a laugh. 'Oh, God. Are we going to have to do it again?'

What? Had he just said that? I looked at him, blood rushing to my face. 'You said there was nothing there,' I reminded him, in a very odd voice. 'Why would you want to re-test now?'

Sam started to blush too. 'No, *you* said there was nothing.'

'I was saying that for both of us! Don't make it my fault!'

Sam was now puce.

FUCK! one side of my brain yelled. *WHAT THE FUCK IS GOING ON?*

There was a pause. *I DON'T FUCKING KNOW!* the other side replied.

Then both sides of my brain ganged up and made me do something completely insane. 'If you're not convinced then I suppose I don't mind re-testing,' I heard myself say. My voice had gone distant and third-personish, as if I were hearing it back in an echo.

Sam was now clutching his Scotch with both hands.

Oh, Christ, I thought. *I've pushed it too far. He knows how I feel. He's disgusted. He wants to run. He thinks I'm insane. He –*

'Maybe we should, just to be sure,' he said.

I stopped short.

And then my hands started shaking. Not just trembling a bit, but fully shaking. I forced them down between my knees in front of me, but my forearms were visibly shaking too. I leaned forward to cover up the shameful spectacle. But, as I did, Sam reached over and plucked one of my hands out. 'Charley,' he said gently. 'It's fine. We'll be friends no matter what.' My hand shook even more. It was like a pneumatic drill. *STOP IT*, I roared at myself. *STOP SHAKING. STOP ACTING LIKE A WAZZOCK.* But the shaking continued.

'I'm not stressed!' I said, as brightly as possible. But

now my teeth were chattering and I sounded like a pneumatic drill too. Sam clamped my hand hard but it made no difference – it simply started shaking Sam's hand up and down on top of it.

Like the last time, we found ourselves suddenly immobile, and for a while we just looked at each other. But, as we did, I felt something shift inside me. I was in love with this man and I couldn't go on pretending otherwise. My hands stopped shaking. I loved Sam. I was about to kiss him. What more was there? And so, without quite realizing that I was doing it, I leaned in and started to kiss him. For a split second, obviously surprised, he didn't respond. But then he was kissing me back. It was very slow, very gentle. In fact, our lips were barely touching. His closed over my top lip, and then moved down to kiss my bottom lip. His hand slid lightly around my waist and a delicious warm tingling began. It filled every part of me.

Sam kissed my lips again, more firmly this time, and then pulled away a few inches to look at me. 'Charley Lambert,' he said softly. I looked back at him and almost immediately looked away. It was quite unbearable to be staring at each other from a gap of less than six inches.

'That's me,' I whispered uncertainly.

Then, to my dismay, Sam pulled away and slid his hand out from my waist. He kept my other hand in his, although it felt suddenly limp. 'Well?' he asked.

And I couldn't answer. I couldn't tell him the truth: that I had enjoyed it probably more than any other kiss I'd ever tried; that I thought I was probably quite a bit in love with him. Because I knew that in spite of the loveliness of our kissing he didn't feel the same. He was Sam Bowes, half of the Most Beautiful Couple in Theatreland.

So I shrugged, as if to deflect the question back to him.

Sam looked depressingly happy. 'I think it's as we thought before,' he said firmly. '*Nada.*'

'YEAH,' I brayed woodenly. 'I bet there's tonnes more chemistry when you're snogging Katia, right?'

Sam nodded. 'Yeah. Tonnes more chemistry. I love snogging Katia. She's amazing! I could snog her all day! Well, I am doing, actually. Ha ha. Yeah, good. So, anyway, we repeated the experiment! And got our conclusion! Cheers!' He chinked my tumbler of Scotch.

I downed about four shots in one go.

Chapter Twenty

I stood back to admire the Christmas tree and beamed. It was a cracker! It was not a modern, spare tree with carefully distributed burnished gold baubles and white lights, it was everything Mum and Dad would want it to be: big, mad and bushy, covered from head to foot with strange baubles, multicoloured lights, chocolate hippos, little wooden boxes and all of the other strange things Dad had accumulated over the years. I laughed as I placed his favourite wooden gecko on the top where any normal person would plant a star.

I could only imagine what crazy treasures Dad was going to dig out of his backpack when they returned next week. I was already bracing myself for the possibility of long grey dreadlocks and a beaded necklace.

Malcolm, who was wearing a pair of festive antlers, avoided my eye as he removed a chocolate from one of the lower branches and carried it off to his bed. Nothing about this bloody house was normal! I'd decided to spend the week before Christmas at home so that I could liberate Malcolm from the Joneses, sort through some of Granny Helen's stuff for Dad and generally make it festive and warm for their return, and I was enjoying being here immensely. I had yet to find anywhere in the world where I felt more at home than in my parents' house.

For the twentieth time today I drifted off into a fantasy about Sam spending Christmas at Lambert HQ.

Far from dying slowly, my feelings towards Sam had become gradually more intense. Every time he emailed me about First Date Aid I felt like my heart was in my mouth, just in case this would be The Email. But it never was. This morning's email, in fact, had been the final straw.

> Chasmonger! How's my long-lost homie? I miss you. Can't believe you're not coming to the opening night tonight. Very bad behaviour, homes. Very bad.

There was a very bloody good reason why I wasn't coming. He was having a romance with Katia buggering Slagface and it would be an act of unforgivable self-harm to go to London and watch them snogging. Especially if they started up at the after-show party.

> Anyway, to work. First I think we should take on more freelance writers. I don't think five is enough. These singles are just rolling in still. Shelley did us such a massive favour with that *Sunday Times* feature in Nov. Shall I put an ad up? Second, I have Big News. We are going to have our first marriage! Remember that dude Robert – the one in Belfast with the paddock full of llamas? He's been dating Jemma pretty much non-stop and he popped the question last night. AWIIIGHT! AWOOOGA! BO! And, finally, we had lunch with William and Shelley yesterday and when Shelley went for a slash William told me he was off to Tiffany's later. That can only mean one thing, Chas, my brother! Amusingly, Shelley still doesn't seem to have any idea I was William's ghost-writer. Very funny being around those two. She talked

about you loads and was quite cross you weren't coming
tonight. As am I.
Anyway, how are you dude? Happy? Sad? Talk to me. Stop
emailing me about bloody work and tell me how you are.

Speak soon.
Xxx

I loved that he talked about Shelley going for 'a slash',
that he still used Kriss Akabusi's 'awiiight' after all these
years; that he called me 'brother'. In general, I just loved
Sam. What I hated was the 'we' who had had lunch with
William and Shelley. It was like a punch in the face.

Our farewell that night in London back in November
had been mercifully brief. Catrina from Reception at the
Mandarin Oriental had obviously got so worried about
ending up with a curry-scented room on her hands that
she'd sent someone to remove the wrappers, which had
provided me with an easy excuse to end the night and
eject Sam from my boudoir. After he'd sloped off, I'd sat
on the floor at the end of my enormous bed for nearly an
hour with my head in my hands, trying to accept that I
had to let him go.

But I couldn't. I'd been unable to eat my five-star breakfast the next morning and had mooned over him every
day since.

'Do you think Sam feels anything towards me?' I asked
Malcolm. Malcolm came over and plonked his nose on
my lap, sighing deeply. I sighed back at him. 'That's not
the response I was looking for, Malcolm.'

My phone beeped with a text message and I was

surprised to see Shelley Cartwright's name on my screen. Since her investor had failed to show up that night she'd cut back on her foghorn-inspired phone calls. Presumably she felt she'd now repaid me for my help – and, having seen the bill on my departure from the Mandarin Oriental, I didn't blame her.

But here she was again, economical of word, generous of bite. *I hear you are not coming to Sam's opening night tonight*, her text announced. *Why?*

I smiled briefly, amused by Shelley's distinctive approach to text-messaging. But the smile was short-lived, for Shelley's question was a good one.

I sighed, and Malcolm sighed back again. Things had really changed for me over the last few weeks. I was sleeping, I was forcing myself to maintain gentle working hours and I was even piecing together a manageable little social scene. It was a daily challenge not to do too much but things definitely felt different. My feelings for Sam, however, remained unchanged. I'd tried everything to get over him, ranging from two Internet dates of my own (very bad) to a *chakra* cleanse with Mad Tania. (Not much better: Mad Tania was a raven-haired healer, East Linton's only hippie, and while her cleanse might have sorted out my *chakra*s it had done bugger-all to dislodge Sam from my mind.)

'I can't see him tonight because it'll kill me to see him with his girlfriend,' I informed Malcolm. 'I need to just keep on plodding on till it passes. Here in Scotland.' Malcolm looked supportive.

I made the same cock-and-bull excuse to Shelley that I'd made to Sam – that I had a prearranged christening dinner for my cousin's baby (who hadn't actually been born yet, but that was by-the-by) – then shoved my phone into the sofa, keen for something to do that would take my mind off the situation.

I pulled over a box of Granny Helen's stuff. Ness and I had been whittling away at her possessions over the last few weeks, using instructions that Dad had left us, but there was still work to be done.

I turned the box over. 'PHOTOS' said Granny Helen's snappy writing. I smiled. Granny Helen might not be here in body but she always would be in spirit. I imagined her now, poking my sloppy jumper (one of Dad's cast-offs) with her walking stick and asking if I was having a breakdown.

The box was filled with a bewildering array of envelopes, all stuffed with small sepia photos. Each had been marked with Granny Helen's formidable scrawl and, thanks to her careful indexing, I found a cracker almost straight away. 'CHRISTIAN'S FIRST DAY AT SCHOOL' the envelope said. I pulled out the photos and immediately started laughing. Little four-year-old Dad was wearing tweed shorts and long socks. He stared at the camera in bewilderment in the first, but by the second he had become Dad again: a monkey. In this one he was hanging upside-down from the tree in their back garden, the contents of his satchel falling to the ground around him. In the third, he was back on the ground with a full satchel and a fearsome scowl on his face. I suspected that Granny Helen had given him a good smack on the bottom in the interim.

I dug into the box, keen for more, and pulled out an envelope that felt rather different from the others.

I turned it over. 'JACK' the envelope stated. I raised an eyebrow.

Granddad Jack was the grandfather I'd never met. He had been a flight lieutenant in Malta during the Second World War and had been shot down and killed when Granny Helen had been six months' pregnant with Dad. It was a tragedy of which Dad spoke little; he'd never known Granddad Jack, of course, and, given his unusually close relationship with his mother, it seemed clear that he had felt the absence of a father keenly.

I opened the envelope, excited at the prospect of seeing my grandfather. But, rather than photographs, I found myself pulling out a tightly folded bundle of papers.

I didn't need to open them to know they were letters.

The first was written in a spidery hand that I'd never seen before, a sweet contrast to Granny Helen's aggressive scrawl. I paused, frowning. Was it OK to read your dead grandparents' correspondence? I asked Malcolm but got only an idle tail thump. After a few minutes' reflection I decided to go ahead. Wasn't this how people discovered amazing things about their ancestry?

'Anyone would do this,' I told Malcolm, unfolding the papers as carefully as I could.

In the centre was a letter that had been carefully wrapped in three different envelopes. It was special. I knew that before I even unfolded it. It was weighted with some strong emotional force that seemed to warm the room before I'd even started reading.

My sweet one, it began, in a neat, sloping hand. I smiled to think of Granny Helen being anyone's Sweet One.

Thank you a thousand times for writing to me, and for the package of Yardley's soap! What a wonderful treat, the lads were so jealous.

I have your letter in my pocket and I feel it there all day and all night, glowing warmly through my confoundedly scratchy vest and into my side. It brings me such comfort, my dear! It keeps me strong in the stillness of night when the noises about me seem hostile and fearful and I find myself longing for the familiar chink of your teacup on a saucer. It calms me when those around me turn to anger and fear and talk to each other unkindly.

I am sorry it has taken me so long to reply to you but sadly we have very little time for sleep, let alone relaxation. My lapse does not indicate a diminution in my feelings for you, Helen darling. You are on my mind when I wake up, you stay with me all day and you are there, a benign and beautiful presence, when I collapse wearily in my bed. I dream of our walks by the sea in April and our summer picnics on the downs.

Oh I do so long to get back to our life together, darling. I must go, Tompkins is calling me.

I love you and I miss you with all my heart.

Yours, for ever,
Jack

I put the letter down, moved beyond all measure. I'd never really given much thought to what it meant to be in love if you were anyone older than Mum and Dad. Somewhere along the line I'd decided that relationships in older generations were formal arrangements based on fondness and regard. How very short-sighted I'd been! I sat staring into the distance for several minutes, quite stunned, then dug around for Granny Helen's reply.

It jolted me out of my reverie pretty quickly.

You didn't bloody write that last letter, Jack, Granny Helen wrote, on 1 December 1941. I was a little bit scandalized: even for Granny Helen this was fairly abrupt. *Think I'm stupid? The letter was pure poetry and you, my dear, are no poet. But you're still pretty dashing and a bit wonderful so I'll let it go. You're my lovable fool.*

I relaxed. This must just be how it worked: Granny Helen sent out a missile but then shot it down before it could cause any harm. I loved the thought of her telling someone they were dashing and wonderful. It was a side of her I'd never seen.

It was nice to hear from you Jack, whoever wrote the letter. I do miss you and think about you every day. It's even more quiet here than usual; most of the women in the town are out in Dunbar helping in some warehouse so I'm stuck here on my tod most of the time. Been designing a machine for making mashed potato though; got to keep the mind sharp. Too many pregnant women become useless jellies.

My sickness has passed and I'm now just eating like that fat horse that the Duries keep.

Last night I had a dream that you were standing in the kitchen playing the harp. How I laughed! I was sad to wake up and remember you were so far away. I'm counting the days to your return. No, I'm counting the hours! Come back safe, my handsome soldier. Your girl, Helen

Looking down at the letter I felt tears pricking my eyes. It had never occurred to me that my grandmother's acerbic tongue could have been capable of such unguarded affection.

But the accusation she'd levelled – that Jack had got someone else to write his love letter – had surprised me. Why had she said it? Had she actually *meant* it?

A thought was beginning to develop. Suddenly excited, I began to search for Granddad Jack's reply.

Darling Helen, of course I wrote it! Doubting Thomas! As it goes I write letters for just about everyone in my squadron. Would be lunatic to let the lads write their own letters, they'd lose their sweethearts in days. No, my dear Helen, I may not be the smartest man on this parade – I had all manner of trouble for the state of my boots this morning – but I write a damn good love letter.

I gasped. It was only a bloody family talent! Not sure if I was about to start laughing or crying, I made a strange noise. It was almost too good to be true. My grandfather had been in the same line of business as me! I dug back into the box, keener than ever to see a photo of him.

I was rewarded soon after. In an envelope entitled 'HELEN/JACK WEDDING' there were photographs of the two happiest people I'd ever seen. Mesmerized, I stared at my grandfather. Granny Helen's handsome soldier obviously loved his young wife more than anything in the world. There was no 1930s reserve here: Granddad Jack had his arm clasped tightly round his bride and was kissing the side of her face in almost all of the photographs. Granny Helen had been unable to disguise her own delight; her smile seemed to infect all of the smartly turned-out people around them.

'Hello,' I whispered to them, a tear sliding silently down on to Dad's old jumper. I turned back to the letter with a large lump in my throat.

> *Why am I so good at writing, you might wonder. What sort of a veterinary surgeon writes verse, eh?*
>
> *The answer, my dear girl, is that I can write like I do because of you. It's you who's turned me into this lily-livered slop bucket. It's you who's turned my clumsy ramblings into poetry. Because I love you, my girl. You consume me! It's not very convenient to love you, I can't deny it. If I were to dream up my perfect girl she probably wouldn't be you. She'd be a bit more bloody respectful for a start! But it doesn't matter, my Helen. You're the only girl for me. And, my darling, leave starts the day after tomorrow! I'm coming to find you!*

Tears now flowing freely down my face, I turned the paper back over to see the date: 13 December 1941. Granddad Jack had been killed the next day. He'd been flying over the Mediterranean shortly after nightfall, looking for aircraft in need of help and – during this act of goodwill – he'd been shot down himself.

I tried to comprehend the extent of this tragedy, knowing now how deeply in love they'd been with each other. No wonder Granny Helen had never remarried. No wonder she had become such a cantankerous old bugger.

'I'm so sorry, Granny Helen,' I whispered. 'You poor, poor thing.'

Next in the pile was a letter from Squadron Leader Tommy Derbyshire, explaining what had happened and enclosing Granny Helen's letters to her husband. He said Granddad Jack had been a brave pilot who had made the ultimate sacrifice for his country. Then he added, in a more personal tone, that Jack had been popular among the boys in 238 Squadron for his help with their love letters. She had many reasons to be proud of him.

I put the letters down to save them from my tears and sobbed. I couldn't bear the tragedy, the timing, the loss. My poor Granny Helen, six months pregnant and madly in love, had never got her handsome young man back. She'd let down her defences and given herself over to Jack Lambert – only to lose him in a flash of light that disappeared into nothingness above the dark Mediterranean. A whole person gone, just like that.

Malcolm gazed at me uneasily as I wept.

I looked back at the wedding photos, at her infectious smile. 'Thank God you knew how much he cared about you,' I whispered. There was some relief in that.

My tears were interrupted by the sound of a text message arriving in my phone. Mopping my face on the sleeve of my jumper with one hand, I opened it with the other.

It was Sam. I sniffed, trying to concentrate: *Just wanted to reiterate how sad I am that you're not coming tonight. You'd love the play, I look like a knob throughout most of it. Speaking of knobs, you're a knob for not coming. I miss you.* XXX

'Leave me alone,' I said aloud miserably. 'Throwing me crumbs from your nice big designer table where you eat stupid Londony breakfasts with Katia stupid Slagface.'

I plunged my hand into the box of photographs, desperate to take my mind off the situation, just as my phone exploded into life once again.

'PISS OFF,' I cried at it. 'I'M IN HIDING!' Then, of course, I picked it up to check it wasn't Sam.

It was Hailey.

I wasn't convinced I wanted to talk to her. She and Ness had gone down to London yesterday morning to do some Christmas shopping before putting on their glad rags for Sam's opening night and I rather feared she was calling to tell me about Sam's new girlfriend.

But, just in case she had some more welcome news, I answered. 'Tits?'

'Hello!' she yelled excitedly. I could hear a busker's interpretation of 'Winter Wonderland' on the street near her and the sound of Londoners being noisily festive. My parents' empty sitting room suddenly felt somewhat remote.

'Um, how's it going down there? You two having a nice time?'

Hailey ignored me. 'Chas,' she said. 'I'm calling because I'm very cross with you. You should bloody well be here! It's really exciting! And Sam's gutted you're not coming!'

I stiffened. The crap excuse I'd given Sam was not the same one I'd given Hailey and Ness. I hoped they hadn't compared notes.

'Just one of those things.' I sighed, trying to sound regretful.

'Oh, you're fucking annoying you are. Remind me why you can't come?'

I changed the subject. 'How's Sam?' I asked. 'Nervous?'

'Oh, bricking it,' Hailey confirmed. 'We had lunch with him yesterday and he had to run off for a shit about twenty times. Poor thing!'

My heart melted a bit. 'William and Shelley came to lunch too,' Hailey added. 'They're a right frigging pair!'

NO! Hailey and Ness had been on the cosy couples' lunch too! Urgh. Shelley and William, Sam and Katia Slagface . . . all being jolly with my twin sister and best friend. That was disgusting. And too cruel for words.

'Right,' I said vacantly. 'How were William and Shelley?'

Hailey sniggered. 'Fucking weird,' she said. 'Noisy, confident, bit like a pair of steam-trains although I'd say Shelley's definitely the boss. What a combo! You did well to get them together.'

I started to ask her about Katia and Sam but she interrupted. 'Shelley kept asking about you,' she said. 'Does she want to lez you up, do you reckon? She didn't bloody stop!'

'No, she's just a bit odd and direct.' I braced myself. 'And, um, how was Katia?'

'OK,' Hailey said doubtfully, 'but she's a right fucking doughnut, Chas. Can't imagine how her husband puts up with her.'

The busker in the background switched to 'Santa Claus Is Coming To Town' and drowned me out as I yelled, 'Her WHAT?'

Hailey moved off down the street a little, cursing goodnaturedly at the singer. 'Eh?' she said.

'Hailey, did you just say that she's married? KATIA SLAGFACE?'

Hailey burst out laughing. 'Oh, now, there's a good name. Yes, she's married. Somehow.'

'She's not shagging Sam?'

'NO!' Hailey cried, genuinely disgusted. 'What are you on?'

'There was an article Shelley mentioned,' I faltered. 'In the *Stage*. About them being the hottest couple in the West End or something.'

'Oh, yeah, Bowes showed me that. But it was talking about onstage, not off! He'd never shag her. She's an absolute prat, Chas! Even the Bowes has limits!'

'Right,' I said, dazed.

Hailey continued, 'In fact, Bowes is having some sort of drought at the moment. He hasn't had sex with *anyone* in three months apparently. I don't know what's wrong with him, he –'

I stopped listening. I'd heard all I needed to hear. Sam was single! *Sam was single!* I ended the call as soon as I could and commenced some serious brooding. Sam was single. Shouldn't I at least *try* to do something? I glanced at my watch, which suggested that I could probably make it to London in time, should I be willing to do a mad dash and pay a huge amount of money for a last-minute plane ticket.

No, I thought crossly. *I can't!*

But why not? I stared at the pile of letters between Granny Helen and Granddad Jack. Granny Helen had lost the love of her life but at least she'd been brave enough to start a relationship with him in the first place. Somewhere along the line she'd decided to take a risk, put herself on the line. Was I so pathetic that I was going to spend the rest of my days wondering how Sam felt?

No, I insisted. *This is not a Granny Helen and Granddad Jack situation. Sam likes girls he can throw around the bedroom! He'd have a prolapse if he tried to pick me up!*

But to my intense irritation I couldn't get Granny Helen out of my mind. I pictured her sitting in this very room seventy years ago, reading a telegram telling her that her husband was dead. And how devastated and furious and alone she must have felt, knowing that the man she loved more than anyone else in the world had been taken from her the day before he was meant to return. It was a tragedy that I could barely even comprehend.

But she knew that he loved her.

Which was why, I saw – with a very sharp stab of fear – I was going to have to go to London and tell Sam I loved him. What if I fell off a cliff today? Or Malcolm ate me? I'd die not knowing!

'Hello, Charleypops,' Hailey chirped, when I called her back a few seconds later. 'Have you changed your mind?'

'YES,' I bellowed. 'I'M COMING TO LONDON!'

'Wow, you sound enthusiastic,' she said, obviously taken aback. 'Everything OK?'

'NO! I'M IN LOVE WITH SAM AND I'M COMING DOWN TO TELL HIM. I'M SHITTING MYSELF.'

There was a short silence.

'I'm sorry?' Hailey asked. 'Did you just –'

'YES. I'm in love with Bowes. Sorry, Hails. Should have mentioned. But, yes, I have to tell him.'

'Oh, God,' Hailey said weakly. 'I think I need to sit down.'

Why the hell shouldn't he love me back? I asked myself, charging up the stairs to get my handbag. *Look at Mum and Dad. They're each other's worst nightmare! Do they love each other? Damn straight they do! They've been together thirty-five years!*

'I'm going to London,' I told Malcolm. 'Be good. I'll get the Joneses to come and rescue you.'

But as I sprinted out of the front door, grabbing Mum's old anorak, I suddenly had a brainwave. A brainwave of the truly ingenious variety. 'Good thinking, Lambert,' I muttered, turning round and running back upstairs where I crammed two very important things into a handbag.

Malcolm watched me go for the second time with his usual kindly smile. 'Stay off the Christmas tree chocolate,' I told him. I ran out of the door and up to the square to get my car.

'Fuck!' I shouted. I didn't have a car. (Almost two months on it still hadn't sunk in.) But without hesitation I turned left and ran up to the high street, making a beeline for the town's taxi office, which boasted one very unreliable Austin Maestro.

'MRS GILBERT,' I yelled, as I ran into the tiny office. 'I need your help! Can you drive me to Edinburgh airport?'

'Ye can piss off, Charley,' she began moodily. 'I need two hours' warning.'

I shifted from one foot to the other. 'Mrs Gilbert,' I said. 'I don't think you understand. There's a boy. He picks his nose and eats junk food but I love him. I have to go and tell him before it's too late.'

Mrs Gilbert looked up irritably from her sudoku puzzle and appraised me.

'He's capering around on a Shakespearean island in six and a half hours,' I cried, as if this would somehow help. 'I have to be there for him! I have to let him know how I feel!' I stared at her beseechingly.

'God's sake,' she muttered. She looked back down at

her sudoku puzzle, as if searching for inspiration. After a few seconds, the puzzle apparently delivered. 'As if anyone from your bloody family would go for someone normal.' She sighed, picking up her car keys from under the counter.

'ALFIE!' she screamed. 'TAKE OVER. ANOTHER BLOODY DRAMA AT THE LAMBERTS'!'

Chapter Twenty-One

I arrived at the Garrick Theatre with less than ten minutes to spare. A small gaggle of paparazzi smoked by the doorway, presumably waiting for the handful of famous actors that Sam had told me were coming. I felt a great surge of pride to think that real-life famous actors were going to watch Sam tonight. My Bowes!

Many people had taken their seats but the bar was still bright and busy with chattering, smiling, well-dressed audience members.

I scanned for Hailey and Ness, who had my ticket, and found a lot of confused faces staring at me. *Oh, fuck,* I thought suddenly. *Oh, triple fuck!* I looked down at myself for the first time in five hours and gasped. I was still wearing my old dog-walking jeans with bright pink socks and muddy walking shoes. Worst of all was Dad's baggy old jumper, which hung down my thighs and looked like half of Malcolm was stuck to it. Mum's winter mac, so grubby and ancient that she'd long since stopped using it herself, completed the picture.

I looked like a farmhand! I began to back out of the door but then heard Hailey shouting my name. I cringed. She was striding towards me on high heels, looking very beautiful in the dress we'd chosen last week. Hailey was still pretty traumatized by her experience with Matty but she did seem to have got over the comfort eating. She looked like Hailey again: curvy, titty and delicious.

'Oh, Hailey, you look amazing!' I said, standing back to admire her.

'You look terrible,' she replied, frowning at my outfit. 'Did you bring a pig and chickens down on your cart?'

'I don't think I can stay here. Maybe I could try and find something to wear . . .'

'Like what? A "Mind the Gap" bikini from Leicester Square? I don't bloody think so.' Hailey took my hand. 'Now, Chas. Are you . . . erm . . . are you *sure* you're in love with Bowes? You're not ill or anything?'

'Not ill. I just love him. I know it's mad, Hailey, but those emails . . . sort of changed everything.'

Hailey studied me doubtfully, trying to make sense of what I was saying. For a few seconds she seemed faintly amused but then concern clouded her features. 'I don't want you getting hurt, Chas,' she said quietly. 'We both know what Sam's like. And I couldn't stand it if you had to go through what I've gone through with Matty.' Her mask slipped and I got a brief glimpse into a fragile, still-broken heart.

'I hear you, Hails,' I said. 'And I know it's a risk. But, honestly, Sam's changed. I think those emails sparked a *massive* change in him. In me too, for that matter.'

Hailey looked unconvinced. 'Well . . . Ness did say they were a bit special,' she conceded.

'They've changed my life,' I said simply. 'And Sam's! Look how different things are now – for both of us.' A nubile teenager stared at me like I was a piece of mad six-foot shit.

Hailey pondered this for a minute and then shrugged.

'Yeah. I can't deny it, Chas. The two of you have done a big fat three hundred and sixty degrees recently.'

'EXACTLY!'

There was a loaded pause. 'OK,' Hailey said slowly. 'But, Christ, this is about as weird as it gets.'

'Tell me about it. Oh buggering hell, I'm scared, Hailey.'

'Come on,' she said, amused, walking off across the foyer. 'Shelley paid about ten million pounds to get you a seat at the last minute. She'll kill me if I don't get you there on time.'

'*Shelley?*'

As we walked up the stairs, Hailey turned round and smiled. She looked rather guilty, which worried me for reasons I couldn't quite put my finger on. 'Mm, yes, Shelley. We're sitting with her. She's got us a royal box.'

'Wow!' I said. 'Although it would be good if you could avoid talking about me and Sam in front of her? I think it'd be a bit weird for a client to know –'

'OH, HOLY LORD,' Shelley Cartwright roared, as we rounded the corner of the stairs and arrived on the first floor. She was clutching William's arm for support. 'She's here, William! It's happening!'

'Charleeee!' Ness cried, hopping over to hug me. She, too, was wearing a lovely dress and heels. I breathed in wafts of her delicate perfume and clean hair and felt part of me die inside. I must smell like a compost heap.

I pulled away from her and looked back at a very excitable-looking Shelley. 'What do you mean, "It's happening"?' I asked her.

'I'm so glad you saw sense, Charlotte!' she said,

completely ignoring my question. She was rubbing her hands together with glee.

Then her face fell and she shuddered in horror, as if I were covered with weeping medieval boils. 'Oh, my God! What . . . What *is* this, Charlotte?'

'Hi, William Thomas,' William said, as if it were not completely obvious. He shook my hand very firmly and I smelt old-fashioned cologne.

'Don't touch her, William!' Shelley hissed. 'She's filthy! Charlotte, your appearance is a disaster! It could ruin everything.'

'What do you *mean*?' I was beginning to feel annoyed, more so because Ness was giggling cheekily into her hand and Hailey looked as guilty as Malcolm had when we'd found him in bed with the remains of our Christmas turkey in 2007. Something – involving me – was going on, but I was not party to any information as to what it might be.

The five-minute bell sounded.

'Please can someone tell me what's going on?' I asked.

'Ha ha!' Shelley cackled, in a *You've Been Framed* sort of a way.

'Ha ha!' William guffawed. 'Played you at your own game! And it worked! You're here, Charlotte! Splendid!'

Half-formed thoughts were flying around my head but I couldn't quite pin them down. Fortunately, Shelley took the matter out of my hands. 'It was all my idea!' she foghorned. 'You and Sam! It worked! Took enough bloody time but you got there eventually!'

'What?' I asked, totally confused. 'Me and Sam what?'

Shelley trumpeted with laughter. 'William and I realized

we'd both used First Date Aid as soon as we saw our testimonies online,' she announced gleefully. 'You put us next to each other on the website! I mean, come on!'

William interrupted. 'Not all Shelleys spell their name like mine does,' he clarified.

'Right,' I said, still in the dark.

'We worked out that you two had been colluding to get us together,' Shelley barked. '*The Pearl Fishers* was bloody inspired. And those sympathetic messages when I was in New York . . . Oh, Charlotte, you bugger! But I'm afraid you didn't cover your tracks perfectly, young lady, and we rumbled you. Ha ha!'

Shelley was not speaking quietly. Theatregoers were staring at us as they made their way into the auditorium.

'We're grateful you went to such lengths to get us together,' William said. 'Some sly manoeuvres! But we were both struck by the messages you and Samuel wrote each other initially. Bit batty and over the top but a great big thumping connection going on there!'

I blinked at them. They were the same person.

'We couldn't believe the two people who wrote the emails weren't an item,' Shelley explained loudly. 'It was like reading a love story!' The two-minute bell was sounding and an usher hovered, wanting to move us on but clearly terrified of the six-foot power truncheon in his midst. 'So,' she continued, 'we decided to return the favour. Do some meddling of our own! Get you and Sam together!'

I blanched. 'What?'

Shelley roared with excitable laughter. 'HA HA! HA HA! Investment dinners, my rump!' she yelled. 'Remember the first one? In the Balmoral? The RBA event? That stood for Right Back Atcha! We played you at your own game! HA HA!'

'She's bloody clever, this woman,' William said proudly.

I stood, dumbfounded, as Shelley crowed about having set up the Balmoral, the Mandarin Oriental and even the bloody *Sunday Times* photo-shoot, all designed to get Sam and me together in romantic situations. 'Was my idea to have you two all tangled up on that *chaise-longue* in the photo-shoot,' she told me. 'I had Kaveh all over it! Bloody triumph! And you kissed each other! Twice!'

'How the hell do you know about that?' I asked, quite shocked. Nobody knew!

'Sam told me. I grilled him yesterday, with force. Ha ha!'

'And?' I asked her anxiously. 'What else did he say?'

Shelley looked uncomfortable for the first time. 'Well, he wasn't exactly forthcoming. He said it was a scientific experiment. But he must feel the same! How can he not after those bloody emails? I mean, my God!'

William led Shelley to the door of our box as the final bell went. 'Come on, darling,' he said soothingly. 'Your plan will work out, I'm sure of it.' I shook my head in disbelief. How was this real?

Shelley dragged me along behind them, her hand clasped round my wrist as if I were an errant toddler. She gloated noisily over how stupid Sam and I were for failing to rumble her. 'I mean, *really*.' She snorted. 'What sort of investor just fails to turn up? In fact, what sort of an investor wants to take on a dating company? Ha HA! And as if I'd pay for you to have a room at the Mandarin bloody Oriental if I didn't want you to seduce Samuel!'

William put an affectionate hand on her back as he stepped into our box. 'She pulled out all the stops, this one,' he said, gazing lovingly at his mad girlfriend.

I was undeniably impressed. Shelley had not only played us but she'd played us very well. And of course she'd sent us to high-end hotels! Of course she'd paid for expensive dinners and champagne! It had Shelley Cartwright written all over it! How could I not have realized?

I felt William looking me up and down. 'We have to go and watch this silly play,' he said reluctantly. 'But don't you worry, Charlotte. We've got tonight all taken care of. You'll get your man this evening, mark my words! Although the outfit may be a problem,' he added, disappearing into the box.

'I'm on the outfit situation,' Shelley told him. 'I just need to make a quick call . . .' She followed him inside without so much as a look in my direction, hissing into her BlackBerry.

'She just sort of attacked me earlier,' Hailey said awkwardly. 'And I found myself telling her you'd fallen in love with Bowes. It was an error. Um, sorry, Chas.'

'You will be,' I told her.

I didn't know what Shelley still had in store for me but I was pretty sure I wasn't going to like it.

It took me a while to get into the action. I wasn't a Shakespeare buff but I knew *The Tempest* well, of course: it was the play from which came Sam's infamous chat-up line. Watching him knock that line out to girls in nightclubs and bars while we were at university, I'd become curious about it and asked Sam to lend me his copy. I'd read the play, failed to understand a word and had had to ask for a tutorial. Sam had talked about it with such enthusiasm that I'd ended up hooked and had read it again and again, declaring it my favourite Shakespeare play. (I skirted round the fact that it was the only one I could understand.)

Sam and I had been to see *The Tempest* a few times over the years and I'd been very disappointed by the crappy, insipid Mirandas I'd seen. 'But, Chas, it's a shit part,' Sam had argued. 'Miranda's got all those lines and yet almost no character. Only an *amazing* actress could bring her alive.' Katia Slagface, it seemed, was that amazing actress. There was a delicate sexuality in her, a subtle strength and steeliness, and furthermore she really owned the stage. *Thank God she's married*, I thought. Never mind Sam, *I* fancied her.

And then Sam walked onstage and my stomach appeared in my mouth. He was laughing as he strolled on, chatting to two other men and looking more relaxed and natural than he did even in our sitting room. The director had set the play on an imaginary island off Egypt shortly before the Second World War and Sam was decked out in a beautiful cream safari suit. His hair was Vaselined off to the side and he carried a slim cigarette. A light somewhere above the stage was dappling him in the warm colours of a late afternoon and not even his dodgy moustache could detract from his beauty. I was expecting the Bowes Actor Voice but when he started to speak I barely recognized the soft, lyrical sound that came out.

I started to smile.

A few seconds later I realized the smile was enormous and I looked sideways to check that Shelley hadn't

414

noticed. But, of course, she had. 'WELL NOW!' she hissed, giving me an uncharacteristically silly thumbs-up. I shook my head.

By the time the curtain fell two hours later, I was even more in love with Sam than I had been before. The audience went wild and a standing ovation started almost immediately. When the actors came back on for their curtain call they were jubilant, ecstatic, even, and Sam was grinning from ear to ear. When it was his turn to take a bow, he came forward quite bashfully but I could see that every cell in his body was happy. I clapped even harder. 'Raaaarr!' I yelled, grinning down at him.

Then he looked up and saw me and his face changed. His eyes widened and, without any thought for etiquette, he waved excitedly at me, beaming like a child. 'No fucking *way*!' he mouthed, much to the delight of the audience. Following his eyeline, a theatreful of people stared at my grubby clothes and greasy pudding-bowl hair. But I didn't care. I fixed my eyes on Sam and clapped even harder, grinning for all I was worth. *I love you*, I thought. *I absolutely love you!*

Feral farmhand I might be, but I had to tell Samuel Bowes how I felt. And, like Frank, I had to do it my way. Not Shelley's way or bloody anyone else's way. I'd had enough of meddling with other people's relationships. I'd had enough of other people meddling with mine. This was my story.

'Sit,' Shelley commanded, pointing to a seat in the corner of the bar a little while later.

I sat, thinking it would be wise to play along with her for now. Our little party sank into chairs around me and an enthusiastic resting actor in a red waistcoat offered us champagne. I took three glasses.

'Now, Charlotte, you don't need to worry. I have a plan,' Shelley said, in tones that were perhaps designed to be soothing. They were not soothing or even close to it. She pulled her chair in closer to me, checking her watch. 'Ah, excellent. There will be a bag of clothes arriving by courier any minute,' she said. 'My friend Araminta is a buyer at Fenwick's.'

There was not even a trace of irony in her face. She was extraordinary.

'Shelley, that's lovely of you but I'm no longer in a position to buy expensive clothes,' I began.

'You aren't buying them,' she interrupted. 'It's taken care of.' She giggled to herself, and William stroked her arm fondly. 'In the interval I arranged for you to use a shower backstage,' she told me. 'We'll have you looking human in no time at all.'

She was mad. They both were.

'So what's the plan?' I asked her, doing my best to look as if I was eager to get cracking.

Shelley tapped her nose. 'You leave the planning to me.' She cackled manically. 'However . . . before I press the green button, Charlotte, I want to know why it's taken you so long to get to this point. I suspect you've liked Samuel for a while.'

I nodded grudgingly. 'I suppose.'

'Well, then, what was *stopping* you?' She looked at William for support. 'Are you mentally retarded?'

I tried to frown but couldn't help smiling. This was vintage Cartwright. 'Well, for starters, Shelley Cartwright, *you* told me he was going out with Katia!' I reminded her. 'I only found out today that it was a lie – that he's single. And what did I do? I got straight on a plane! I don't think I'm entirely to blame.'

Shelley reddened. 'Ah,' she said spiritedly, staring at her expensive bracelet. 'Yes. Was hoping to stir up a bit of jealousy. Make you fight for him. Possibly an error.' She recovered from her embarrassment soon enough, though. 'Well, you came round in the end, Charlotte! I suggest you sit back and let me take care of this. OH! AHOY THERE!' A motorbike courier with four Fenwick's bags stood in the doorway and Shelley strode over to him without so much as a glance in my direction.

I watched her go and marvelled. It was touching, of course, that she was so desperate to get Sam and me together, but alarming to witness the extent to which the challenge had taken her over. *Thank God I'm not like that any more*, I thought, shuddering. Thanks to Sam, it had been nearly two months since I'd walked out of Salutech and the life that came with it.

Sam. My palms prickled. *I have to find Sam before Shelley gets to him.* I watched her sign for the delivery while yelling into her BlackBerry, and knew that it was now or never.

'Just going to the loo,' I said to the others. Hailey waved me off and nicked one of my glasses of champagne.

I ducked under the velvet rope which was across the entrance to the stairs and scampered up towards our box. If my plan was going to work, I had to act fast. I drew level with the door and then, checking no one was watching, snuck through the one next to it, a narrow, heavy door marked 'Private'.

It opened into a narrow corridor with black curtains on either side, lit softly by blue-painted bulbs, which I'd seen a technical person disappear down during the interval. For a moment I paused, weighing up the probability of being caught and thrown out. But I had a plan and I wasn't afraid to use it. I wasn't Charlotte Lambert the Scottish Amazon any more: I was Charley who wanted to do her best for herself.

I followed the little corridor around a corner and down some stairs. And there it was. Bingo. Dimly lit and blissfully quiet: the empty stage.

I wandered to the edge and stared out into the gloom of the auditorium.

For a few minutes I breathed in and out, feeling strangely empowered by the silence and the stillness around me. But then my head started chattering. *Your plan is stupid and mad*, it told me. *It's about as romantic as a fish finger!* I tried to ignore it but the volume just increased. Fear scrunched up my digestive system and I felt suddenly weighed down by the contents of my bag. *You are a pillock*, my head informed me. *Sam's probably drinking champagne with his luvvie friends right now – what are you going to do, barge into their dressing room, drag him off to a toilet and show him what's inside your bag like a crazed gypsy?*

I sat down on the edge of the stage, dangling my legs into the orchestra pit, and wondered if it would be best to ditch my plan and sneak off. I looked like a tramp, I smelt like a dog and my hair looked like it had been attacked by a block of lard. I couldn't talk to Sam like this.

'Wow,' said a voice behind me, causing me nearly to jump out of my skin.

It was Sam, standing in the centre of the stage. He'd obviously just showered and was wearing a beautifully cut shirt with super-smart trousers, all ready for his big glittery party. He looked edible.

'That's a very special outfit,' he said, appraising my attire with awe.

I nodded. 'I spent hours shopping.'

Sam walked over and plopped down beside me, smelling clean and masculine and gorgeous. I was painfully aware of my canine aroma.

'I did shower this morning,' I blurted.

Sam sniggered. 'We have little monitors in our dressing rooms, showing what's going on onstage,' he told me. 'I saw this bizarrely clad creature roaming round.'

'Just sizing it up,' I told him. 'Thought I might give the acting thing a go some time . . .'

Sam smiled indulgently. I couldn't bear how handsome he was.

'Where's your colonial moustache?' I honked, into the ensuing silence.

'It's a fake,' he replied. 'I spent six weeks trying to grow a moustache – or any sort of facial hair, really – and just ended up with patchy bum-fluff. The wigs mistress designed it especially for me. You like?'

I nodded, unable to think of anything to say.

And here we go again, my head said. *It doesn't work in the real world. It only works when we're emailing.* WE CAN'T COMMUNICATE. IT'S DOOMED.

For once, my head had a point. I was sitting alone with Sam, bursting with things I wanted to say, yet I was mute.

Which meant – another scrunch of fear in my stomach – that I was going to have to put my plan into action.

In slow motion, I put my hand into my bag and pulled out my laptop, which I handed to Sam. It was all ready to go.

He took it, clearly confused, as I dragged out the gigantic black spaceship that my parents called a laptop on to my own knee. I opened it up and there on the screen was an instant messenger dialogue box with a cursor flashing patiently. *Charley says*, it read.

'Er . . . ?' Sam said. I nodded to indicate that he should open up the laptop on his knee. Which he did, with a slightly bemused smile.

'Chas . . . ?' he said, peering at the screen, which looked very similar to mine. 'What's going on?'

I ignored him and started typing.

Charley: Hello

I screwed up my eyes, praying he'd jump on board. And a few seconds later, I heard the sound of fingers typing.

Sam: I repeat. What the fuck's going on, homie?

What the fuck was 'going on' was that I was going to tell him how I felt. Using a very romantic mode of communication known as instant messaging. I didn't care if it was the most soulless expression of love in the universe:

the fact was our lives had changed for ever because of our online conversations.

Email worked for us. Talking didn't. Not yet.

As the Heathrow Express had powered towards Paddington earlier, I had created instant-messenger accounts in anticipation of this chat. And the lovely thing was that I felt no compulsion to plan what I was going to say. I knew that, when the time came, my fingers would start typing, just like they had during those spine-tingling hours in October when 'William' and 'Shelley' had been emailing each other. It had been as effortless as breathing.

So here I was, facing a darkened sea of seats, ready to send a message of sweet love on Dad's gigantic boulder of a laptop. Shelley probably had a search party out by now and I had to move quickly.

I took a deep breath.

> Charley: So, I wanted to talk to you about us.
> Charley: don't seem to be able to do it face to face
> Charley: and, erm, I devised this little plan.

There was an excruciating pause.

> Sam: I'm listening.
> Charley: Bowes, I
> Charley: sorry. SAM.
> Charley: Sam, I'm afraid our emails back in October have turned my head.
> Sam: Oh come on Chas, me too! You know it wasn't just you! Look at all the changes we've made!

Charley: hang on. I'm not just talking jobs 'n' lifestyle 'n' shit.
   I'm talking
Charley: erm
Charley: feelings.
Charley: specifically, feelings towards you.

There it was. I couldn't turn back now.

Sam removed his hands from the keyboard, which threw me. Was he about to run? Or was he just ready to listen?

He picked up his hands again and put me out of my misery.

Sam: I'm still listening. X
Charley: I sort of fell a bit in love with Willia,
Charley: sorry, Williannm
Charley: ARRGH! W I L L I A M
Charley: fucking messenger
Sam: it's ok Chas. I'm right here dude, you don't need to stress
Charley: thanks.
Charley: William. And when I realized it was you, I thought Oh well
   that's over then

I inhaled slowly. I knew it was going to be nerve-racking. I just had to do it.

Charley: but it seems that it's not over
Charley: and that it sort of doesn't matter who wrote those emails
Charley: I feel the same way about the writer whoever he is.

Sam didn't move or say anything. Turning ever so slightly I could see there was a blush on his neck, spreading out underneath the soft downy hairs where his hairline ended and his neck started. I longed to throw my laptop into the orchestra pit and hug this soft downy neck.

However, my more pressing concern was that Sam wasn't saying anything. And so I took things up a level. A substantial level.

> Charley: basically Sam I'm saying that I've come to realize that I'm in love with you.

Still nothing.

> Charley: I know you don't feel the same, that's ok.
> Charley: and I don't expect anything from this conversation other than
> Charley: I dunno. Confirmation that you don't feel the same. Just for my records, you know . . .

I stopped typing, even though I wanted to add two thousand more sentences persuading Sam to love me. But I'd promised myself: keep it simple. Say what you need to say, and if he's not forthcoming, get the hell out. Put a few hundred miles between you. Get back to Malcolm.

After what seemed like several lifetimes, Sam began to write. I felt like I was having a heart attack.

> Sam: you smell of Malcolm.
> Charley: You are jealous.

Sam sniggered.

How the fuck can you be sitting there cracking jokes? I thought desperately. *Are you mad? Blind? Did you not just see what I wrote?*

Sam started writing again.

'THERE THEY ARE,' hissed a loud voice.

Sam stopped writing.

The voice had been a full-on pantomime whisper and it had come from somewhere above me. With a sinking feeling, I looked up and saw two heads poking out from the box we'd sat in tonight, staring furtively down at me. Of course it was Shelley and William. And of course they were goggling at us.

I looked back at my computer, which had just pinged a message in.

Sam: We have company

Charley: Permit me to deal with this

Sam: Actually Chas, I don't think I can do this.

Sam: this conversation.

Sam: I think I have to stop it here, I'm really sorry.

NO! I thought desperately. *No! Shelley is not ruining this for me!*

I put the computer down and stood up.

'Shelley, bugger off,' I shouted. 'And William too.'

There was a stunned silence as the two protruding heads looked at each other, then back down at me in astonishment. 'Us?' Shelley barked.

'Yes, you. Bugger off.'

Nothing happened.

'ARE YOU DEAF?' I was getting angry now. 'BUG-GER OFF. I don't want or need your help. Or your interference. Just leave us alone, OK?'

'Of all the ungrateful . . .' Shelley began, in outraged tones.

'Pah,' William added helpfully.

They went, shaking their expensively coiffured heads.

I closed my eyes for a split second before turning back to Sam. I needed to be calm while we had this conversation.

But when I turned round, Sam had gone.

My laptop sat silently on the floor, abandoned.

My insides plummeted out of me and down through the stage, landing in a stricken pile in some dank underground wardrobe store. I had just told Sam I was in love with him and he'd fled. I felt my face go red. And then it crashed down on me, an awful, terrible shame.

It took me over. How could I have been so stupid? How could I have believed, for *one millisecond*, that Sam would be interested? I passed my hand over my face. I had to leave this place, fast.

I hauled the laptops into my satchel and slid off into the wings, checking one last time that I hadn't left anything. Satisfied, I turned to go, but something caught my eye.

It was Sam, walking back onstage. 'No, wait, Chas!' He laughed, as if we'd just been giggling over some sherry and shortbread together.

'I have to go,' I said tightly. 'Forget what I said. Bye.'

I turned and left.

I heard Sam begin to trot after me and, accordingly, I broke into a run. I was not going to allow him to embarrass me any more than he had done. I shot off up the stairs I'd arrived down and made it almost to the top before he managed to grab one of my mud-caked walking shoes. I pulled against him and the shoe came off; I scrambled up the rest of the stairs towards the door.

'STOP!' I carried on without my shoe. 'Oi! Cinderella! Get a grip!'

I sprinted on up but, just as I got to the door, Sam rugby-tackled me. 'Chas!' he yelled, half laughing, as I crashed to the floor with him wrapped round my middle.

'Get the fuck off me,' I hissed. I wriggled hard but he wouldn't let go.

'Fucking stay still!' He was properly laughing now.

How dare he? Did he think this was *funny*?

'Charley,' he said, struggling to contain me, 'when I said I couldn't do it, I meant I couldn't have this conversation with you online. I wanted to have it face to face!'

'Bullshit,' I replied angrily. 'You got up and walked off.'

'FUCKING STOP WRIGGLING!' Sam yelled. 'FOR THE LOVE OF GOD!'

I stopped. I had very little fight left in me anyway, plus I couldn't guarantee that the crotch of my dog-walking jeans wouldn't split open if I carried on in this manner. They'd been wearing thin for a very long time.

'Thank you,' Sam said. 'If I let you go, do you promise not to run?'

'S'pose.' I sounded so sullen that Sam burst out laughing again. He let me go and pulled himself up, holding out a hand to pull me up too. I ignored it and stood up under my own steam, eyes fixed on the black wall opposite me. This was far too narrow a corridor to be trapped in with Sam.

There was a pause while he waited – in vain – for me to meet his eye.

'Chasmonger,' he said quietly. He took my hand and I flinched. 'Please stop being angry. I went to turn off the little camera onstage. Otherwise all of the cast would be watching and listening to us from the dressing-room monitors. Look.' He led me to another private box that overlooked the stage. It was full of screens and dials and switches, and there was a large microphone sticking out of the desk.

'This is where the deputy stage manager sits,' Sam explained. 'She tells everyone when to change the scene and the lights and the music and stuff. And look, here's the monitor where everyone'd be able to watch us and listen to us.'

Grudgingly, I looked. There was indeed a monitor, showing the empty stage. 'OK,' I said. 'Well, please tell me what you wanted to tell me and then I'll be off. I need to shower.'

'Tell me about it,' he said. 'I feel like Malcolm's here with us.'

I tried very hard to keep a straight face but it was difficult. Sam was still clutching my muddy shoe, I was covered with dog hair and both of us had broken a sweat from our wrestle.

And once I'd started laughing, I couldn't stop. I sat down, rested my head against the deputy stage manager's desk and shook with mirth. 'I came down and told you I was in love with you using Dad's spaceship,' I cried. 'And then you rugby-tackled me. And I smell. And we had a shouting match. Bowes, I'm so sorry. Of course we're not meant to be together.'

Sam laughed, but then stopped. Without warning he stuck a finger out and trailed it down the back of my hand.

It was like receiving an electric shock.

He withdrew it but I continued to stare at my hand, enchanted, as if waiting for a silver line to appear where his finger had been.

Sam was leaning back in his chair, watching me. I tried to look at him but I couldn't. I had no idea what was going to happen.

'You don't need to say anything,' I said, after a charged pause. 'I understand.'

Sam smiled kindly at me.

'And no kindly smiles,' I added. 'I'll survive this. I've survived worse.'

There was another electric shock, this time on my left hand. I looked at it and saw that Sam had put his over it. He looked nervous but also quite happy. 'Charley,' he said quietly. 'You've changed my life.'

'Yes yes yes. But you only like small girls. We've been friends too long. Rah rah rah WHATEVER.'

There was a pause. 'Have you quite finished?' Sam asked.

I thought about it, shrugged and nodded. Yes, that seemed about enough.

'And – Chas, will you look at me, you freak?'

I looked at him.

'And stop looking like you couldn't care less what I was saying?'

In spite of myself I was smiling again.

'Your emails made me realize I was wasting my life. Job-wise,' he added hastily. 'I'm not taking any shit from you about my Nutella.'

I waved him on.

'But the rest,' he continued, 'the rest had to change. All because of you. And the thing is, bruv, I did try to fight it, when I found out it was you. No offence but it's not convenient to be in love with someone like The Chasmonger.'

Before I even processed what he'd just said, I was taken back to the letter I'd read this morning from Jack to Granny Helen: *It's not very convenient to love you, I can't deny it. If I were to dream up my perfect girl she probably wouldn't be you. She'd be a bit more bloody respectful for a start!*

And then my mouth dropped open as I realized what Sam had said. I looked up at his face, which was suddenly vulnerable. I hadn't known he had a vulnerable face.

I had to be certain. 'Sorry, Sam. Did you just say it wasn't convenient –'

'To love you,' Sam said quietly. 'Yes, you knob. That's what I said.'

I felt a delicious tingling somewhere inside me. Not somewhere rude: somewhere pure and lovely, where cherubs romped. Sam sensed it and relaxed. He gave my hand a squeeze.

'Could you just confirm precisely what you're getting at?' I asked him. My smile was getting a bit out of control.

Sam sighed. 'Oh, you're a knobber,' he remarked. 'But a funny one. A challenging one, a clever one. The kind of knobber that people can't take their eyes off. You have no idea how much you brighten up a room just by being in it, Chas.' As well as pleasure, I felt relief at his words. Of

429

course Sam and I could talk to each other face to face. Of course we didn't need emails to communicate. We just needed honesty.

Sam sat forward on his chair again so that he was closer to me. He slid his hands to my forearms, which went a bit barmy. 'To confirm, Chasmonger, I've gone and fallen in love with you. My poor innocent heart has been stolen. By a bloody Lambert!'

Somewhere in the distance, a great cheer went up, followed by the sound of clinking glasses and excitable laughter.

'You're missing your party,' I heard myself say. I was so happy I might explode. Sam ignored me.

'I think we should do one third scientific experiment,' he announced. 'We've kissed twice already, how's about best of three?'

My insides somersaulted. 'Good idea. Although I was pretty sure after experiment number one,' I admitted.

'Me too. What's *wrong* with us? Why the hell didn't we just say?'

Further cheers erupted in the bar downstairs, followed by the rather unexpected sound of running feet. I looked nervously into the still-empty auditorium but Sam reached over and turned my face back towards his. 'No one can find us here,' he said confidently. 'This is our secret science lab. Where we conduct important experiments.'

I shivered as he touched the side of my neck.

There was a long pause, during which I felt as if I was fizzing over like champagne.

'Are we having another standoff?' I asked eventually.

Sam grinned. 'No.' And then he kissed me properly.

It felt right. More than right. I slid my arms round his neck and we leaned in closer, kissing even more deeply. It was the nicest kiss I'd ever, ever had. It was full to bursting with loveliness, with kindness, understanding, humour. It was a little bit beautiful. No, it was extremely, supremely beautiful.

Sam stopped kissing me and hugged me tightly. His head was buried in my not-very-lovely hair, and I could feel his warm breath on my neck, which meant he must be getting whiffs of Malcolm but it didn't matter.

I pulled back to kiss him again, just as I heard a door smash open and a familiar foghorn of a voice yell, 'THERE THEY ARE!'

Sam and I sprang apart, peering over the edge of the box at the auditorium. Shelley was standing at the door, jumping up and down, pointing at us, and pouring in through the doors to her left and right were champagne-wielding audience members. All cheering, whooping and pointing at us.

Hailey came thundering down the central aisle, shouting, 'That was like the fucking Archers on acid! Amazing!'

I looked at Sam, bewildered, as someone started doing three cheers. For a few seconds he seemed as confused as I was but then, finally, something dawned on him. He moved my elbow, which was resting on the stage manager's desk, and grimaced. 'Oh dear,' he said. 'Oh dear, dear me.'

'What?'

The whooping downstairs was continuing unabated. 'HAVE ANOTHER SNOG!' someone yelled. How the hell did they know we'd been kissing?

431

Sam pointed to a switch with a red light glowing under it. 'You flicked the switch when you did your dramatic collapse on this desk a few minutes ago. That's what the deputy stage manager uses to talk to the audience when they're in the bar. That switch and this microphone.'

I stared in horror at the microphone, which was inches away from where our mouths had been during the preceding conversation. 'So we just broadcast everything across the bar?'

'Sod it!' Sam shouted, before I had a proper panic attack. 'Who cares? I love you! I want the world to know!' He leaned into the microphone and said, 'I repeat, I love Charlotte Lambert.' And then he grabbed me and kissed me again, to thunderous applause. The stalls were filling up: a second standing ovation was under way.

'Who *is* she?' someone yelled.

'My fucking sister,' Ness yelled back. I didn't think I'd ever heard her swear. 'She's the fucking best,' she added.

Sam tucked my doggy hair behind my ear. 'Blimey,' he said, looking at the chaos below us. We both grinned, first at the crowd and then at each other.

'IT WAS ALL MY IDEA!' Shelley yelled hoarsely. Someone had hijacked the sound desk and 'I Wish It Could Be Christmas Every Day' filled the auditorium. Half the drunken crowd were jigging along, the rest were pointing to the stage demanding we come down and make a speech.

'Come on,' Sam said, taking my hand.

'No way! Look at me!'

He pulled me out of the box and the door shut behind us, blocking out the music and the cheering.

'I didn't mean "Come on, let's go and make tits of ourselves onstage," ' he said, breaking into a trot. 'Bugger that! I meant let's get out of here! They're all drunk, they've got some music, they'll have forgotten about us in two minutes.'

I squeezed his hand. 'Thank you,' I said gratefully, and he kissed me briefly, doffing an imaginary hat. Even a one-second thank-you kiss gave me stomach somersaults. Me and Sam! Chas 'n' Bowes! My world danced.

Sam smiled at me, then slowed his pace, holding my hand.

He pulled me down some steps and out through the stage door, where a man was listening to Mahler with a burger in his hand. We exploded out into the chaos of Charing Cross Road on a Friday night, with drunk, singing foreigners roaming in packs, brightly lit kiosks knocking out lukewarm pizza; music pumping from rude-boy cars waiting for the lights to change. Almost straight away Sam trod in the remains of a Chinese takeaway and a group of drunken stags lurched into me, sending my satchel flying. We stopped, laughing, to straighten ourselves out, and Sam kissed me again. 'I'm excited about us,' he announced, hugging me tightly.

I saw how much he meant it and I felt wonderfully, madly happy. 'Me too, Bowes,' I told him, squashing down a funny corner of his hair that had sprung up in the sharp winter wind. 'I think we might just be OK, you know.'

'Seconded.' He kissed me again, running his thumb slowly along my jawline and smiling at me in a way that transported me far from the noisy drinkers and revving engines of Charing Cross Road. 'Come on,' he said, taking my hand. He paused, looking left and right with a comically furrowed brow. 'Although I've got bugger-all idea where to go, Chas,' he said eventually. 'Fancy a kebab?'

And that's when I knew that my life was not, and would never be, perfect. But it was pretty damn good.

Acknowledgements

Writing a novel is a wonderful challenge. As is backpacking around South America.

Doing both of these things at the same time, however, is downright foolish and it is therefore a testament to all of the brilliant people in my life that I was able to pull it off and not go mad. So thank you, first of all, to everyone I met during my travels, fellow itinerants and locals alike, for the craic, the stories and the space when I was being writerly. Thanks in particular to the many people who helped me when I was ill, especially Hannah Coffin, Amy Phillips and the folk at the Secret Garden hostels in Cotopaxi and Quito. Thanks also to my handsome man, George, for understanding that I had to go off and write some of this book on my own . . . and for being such a brilliant travel buddy when we were on the road together. The same to Tania and Bert.

Thank you to Chris Parkin for emailing me that newspaper article. I hope you'll agree that it was worth a little more than a blog. Thank you too to Rory McClenaghan for help with my questions on ghostwriting!

Thanks to Cressida Toro for her invaluable help with the world of Pharmaceutical Comms and to Ellie Tinto for getting me started. Thank you to Doctors Alpesh Kothari and Michael Rayment for help with broken legs – if there are still mistakes they are definitely my fault!

Thank you to Jennie Green and the Great Leap Forward girls for their Edinburgh help and hospitality.

Thank you to my lovely family for being so cool about my travels – and for all the support around my new writing career. And to my friends, for their excitement and willingness to push my book on anyone who'd listen.

THANK YOU to my agent, Lizzy Kremer at David Higham Associates, who is simply the best agent in the world. Sorry that you got Spanish-speaking hostel owners every time you tried to call me.

Another large thank you to my editor Celine Kelly for absolutely everything, especially for helping me to really believe in this book. And to the excellent folk at Penguin with whom I've worked with over the last year – Liz Smith, Francesca Russell, Anna Durkacz to name but a few. Your enthusiasm and determination to get me out there has helped me so much. Thank you also to Ania Corless, Tine Nielson and Stella Giatrakou at David Higham for getting me published in so many languages and to Harriet Evans and Laura West for the other bits.

I am well lucky, me.

Discover Lucy's
other laugh-out-loud novel
The Greatest Love Story of All Time...

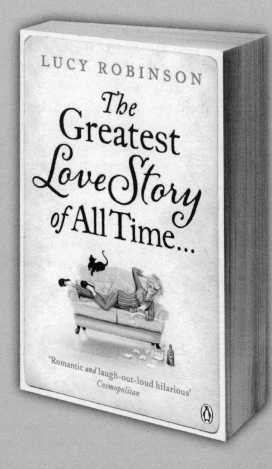

Read the first chapter here

Prologue

My friends broke into my flat.

They stood scrutinizing me for a few seconds: Stefania, a vision in purple dungarees; Leonie in a massive fur coat with an inexplicable gin and tonic in one hand. Dave, wearing a patchy deerstalker, rolled a cigarette while my cat Duke Ellington sat next to them on the floor, watching me with open contempt.

Stefania spoke first. 'Ve have decided to hold Gin Thursday here at your house.'

'I love you, Franny,' said Leonie, taking a sip of her gin. 'But this has got to stop, darling. You stink.'

Dave merely laughed, shook his head and murmured, 'Fuckin' hell, Fran. We left Gin Thursday for *this*?'

Duke Ellington looked up at them as if to say, 'See? See what I've been up against?' He stood up and stalked delicately out of the room with his tail twitching. 'Whatever, Duke Ellington,' I muttered in his wake. He ignored me.

I looked up at my friends again and tried to organize my features into a calm, spiritual sort of expression. Something that said, 'Dudes! Sorry I couldn't answer the door! I was just too blissed out to hear you knocking!' *Please make them go away,* I prayed. *I just want to live like a feral animal. Please.*

'Get out of bed,' Stefania commanded, striding over to the window and opening my curtains. 'You look like someseeng zat Duke Ellington has seecked up in ze flowerbed.'

Not having seen daylight in some time I shot back under the covers, swearing. Dave muttered something about me being a nasty little ferret.

I wriggled further down my bed and fumed. What the hell did Dave know about heartbreak anyway? He lived with the most beautiful woman in London. How dare he judge me? The injustice of it! I balled myself up into a foetal position and waited for them to leave, vowing to stay in the warm fug of my bed for ever.

But it was not to be. The duvet was swept from above me, the interior of my bed was exposed and all hell broke loose. Stefania shrieked, 'YOU DISGUS-TEENG ANIMAL!' Leonie downed the gin and tonic and Dave, who was well known in war zones for dodging enemy fire without so much as a raised eyebrow, dropped his half-assembled roll-up and covered his face with his hands.

The sight that had greeted them wasn't nice. Even I could see that. A half-eaten tub of ice-cream had welded itself to the sheet and was growing fur. My pillowcases were rigid and peaked where I had let snot dry on them, and photos of Michael lay under an abandoned piece of rock-hard Cheddar. A small bottle of Morrison's brandy was resting against my feet. Scattered everywhere were crumbs, crisps and knickers.

Stefania stormed out to the kitchen, shrieking over her shoulder, 'Zis place needs to be decontaminated! Get OUT OF BED!'

I didn't move.

Dave sat down at my dressing-table and stared at me, while Leonie climbed over to my bedside table and took my phone. 'Give it back,' I mumbled feebly. She ignored me and started pressing buttons.

'Give it *back*,' I said again.

'Oh, bloody hell, Fran, what have you been doing?' she asked, taking off her fur coat. She passed the phone to Dave, who looked at it and shook his head with a mixture of pity and amusement.

'Fran, you can't send him messages like this,' he said, trying not to smile. 'That's just . . . it's just fucking madness, love.' He started chuckling. Leonie retrieved the phone and recommenced fiddling.

'I'd like to know what you're finding so funny, Dave,' I said, pulling my hood up to keep the draught out.

'Fran, where would I even start? Oh, love, you're a fuckin' basket case sometimes. Have you been sending him messages like this every day?'

'I never *sent* them,' I mumbled, tears of shame welling. Why was Dave laughing at me when my life was falling apart? Did he really believe I needed to feel any more stupid than I already did? 'Stop it,' I whispered. Tears fell off the side of my nose and into my crusty sheets. Leonie was still fiddling with my phone and Dave sat back and roared with laughter, oblivious to my breakdown.

But when I started to sob he stopped laughing and jumped up from the dressing-table, arms outstretched. 'Oh, no, Fannybaws, I was just joking . . .' My sobs upgraded to roars in anticipation of one of his big hairy-bear hugs.

But just as he reached down to scoop me up, Stefania re-entered the room and yelled, 'STAND BACK, DAVE! DO NOT TOUCH HER! SHE IS RADIOACTIVE!'

Through my tears I saw her standing in my doorway wearing long rubber gloves and one of my anti-dust face masks. She had even found the plastic goggles the plumber had left under the sink a couple of years ago. In one hand she held a bottle of anti-bacterial spray, in the other, a bin bag.

Leonie came and sat on my bed, ignoring Stefania. She took one of my grubby hands in hers. 'Now listen here, Franny darling. We've come because we care about you. We want you to be happy, and that's not going to happen if you're drafting crazed messages to Michael and rotting in bed.'

I gulped and sniffed but the crying wouldn't stop. *Happy?* Were they mad? My life was over. In thirty years I had never felt more lonely and hopeless. How in the name of God was I going to achieve happiness without Michael? Dave sat down and stroked my greasy hair with one of his great big paws.

'I just want my boy back,' I cried.

Leonie squeezed my hand. 'I know, darling. I know. And that might just happen!'

I howled.

'Franny! Come on. It's not like he's said he never wants to see you again, he's just asked for three months apart. It's ninety days, Franny! You can get through ninety days, can't you?'

I shook my head hard. I most certainly could not. Every part of me was in pain.

'Well, from the sounds of it you don't have any choice. But I can tell you right now, Franny, he's not going to take you back if you die of malnutrition in your bed.'

More sobs, with snot this time.

Leonie sighed, then ploughed on: 'So we've come up with a plan for you, Franny. A plan to help you get better. It's a sort of dating rehab. And if at the end of it you still want to fight for Michael, you'll be ready. We'll even help you. OK?'

I made a snotty noise. Dave smiled and continued to stroke my hair. Stefania stood in the doorway, looking like a pest exterminator. Leonie gazed down at me in an uncharacteristically kindly fashion and squeezed my hand again.

I nodded. I'd do anything it took to stop feeling like this.

'Great. Good girl! We'll have you better in no time! Here's the plan . . .' Leonie began.

Chapter One

February 2008: two years earlier

I'd always wanted to be a journalist. In reception class at primary school, while all of the other children told Mrs Grattan that they wanted to be a fireman, a princess or a singer, I had announced coolly that I wanted to travel to war zones and do brave things on the telly. In retrospect I can see why Mrs Grattan told Mum and Dad at parents' evening that she found me a precocious arse.

It had been a little disappointing when the only job I'd been able to get after my broadcast journalism master's was a position as general gimp to the rugby union team at Sky News. For three years I spent every Saturday hunched in the corner of a broadcast truck parked up outside the nation's rugby stadiums, transmitting live scores while the boys talked about anal.

After a particularly sordid Saturday in 2005, during which I was asked to judge a Largest Bollock competition during the Wales v. Ireland decider, I resigned and managed, against all odds, to get a job as a general gimp on the six thirty p.m. news at ITN. (I strongly suspect that I got it because Stella Sanderson, the senior specialist producer who was responsible for hiring me, had also begun her career judging testicles for the Sky rugby team. 'Is there still quite a strong crotch theme in those broadcast trucks?' she asked in my interview. I went red and talked about my overwhelming passion for current affairs. She nodded sympathetically and scribbled in the margin of my CV.)

I was twenty-five when I finally got my break; the age when my friends were beginning to settle down and do grown-up things like having relationships and getting pregnant. I started a wild and passionate affair with my career and moved into a strange little converted car mechanic's garage in a backstreet off Camden Road. It was affordable only because the conversion – involving ceilings that sloped down to the floor – had been designed solely with dwarfs in mind. But it had an *actual* wet room and a big yard where Duke Ellington could terrorize the local mice and birds, so I took it on the spot and convinced myself that Big Things were coming my way.

My job was on the entertainment and culture desk, trailing around London in the wake of our correspondent; carrying his discarded Starbucks cups and broken tripods. Occasionally I'd look after studio guests, and Pierce Brosnan once complained that my hospitality had had a lot in common with sexual harassment.

It was pretty unglamorous stuff in spite of what Leonie and my mother believed: as often as not, I'd

spend shoots on bag-watch duty down a smelly alleyway with a coterie of crack addicts. But I loved my
job and I gave it everything. It made me feel alive,
challenged and useful. I entertained fantastical
notions of one day being a foreign correspondent
wearing linen trousers in a dusty land far away and in
the meantime I plugged away merrily on cuts in arts
budgets and the odd celebrity scandal.

Soon after starting I struck up a friendship with a
cameraman called Dave Brennan. He was a big scruffy
bear of a man who had been born with a camera in
one hand and a roll-up in the other. He was renowned
for his strange tastes: once I found him sitting in his
van eating jellied eels and singing along loudly to soft
rock; another time he turned up to a shoot at Buck-
ingham Palace wearing a jumper that was covered
with mating gnomes.

Dave was Glaswegian, tough as fuck, and had just
transferred to domestic news after a long stint in Iraq.
In spite of losing one of his fingers to a piece of flying shrapnel and being holed up in a besieged town
for ten days without food, he hadn't wanted to come
home; he'd only done so because his girlfriend had
threatened to further dismember him if he didn't. I'd
never quite worked out how old Dave was because of
his sun-abused face and poor control of facial hair,
but I suspected he was in the late-thirties bracket.
Regardless, at ITN he was a legend, the best and
bravest cameraman we had and generally believed to

be the wisest man in the world. Given the rather different nature of our news desks, I got to work with him only rarely but when I did I always sensed I was in the presence of a genius — a slightly hairy, unpredictable genius, but a genius all the same.

Dave and I bonded when he found me necking sausage and mash in a pub near work because I was too embarrassed to do so in front of my slim, tough, salad-eating colleagues. He had retreated to the same pub to down a pint of Stella after a particularly harrowing day at a murder scene. 'Well, well, well. Another outcast. Welcome to my team of one,' he said.

I blushed, mortified, while Dave got to work on his pint, drinking it like Ribena and finishing with a long, mellow belch. 'Sorry. That came out wrong. It's just nice to see someone round here who's a little . . . a little less *corporate*,' he said, and belched again. I smiled bashfully, feeling slightly less stupid.

Most weeks, unless he was in trouble with his girlfriend, Dave would join Leonie and me on Gin Thursdays, an institution the two of us had founded at the tender age of fifteen. The general rule for a Gin Thursday was to get drunk on gin on Thursday. We weren't a complex organization. Ten years on, Gin Thursdays took place at the Three Kings in Clerkenwell, not too far from work. As per our remit, we would drink a lot of gin (Dave added it to his Guinness) and as a general rule Leonie would cop off with a hot lawyer while Dave tried to encourage me to do the same. I always refused. 'I'm after something a little more special than a one-night stand with a man in a pin-stripe suit,' I had announced airily, a few months after we'd met.

'Rubbish,' Dave had replied. 'You're just shite at pulling, aren't you?'

'Yes,' I said meekly.

He smiled and ruffled my hair. 'Aye, I thought as much. Never mind. I'm sure some little scamp will whisk you off your feet soon,' he said kindly.

'Unbloody likely. Last time I tried to pull someone in here I pelvic-thrusted a Greek Cypriot and then asked him to take me home and feed me halloumi.' Dave roared with laughter. 'Oh, Fannybaws,' he said. 'You wee disaster!'

The only time I didn't really enjoy Dave's company was when his partner Freya turned up for a cheeky glass. This was not because she was anything other than nice; it was solely because she was so attractive that in her vicinity I felt like an animated rubbish dump. It was preposterous, a woman like her being let loose on an unsuspecting pub: all conversation shut down and everyone just *stared*. Freya was slim and horribly healthy; she possessed beautiful peaches-and-cream skin and gently waving hair. She wore things made of linen and always smelt amazing.

I had expected Freya and me to become excellent chums, but after a few months of stilted conversation I'd had to admit defeat. I wanted to blame this on her but, deep down, I knew it was my fault: she was calm, spiritual and smooth; I was noisy, clumsy and foolish. I just wasn't her cup of tea. Nonetheless, she tolerated Leonie and me – and our bawdy, studenty drinking – with remarkable patience. Once when he thought no one was looking I saw Dave plant a gentle kiss on her summery shoulder. I was envious. I wanted to kiss it too.

After three years in my rather junior job, I was fantasizing daily about becoming a fearless correspondent with a bullet-proof vest and a string of exotic admirers. 'What do you think the chances are of me being able to apply for a job on the foreign affairs desk?' I asked Hugh, the assistant programme editor, one day.

He looked up briefly from his computer. 'Zero.'

I carried on plugging away with my ideas and late nights, and eventually Hugh came good. In February 2008 he summoned me to his glass fortress at the top end of the newsroom floor. He told me that I was 'a lucky little fucker' and that I was being given a chance to audition for Foreign Affairs by going out to help them cover the aftermath of Kosovo's Declaration of Independence. I'd 'better be fucking outstanding' or 'you'll be working in the fucking canteen for the rest of your fucking life'.

Hugh Gormley was an enormously intelligent man with a swearing habit even worse than mine and a reputation for being a monster. Normally I was terrified of him, but the day he sent me to Kosovo I loved him madly. It was all I could do to stop myself jumping into his lap and kissing him passionately.

As I left, gasping promises of outstanding journalistic vigour, Hugh softened a little bit and smiled. 'You're fucking good news, Fran,' he said. 'You're doing really well. Now fuck off to the Balkans. And be careful. Spend the next two days in hostile-environment training, please.'

I punched the air discreetly and ran off to buy a celebratory can of Vimto, as I often did when life felt good. At last! Fran the Balkans correspondent had been born! I knew nothing about the Balkans, but who cared?

'Don't get any big ideas,' said Stella Sanderson, as she strode past me at the vending machine with a huge folder marked 'Kosovo' under her arm. 'You're at the bottom of the pile. We're going only because the main team out there need a break. It goes them, then me, then our correspondent, then Dave, then the entirety of Kosovo, then you. OK?'

'OK,' I said, nodding enthusiastically. I'd wipe Stella's bottom if I needed to.

After two days' training in hostile-environment filming I began to read about Kosovo. A few moments later, I gave up and called Dave. 'Who'd have thought it, eh? ITN's promising new talent learning her stuff from the cameraman.' He chortled.

I could hear Freya's pots and pans in the background.

'You're not a cameraman, you're a legend,' I said, feeling a bit silly. 'Of course I'm trying to learn from you.'

After a pause, Dave started talking. I listened intently. By the end I was feeling pretty scared.

'You'll be fine, kid, I'll keep an eye on you,' he said at the end, stopping to puff on his fag.

I sighed. 'Dave, I *wish* you wouldn't smoke.'

'Cut the wee princess act, Fran.' He snorted. 'I'm off for my tea now anyway. Pork chops. What are you having?'

I looked in my empty fridge. 'Um, probably some dry Weetabix.'

'You're the fuckin' pits, Fannybaws.' He laughed, hanging up.

I made my nightly call to Mum, who was drunk and complaining about something to do with the gardeners, then packed my bag, wondering how she would cope over the weekend without me coming over to do her shopping and clean her house. Well, she'd have to. If this foreign-affairs thing took off, I'd be going away a lot more. I filed my prickly sense of guilt into a remote drawer in my head and wrote a Post-it note for when I got back: *sort out Mum*.

In spite of having spent his life either attacking me or pretending to hate me, Duke Ellington always got into a panic when I went away. Tonight was no exception. Every time I turned round to put something in my bag he was sitting in it, refusing to meet my eye. 'Duke Ellington, if I ever love a man the way I love you, he will be very lucky,' I told him. He ignored me and moved over to sit down on my clean pants, purring loudly to indicate that he knew this was a bad thing to do. Cursing him, I braved a hand underneath him to fish them out but was unable to escape without toothmarks. 'Why are you such a little bastard?' I yelled, as I washed my hand. I kept a box of plasters by the sink for Duke Ellington attacks.

'You'd better behave yourself when Stefania comes round to feed you,' I told him, just as she arrived at my back door. His purring got louder. For the purpose of driving me mad, he *always* behaved himself with Stefania. I watched in frustration as he trotted flirtily over to her and sat, purring, while she stroked his head and crooned to him in an unidentifiable language.

After talking to him for a good thirty seconds, she glanced up. 'Oh, Frances. Greetings. Have you been drinking ze barley grass like I said?'

'No. It tasted of shit,' I replied.

My neighbour Stefania was simultaneously the best and most ridiculous human being I'd ever met. Since she had barged into my kitchen the day I moved in, bearing a 'dish for health' in an earthenware pot – 'It vill grow ze hairs on your chest' she hissed – she had become my friend, cat-feeder and source of inspiration.

The converted garage in which I rented my flat had retained the inspection shed that was used to assess cars on their arrival, and this shed, just inside the lop-sided wooden gates, was where Stefania lived. By anyone's standards it looked from the outside like a shack in a Comic Relief appeal, but inside it was delightful – a childhood fantasy den full of exotic silks and mad plants and just about enough floor space for her to contort herself into strange yogic shapes.

Stefania's country of origin was nebulous: when I'd first met her she'd told me she was a Yugoslavian princess; another time she'd claimed to be related to the Polish prime minister, and recently I'd heard her introducing herself to another neighbour as a descendant of the oldest family in St Petersburg. Whatever the grandeur of her past, however, the reality of her present was not so impressive. Apart from making enormous pots of stew for the local homeless shelter, she appeared to have no job and even less desire to discuss the matter. I knew that I was probably paying her gas and electricity bills but I couldn't give an arse. I loved her and her barmy ways: I wasn't prepared to lose her over a detail as minor as money. I *wanted* her there. Apart from anything else, Duke Ellington worshipped her.

'How are you anyway, Stefania?' I asked, as she removed my house key from the bunch of spares.

'I am blessed,' she replied, putting the keys down and placing her hands flat on the work surface. Just to emphasise the fact, she closed her eyes.

I smiled. This was textbook Stefania. 'Oh, good. Are you in love?'

'Do not be silly.' She kept her eyes closed.

'Well, then, what is going on?'

'Today I make the perfect seaweed lasagne. It is touched by ze hand of God, I tell you, Frances.'

'That's amazing. Congratulations.'

Stefania nodded. 'Sank you. It is truly amazing. As I tell you, I am blessed.' She scooped up Duke Ellington, who put up no fight whatsoever, and left my house, shouting, 'Take peace viz you to Kosovo, Frances!'

On the train to Gatwick, Dave was unlike his usual self. He was quiet and serious, even rougher round the edges than usual. 'You OK, Dave?' I asked, fishing a fag out of his mouth before he got us thrown off the train.

'Yep,' he said briefly. 'Yep, all good. Just up late with the missus. Tired.'

This was obviously Serious Dave, the Dave who'd lost one of his fingers in a war zone. I resolved to be Serious Fran during the trip, although I was less keen on losing part of my hand. As if he'd read my mind, Dave picked up my bandaged thumb and raised an eyebrow. 'Duke Ellington?' I nodded. 'He's a little fuckwit, that one.' Dave grinned, and returned to his paper.

I'd been sitting at the MAC counter in Duty Free for about fifteen minutes when Dave strode in looking agitated. 'What's up?' I asked him as a pearlescent black eye shadow was brushed into my eye sockets.

'Stella,' he replied, staring at my glam-rock aesthetic with confusion. 'Get out of here, Franny, we're in trouble.'

I shrugged guiltily at the makeup girl as Dave strode off. She gazed at me stonily. Not only was I leaving in the middle of her story about having it off with a minor league football player but I was scarpering without buying any makeup. 'Sorry,' I tried. 'We're journalists. There's an emergency in progress.'

'You – you are *journalist*?' she asked, with a raised eyebrow.

Damn her! 'Yes,' I said, drawing myself up to my full height of five foot four. 'Actually, I'm a foreign correspondent.'

The girl looked me up and down and smiled. 'No. I think you lie,' she said, handing me a face wipe.

When I met up with Stella in the Ladies, I saw why we were in trouble. She was crouched around the toilet bowl with a grey face and shaking hands. 'Crayfish,' she muttered in anguish.

'Oh dear, I, erm . . .' I said, dabbing ineffectually at her brow. It was cold and clammy. I withdrew my hand swiftly and ran as she heaved.

I left the loos to find Dave outside, his phone in his hand. 'She's not flying, is she?' he said. I shook my head. 'No. Let's get on to the office urgently. If someone leaves now they'll get here in time.' He peered at the departures board. Our flight was to leave in under two hours. 'No, they won't. I think we should go alone, Fran,' he said.

'*What?*' I froze. 'Dave, I'm a gimp. I'm just a junior producer! I'm the lowest of the low – I wouldn't have the first idea how to do Stella's job! I . . . can't. It'd be like asking Stephen Fry to stand in for one of Girls Aloud just because he's an entertainer. No way.'

Dave smiled briefly. 'You *can* do this and you will,' he said. 'There's only one direct flight each day. By the time anyone else gets out there we'll be going home again. Come on, Franny. Stop being a fanny.'

I gulped. Dave grinned more encouragingly. 'Are we good to go, Producer Fran?'

He just wanted a decent book to read ...

Not too much to ask, is it? It was in 1935 when Allen Lane, Managing Director of Bodley Head Publishers, stood on a platform at Exeter railway station looking for something good to read on his journey back to London. His choice was limited to popular magazines and poor-quality paperbacks – the same choice faced every day by the vast majority of readers, few of whom could afford hardbacks. Lane's disappointment and subsequent anger at the range of books generally available led him to found a company – and change the world.

'We believed in the existence in this country of a vast reading public for intelligent books at a low price, and staked everything on it'
Sir Allen Lane, 1902–1970, founder of Penguin Books

The quality paperback had arrived – and not just in bookshops. Lane was adamant that his Penguins should appear in chain stores and tobacconists, and should cost no more than a packet of cigarettes.

Reading habits (and cigarette prices) have changed since 1935, but Penguin still believes in publishing the best books for everybody to enjoy. We still believe that good design costs no more than bad design, and we still believe that quality books published passionately and responsibly make the world a better place.

So wherever you see the little bird – whether it's on a piece of prize-winning literary fiction or a celebrity autobiography, political tour de force or historical masterpiece, a serial-killer thriller, reference book, world classic or a piece of pure escapism – you can bet that it represents the very best that the genre has to offer.

Whatever you like to read – trust Penguin.